Praise for De

Unholy Secrets

"Delphine Boswell's debut mystery, UNHOLY
SECRETS, is a deliciously creepy, devilishly clever nail-
biter. Set in the 1950's, in a New England town that makes
Peyton Place seem like Mayberry, this thriller grabs you
from the very start and doesn't let go until the startling
finale. Private Investigator, Dana Greer, is a smart,and
resourceful heroine you can root for. Throwing one twist at
you after another, author Boswell deftly spins a hair-raising
tale of murder, deception, secrets and lies. Once you pick
up UNHOLY SECRETS, you won't be able to put it
down."

—New York Times Bestselling Author: Kevin O'Brien

Books by Delphine Boswell

Unholy Secrets	**April 2018**
Silent Betrayal	**October 2018**
Bitter Wrath	**April 2019**

Published by Jujapa Press

UNHOLY SECRETS

A Dana Greer Mystery Series

DELPHINE BOSWELL

jujapa   press
hansville   washington

ISBN-13: 978-1985066076
ISBN-10: 1985066076
Library of Congress Catalog Number: 2018934571

Published by:
Jujapa Press
PO Box 269
Hansville, Wa 98340

Cover by: vibrant_grafiz (fiverr.com)
Illustrations by: watercolorcirp & poroshm (fiverr.com)

This is a work of fiction. Names, characters, places and
incidents either are products of the author's imagination or
are used fictitiously. Any resemblance to actual events or
locales or persons, living or dead, is entirely coincidental.

Acknowledgments

Writing a novel is like wandering in the woods for a year. Sometimes you come across the most glorious moments of discovery, and sometimes you cower in fear of the dark and unknown.

This is my opportunity to thank those who got me started on my journey, helped me along the way, and brought me to the clearing.

A special thank you to my friend and former director of the Northwest Institute of Literary Arts MFA program, Wayne Ude. From suggesting what I needed to pack in my literary backpack, Wayne was my moral compass from start to finish.

I thank my son, Brendan C. Boswell, a former United States Navy sailor, for his encouragement in helping me find the story I wanted to tell.

Thanks to Clark Parsons of Jujapa Press, who enabled me to get my book in print, for his time and tech savvy knowledge.

I owe gratitude to my friend New York Times Bestseller Kevin O'Brien, who read my manuscript and offered me a blurb.

Lastly I thank my family who offered me respite on days when, as writers, we become thirsty for reassurance and motivation.

To those I have unintentionally overlooked, know that you, too, were part of my process.

And, as I look forward, a special thank you to my readers, who bring me the greatest joy knowing my words have traveled the distance to reach each and every one of you!

Prologue

October 25, 1952

Something was wrong; Raymond McGregor could sense it. He blew his breath into the palm of his hands and rubbed them together. Even his sage green hunting jacket and insulated long-sleeved shirt could not deter the dampness from seeping through to his very bones as the sun began to settle on Cape Peril off the coast of Maine. The days were getting shorter. Anytime now, snow would be in the forecast.

"Cocoa. Cocoa," Raymond called, and again a third time. He scanned the wet fields before him.

McGregor's brown lab always responded to his name. He was an experienced hunter, as was Raymond, and had retrieved many a duck, dropping them at his master's feet. Raymond would find the dog; he was determined not to go home without him.

Overhead a flock of geese honked, their pitch shrill and deafening. Once they passed, Raymond heard a muffled, faint bark. He turned and headed toward the darkened shadows under a forest of pines, surrounded by the sound of twigs snapping and branches cracking. His tall leather boots squished as he made his way through the swampy terrain, further and further from where he had parked his Ford truck.

"Cocoa," he yelled. "Come here, boy." Raymond clapped his hands. The dog's barks grew louder. Raymond could see him now, several feet in the distance. He looked to be sniffing and scratching, oblivious to Raymond's nearing presence.

"Whatcha got, boy? Find yourself a duck?" It was not unusual for the dog to find a bird someone had shot and left to rot. The kind of hunters who killed merely for sport.

As Raymond got nearer to the animal, he could see Cocoa hovering and snarling at something. Raymond bent down to get a closer look, kneeling in the muddy, cold dirt. With the tips of his shivering fingers, he whisked aside some brush. "What the hell is this?" Cocoa pawed at Raymond's hands. The dog began to bark. Raymond pushed him aside. "Back, boy, back." Taking out his pocket knife, Raymond cut prickly thistles and scratchy branches covered in shriveled purple berries. He closed the blade, stuck it back in his rear pocket, and yanked off the flashlight clipped to his belt. He flicked on the light, rested on his forearms, and peered into the dark hole. Feverishly, he ripped at a sheet of dew-covered cloth, the fabric saturated with blood. "My, God. It can't be!"

Like a monstrous Halloween mask, a small face stared up at him. At first, Raymond thought it was a doll. . .some kind of ghoulish prank, but as he focused the light one more time, he could see tiny larvae squirming across the face of a young child.

Raymond straightened his shaking body and shut off his flashlight. "C'mon, Cocoa. Let's get out of here."

Chapter One

There are those who are afraid of water, who fear the white-capped waves and royal-purple depths of the sea, those who see the ocean as if staring in the face of death itself. Dana Greer almost drowned when she was seven-years-old. Most thought it an accident the day she fell overboard off her uncle's motorboat, but only she and her uncle knew otherwise.

Now twenty-three years later, Dana was headed to Cape Peril, one of many islands off the Coast of Maine, aboard the Seaside Ferry. Almost dusk, the view from the finger-printed and smeared windows announced the coming of winter. Sharp, white points of the steel-colored ocean crisscrossed the surface, and off the coast in the distance, the last of gold-leafed trees swayed. As the barge shoved out to sea, a lone seagull sat at the edge of the weathered dock, droplets of mist upon his wings.

Dana sat on a torn vinyl bench, its cotton stuffing scratching at her nylon hose. Around her neck, she twirled a string of fresh-water pearls, a token of her mother's, the 'something borrowed' Dana had worn on her wedding day. As quickly as the beads spun through her fingers, so too did the endless questions she asked of herself. Why was she really leaving Bay View? She had, after all, worked as the principal private investigator there for the last twelve years, ever since 1940 when her father, who was Chief of Police at the time, opened the Dana Greer, P.I. Agency. Upon graduation from high school, while many girls her age married and started families, Dana's life took quite different turn, taking her into the dark world of crime. But her father had retired and headed for Florida, and she wondered if that was the reason for leaving her childhood home and its memories behind. A woman by the name of Fiona Wharton, one of the best private investigators when it came to working crime scenes and who had mentored Dana, had passed away suddenly of a heart attack only last year. Did the loss of her teacher make Dana think she needed a new start, a new job? No one forced her to answer these questions, yet she knew it was important for her to confront the answers, to face the truth. In her heart, she acknowledged she was running. . .running from a childhood she had never come to terms with, running from a failed marriage she had too long repressed, and running from the Myra Pembroke case involving a young prostitute whose body was found in an abandoned motel—a case gone cold. Dana felt in some way responsible for all of these, and much like Hester Prynne in *The Scarlet Letter*, Dana wore the blame.

She reminded herself what was important was from this day forward, her life would be a clean slate. She would be a woman with no background, no history. Only days ago, Bishop Walsh of Bay View and a long-time friend of the family had asked for Dana's input in solving a murder case involving a seven-year-old child, who had attended the Holy Name Academy. Her body was found in a remote part of Cape Peril. Dana slipped her fingers into her bag and lifted out the tiny tattered Bible she had received at her First Communion, the one her uncle had given her. Although she had fallen away from the church long ago, she carried the miniature Bible, with its miniscule print, everywhere she went. She rubbed her fingers across its white, leather-like cover. The book provided her comfort.

The ferry's horn blasted three times, forcing her thoughts back to the present. Dana had never been to the island, one of many off the Coast of Maine, but had heard the trip took about an hour. She headed to the dining area, following the sounds of banging pots and pans and clanking cups and plates. She ordered some scrambled eggs, toast, and coffee—she had always been a breakfast person—and found a seat by a gold Formica table. From her handbag, she pulled out the fliers that she obtained from the Better Business Bureau.

Cape Peril offers the amenities of small-town living with one of the lowest crime rates in the Northeast. Dana smiled. That would be a change. Bay View wasn't exactly like Chicago or Detroit, but its statistics on violent crimes had increased since she had first taken over her private investigative agency.

Holy Name Academy boasts the highest test scores in the region, staffed by the Sisters of the Immaculate Heart of Mary. Dana had gone to Catholic schools all her life, taught by the IHM nuns. Since her marriage to Nate, she had not set foot in a church. Someday, she hoped that might change.

Beautiful, ocean-front cottages available for sale. Dana glanced at the pastel-colored homes, dollhouses dotting the shore, yet she was grateful she wouldn't have to be anywhere near the sea. Bishop Walsh had contacted Sergeant Logan of the Cape Peril Police Department. The officer had found a room for rent with a couple named Harrison. Jay Harrison was a teacher at Holy Name Academy and his wife, Loretta, worked in an antique shop. From what the bishop had told Dana, the Sergeant explained he had ulterior reasons for choosing this couple. Five years earlier, Jay's wife, while in her early teens, had performed a self-inflicted abortion and almost died from complications. Dana wondered why the background of the woman would be of any importance but assumed she would find out soon enough.

Dana paused momentarily to glance away from the brochure. The rocking movement of the ferry and her reading had suddenly begun to make her feel nauseous. She realized she was not alone. An elderly woman had joined her at the table and was peering at the flier in Dana's hands.

"Don't mean to intrude, honey, but I see you're reading about Cape Peril. Are you a visitor? We sure get a lot but not this time of year." The aged woman's face resembled a neatly creased Venetian blind, complete to a light coating of powered dust, and her voice was a high-pitched alto.

Dana swallowed the crust from her bread, hoping it would settle her motion sickness. "No," she said, "I'm moving here." Early on, Dana had learned not to reveal what she did for a living. The public had a million and one questions to ask once they heard she worked the murder scenes.

"How nice," the woman said, her cheeks rosy red, forming two circles which were too heavily rouged.

"Are you from Cape Peril?" Dana asked the woman, feeling her eyebrows rising. She drank the last of her coffee, swallowing the leftover grounds, and set it on the tray.

"Born and raised."

"Like it?" Dana asked as she put the flier back in her handbag.

"Hmm. You know islands."

"No, not really. I'm from Bay View."

The woman went silent. She rubbed her thumb with her index finger, her cuticles ragged and torn. Dana's investigative instinct told her the old woman was refraining from telling her something, something she was reluctant to share.

"What did you mean about islands?" Dana asked.

"Nothing really. People just know people. Word travels quickly. That's all." The woman nodded her head; large hooped earrings, which looked out of place on an elderly woman, dangled from her earlobes. She wore a blue-and-pink flowered shirtwaist dress, and up and down her thin-skinned arms, she wore rows of beaded bracelets.

"You mean gossip?"

"Rumors."

Dana glimpsed out the ferry windows and noticed the darkened sky. A straight-lined rain had begun to fall. It reminded her of pins her mother had used to hold her Simplicity patterns in place. As a child, Dana's whole wardrobe consisted of clothes her mother had sewn for her on an antique Singer sewing machine. Her mother had died when Dana was only twelve years of age.

Dana turned toward the woman. "Any in particular I should know about. . .rumors, I mean?"

The woman pressed her knuckles to cover her lips, a smudge of red. She suddenly looked like a child hiding a secret better left untold. "Can I trust you with one?"

Dana nodded. She wondered if it had something to do with the young child whose body was found in the marshy bog. Without a doubt, it would have been the talk of the island, and one could only speculate on what stories might be circulating.

"A little girl, a second-grader, at Holy Name Academy, was murdered. There's talk that I may have had something to do with her passing," the woman said, as she spun a loose thread around one of the buttons on her dress.

Images are deceiving, but Dana could not bring herself to believe any person would point fingers at the old woman across from her. She looked like anyone's grandmother, one who spent her time in the kitchen baking chocolate chip cookies, not someone involved in a murder case.

"That's impossible to believe."

"Perhaps, but someone started the rumor."

"But why?" Dana bit down on the knuckle of her index finger.

"Name's Opal." She reached out her liver-spotted hand and shook Dana's. On the ring finger of her right hand, she wore a stone matching her name. "I'm a reader. . .cards. . .Tarot."

"Interesting. I'm Dana. . .Dana Greer."

"Not everyone thinks what I do is interesting. As a matter-of-fact, there are a small group of people who call me a devil worshipper and go so far as to say I cast spells."

"But why would these people believe you were involved in murdering a child, for heaven's sake?"

"Someone said one of my Tarot cards was found with the body of the child." The woman shook her head in dismay. "Can you believe that?" In the same breath, Opal said, "Would you like your cards read?"

"Here? Now?"

Opal nodded.

Right then, the bus boy came to remove Dana's tray. Her half-eaten toast and leftover scrambled eggs sat on it as she handed it to the young boy. He stared at the tray and then at Dana. She fumbled in her handbag and put a dime next to her dish. He grinned and went about his work.

"So, should we proceed?" Opal asked.

Dana never put faith in superstitious beliefs. A scene from her past played before her. She had been a second-grader at St. Michael's, and the nuns had been readying the children for their first confessions. They had memorized the Ten Commandments. Dana recalled the first—the one about false gods. Carrying a good luck charm in one's hip pocket, following the astrology of the stars, and professing to believe in fortune tellers and card readers were all looked upon as false gods. Yet something inside of Dana, possibly her curious nature, urged her to go ahead. Before she answered, she furtively reached into her bag and rubbed the grainy cover of her Bible, as if somehow the motion would absolve her of the sin she was about to commit. "I guess. I mean, it wouldn't hurt any."

Across the aisle from the two women, a man sat listening to their conversation. He quickly cast his gaze aside when he saw Dana browse in his direction. Dana knew there were those who thought her paranoid, overly aware of her surroundings, but she attributed it to her years in the crime field.

From a woven handbag, the woman pulled out a small, black velvet draw-string pouch. Her hands involuntarily shook. She shuffled a deck, dog-eared and worn. Then, she spread the cards in a fan shape across the table. "Pick any three, dear."

Dana kept telling herself if she didn't believe in fortunes, the reading couldn't do any harm.

Opal turned the first card over.

She fixed her eyes on it as though she had never seen the image before. "The Hermit. Do you know what that means?" Her voice rose as if she was expecting Dana to give her the answer.

Dana shook her head.

Opal spun her index finger, circling her round, rosy cheek. "You will need to be cautious. Use your discretion before you jump to conclusions. Does that make sense to you?" Her eyes widened, and Dana saw one of the woman's pupils was larger than the other; it gave her an owl-like appearance.

"No, not really," Dana said. She didn't want to give the woman the satisfaction that her advice might just be helpful to an investigator. Dana folded her hands and set them in her lap.

"Here, let's turn over another. Death."

Dana cupped her hand under her chin. She opened her mouth, but no words came.

Opal took a deep breath. "Ah,

don't look so frightened."

"But it says death."

"Death to the old, and life to the new," Opal said, her voice rising with optimism. "Are you starting a new job, honey?"

"As a matter of fact, I am," Dana said.

"Mind if I ask you what?"

If Opal was the reader, shouldn't she know the answer? Dana wondered. She pretended to ignore the woman's question, and Opal turned over the next card.

"Oh dear. The Moon, and it's reversed."

Opal tugged on her earring. "Be careful. The reversed moon means there will be insincere people around you. They will try to deceive you. You mustn't believe them."

Dana began to fidget in her seat, reminding herself a deck of cards in no way could predict what was to be, and to think they could was nothing short of preposterous.

"As the hermit warned, just be cautious. You mustn't make any hasty decisions." Opal twirled her finger through the air.

"That's helpful to know. Thank you." Fiona Wharton had taught Dana early on in her career it's better to second guess yourself than to jump on a lark. The interpretation of the hermit card was nothing new to Dana.

SWORDS

Opal placed her trembling hand over Dana's. "We're not done yet, dearie. Make a wish."

"I'm afraid I don't—."

"Do it." Opal demanded.

Dana wished for the obvious— that her new position would go well.

Opal gathered up the deck and shuffled and cut the cards three times. "Pick one."

Dana did as Opal said. Her face appeared drawn; she nibbled on the tip of her thumb.

"Is something wrong?" Dana asked. She stared at the card lying upright.

It was a picture of crisscrossed swords, ten of them. Where they met in the center, droplets of blood filled the diamond spaces.

"It's the ten of swords, the lord of ruin."

"Meaning?"

Opal softly grabbed Dana by the arm. Her voice a whisper, she said, "Many readers believe the ten of swords depicts the saddest card in the deck. The swords represent your conscious mind. When things get as bad as they can, and there is nothing more that can be done, you must release the problem. Do you hear me? Let go!" Opal's eyes got watery; she stopped blinking and stared straight ahead as if she saw something not there. Her voice grew quiet again. "Don't let those around you play with your mind. And, you know. . .they will."

A groan of thunder and a streak of silver light interrupted the woman. The winds began to howl, first swaying, then, bouncing the ferry from side-to-side. Dana's stomach grumbled; her breathing quickened. She dug her nails into the vinyl seat, leaving impressions in the red upholstery. At that moment, the captain came on the intercom apologizing for any discomfort his passengers might have experienced and announcing the ship would soon be pulling into port.

"Here, dearie," Opal said, as she pulled a pencil from her handbag and scribbled something onto a small scrap of paper. "This is my phone number. Don't hesitate to call. I live above the Rexall Drugs, right next to the police station, with Felix and Jinx."

"Felix and Jinx?"

"My cats."

Could it be possible the woman did have a gift? That she could see what lay in the future merely by discerning the meaning of the chosen cards? "Perhaps I will. . .call you sometime," Dana said.

"No *perhaps* about it. I know you will."

Dana took the paper, turned, and followed the crowd rushing to the stern of the boat, where one of the deck hands helped those needing assistance exit the ferry.

"Be careful," he said. "Might be a bit slippery."

Dana stepped onto the wet dock and looked back at the endless sea, her past separated from her future. A new beginning, or so she hoped.

Chapter Two

A young boy in khaki knickers and a baseball cap sitting sideways on his head yelled out, "Read all about it. Get the *Cape Peril Post*. Body identified."

The boy wore red knitted gloves and a muffler to match. His cheeks bore the same color, his breath like a puff of white smoke in the dark air.

Dana set her bag down, paid the lad twenty-five cents, and hurried to find a coffee house to escape the pouring rain. The Sip 'n Stay, conveniently located on the corner, looked inviting with a steaming orange cup on the front window. Upon entering, the scent of honey roasted nuts and cocoa beans greeted her.

The waitress, a middle-aged woman, came to Dana's table. The bridge of the woman's nose crinkled as she squinted over her spectacles inlaid with scattered glitter dust. "You new here?"

"The name's Dana Greer." Dana reached out her hand.

"I thought so," the waitress said, ignoring Dana's attempt at friendliness. The woman studied Dana's face as if looking at an old high school yearbook.

"What do you mean?" Dana's shoulders nudged forward.

"Thought I remembered seeing your picture in the 'Post.' You're here to work on that case."

"Yes, I am."

"I sure hope you find whoever did such a horrible thing to that innocent child." The waitress wagged her index finger. "Someone like that should be shot at sundown."

"I'll have a coffee. . .black, please." Dana settled back into the bench. The waitress, a busy-body, for sure.

The woman walked away, mumbling something to herself.

Dana pulled the paper out from under her arm and began to read:

A young girl's body found in a shallow grave in a marshy flat land has positively been identified by coroner Red Tanner as Bernadette Godfrey. Bernadette was a seven-year-old child who drew suspicion when she failed to arrive for her Monday classes at Holy Name Academy.

The waitress brought Dana's cup of coffee, and without being asked, sat down. She peered over Dana's shoulder, onto the paper. She tapped her red polished nails on the Formica table. "See the authorities know the girl was a student at that Catholic school. Heard she was found in her uniform." Glimpsing over her glasses once again, the waitress said, "And can you believe she still had her school bag with her? The poor, sweet angel. They say some fortune telling card was found among her school stuff." The waitress's face scrunched up. "Just bet that ol' witch had something to do with it."

It confirmed Opal's rumor speculation. There were those who were accusing her of being involved in the case, but at this point that's strictly what it was: mere speculation. Dana, for one, had no intention to foster such talk until she had a chance to look into the matter for herself. She kept her focus on the newspaper article. Her plan to ignore the woman worked; the waitress got up and moved to the next table. While she took a customer's order, the waitress glanced back and forth at Dana like a vulture eyeing its prey.

Dana read on:

The Godfreys are new residents, having moved to the Cape last April. Bernadette, their adopted daughter, had started second grade. Bishop Walsh of the diocese of Bay View recently hired Dana Greer to investigate the crime. Miss Greer comes from the mainland with twelve years of private investigative experience. She is best known for her involvement in the Myra Pembroke case which involved the murder of a juvenile prostitute.

Dana's desire to remain a blank slate evaporated. The Pembroke murder had made front-page news two years ago in the Bay View newspaper, but as it stood, the case was never solved. It certainly hadn't won Dana any fame, and on the contrary, the case served only to humiliate her. She and her former husband, Nate a police officer, had worked the case together. Months after the body of the young prostitute was found, Dana learned the dead woman and Nate had been lovers. Had been ever since Nate and Dana married. She had never bothered to mention the case when the bishop had interviewed her for the job, nor when he asked her for a resume of her past work experience. Why news of it appeared in the *Peril Post*, she had no idea.

Dana stopped at the register on her way out of the coffee shop and asked the cashier if he might know the Harrisons.

He cupped his ear to better hear Dana over the chatter of the patrons' voices and the banging of dishes in the kitchen. "You kidding? Everybody knows everybody on the Cape. That where you're headed?" He pulled out an old receipt and started to scribble some directions on the back of it. "Can't miss it; three-twenty

Captain Cove, a purple Victorian with a steeply pitched roof and the longest spindled porch you'll ever see in your lifetime."

"Glad to hear it's so close; I don't have a car."

"Won't really need one; in fact, the only people who bring autos over from Bay View are those highfalutin folks up on the Pointe."

Dana pulled up the collar on her tan raincoat, wishing she had purchased that cashmere number she had seen advertised in the Penney's catalog, the one with the brown mutton fur trim. Eleven dollars had seemed like too much at the time. Cape Peril sat at the most northern point before entering Canada; she should have guessed the weather here would be much blusterier than in Bay View. A light crusty drizzle fell onto the concrete and quickly turned to patches of ice.

On Dana's way toward the Harrisons, she passed homes constructed of clapboard, covered in cedar shingles, and embellished with wooden shutters, all sparsely situated on plots of land, in keeping with the way New Englanders prized their space. Many of the homes were already decorated for Halloween, less than a week away. White gauze ghosts hung from tree branches while rubber bats swayed beneath porch lights. Carved, lit pumpkins with gruesome faces stood on several of the porches. Someone had even taken the time to crepe paper a pine tree with black and orange streamers, a mischievous looking crow perched on top.

Dana found the Harrison's house only a couple of blocks away. It sat off the road by several yards—a stately, three-story Victorian surrounded by hemlocks, spreading junipers, and the barren branches of several lilac bushes. A white, spindled porch graced the front of the house and disappeared around the sides just as the cashier had described it. Dana puffed up her hair with one hand and rang the bell with the other. She could feel her heart fluttering as it always did when she found herself in new situations.

A handsome man with a thick head of brown hair, a somewhat long nose that looked like those found on Greek sculptures and a scruffy face in need of a shave greeted her. "You must be Dana Greer. I've been expecting you. How was the ferry over?"

There was something about the man's enthused voice that instantly made Dana feel welcome. After the card reader and the waitress, she needed a greeting like Jay Harrison's.

"Come on in. Glad you found our place," he said. "My wife," he turned, the woman right on his heels. "Oh, here she is." He reached for her hand. "This is Loretta."

"Pleased to meet you," Dana said. She eyed the spiral bannister with its mahogany railing and the multi-tiered chandelier above her head. "Beautiful place you have here."

The woman, who looked to be at least ten years Jay's junior, resumed her position behind her husband, appearing almost as a child playing peek-a-boo. Probably shy. After all, Dana thought, here she was a total stranger to the Cape, come to investigate a murder, and planned on living in the Harrisons' home.

Loretta spun a lock of her curly brown hair, which looked mousy and lacked luster, around her index finger. "Excuse me." The woman stared at the Oriental rug beneath her feet. "I was just getting ready for bed," she said.

Dana glanced at her watch. Seven-thirty.

"We're happy you're here," Jay said. "Let me show you to your room." He grabbed Dana's bag, and she and Jay followed Loretta up the creaking steps, winding around the turret like the letter *S*. The young woman turned into the first room at the top of the stairs and closed the door, never bothering to say goodnight to either of them. Jay led Dana to a large room located at the front of the home, where gold and crimson flowered paper covered the walls. "Tomorrow, you'll get to appreciate a view of the cove," he said, gently pushing aside the cream lace curtain, pointing out the large bay window. A red velvet window seat enhanced the early 19th century look. A pillow of embroidered daisies sat on a yellow-painted rocking chair. Next to it stood a bookcase, its shelves filled with miniature porcelain dolls dressed in various Victorian fineries. A faint smell of a sweet floral perfume lingered. A lace crocheted canopy and a matching spread graced the large bed in the middle of the room. Covering the bed, from end-to-end, sat stuffed bears of various sizes and colors. Other than in a toy store, Dana had never seen so many in one place as they toppled over one another as if trying to gain a position of prominence. When Jay noticed Dana eyeing them, he said, "My wife's collection. I've told her. . . . Here, let me help you. Just throw them in a pile." Briskly, he grabbed armfuls of the animals and threw them across the room. "Sorry," he said. His face spoke more of frustration than of repentance, his breathing heavy.

A roll-top desk and a spindled-back chair stood near the window. "Imagine you'll be needing these," Jay said, as he pointed to the spot. A large bath tiled in gold marble with pedestal sinks, gold-inlaid faucets, and a claw-footed tub adjoined the room, complete with a walk-in closet.

"If there's anything else you'll need, please let me know. Of course, you're free to relax anywhere you like downstairs, so don't feel quarantined up here. Help yourself to the kitchen; the pantry and ice box are full." He started to leave the room but turned abruptly, his profile rigid and sharp. "By the way, don't feel insulted by Loretta's behavior. She's not been very happy ever since I brought her to the Cape from South Dakota. That was five years ago."

"I see. Where in South Dakota?"

"Aberdeen. . .lived there her whole life."

"Nice place," Dana said, having never been there. Another trick-of-the-trade she'd learned from Fiona. It pays sometimes to act like you know more than you do. People often will fill-in-the-blanks for you.

Jay turned back one more time. "Help yourself to the basket of fruit on the night table if you like."

A small, white wicker basket held three red apples, two oranges, and a vine of purple grapes. "How kind. Thank you," Dana said. Before Jay left the room, he snatched two spoiled looking grapes from the vine and left the door slightly ajar.

In the morning, Dana would meet with Sergeant Logan. Although this was to be her case, she knew from experience, it never hurt to befriend the Chief of Police. Tonight she would make a list of the thoughts already whirling through her mind. She pulled a pen out from her bag, found some lavender-smelling stationery in the top drawer of the desk, and began to write:

October 27, 1952
- *Meet with Sergeant Logan*
- *Meet with Red Tanner, the coroner, to view the body*
- *Do some background work on Jay Harrison*
- *Check into Opal, the card reader's background*
- *Question the Sip 'n Stay's waitress*
- *Find out who the highfalutin folks on the Pointe are*

She might not get to all of these tomorrow, but at least it was a start. Tired from the long ferry ride over to the island, Dana quickly unpacked. Before climbing into bed, she took her Bible out of her bag and glided her fingers across the grainy cover. About to turn out the lamp, its base a Victorian woman complete with parasol, Dana tossed a couple grapes into her mouth as she examined, once again, the hill of stuffed bears in the corner of the room. Some looked tattered and worn, with missing ears or eyes. Others looked to be brand new, dressed in satin vests and shiny bowties and velvet dresses trimmed in lace and ribbons. Human-like, they stared at her as if they longed to speak, as if concealing secrets their stitched mouths would never reveal.

Chapter Three

The red-brick police station in the middle of town, with its American flag flying proudly, was sandwiched between the Rexall Drugs and a Polish bakery. The scent of glazed donuts and coconut macaroons came from the exhaust fan out front. The station was only a short walk from the Harrisons' home. Parked out front were two black-and-white cruisers with the words Cape Peril Precinct Police scrolled along the side. Dana wondered on an island the size of the Cape, sixteen miles in circumference and a total of seven point six square miles, how many police officers there might be. From what she had read, the Cape boasted a population of two hundred seventy-two people with eighty percent of them living less than three miles from Port Avenue, the main road which ran east to west across the island. Dana found the residents of the small island appreciated its open spaces as did most of the people of Maine, yet the islanders enjoyed the closeness and camaraderie that allowed rumors to spread and promulgate.

Dana entered the building and was welcomed by the smell of fresh coffee brewing along with a disgusting scent of nail polish. A girl who looked to be in her late teens sat at her desk. She carefully brushed a shade of hot pink onto each of her nails and chomped on a stick of gum. "Help you, Ma'am?" she asked.

"I'm Dana Greer, the new private investigator. Is Sergeant Logan around?"

The receptionist blew a large, pink bubble from her gum, matching the color of her polish. "Oh, you're the one he hired," she said. "Go on in." She pointed to an open door across from her desk. "By the way, you sure don't look none like your photograph in the paper." As an afterthought, she added, "Must have been an old picture."

"Thank you," Dana said, feeling indignant. She knocked on Logan's open door. He was speaking with a man whose back was turned away from her.

"Dana, glad to meet you. You look in person just like the photo you sent."

After what the receptionist had just said, Dana felt relieved.

"I'd like for you to meet Red Tanner, our coroner on Cape Peril."

"Pleased," Dana said, looking at the man with the bushy head of bright red hair. Tanner wiped his palms onto his pants and extended his freckle covered hand.

"Not exactly the way I'd like to introduce someone to their first day on the job, Dana, but Mr. and Mrs. Godfrey want to bury their daughter as soon as possible," Logan said. "Red'll take you to the morgue, let you do some examining, and see what your thoughts are."

Red made small talk with Dana as they crossed Port Avenue and made their way north down Starboard Street, asking her about the ferry ride over from the mainland, about the weather in Bay View, and whether or not she liked crab. She wasn't sure what the latter had to do with the first two questions but figured he had run out of things to say. They turned into an alley, a shortcut Red said, a dead-end. How appropriate a location for a coroner's office. He quickly led Dana to a back room that housed the morgue. In her twelve years of crime, she had looked at lots of bodies from the wrinkled skinned ones with gaping mouths and no teeth to the strikingly beautiful ones like Myra Pembroke whose nude body looked more like a model than the prostitute she was. Then there was the nine-year-old negro boy who first was thought to be the victim of a murder. Later, she was to learn the boy had jumped from a bridge, a suicide when he feared his parents would learn he had robbed some mom-and-pop store. His body resembled a blow fish, all swollen and distorted.

When Red Tanner pulled the sheet on Bernadette Godfrey, Dana encountered the youngest deceased child she had ever seen. Her sweet face, though partially chewed by the typical insects of death and colored a bluish-grey, still looked like a sleeping angel. Blond, tightly woven curls graced her face giving her a strange resemblance to Shirley Temple, and Dana could picture the young innocent rising to sing "On the Good Ship Lollipop." For a moment, she turned away, swallowed hard, and caught her breath. When she returned to glance at the girl, she reminded herself this was a corpse so she could restore her objectivity. Still in the green and blue plaid jumper, the uniform of Holy Name Academy, the fabric was saturated in blood as if whoever murdered her had randomly stabbed her multiple times in the chest. The child's white Peter-Pan collar was soiled, the top buttons missing. One of her white anklet stockings was gone as was her saddle oxford.

"Any evidence collected?" Dana asked.

"Only this," Red said, showing her a large plastic bag marked 'Exhibit A.'

In the bag, Dana viewed a small green school bag with brown clasps. "Anything inside?" she asked.

"Typical stuff. You know, books, paper, crayons."

"Could I have a look?"

From a squeaky drawer, Red pulled out some smaller plastic bags marked 'Exhibit B,' 'Exhibit C,' and 'Exhibit D.'

"No need to wear gloves," he said. "Everything's been checked for fingerprints, and there ain't a one."

Dana opened the bag marked 'Exhibit C,' the one with the loose-leaf paper. Typical school math problems filled the wide blue lines. Another sheet looked to be a poem the child had started. Written in perfect penmanship, the straight letters touching the blue and pink lines, it read:

I love the sea.

Its waves calm me.

I love the sea.

It's here

he waits for me.

"Mind if I keep this one?"

"Feel free. Whatever it takes to nail this guy."

Dana replaced the paper into its bag and put it in her satchel, the one she always carried when investigating crimes. In the other two exhibit bags, she found exactly what Red had said. 'Exhibit A' held a small Catechism of Christian Doctrine and a Think-and-Do Workbook. She flipped through the pages, pencil markings circling the hidden pictures of Puff the cat and Spot the dog. 'Exhibit B' held recently sharpened number two pencils and a box of twenty-four Crayolas, still pointed and new.

Dana wondered about the comment Opal made earlier that suggested she may have played a part in the murder. Most likely, an ugly rumor began by someone who saw the reading of cards as the work of Satan, but to be a thorough investigator, Dana asked Red, "By chance, did you happen to come upon any Tarot cards?"

"Ah, so you, too, have heard the rumors, huh?"

Dana nodded and waited to see if the man would confirm the story or laugh it off as some silly island gossip.

"You're referring to the High Priestess card, I suspect."

Dana wasn't sure if Red's comment was a declarative statement or an interrogative one, but she decided to further his thought with a question. "So, a Tarot card *was found* with the body?"

"Nonsense, I'm sure," Red answered, with a hint of sarcasm and laughter in his voice. "Do you actually think if the old fortune teller had anything to do with the crime she'd have been stupid enough to put one of her cards with the body? I felt no need to further such idle gossip."

"You mean you no longer have the card as evidence?" Dana could hear the disbelief in her question.

Red shook his head, then looked at Dana with discerning eyes, "If you choose to believe such mumbo-jumbo, the High Priestess sits in front of the Tree of Life, which represents the mystery between darkness and light. In later years, some thought the Priestess to be the Virgin Mary. You tell me how that ties in with the little's girl's murder. There are those of us on the island who believe whatever comes out of Opal's mouth is sheer rubbish. I might suggest since you're new around here you do the same."

Dana did not bother to comment but only thought, *I'll come to my own conclusions, thank you.*

Red picked up some medical instruments on the pea-green counter and tossed them into a nearby sink. He whistled the tune "Singin' in the Rain" from a Broadway musical. Dana assumed his nonchalance might be his coping mechanism for a grim reaper's job.

"Could I take a few photos?" she asked, taking out her AGIfold 6 X 6 with uncoupled rangefinder, one of the best cameras on the market. Without waiting for Red's answer, Dana began snapping shots of the child from multiple directions.

"I can get those developed for you if you like," Red said.

"I appreciate that, but I've got a few more to take on this roll. I'd like to see the crime scene. . .the bog where the child's body was found."

Red and Dana walked back to Logan's office. The station was so different from the bustling one in Bay View. It was apparent to her life went at a much slower and more casual pace on Cape Peril. Two police officers, smoking cigarettes, met her at the door.

The receptionist sat filing her nails. "You met Officer O'Neil and Boyle yet?" she asked, blowing emery board dust off her desk.

"No," Dana said, as the two men introduced themselves to her.

"Boyle. . .Carl Boyle here."

"Frank O'Neil," the other said, shaking Dana's hand.

Dana was about to introduce herself when the taller of the two men, Boyle, said, "Logan's told us detectives run cheaper than a uniformed officer." He laughed along with O'Neil.

At that moment, the door to Logan's office opened. "See you've met my force."

"None too busy, I see," Dana said.

The two men took another puff on their cigarettes and stepped outside.

Logan smiled revealing a gold-crowned incisor. "Come on in, have a seat."

"I was looking over a flier about the island. Read about your crime statistics. . .almost non-existent, I see."

"That's why you're here."

Dana cocked her head to the side. "Guess, I don't understand what you mean."

"I need someone who's good at finding a needle in a haystack. We don't lose too many around here."

"Chance we might go out to see the crime scene of the Godfrey child?"

Logan plopped his officer's cap on his nearly bald head. "I was just going to ask."

***

As they drove to the site, low-lying grey clouds fringed the peaks of purple mountains in the distance, and a howling wind blew, sounding like a far-away wolf's cry. Logan stopped his rusted truck, missing all of its hubcaps, at the end of a dirt two track. "This is as far as we go with wheels," he shouted over the sounds of the blustery gusts.

Dana was glad she had worn boots, the kind horseback riders wear. . .real leather, up to her knees, and highly durable. They walked through the marshland, wet mud oozing from the swampy bottom. Overhead ducks squawked, the location isolated, tucked away for only a few to find. Besides an occasional hunter, Dana wondered who would even know the spot was here. She and Logan continued walking until they neared a sparse collection of Pitch-Pines, the type so commonly found in swampy regions.

"Right this way. Over here," Logan said. "Watch your step." He lowered his body toward the open grave.

Dana took out her camera and got down on the damp ground. The makeshift grave looked tediously carved as if someone had taken great pains to smooth and chisel the hole, leaving not so much as a stray rock or weed. She took one photo and then another.

Dana turned to face Logan. "Body was found by a hunter, right? Know anything about the man?"

"Raymond McGregor. Duck hunter in his spare time and a newspaper columnist by day."

Just then, a gun popped in the distance. "A Remington 870," Dana said.

"There aren't too many men who'd know what barrel that shot came from. Impressive for a woman," Logan said.

Dana chose to ignore his comment. One thing Logan would soon learn about her is a good detective had nothing to do with gender.

"We're right in the range of fire; I suggest we head back. Peak of duck season." He stood abruptly.

"Anything else I should know about this?" Dana asked, pointing to the four-foot by five-foot hole. Logan extended his hand to help her up. She pretended not to notice and stood without his assistance. "Body was covered with a white cloth. Like everything else, no fingerprints," Logan said.

"Interesting. . .a white cloth? Red never mentioned that to me." "The covering over the body? Assuming, he might have even gotten rid of it," Logan said. "From what Red told me, it was soaked with the girl's blood."

The randomness with which Tanner had handled the evidence bothered Dana. . .a Tarot card with the body, a white cloth soaked in blood. If Tanner were a coroner in Bay View, he would have lost his job with such careless actions. Dana thought some more about the cloth that supposedly covered the child's body. "Almost like a last attempt to give the child a token of affection," Dana said, more to herself than the sergeant.

"I saw it as a protection from the elements, but yeah, you might be onto something there."

Dana took one more look at the shallow grave before Logan and she left the crime scene and headed back into town.

Dana wondered what Logan had in store for her next when he said, "Know this isn't typical for your line of work, Dana, but I was wondering if you'd like to accompany me to Holy Name Church tomorrow?"

"But it's not Sunday."

He laughed, this time showing a row of bottom teeth squeezed together like too many men on the seat of a bus.

"Angela Artenelli, Bernadette Godfrey's teacher, is professing her final vows tomorrow morning. Just about anyone Catholic will be there." He laughed again, this time a nervous kind of laugh. "Might give you a feel for some of the folks who live here."

"I'd be pleased to join you." Without thinking, the words, "As a child, I always wanted to be a nun myself," slipped out.

"Well, that's sure a blessing," Logan said.

"What do you mean?"

"Men weren't meant to suffer by sacrificing beautiful women to the convent."

Dana could feel a warmth rising upward from her neck until it landed across her forehead. She never did take to compliments. Maybe it had something to do with her upbringing. Neither of her parents offered any positive reinforcement for anything she did, but then again, they weren't exactly what she'd call critical of her either, so typical of the times.

Changing the topic, she said, "By the way, what's the percentage of Catholics on the island?"

"At least ninety percent, I'd say, at a quick estimate. When the French Canadians populated this area, they brought their religion with them."

Just one more thing Dana planned to jot into her notebook.

Suspect likely a Catholic with no conscience.

Chapter Four

Holy Name Church, a white wooden building adorned with stained-glass windows of the seven archangels on one side and the seven sacraments on the other, was founded in 1848 by an order of Jesuits who came from Quebec. The church's steeple rose majestically, the tallest fixture on the island, and the bells in the tower chimed faithfully the hours all religious recited the Angelus Prayer: six a.m., noon, and six p.m. Two marble angels stood on either side of the heavy wooden doors, a sign of welcome to the congregation.

Logan and Dana entered the church and selected a pew behind those marked *Reserved*. Each of the heavily stained mahogany pews was adorned in blue carnations and baby's breath with large navy satin ribbons. Dana nodded to Jay and Loretta Harrison, seated in the pew behind them, and they smiled.

True in most Catholic places of worship, the scent of incense and melted wax was strong. From the side altar a choir of postulants, those girls who had just entered the religious order, sang "Regina Mundi," "Ave Maria," and "Holy Queen." The lyrics brought back fond memories for Dana of the years spent in Catholic schools. There was something to be said for the reverent traditions. As she had told Logan, when she was a child, she had been convinced the religious life was for her. All of Dana's friends agreed they wanted nothing more than to be nuns when they graduated from high school and some as early as eighth grade. The idea of becoming a religious and devoting oneself to a life of servitude had a certain appeal and definitely a role of respect in the church community. Certainly, Dana's upbringing spoke of faith-filled rituals, such as gathering around the radio with her family and reciting the rosary out loud during the months of October and May; and on Fridays during Lent, Dana and her family fasted, refrained from meat, and gave up such desserts as ice cream and chocolate cake. Dana liked to believe if it had not been for her failed marriage, she might just be a member in good standing in the Church, yet she continued to blame her former husband and his affair as responsible for her decision to leave.

Dana watched as people continued to file into the quaint church and as Logan had predicted, the place of worship quickly filled to capacity. Two ushers attempted to seat late comers, asking people to move toward the center of their pews. The front pews, marked *Reserved*, were saved for families of the religious as well as the nuns.

The postulants turned toward the main aisle and began to sing "Holy God" as the choir director motioned for the congregation to stand. As they did, a procession of nuns came in through the back doors of the chapel. First came those who had already made their final vows. Dana could tell because these women wore the black veils. Following them came the novices in their white veils and white habits, looking like the brides of Christ they professed to be. Each carried a single white rose. The image of the women gave Dana chills.

Logan nudged Dana. "There she is. . .Angela Artenelli. That's her coming now."

Dana turned and was stunned. The woman, incredibly beautiful, had a pale complexion, like that of porcelain, large dark eyes, and a few wisps of black hair falling innocently from the corner of her veil.

"She's gorgeous."

"Ah, yes. A pity to surrender herself to the nunnery," Logan said.

The sisters processed into the front reserved pews. Through the sanctuary door entered the red-capped bishop holding his staff, the official symbol of the shepherd, along with two altar servers dressed in red and white cassocks. The last time Dana had been in the presence of a bishop had been at her fifth-grade confirmation. It had been the first time her mother allowed her to wear nylon stockings. She had felt so grown-up—near to God—even if she told herself, God, after what happened that day on her uncle's boat, might not have felt the same way about her.

Standing before the crowd, the bishop began. "Welcome all family and friends on this special day when our brides of Christ profess before us and God Almighty the vows of poverty, chastity, and obedience. Please be seated."

The postulants began to sing again in the softest of voices as the professed nuns rose and formed a semi-circle around the altar, which was covered in glowing candles and vases of fresh white roses.

"I will begin by calling each novice by their Baptismal name. First, Angela Artenelli."

The young nun walked to the altar, genuflected, and lay prostrate before a huge crucifix one of the altar boys held. Even from the pews, the marble floor glistened from the reflection of the stained-glass windows.

"Angela Artenelli, do you know, my daughter, the severity of the covenant you are entering today?"

"Yes, bishop."

"Do you wish to become a Sister of the Immaculate Heart of Mary, following in the footsteps of Mary, the Mother of God?"

"Yes, bishop."

"Then you may rise."

At this point, the other altar boy reached into a box. He held up the dark blue habit of the professed nuns of the order and slipped it over Angela's head. Next came the monastic tonsure, a small woven belt.

One of the nuns in the front pew arose carrying a small basket.

"That's the Mother Superior," Logan said.

The organist continued to play hymns while the young nuns hummed.

The altar boy removed the white veil from Angela's head.

Soft "ahs" could be heard from the congregation as Angela undid some pins and let her black hair fall upon her shoulders.

The older nun removed a pair of scissors from the basket and gently held a lock of Angela's tresses as she snipped it short. In a matter of minutes, Angela's long hair became a thing of the past. The altar server covered the nun's head with a black veil.

The bishop commented, "Symbolically, you have renounced all vanity, pride, and materialism to enter a community of spirituality." He continued, "In the same way you are to leave your past behind you so, too, you will leave your baptismal name and today take the name of a religious. What will that name be?"

"I choose the name of Mary Rose, Bishop."

"So shall it be, Sister Mary Rose. Before those who will serve and before God Almighty, do you accept the vow of poverty, leaving behind you all unnecessary for your new journey in life?"

The young nun answered, "I profess the vow of poverty, Bishop."

Dana harbored a feeling of utter amazement at the sacrifices these young women were willing to make. She knew what came next. The vow of chastity. Her talk as a young child of wanting to be a nun quickly vanished after that day she had spent with her Uncle Lou on his rowboat. Although she never spoke about wanting to be a nun again, the desire to join the order of nuns who taught her remained hidden away in her heart, but she felt she was impure, soiled, dirty, and in the eyes of God, she would never be clean enough to be a bride of Christ.

"Do you, Sister Mary Rose, accept the vow of chastity, leaving behind you all need for sexual pleasure on your new journey in life?"

Dana heard a rustling from behind. The others in the chapel turned to see what the noise was about. A man in his early twenties dressed in a plaid flannel shirt, a pair of Wranglers, and some scuffed cowboy boots was making his way down the center aisle. He held both arms in the air, his hands in balled fists. "Stop right there! I know this woman!"

"What? Who's this?" people were heard whispering in the pews. "Someone grab an usher," another said.

Dana glanced at Logan who sat shaking his head, obviously as confused as the others.

"My name's Eddie Vineeti. I know this woman."

Two of the ushers ran up the aisle and grabbed the man under his arms. Logan shot up and accompanied the ushers.

"Get your grubby mitts off me, all of you!"

The ushers and Logan dragged the man to the back of the chapel as he began to blast obscenities. Sounds of "oos" and "ahs" came from the distressed crowd.

From where Dana was seated, she could see the beautiful nun's face coated in a crimson haze. The arms of the Mother Superior surrounded her.

One of the altar servers left and came back with a glass of water for the young nun.

She sipped at it and ran her fingers over her forehead.

A woman in the front pew, dressed in a yellow suit with a purple orchid pinned to her lapel, raced out of the pew and scurried to the altar. She said something to the Mother Superior and hugged the young nun.

Dana assumed the woman was the nun's mother. Under her maize pillbox hat, long, black curls fell; her complexion seemed as pale as her daughter's. Dana, in a soft voice, said "My God. What a scene!"

The woman spoke to her daughter for what seemed several minutes and then returned to her seat, her composure one of self-confidence and assuredness.

The service continued as normal with Sister Mary Rose responding, "I profess the vow of chastity." She also answered positively to the vow of obedience, took her seat among the others waiting to recite their vows, and an hour later, the entire order of nuns marched out of the chapel.

Next, the congregation left and gathered in the lobby of the chapel. Dana could hear them whispering, "Who in the hell was that guy?" Another muttered, "What made him so bold as to disrupt the whole service?" A woman in a derby hat with a green feather mumbled, "Did you see Mrs. Artenelli? Beautiful as always."

Standing off to one side, alone, was a priest who Dana assumed to be the pastor of Holy Name parish although she had not, as of yet, been formally introduced to the man. In the shadows of the stained-glass window, he watched Sister Mary Rose and the people who came up to congratulate her, to hug her, and to plant kisses on her porcelain face. Although he made no attempt to approach the young woman, his gaze remained fixed.

Dana couldn't wait to hear Sergeant Logan's explanation of the disturbing events. Who was this Eddie Vineeti character, and why the need to disrupt the ceremony? Out front, she could hear the wailing of a siren.

Chapter Five

Only two days earlier, Angela Artenelli had made her profession of final vows, and many of the same people who had attended her celebration now stood at the open grave of an innocent child whose life had been cut short by the hand of an unknown murderer.

The end of October and already the snow-filled clouds lay low in the sky. Intermittent piles of golden leaves lay like a blanket over the dry and brittle grass, the earth cold and hardened. Only a lone crow, its feathers covered in dust, hovered in the bare branches of an oak tree. Surrounding the crowd on all sides were tombstones as varied as the people beneath them. Some gravestones held blurry, glass-covered photographs of the deceased, who had passed on more than a century ago; while others were honored with plaster angels and sculpted crosses. In memory of those gone on, the living had left behind potted mums, eucalyptus wreaths, and tiny flags. There were also the forgotten souls whose stones were almost hidden behind prickly thorns and overgrown weeds.

Dana was grateful that Sergeant Logan had asked her to go with him; she never did do well with cemeteries. If one were supposed to believe that, indeed, there is an afterlife then she never quite understood the whole point of funeral arrangements, burial rites, and all of the ugly fake bouquets and floral wreaths. To Dana, it made a mockery of one's life more than it did to honor one's dead. But to each his own, and looking at the large gathering standing with her at the grave of Bernadette Godfrey, Dana was sure Bernadette's parents appreciated the support that wrapped around the burial site like outreached, embracing arms.

Most criminal investigators appreciate the opportunity, if one can call it that, to be present at a wake. Fiona Wharton, when she was Dana's mentor, used to say, "There's no better time to study the reactions to death than at a funeral service." Abiding by these thoughts, Dana consented to come. Slowly, she began to tune out what the good-looking priest, the one she had seen only yesterday in the vestibule of the church, mouthing the burial words from his black leather breviary was saying. She let the image of him standing at the front of the gravesite become nothing more than a blur in her eyes.

Instead, Dana decided to take Fiona Wharton's advice and to scan the crowd, making mental notes. She told herself that it would be rude to bring her notebook with her to such a somber occasion as this, yet she wished that she had made an exception to Emily Post's protocol.

Mrs. Artenelli, an obvious fashion statement, wore a black, knee-length coat with large loose sleeves, and a red fox around her neck. She wore a mauve velvet hat covered in beads and pearls with a black net veil covering her face. She stood with her arm draped over her daughter's shoulder. Sister Mary Rose, dressed in a black wool coat, huddled close to her mother and sobbed into a lace handkerchief that her mother held for her. The nun's eyes, red and swollen, tears rolled down her cheeks. Next to them, a man in a grey flannel suit, like one Dana had seen Gregory Peck wear, stood with his hands in a quasi-prayer mode, draped at the end of his long arms. His bearded face made him look distinguished, yet his red, bulbous nose and his protruding stomach which folded over his belt buckle spoke to a history of alcohol abuse. Someday Dana told herself she should write a book about how appearances and behaviors are key components in criminal investigations. She would call it profiling. It never failed to amaze her how her personal observations spoke volumes. Looking at the man one more time, she assumed he was Mr. Artenelli, yet she had not recalled him at the service yesterday. Odd he wouldn't be at his own daughter's important day.

Across the lawn, hovering together like two birds, sat Jay and Loretta Harrison on a white ornate metal bench. Even from this far away, Dana could see Jay crying uncontrollably, wiping his face with a large handkerchief. How horrible it must be for Sister Mary Rose and Jay to have seen Bernadette Godfrey only days before as a second-grader at their school and to stand before her casket today.

Several nuns from Holy Name Academy patrolled a group of about fifteen young children who stood in their school uniforms, each fingering black beaded rosaries. Bernadette's classmates no doubt. Logan told Dana that the second graders had assembled at the Godfreys' home earlier that morning to *see* their friend for the last time. According to Logan, Mr. and Mrs. Godfrey buried the girl in her First Communion dress and veil as she would not be among her fellow students the following May on their important and memorable day. Dana wondered how the children made sense of death at such a young age and could possibly be expected to process that one of their own classmates had her life ended so tragically. Certainly, their lives would be tainted forever.

Dana mingled through the crowd, attempting not to disturb the service nor the mourners. Kneeling on the hardened ground next to the casket, Dana assumed, was Bernadette's mother. Dana hadn't met her yet, but it was obvious who she was. The woman, dressed all in black including a veiled hat that covered most of her face, bent over the ivory coffin embellished with gold angels, tears falling onto her crocheted shawl, crystal beads entwined between her fingers, her lips quivering the prayers of the rosary. The man next to her, who Dana assumed to be the father of the child, stood rigid like a tree trunk. The two of them appeared to be middle-aged, and from what Sergeant Logan told Dana during her interview for the job, they had adopted the child and only this year had moved from Bay View to the island to provide the child with a safer living environment. How ironic.

"Always eliminate family members first," Fiona used to warn Dana. Looking at Mrs. Godfrey bowed over the casket of her only child, Dana likened the woman's emotions to raw open wounds. Mr. Godfrey, on the other hand, distanced himself from the anguish around him. Dana could not bring herself to see how any parent could willingly choose to end the life of his or her child. The parents would be suspects, however, just like anyone else who was associated with the girl, as difficult as that was for Dana to accept.

As for the rest of the faces in the crowd, she had no idea who they were. Could one possibly be wearing the mask of a murderer? After all, perpetrators were often known to attend the funerals of their victims.

In the background, Dana heard the closing prayer of the priest and the sounds of people rustling. The wake over, Dana turned to

Sergeant Logan, who said, "Did you notice anything out of the ordinary? Anyone in the group who looked conspicuous?"

"Don't know if you'd call this conspicuous or not, but I noted a few things."

"Like?"

"Sister Mary Rose. . . ."

"What about her?"

"She was blowing her nose into a lace handkerchief. A small thing, I guess, but it does seem odd that a nun who had just taken her vow of poverty wouldn't have had just a plain linen handkerchief."

A small smile covered Logan's face. "And?"

"The man in the grey flannel suit?"

"Oh, Gino Artenelli. . .Sister's father."

"Strange to see him at the funeral yet not at his daughter's profession of vows, don't you think?"

"Good point. I figured it had something to do with him not agreeing that his daughter enter the convent."

"I see. Then as for the father of the murdered child, well. . .why, he stood straight as an arrow through the whole service. I watched him; he never shed a tear, never showed any emotion. He made no attempt to even comfort his wife."

"Keen observations, Dana. You've proven one thing to me already."

"What's that?"

"You've got the eye of a good investigator."

Dana felt a warm glow hover across her face.

She and Logan turned to make their way to the cruiser when he whispered in her ear, "Over there. . .beneath the black maple."

Dana looked over her shoulder. "The card reader. . .Opal."

"You know her?" Logan asked, his eyebrows shot up like pointed arrows.

"Yes, met her on the ferry over to the island."

"Let me guess. She offered to read your cards?"

"Why yes, that's exactly right."

"And?" Logan opened the car door as Dana sat down on the front seat of the cruiser.

He walked around to the other side of the car, opened the door, and before he had a chance to slam it shut, Dana said, "She warned me to be wary of those who might hurt me because I tell the truth."

Logan grabbed at his chin. "That's interesting." He closed the door and started the engine.

"What's that?"

"She told me to embrace the truth, too." Thin horizontal lines formed at the corners of his eyes. "She also told me something else."

Dana waited.

"She told me several months back that I'd be burying a child. I'm not even married. I had no idea then who she meant."

"But you believed her?" Dana asked.

"Why not? Everyone on Cape Peril knows Opal's predictions are right on the money. You'd be a fool not to."

Chapter Six

Dana sat staring out the kitchen window intrigued by two grey squirrels with long, bushy tails that playfully chased each other around the Harrisons' back yard. A pile of burnt orange and gold-raked leaves braced itself against the trunk of a birch tree until one of the critters dashed over the mound, scattering leaves in his wake. "Such a beautiful place," Dana said to Loretta as she came into the room. "You must love this area."

"Not really. Dakota is my home." Loretta, dressed in a floor-length robe of vivid green with a satin front of fire red and aquamarine, forced a smile and poured some coffee into a dainty floral teacup.

"Mind if I ask why you ever left?"

"It was Jay's idea." The way she pronounced her husband's name told Dana that not only was it his idea but that Loretta also held him accountable and blamed him for the move.

"A job, I suppose?" A ploy, Dana was hoping Loretta would expand upon.

"Yeah, a job."

Obviously, Loretta wasn't going to go any further. She started to leave when Dana said, "Won't you join me?" Dana pointed to the empty seat across from her.

Loretta sat down across from Dana on the chrome kitchen chair, upholstered with a bright yellow vinyl seat. Loretta's jaw clenched; she picked on the cuticle of her thumb. Periodically, she peeked out at the back yard, mumbling something about Jay never having raked the leaves.

"Loretta, I don't know how better to say this, but I hope you don't find me an intrusion in your life. After all, here I am a total stranger, and I just move into your home."

Loretta shook her head and lowered her gaze onto the ecru lace tablecloth. She ran her fingers over the pattern, catching her nails on the loose threads.

"Sergeant Logan's the one to blame." Dana tried being more lighthearted, thinking she would force at least a chuckle out of Loretta.

Loretta brushed her hair behind her ears, diverted her sight into her teacup, and appeared non-responsive to Dana's attempt at humor. Slowly, Loretta sipped at her coffee.

Dana's plan to break the silence seemed to be going nowhere when Jay came in the back door, his cheeks a warm pink from the brisk fall day. He pulled off a home-made crocheted stocking cap from his head and unbuttoned his overcoat. "Brr, it's a cold one out there today. I got all the way to my appointment and realized I forgot something."

He quickly glanced at Loretta, who averted her gaze. Looking at Dana, Jay said, "Good morning. See you're still here. Thought after the funeral you'd have had second thoughts about wanting to work the case." He poured himself a cup of coffee, fumbled through some mail next to the sink, and turned on the Zenith radio, standing in the corner. He turned the knob until he found a station with clear reception. Rosemary Clooney's smoky voice echoed over the air.

Dana thought it odd that Jay's graciousness only days ago had suddenly changed to irritation, sarcasm, and a definite hint of arrogance. Jay didn't think women had enough guts to handle the seedier parts of life; that was obvious from his comment. "I don't get scared off that quickly; though, the case is tragic," Dana replied. Her intention was to put Jay in his place as she was not about to be treated as a second-class citizen based strictly on gender.

"Agreed."

"From what I've learned so far, Bernadette was the Godfrey's only child," Dana said.

"Adopted from some orphanage. A small town off Highway 202...Waterville, I think. The Godfreys came out to the island to get away from the crime scene in Bay View, and who would have guessed something like this would have happened?" He took a gulp of his coffee and set the cup down.

"Know much about the Godfreys?" Dana asked.

"The Mrs. is a caring woman. Not a thing she wouldn't do for the child."

"What about Mr. Godfrey?"

"Can't say I know him too well. He's a deckhand on the ferry. Quiet guy." Jay began to move the cookie jar and a set of rooster canisters from their position on the counter next to the sink.

Dana was about to ask him more when he said, "Listen. Don't mean to cut this short, but I've got to be on my way. Anyone notice a key around here?"

Loretta looked at Jay, a longing in her eyes. In a monotone voice she replied, "No, I haven't."

"Humph." He opened a kitchen drawer stuffed with hand towels. "Ah, here we are." On his way out, Jay turned. "By the way, Dana, thought you might like to know. That old woman came by last night looking for you."

"Old woman?"

"The devil worshipper."

Loretta's mouth opened, and for the first time, Dana thought she might have seen a hint of anger in the woman's face, yet she said nothing to her husband.

Dana began to speak. Suddenly, Jay interrupted her. "See you two later. Oh, and by the way, I'd prefer you not invite that card reader into my home."

It had to be Opal, but Dana had no idea why Opal would have come looking for her at the Harrison place. The woman had given Dana her phone number and told her where she lived should Dana have to speak with her again.

Loretta stood up and took her cup to the sink. She poured what was left of her coffee down the drain and took a glass out of the oak cupboard. She filled it with water and soaked the ivy plant on the windowsill. Dana could feel Loretta's sense of abandonment; she radiated it.

"Loretta, mind if I ask you something?" Dana asked.

Loretta's face spoke of mistrust. Dana had seen the look many times before in her line of work. The face that says, 'What do you want from me? Why are you pulling me into this?' Most people like that would just tell Dana to stay out of their business, but she knew

Loretta was not that type. Loretta would feel obliged to answer her if for no other reason than to be polite.

"How well did *you* know the Godfreys?"

Loretta turned and said, "You mean Bernadette?" She bit down on her lower lip and tears glistened in her brown eyes. She tightened the knotted belt on her robe. "She was like. . .our own. Jay and I can't have children."

"Oh, I'm sorry to hear that."

"Bernadette was a second grader in Sister Mary Rose's class. Jay'd bring her over lots of times. He'd help her with her homework; she'd stay for supper. I just can't imagine anyone wanting to hurt her." Loretta sniffled. Too embarrassed that she had even offered that much insight into her emotional make-up, Loretta hurried out of the room.

Bernadette was more than a student; she was a part of the Harrisons' family. Interesting, Dana thought. A replacement, perhaps, for the child Loretta had done away with.

Just then, a radio announcer interrupted the station and in a staccato-type voice said:

We interrupt station WXYZ to bring you this important message. A mysterious package found on the steps of the radio station early this morning included a child's shoe along with a note, stating that the saddle oxford might very well match that of Bernadette Godfrey, the seven-year-old child whose body was found only days ago on Cape Peril.

Dana wondered if Opal might not have seen this coming in one of her card readings. Could it be that was the reason for her sudden, unannounced visit to the Harrison home? First, Dana would call

Logan, a number she had already chosen to commit to memory, and then she'd stop by to see Opal.

Logan picked up the phone. "Just heard the radio announcement. Bernadette Godfrey's shoe was found."

"You read my mind," Dana said.

"I spoke with the station's manager, a guy by the name of Lloyd Briggims. He said the shoe was carefully placed in a cardboard box and whoever left it, wiped it clean of any fingerprints. Not only that, but whoever left the box timed it just right, so there would be no witnesses around."

"What about the sole of the shoe?" Dana inquired.

"Interesting that you should ask. According to Briggims, it looked as if someone attempted to wipe it clear, yet he said there was some dried mud and what looked like a broken pine needle on the heel."

"So, the shoe was worn."

"Sure was."

"This could mean a couple of things," Dana said.

"One?" Logan asked.

"If it is Bernadette's missing shoe, it could imply that the child walked to her own grave and was murdered on site."

"And, two?"

"Whoever sent the shoe is directly involved. Let's face it, Logan, the paper never leaked a word about the condition of Bernadette's body let alone that her shoe was missing."

"I hear you," Logan said.

"Either this person wants to be caught, or else is feeling guilt over his deed."

"And, third," Logan said, "we have a real sick mind on our hands here."

"Agreed."

"What's up your sleeve next, Dana?"

"I'd like to pay a visit to the Godfreys. Could you give me the number?" Dana grabbed a nearby napkin and jotted it down. "Oh, and one more thing. Is Eddie still around? I'd like to talk to him."

"Sure is. I'm keeping him in the clink for thirty-six hours. No way I'd charge him with any fine. Guy looks like he doesn't own more than the shirt on his back. Anything else?" Logan asked.

"Oh, there is. The card reader. . .Opal."

"The best that there is. Like I told you before, don't be swayed by what others have to say about her. She's been right too many times; that alone scares people. If you're interested in speaking with her, I'd just go down to her place; the woman loves visitors, lives right above the Rexall Pharmacy."

"I'll do that."

Dana was about to hang up when Logan said, "By the way, I can tell already that I like the way you're handling this case, particularly, your attention to the small details." Then, he added, "That's got to be a woman thing."

She thanked him and dialed the number for the Godfreys. "Mrs. Godfrey, my name is Dana Greer. I'm a private detective. . . ."

"I saw your picture. . .in the 'Post.' You were at the cemetery."

"I'm so sorry about your loss. I'm hoping, though, that I can help."

Mrs. Godfrey cleared her throat and in a scratchy voice said, "There's nothing you can do. No one can."

Dana could hear the hopelessness in the woman's voice. Dana wished there were something she could do. . .something far beyond trying to find the person guilty of murder, yet trying to solve the crime was supposed to be her area of expertise; however, it did not rule out the compassion she felt for the woman. "Could we at least talk?" Dana suggested stopping by in the morning and asked the woman's address.

"No, I'm afraid not; that won't work. My. . . ."

Dana gave the woman a chance to complete her thought, but Mrs. Godfrey stopped there. "Could we meet elsewhere, say the Sip 'n Stay, about ten?" Dana thought it odd that the woman did not invite her to her home, a more private setting than a coffee shop. Dana made a mental note.

"I'll see you then," Mrs. Godfrey said, and hung up the phone.

Dana hurried up the stairs to her room; her mind a whirlwind. As she rounded the corner, she heard faint sobs coming from one of the bedrooms, where Loretta was sitting on the floor by an open cedar chest. When she noticed Dana standing in the hall, Loretta quickly stashed what she had in her hands and slammed the lid of the chest. "Everything okay?" Dana asked.

The young woman whimpered a meek, "Yeah."

A part of Dana wanted to reach out to Loretta, to tell her she understood, to let Loretta know that whatever she was shedding tears over, Dana felt for her. Dana never forgot the day she learned that Nate had been unfaithful to her the entire time they were married.

Something about her sense of pride wouldn't allow her to admit to anyone she had been blind enough not to have seen the truth long beforehand. In the same way, Dana never told anyone about her uncle's abuse of her as a child. Psychology books call the defense mechanism repression; Dana called it running, something she had become quite adept at.

From what little Logan had told Dana about Loretta's past and her self-inflicted abortion, Dana knew Loretta, too, was running. Her method of handling things was to purposely keep herself a closed book. But, not for long.

Turning down the L-shaped hall toward her room, Dana realized there was yet another bedroom. The spread looked rumpled as if someone had gotten up in a hurry and failed to make the bed. The bed was a single. Might the Harrisons be sleeping in separate rooms? Dana wondered if that might explain why their relationship appeared to be so distant, so cold. Unlike Dana's relationship with Nate, there never was a moment when Dana found Nate withdrawn or unresponsive toward her, not even when he was sexually involved with another woman.

She sat down at her desk and hurriedly jotted in her notebook:

November 1, 1952

- *Meet with Mrs. Godfrey at the Sip'n Stay at ten*
- *Question Eddie Vineeti*

Dana decided to put Eddie first on her list before he had a chance to leave the area. Something about his erratic emotional state made her wonder about him.

- *Continue to learn more about Loretta and Jay's marriage*
- *Talk with Sister Mary Rose*

- *Talk with Mrs. Artenelli*

She looked at a previous item in her notebook about the highfalutin folks who lived on the Pointe. Remembering the stylish attire of Mrs. Artenelli made her think that maybe, just maybe, she was one of them.

In addition, Dana still hoped to speak with Opal. According to what Logan told her, Opal had a respected image on the island; at least there were people who believed what she saw in her cards to be true. That said a lot about Opal's ability on an island where the majority of people were Catholic and were indoctrinated with the belief that to have one's cards read is a sin. Dana was not about to rule out Opal as a potential prospect in helping her with the case. On the other hand, Dana told herself that she must not forget to investigate the rumor spread by the naysayers who believed that Opal had something to do with the death of Bernadette.

Tomorrow before she met with Mrs. Godfrey, she'd see if the nosey waitress was on duty. Like Opal had told her on the ferry, people were well connected on the small island. Who was to say who knew what?

This early in her investigation, Fiona had taught her that it was much better to have too many leads than not enough.

Chapter Seven

S hortly after Jay left for classes at Holy Name Academy and
Loretta went to her job at the antique shop, Dana was finally
alone in the house and could wait no longer.

The cedar chest lid in Loretta's room squeaked as Dana raised its
copper hinges. The comforting scents of cedar mixed with lilac and
roses came from inside. Layers of white lace covered in crystal beads
lay near the top, and as Dana lifted the piece, she saw that it was a
wedding veil. Beneath it were yards and yards of white satin graced
with shiny rhinestones and white petaled roses of the same fabric.
Loretta's wedding dress, Dana assumed. She carefully laid the weighty
dress and its incredibly long train on the carpet next to her, trying to
imagine Loretta of such tiny stature wearing the attire. Her parents
must have wanted her to appear as the blushing bride she wasn't,
having her walk down the aisle dressed in white. A creased and
folded document lay beneath. The words embossed in a fine and
detailed gold pen spoke of the marriage of Loretta Amhurst and Jay
Harrison on the 5th day of June 1947. Like a child snooping in an old
attic chest, Dana's curiosity intensified as she dug deeper to find
more hidden treasures; or, in this case, hidden secrets that might help
her to understand the quiet ways of a woman of so few words.

Dana expected to find family photographs in the velvet-covered
album tied together with black shoelaces. She lifted the cover and
several small pieces of paper fell onto the floor: one a newspaper
clipping from 'The American News,' announcing Jay and Loretta's

marriage in Aberdeen, South Dakota; another from the same paper congratulated Jay on his magnum cum laude graduation from Northern University. Dana set the articles down and looked at the last clipping:

Dr. Hayes Talbot, a surgeon in Aberdeen, confirmed treating a fifteen-year-old girl, in her second trimester, who had performed a self-inflicted abortion. Dr. Talbot stated that in all twenty-five years in practice, he had never seen such a tragic case. He claimed, "When the girl entered my office, her intestines were hanging from her body." Thanks to the immediate care of Dr. Talbot, the girl recovered. No charges were brought.

Dana's mouth opened in awe. So, Loretta had caused her own abortion and had not been prosecuted for her deed. Although the reporter had deliberately left out Loretta's name from the article, true to small towns, rumors must have spread that the patient came from a well-to-do family, a professional's family, who would not want their dirty laundry out on the line for all to see. Some bribe must have occurred under the table, or else someone with influence was able to keep things hushed up. These were the only explanations Dana could come up with that might explain why Loretta was not prosecuted.

While at it, Dana decided to browse through some of the photos in the album. Nothing looked to be unusual: typical photographs of what appeared to be family and friends; that is until she got to the back of the book. In a pocket, she found two colored photos. They looked to have been taken on the grounds of Holy Name Academy. One photo showed Bernadette Godfrey with Jay Harrison, his arm wrapped around the girl's shoulder. The two were smiling for the camera. The second picture was of Sister Mary Rose, still in the white veil of the novice, and Jay, their arms around each other's waists. From what Dana knew about novices, religious orders forbade them from the vanity of a camera's lens. Attempting to figure out which of the items in the chest might have triggered Loretta's tears proved pointless. Clearly, the memories in the chest represented Loretta's sorrows, and to do away with their contents would be comparable to doing away with Loretta's life.

Dana's snooping had more than paid off for the day. If lucky, she could make it to the woman's apparel shop down the street from the police station to get some warm boots and a heavy coat, head over to the Sip 'n Stay to speak some more with the waitress, and meet with Mrs. Godfrey by ten.

The blustering winds coming in from the ocean made it difficult to walk. Dana found herself zig-zagging down the sidewalk. Falling snow showers began to stick to the pavement, painting it a slick white. The Seaside Ferry's horn blasted its arrival at the pier, and, ultimately, another day was underway on the Cape.

Dana brushed off the snow accumulated on the sleeves of her coat and entered the woman's shop. Surprised, Dana saw Opal talking to one of the sales help.

"We meet again," Opal said.

"Nice seeing you."

Instead of stopping to chat, the old woman hurried from the store, looking back to say, "By the way, buy the red one. It'll look great on you."

"May I help you?" the sales girl asked, pinning a sales tag on a green-and-blue striped dress.

"I'd like a warm coat."

"I have just the thing for you. Follow me." She led Dana to a rack at the back of the store. "It's called poodle cloth. You know, those adorable little breeds? Well now, Jacques Lesur has taken the idea and designed a perfect fashion statement of curly wool. Here, let's try this one on." She slipped a blue plaid coat off its hanger.

Dana removed her raincoat and put her arms into a double-breasted, wide lapelled coat with a thick belt. She looked at her image in the mirror. Rather pretentious, she thought, for a detective. She pulled the collar up and let her shoulder-length blond curls rest on it. She puffed up her pompadour and tightened the bobby pins just above her ears.

"You've an attractive woman. The coat makes you look like a million. Are you a model by chance?" the sales girl asked.

"Heavens no," Dana said, surprised by the compliment and by the fact that the sales woman had not recognized her from the newspaper article. The clerk stood back and admired the coat and said, "Opal told me you were someone very important; I figured you were in fashion. Here, let's try on the red one. It'll look great with your pale complexion, blond hair, and big blue eyes."

It certainly was warmer than the raincoat Dana had, and with the weather only getting worse, she decided to purchase the red, poodle-like coat and a pair of black knee-high galoshes lined in white rabbit fur. If only she had gotten that coat from the J. C. Penney Catalog, she would have saved twelve dollars. Now, with the galoshes, she'd spent twenty-eight! Opal was right, though. The red did look good on her.

Dana hurried over to the Sip 'n Stay. The waitress, who Dana had hoped to speak with, was delivering two pieces of French toast to a man in the front booth. The woman nodded at Dana.

Dana sat down in the last booth, hoping it would give Mrs. Godfrey and her some privacy when the woman arrived. The Sip 'n Stay drew its share of business; that was for sure.

"My! My! Don't we look fancy," the waitress said, walking toward Dana. "Headin' anywhere in particular?"

Dana smiled. "No. Just trying to beat the cold."

The waitress lowered her voice and covered her mouth with one hand. She asked, "How's the case comin'? Any leads on who did that god-ugly thing to the little Godfrey girl?"

"No, no leads, just many unanswered questions."

"Well, let me tell you this. I heard you're staying with the Harrisons?"

As Opal had said, word traveled quickly on the small island.

"Better I warn you to watch out for Jay Harrison's wife." The waitress slipped into the booth and sat across from Dana as if they were long-lost friends.

Dana deliberately stayed mute. She had found, over the years, that besides learning much from one's body behavior, one also learned from listening.

"She's got secrets, that one. Just 'cause her daddy was some big shot, the woman got away with murder. And, I mean, murder." The woman coiled her hand around her lips.

"Could you explain?"

"Let me take your order, and I'll be back."

Dana ordered a raspberry jelly donut and a cup of coffee and stared at the people coming and going from the shop, her curiosity piqued by what the waitress was about to tell her.

When the server returned, she placed the donut and cup of coffee in front of Dana, and once again sat across from her. "That Bernadette Godfrey child was a replacement for the one Loretta killed," the waitress said, in a voice so faint Dana could hardly hear.

"Killed? How sure of all this are you?"

"I'm positive. Rumors have it that the story made the front page of 'The American News' in Aberdeen, South Dakota. The woman used a hanger. As quickly as the murder made news, it just as fast went by the wayside."

"What about Jay, her husband? If this were true, why would he have married Loretta?"

The waitress pointed her red enameled nail at Dana. "Why do people do the strange things they do, Miss Greer? For money!"

Dana could feel her eyes widening and her brows raising, not her usual facial expression when someone told her something shocking. Normally, she maintained her objectivity.

"Loretta Harrison comes from money; money is what closed the case as fast as it opened; and money is what bought that pretty Victorian home they live in. Daddy saw to it all. Probably wanted to get the two of them as far away from Aberdeen as he could. Can't say for sure, but I wonder how Jay landed his job at the Academy. Maybe, that was an inside deal as well." The waitress looked over toward the kitchen. "My boss is motioning me; I gotta go."

"Oh, just one quick question."

"Yeah?"

"Loretta. . .she's so quiet."

The waitress nodded her head. "Sure is. And she's got a reason to be. Her handsome husband and her don't got much going for them." The waitress turned her face to the side and covered her cheek with her hand. "You know. . .in the bedroom."

"But wait." Dana reached across the table for the waitress's hand. "Why would he stay? It can't just be his job that keeps him on the Cape."

"Money."

The waitress got up and headed to the kitchen. No sooner had she left, then Dana saw Mrs. Godfrey perusing the coffee shop. Dana stood up. "Mrs. Godfrey, over here," Dana waved.

The woman walked toward her with stooped shoulders. Her head was covered in a black shawl. Several grey hairs poked through the knit, like straws in a hay field. The woman's brown wool coat, worn on the elbows, appeared two sizes too big for her, and her rubber boots were cuffed with dirty gray fur.

The two shook hands, and Dana noticed the woman's skin was red and chapped, some of her knuckles cracked and bleeding, and her fingers shook. Dana watched as the woman scooted into the booth, sitting up against the red-tiled wall. Evidently, she had been crying for some time as her eyes were puffy and her nose red and swollen. In a soft voice, she said, "What was it you wanted to tell me, Miss Greer? Who did this to my baby?" She pulled a linen cloth from her coat pocket and began to rub her nose.

The woman's forthrightness surprised Dana. "No, Mrs. Godfrey. . . not yet anyway, but I intend to find out." The thought of the Pembroke case that went cold crossed Dana's mind. She wanted to promise Mrs. Godfrey that the same would not be true this time but couldn't quite bring herself to say so. Dana stared at the jelly donut in front of her and pushed it aside as she sipped on her coffee. "Would you care to order something?" Dana asked Mrs. Godfrey.

"No, not hungry," the gaunt-looking woman said.

Dana returned to her thoughts about the missing child. "Is there anything you can tell me about the day your daughter disappeared?"

The woman stuffed her handkerchief in her pocket and spread the palms of her hands across her cheeks. She shook her head. "No. It was like any other day. Bernadette walked to school every morning, left at 7:45 and never showed up."

"Did she walk with other children?"

The woman clutched her hands together, twisting the fingers on her right hand. "No, Bernadette was shy. She didn't know too many children. We only moved to the Cape seven months ago. I never should have let her go alone."

"Don't blame yourself. It's not your fault. You know that, don't you?"

"It's why we left Bay View. I wanted her to be safe." Mrs. Godfrey paused, her face deep in thought. Fine, carved lines outlined her eyes and her upper lip trembled. "I should have known better."

"Known what, Mrs. Godfrey?"

"God. . .It was God. He punishes." She nodded. "That's why He took my Bernadette."

Dana thought it odd how the woman had changed her thoughts about leaving Bay View to abruptly shifting her blame on God.

Mrs. Godfrey fumbled with the brass buttons on her coat. "It was him who took her from Joe and me. He made us pay for a poor choice." Tears flowed down the woman's face, and her eyes blurred. She looked toward the wall and ran her hand over her lips.

Dana got up and sat next to the woman. She attempted to put her hand on her shoulder, but she coiled away from her like a garden snake, nestling close to the wall. Still unclear as to what Mrs. Godfrey was saying, Dana asked, "Why do you think God would want to punish you?"

In a muffled voice, hardly discernible, the woman went on, "Joe and I weren't able to have children. We decided to adopt. Never should have, never." In between her sobs, she said, "I should have known better. If God had wanted for me to be childless, I should have accepted his plan, offered it up for the sins of the world."

"Do you think God would actually punish you for adopting a child?" Dana had no idea where the woman was going with this self-accusation.

The woman turned toward Dana and muttered, "Like I said, He never wanted Joe and me to have children. I went against His plan. Now, Bernadette had to go back to God."

Before Dana could think of what to say next, the woman shoved against Dana's sleeve. "I have to go now," she said. "Joe would be mad if he knew I was here talking to you."

Dana got up and watched the woman, bent nearly in half, leave the coffee shop. The woman's thoughts, far from making any logical sense, puzzled Dana. She placed fifty cents on the table.

The waitress arrived. "Something wrong with your donut? Stale?"

"No, just lost my appetite," Dana said, heading for the door, her intentions to make it to the station to speak with Eddie Vineeti next.

Walking down Port Street, Dana thought about how much she had grown to like the Cape after only having been on the island for a week. Something about the size of the place appealed to her. The main street through town consisted of four blocks, yet it had everything one could want from apparel shops to a five-and-ten, to a library and medical center, as well as a mom-and-pop hardware and a service station for those bringing cars to the island. The Holy Name Academy with its church, convent, and rectory occupied an entire city block of its own. As Dana neared the police station, the Polish bakery sandwiched next to it scented the chilly air with the sweet smells of cinnamon rolls and vanilla wafers. The Rexall Drugs on the other side of the station was running its Christmas sales a month early. In the window, the newspaper clipping announced some of its best deals:

Bath Powder $1.25

50 Christmas Cards 98 cents

Brush and Comb Set $1.39

Dana entered the station and noticed Janet, the receptionist, was not at her desk. The place sounded exceptionally quiet except for the flapping of playing cards. She peeked into Logan's office and found the young secretary and Logan playing a game of War. It appeared the receptionist was winning, evidenced by the high stack of cards in front of her. Dana decided not to disturb them and, instead, meandered toward the jail cell in the rear of the station.

The six-foot by eight-foot room, painted lime green, contained a narrow cot bolted to the wall, a toilet with no lid, and a small stool that looked like the type used to milk cows. Near the ceiling, a window the size of a loaf of bread, covered in thick, rusted bars prevented any prisoner from even imagining an escape. In the cell, she found Eddie Vineeti. Still in his wrinkled leather cowboy boots, his overly tight jeans, and a plaid flannel shirt, he lay on his cot, his head propped under his hand, flipping through a *Life* magazine. He hummed "Unforgettable," a Nat King Cole tune.

"Go on in," Logan said. Dana jumped at the sound of his deep voice coming from behind her. "He's expecting you; I left the cell open." A bit of an oxymoron, Dana thought, or else a bit more trusting than she would have been.

Eddie looked up. His blond head buzzed like a sailor's made his ears stand a bit too far out. In the pocket of his shirt, he kept an opened pack of Camel cigarettes. He had the kind of sparkling eyes that made his face look friendly, far from what Dana expected to find after his uproar at Sister Mary Rose's profession of vows.

He got up from the cot he was lying on, throwing the magazine onto the tiled floor. "Yeah?" He eyed her with a suspicious look, yet with an air of arrogance.

Dana sat on the short wooden stool, and he sat back on the cot.

"My name's Dana Greer. I'm the new private investigator on Cape Peril. I've been hired to work on the Bernadette Godfrey case."

Vineeti picked at the tip of one of the cigarettes, small pieces of tobacco landing on his shirt. He lowered his chin and blew the crumbs into the air.

"What'd ya want from me?" He curled the corner of his lip.

"The ceremony the other day. . .in the chapel?"

"Yeah, the ceremony. . .what was that. . .five days ago. When in the hell do I get out of this joint?"

"That's a decision Sergeant Logan must make. Like I said, I'm here to solve the murder of Bernadette Godfrey," Dana said.

"What's the church thing got to do with a dead kid?" He wrinkled his face until his lips and nose became one.

"Nothing, I suppose," Dana said.

"Then, why you askin' me?"

"I just wondered why you felt it necessary to disrupt the service."

He smiled, his teeth stained yellow from one too many cigarettes.

"Wouldn't you?" He looked at Dana with a cocky expression.

"I'm not sure what you mean."

"I mean Angela Artenelli and me? We were a thing, man, going steady and all." He rolled his shoulders and ran his hand through his buzzed head.

"You say *were?*"

"Angela was forced to join the convent. Her mother made the decision, plain and simple. Angela had no say in the matter."

He was trying to blame Mrs. Artenelli? She coerced her child into becoming a nun? Just as Dana had expected, Eddie was voluntarily providing more information than she had asked. As if saying a silent prayer to a saint, Dana thanked Fiona once again.

"She never wanted us going together in the first place. Against some God damn commandment or something, she said." He pulled a cigarette from the pack and let it hang, unlit, from his bottom lip.

Dana noticed a purple tattoo on the side of his neck. A heart with the letters *AA & EV* in the center of it.

"Why did you wait until now? I mean, Angela was professing her final vows. If you wanted her to reconsider, why didn't you do something before?"

"Lady," he said, looking at Dana as if she were a moron, "let's just say it was a last-ditch effort."

"Did you really think you could have prevented Angela from going through with her final vows?"

"Ain't it worth a try?" Eddie cocked his head to the side and tapped his fingertips along the purple-stained letters on his neck.

Dana studied Eddie's demeanor. Probably in his mid-twenties, a cute kid underneath it all, but one who was putting on an air of toughness, of belligerence, but to what avail? she wondered. She couldn't see extending her questioning any further. That is until Eddie stood up, stared her right in the face, and in a quiet voice so as not to be heard by Logan or the jail receptionist, said, "I ain't through with Mrs. Artenelli yet. That bitch owes me one."

"Is that a threat?" Dana hoped her voice didn't reflect the fear that she suddenly felt. . .his words icy, cold-blooded.

He pulled the cigarette from his lip. "Guess, you'll just have to wait and see, won't ya?"

Something about his boy-like, innocent face not matching with his combative nature didn't add up. Anger? Revenge? The two never made a good combination. Who knew just what Eddie might be capable of given the right circumstances?

On the way out, Dana stopped in Logan's office. "Got *any* background on this guy?"

"Some petty larceny stuff. A fist fight. Some shoplifting. A high school dropout. Pretty tame by law-and-order standards."

"Hmm."

Logan put up his hand in the air. "Oh, there is one other thing. About five years ago, he married some pawn dealer's daughter. Girl by the name of Rayna Milton from some little town in Maine."

Dana looked at Logan. "He still married?"

"Far as I know, yeah."

Dana started to leave when Logan said, "Why the look on your face?"

"Why the interest in an ex-girlfriend who became a nun if the guy's got a wife?" she asked.

On her way to the Harrisons', Dana was more convinced than ever that speaking with Sister Mary Rose and Mrs. Artenelli would be high on her list of to-dos. Dana hoped the nun could tell her what part Eddie played in her past. Dana wasn't sure how Mrs. Artenelli could figure into the death of little Bernadette, but now was not the time to rule anyone out.

Chapter Eight

Eddie was shoved out of the Cape Peril Police Station by Officer Boyle who treated him like a piece of raw meat. Eddie slid across the sidewalk, bumping his head into a fire hydrant. "And don't let us see your God damn ass around here again. Ya hear me?" Boyle growled. He spit onto the pavement and placed his hand on his holster.

"Yeah, sure, man. Sure." Eddie got up and brushed himself off. When he was out of earshot, he cursed the officer and hobbled to the ferry, realizing that he had broken the heel on his right boot. He occupied his time on the ride back to the mainland with bitter thoughts of how he'd seek revenge, not only against Mrs. Artenelli but anyone else who got in his way.

When he finally got back to Waterville and opened the front door, Rayna was waiting in pink baby-doll pajamas. Her red hair was in pigtails tied with white satin ribbons.

"Where you been, handsome?" She tried to put her arms around Eddie's waist, but he pushed her aside.

"Ain't none of your beeswax," he said.

"I've been worrying 'bout you, baby. You've been gone for days." She played with three tiny buttons that ran down the front of her pajamas.

"I don't need no one worrying 'bout me. I can take care of myself."

"But, baby, I missed you." Rayna stood on tiptoe and planted a kiss on Eddie's cheek.

Eddie pretended to spit on the palm of his hand and then wiped his cheek. "I've been in the graybar hotel." He flopped down so hard on the sofa that a spring popped.

"Where's that, honey?"

"For God's sake, Rayna, are you that stupid?" He watched as the complexion of her face turned to a shade of cherries. "Ya never heard that term before?" He twirled his little finger in his right ear, and with a flick of his thumb, he shot a piece of earwax onto the carpet.

She shook her head.

"Think about it," he snapped.

"You ain't been in trouble with the law again, have ya?" She sat down next to him and nuzzled as close as she could.

"Well, my, my. You been listening to Sam Spade again, that radio detective guy?"

"What are you talkin' about, Eddie?"

This time he shook his head. He picked up an old newspaper on the coffee table and read:

Socialite Family on the Cape Marry Off Their Only Daughter to...Christ Carmelina Artenelli attended Holy Name Church on Cape Peril on October28 to participate in her daughter's final profession of vows in the Immaculate Heart of Mary religious order of nuns. Angelina Artenelli, a second-grade teacher at the Holy Name Academy, took the religious name of Sister Mary Rose.

"Just like I figured," Eddie muttered to himself. "Her old man didn't have a say in the matter. If he had a choice, you can be damn sure his daughter would never have been a bride of Christ." Eddie ran his dirty thumbnail through his front teeth.

"What cha readin', Eddie?" Rayna peered over his side. "Who got married? Do you know the girl?"

"Know her? You bet your ass, I do. Ain't you ever heard of the Artenelli family?" He threw the paper back on the table.

"No."

"Used to live over on Gardenia Circle in one of those houses that almost take up a whole city block. Sold that place and moved to the Cape. Hear they got a real pretty mansion up there on the Pointe."

"Rich, huh?"

"You better believe it, girl. More money than me and you could count," Eddie said, with a sneer on his face.

"How'd they get so much money, honey bunch?"

"The old boy, Gino Artenelli, is a mobster. Been involved with the gangsters for as long as I've known."

"Why don't the police arrest him?" Rayna asked, in a child-like voice.

"The police?" Eddie laughed. "They ain't gonna touch someone as powerful as Gino. Oh, no. They prefer to look the other way. Wouldn't surprise me none if they didn't get a little cut from the guy just from keeping their damn mouths shut."

"But ain't that illegal, Eddie?" Rayna picked up the article that Eddie had set down. "Who's Sister Mary Rose? Do you know her?"

"Used to. A long time ago."

"Is she pretty, Eddie?"

Eddie thought for a moment. "Hell no, she ain't pretty. She's all bundled up in those blue robes with a veil to her knees." He thought to himself, *But under those robes, oh baby! She's got the body of Rita Hayworth, the face of an angel.*

"I don't get it, Eddie."

"What's that?"

"Why girls decide to become nuns. Ain't they the least bit interested in men?"

Eddie exhaled a stream of hot air. "Sometimes, they don't got a choice." He propped his feet up on the coffee table, a chunk of dirt fell onto the glass.

"Eddie, honey, how cha break your heel?"

"Huh?" He pulled off his boots and socks. "Rayna, honey, get me a cold beer, won't cha?"

"Sure will, Eddie." She started to walk toward the kitchen and turned. "I'm glad you're back, honey. It sure was lonely around here without ya."

"Yeah, yeah." While he waited, he tried to pick up a checker piece from the table with his left foot. He placed the game piece on his right knee and continued to play the balancing act until Rayna returned from the kitchen. He had always been double-jointed, and his mother used to say she wanted to put him in a carnival act.

Rayna returned with a frosted mug filled to the brim with beer. "While ya was gone, you got a phone call, Eddie." She sat back next to him.

"From who?" He let the checker pieces fall and took a long slug of his beer.

"You really want to know?" she asked, trying to egg him on.

"Yeah."

"You'll have to catch me if you do." Rayna stood up and playfully started running around the living room, into the kitchen, and back to the living room. The two chased each other like children playing tag until Eddie finally cornered Rayna who fell laughing onto the sofa.

"So, tell me. . .who called?"

"Your mother."

"What? You've got to be kidding me? I chased you all around this house only for you to tell me my mother called?"

"What's wrong with that?" Rayna asked, out of breath.

"I haven't heard from that bitch for at least five or six years. If you remember, I had to throw her out of the house that Christmas she came over drunk as a skunk."

"Oh, I remember. Think we were only dating then."

"If you recall, she started calling you all kinds of names and cussin' like a drunken sailor. The woman should talk; she's nothin' more than a street walker who cleans up other people's shit on her days off."

"Eddie, that's a terrible thing to say about your mama."

"It's true, every damn word of it. I don't need her puttin' her nose in our business. No, she'd better leave us alone." Eddie sat back down and sipped on his beer. After a few moments, he said, "Did she say what she wanted?"

"Who? Your mother?" Rayna asked. "Just said she needed to talk with you."

"Hmm." Eddie had absolutely no idea what she would want, and he wasn't sure he cared to find out.

Chapter Nine

After going through reels and reels of microfilm, spending hours at the Agatha Christie Library on Cape Peril, all Dana came up with was the same clipping that she had found in Loretta's cedar chest. The unobtrusive article did appear on the front page of the Aberdeen, Dakota newspaper as the waitress had said, but anything more than that Dana couldn't find. The explanation the waitress offered her at the Sip 'n Stay was the only one she had and not a bad one at that. If Loretta's father became mayor at the time that Loretta aborted her unborn child and no charges were made, one of the most logical things to assume was that the mayor paid off the media to keep their mouths shut. As for what the waitress told her about Jay and Loretta's relationship, this was definitely something Dana would look into. The two unmade beds in two separate rooms had made Dana suspicious, not to mention the lack of communication between the couple. From all Dana saw of their relationship, it seemed Jay did little to tolerate his wife and, in fact, preferred to be out of their home as much as possible.

The only time Loretta appeared the least bit interested in carrying on a conversation with Dana was when she spoke about Bernadette and how she enjoyed having the child in their home. Could it be that the Godfrey child reminded Loretta of the unborn child she aborted? Would that alone give Loretta motive for her wanting the child dead? Would it be strong enough reason for her to eventually do away with the child?

Dana fixed her eyes on the photo of Jay with Sister Mary Rose that she had found in the chest: the young nun as a novice in her white habit with a male teacher, and the two hugging. Dana told herself that she was letting her imagination get away from her, but then wasn't that what every good investigator did? What if Jay and Sister Mary Rose were more than just teachers at Holy Name Academy? What if Loretta suspected that? Certainly, one way of punishing Jay would be to do away with the child that Jay so much loved. Dana wondered who might have taken the picture of Jay and the nun. Surely not one of the other nuns or the priest. That might have been Loretta's first indication that Jay and the nun were more than just colleagues at the Academy. As farfetched as these theories sounded, Fiona Wharton had taught Dana early on that it was better to consider all options when working a case than to let something slip between the cracks.

In the same way, Dana didn't understand why Eddie would disrupt the nun's religious ceremony. Was he really thinking that he could woo Sister Mary Rose back? That explanation sounded weak to her in that Eddie was married now. What difference would it make? His threat against Mrs. Artenelli was a serious one, though. No doubt he appeared erratic and emotionally unbalanced, but was that a strong enough motive to shed suspicion on him as a murderer of the Godfrey child?

Dana rubbed the back of her neck, which had gone into a miserable spasm. Too many questions without answers and more to come, she was sure. Slowly, she began to put the individual rolls of film into their responding canisters. She looked at her watch. Four o'clock and she had arrived at the library at noon. She returned the canisters to their appropriate shelves, put on her red coat, and tied a woolen scarf around her neck.

As she stood to leave, a mural of fishing vessels and lobster traps painted on a soft blue palette caught her attention. Such a peaceful scene. Dana knew she would have to find some way to relax as well. Only a little over a week since she arrived on the Cape and every minute her mind raced with unanswered questions. She knew that many private detectives found themselves so obsessed with their cases that they eventually quit their jobs or ended up committing suicide.

Dana shook her head and rubbed her forehead, her headache intensifying. She would go back to the Harrisons' and return the items she had taken from the chest. Then, she'd see if they had a phonograph and some relaxing albums. If lucky, they might even have some records by Eddie Fisher, her favorite. Listening to music sounded ideal.

As she was about to pass the research librarian's desk, Dana noticed Opal seated at a table, her nose buried deep in a book. Her first impulse was to leave unnoticed, but then she remembered what Logan had told her, "Everyone on Cape Peril knows Opal's predictions are right on the money." Dana decided to take whatever help she could get in solving the Godfrey case even if it meant taking it from a card reader.

She went over to Opal and tapped her lightly on the arm. The old woman looked up from her book, which bore the title *Trust Your Mind*.

"How nice to see you again. Love the red coat. I told you that was your color."

"Indeed you did."

"Join me, won't you?" Opal motioned for her to sit across from her at the table. "I stopped by the Harrison house the other day to see you, but you were out."

"So I heard. I had planned to stop by your place, but. . . ."

"No matter. We can speak here just as well as anywhere else."

All Dana wanted was an aspirin and some rest, but she could tell Opal would be offended if she didn't give her some time.

"You know I'm a card reader, but there's more to it than that. Sometimes, I get these. . .well, feelings, I guess you could call them. I had one of them the other day."

"Really?"

"I could tell just as sure as shootin' that someone was feeling guilty over that little girl's death. I got out my deck and sure enough."

"What happened?" Dana wondered if there might be any connection with the radio report of an anonymous person leaving a girl's saddle oxford at the station.

"I shuffled the deck, concentrated upon it, and pulled out one card from the stack."

"And?"

"Here let me show you," Opal said, as she pulled out her Tarot cards from the black pouch. She put the deck face-up and fingered through the cards, zealously searching for one in particular, Dana assumed. Several minutes later, Opal laid down one of the cards:

"The Nine of Swords," Dana said, feeling confused.

Opal squinted, then widened her eyes, revealing the unusually large pupil in her left eye. "The card of self-loathing and guilt, but that's not all."

"What do you mean?"

"No matter how many times I shuffled the cards and randomly chose one from the deck the same card appeared: the Nine of Swords."

Dana asked Opal whether she had heard the announcement on the radio about the box with a lone shoe in it.

"No, no I hadn't. When did you hear this. . .about the shoe?"

"A couple of days ago. Why?"

The woman fanned her fingers across her lips. "That's odd. Two days ago is when I drew the card repeatedly from the deck."

"You're saying you think the person who dropped the box off at the radio station in Bay View is the same person who murdered Bernadette Godfrey?" Dana studied the old woman's complexion covered in heavy pancake makeup with rosy, round circles over her cheeks. Her gray brows were penciled in with a harsh brown. The wrinkles on the woman's face overlapped, making her face appear to be made of modeling clay. The woman's warm breath on Dana's face smelled of bitter coffee.

"Who else?" Opal said.

Although it did seem strange that Opal would have her feelings on the same day that the mysterious person dropped off missing evidence, it in no way brought Dana any closer to understanding who might have wanted the girl dead. On the other hand, it did reassure Dana that Opal was not a devil worshipper as Jay and some of the other islanders thought. No, as Logan had told Dana, "Everyone on the Cape knows Opal's predictions are right on the money." Could it be that the murderer would eventually be overcome by his self-hatred and guilt and turn himself in? Dana would have to wait and see.

Chapter Ten

A light dusting of snow, like powdered sugar covered the streets, and the darkness from the night before had not dissipated. The harsh climate of Northern Maine ushered in winter conditions long before even other New England states. On the way to Holy Name Academy, at seven a.m., a brisk four-block walk, Dana and Jay ventured in silence. Dana had asked Jay if he might introduce her to the nun. At first, Jay had appeared uncomfortable with her request, questioning its purpose, assuming that Dana was after more than she told him. When Dana explained that speaking with Sister Mary Rose might help her to better understand the Sister's former second-grade student, Jay had consented.

The dull street lights shone on the snow and helped to light the way, and the headlights from an occasional car served as beacons in an otherwise black morning.

As they meandered along, Dana could sense tension. Jay's attempt to remain silent, Dana felt, was his way of protesting her insistence on meeting with the nun. As was true of many men, Jay believed a woman's place was near the oven baking chocolate chip cookies or by the fire mending torn socks, not putting her nose into other people's business even if the purpose was to bring justice. It didn't take Dana too long to realize that maybe, just maybe, there might be more to Jay's makeup than she had originally seen. For one thing, he sure didn't know how to treat his wife lovingly, and for another, he had a need to show masculine superiority, so common in the day's patriarchal society.

They stomped the snow off their boots and entered the school, scents of chalk dust, lemon air freshener, textbook ink, and, of course, the all too familiar smell of Crayolas.

"Mass starts in an hour, so Sister might not be here yet," Jay said as he led Dana into the faculty lounge and switched on the lights. A few wine-colored upholstered pieces filled the space, along with several oak tables, and lamps with brown-leather type shades, shielding bright light bulbs. On the wall above the couch hung an oak framed picture of Pope Pius XII, standing in the portico of St. Peters waving to a crowd of people. In a small alcove adjacent to the room stood two small desks with chairs. Pictures of the Sacred Heart of Jesus and the Sacred Heart of Mary hung crooked on the wall above, their frames covered in dust. Opposite the door a bulletin board stuck with red and yellow headed pins posted the week's events:

Monday	*Dr.Polly Thatcher speaks to school assembly*
Tuesday	*Visitor from the Bay View Zoo*
Wednesday	*Parent/Teacher Open House*
Thursday	*Mother Superior speaks on vocations*
Friday	*Prayer for the end of Communism in Russia*

"Who's Doctor Thatcher?" Dana asked.

"She's a school psychologist who's to speak to the kids today about loss."

"Anybody speaking to the children on personal safety, not speaking to strangers, things like that?"

"Maybe you'd like to do that," Jay said, his voice rising at the end of his sentence, his eyebrows like upside down V's.

"No thanks. My job is solely to find out who did this horrible thing to Bernadette Godfrey, not to tell youngsters how to protect themselves from a murderer on the loose."

"But don't you think that would be important for them to know? All I'm saying is how do we know *if* Bernadette will be the last victim?" Jay asked, as he ran his thumb across his Adam's apple.

Something about the way Jay put his emphasis on the word *if* made Dana question what he was getting at. "Perhaps, you're right, but hopefully, I'll track down whoever murdered the girl, so there won't be a chance that whoever did this will strike again."

"Do you think that this person specifically went after Bernadette?" Jay asked.

Dana and Jay both turned when the door opened, and Sister Mary Rose entered. She wore a heavy black woolen cape over her shoulders and carried a stack of books in her arms. Tiny snowflakes caught in her long, black lashes. Sister Mary Rose and Jay exchanged glances.

"Sister."

"Jay."

"This is Dana Greer, the investigator. Here to ask you some questions."

"Certainly. I'm pleased to meet you." The delicate, fine-featured nun put her books on the table and shook Dana's hand. "Let's all have a seat. I remember seeing you at the funeral. Thank you for coming. It meant a lot to all of us, especially, the Godfreys, I'm sure."

Before they got any further, Dana could see pain in the young woman's face. Her expression reminded Dana of one of the paintings on the church wall where Nate and she were married. It was a scene of the souls in purgatory, their faces pleading and begging to be released from the agony they were enduring. Their greatest longing was to be freed to see the face of God.

"Sister, this must be a difficult time for you. I know that Bernadette was a student in your second-grade class."

The young nun nodded. She ran her hand across her cheekbone.

"Mrs. Godfrey told me that Bernadette had left for school at 7:45 a.m. but never arrived in her classroom."

"That's what I've been told," Sister said, as she fingered the silver crucifix that lay on her heavily starched white wimple.

"What's this got to do with anything?" Jay asked.

Dana looked from Jay to the nun. "You say this is what you were told, Sister. Don't you know for sure?"

"No, actually I don't. I was ill that day and asked for a substitute."

"I assume the substitute did take attendance, then, correct?" Dana felt a tightness in the room like a large rubber band ready to snap.

"Yes, substitutes are expected to follow a teacher's plan."

Jay's lips moved as if he were saying something, but no words came out.

"And no one from the Academy. . .an attendance clerk or someone from the office. . . called Mrs. Godfrey to say the child never arrived that morning?" Dana found this incredulous.

"That is not our standard procedure, no."

"Well, certainly, it should be. If someone had made that call. . . ."

"I hear what you're saying, Miss Greer. It's true. Bernadette could still be alive today." The nun stumbled over her words.

Dana turned her attention toward Jay who sat across from her. "Jay, Mrs. Godfrey told me that Bernadette was almost a part of your family."

"That's correct. Let me guess. Do you want to ask *me* where I was at the time Bernadette went missing?" Jay's caustic voice grew louder, his hands clenching.

"As a matter-of-fact, where were you, Jay, the morning Bernadette never showed up at school?"

His shoulders stiffened, and his breathing intensified. He rubbed his thumb over a jagged nail on his middle finger.

"Are you trying to accuse me, Miss Greer, saying I had something to do with the girl's death?"

The hostility in the man's voice made Dana feel as if he would have taken a swing at her if he could have.

"Jay, Miss Greer is only doing her job," Sister Mary Rose said. Her good intentions went ignored. Jay sat rigid, only his fingers moved, tapping the armrest of the chair, his teeth anchored into his lower lip.

"No, Jay. Of course, I'm not trying to accuse you or anyone. Can you answer the question, though?" Dana smiled.

"Of course, I can. I got to school late that day. I realized I had forgotten my geography book and went back home to get it. I didn't get back to school until around 8:15."

"And the children. . .your class?"

"Sister Mary Rose's substitute took both classes to 8 a.m. Mass."

"I see." Dana repositioned herself to face Sister Mary Rose.
"Sister, let's get back to Bernadette."

The palm of Sister's hand rested above her lip as she bit down
on her thumb. The gold band on her right hand, marrying her to the
Church, shone in the light.

"What kind of student was Bernadette?"

"One of my best."

"How's that?"

"A conscientious student. A perfectionist. Always wanted to
please."

"I can vouch for that," Jay said. "Came over almost every night
to get help with her homework."

"Hmm. How about her grades?"

"Bernadette had come to Holy Name at the end of the school
year. Her parents had just moved to the Cape from Bay View. She
got right down to work, no monkey business about her," Sister said.

"How well did you know her parents?"

"Sweet people. Moved here solely for the benefit of the girl.
Wanted a safe environment." The nun began to sniffle. "Pardon me,"
she said. She pulled a white linen handkerchief from a side pocket in
her habit and blew her nose. Dana noted that the cloth was
embroidered with the letter *A* and had lace trim.

Jay rose from his chair and sat down next to the nun. He patted
her gently on her hand.

Something about the way the nun looked up at Jay made Dana uneasy. For a moment, she could have sworn their body language spoke of more than just comforting.

"Maybe this is enough for now, Dana. This is a trying time for all of us." He bit down on his inner cheek. "Why, you can well imagine what Sister here is going through."

"I understand, but this is a murder investigation. Perhaps, you'd like to get to your classroom to prepare for the day. I'm sure Sister Mary Rose and I will do fine in your absence."

Jay shrugged and left, slamming the door behind him as an angry school boy might do.

"Now, just a couple more questions. . .please. This Polly Thatcher. . .coming today to speak on loss. Where is she from?" Dana asked.

"She's a leading authority on grief in children, one of less than a handful in her field. Comes from Boston. She actually offered to come free of charge to speak to the school children," Sister said.

"How kind of her," Dana said. "How did you find her?"

"She was seeing Bernadette as a client."

"Oh?"

"You know, it isn't always easy for children to move and to transfer to a new school, especially, at the end of a school year. It can present adaptation problems—emotionally, socially."

"How so?" Dana rubbed her forehead, feeling a dull ache. She hoped one of her headaches wasn't coming on again.

"Bernadette needed lots of approval. She would get her feelings hurt for the slightest of things. You know, she acted like she was being shamed when she really wasn't. Bernadette was a shy child, seemed as if it took her great effort to mingle with the other children."

Dana quickly jotted these points into her notebook. She was getting a good profile on this child called Bernadette.

"Helpful, quite helpful. Sister, when will Doctor Thatcher be meeting with the children today?"

"Second hour in the school auditorium."

"Mind if I come?" Without waiting for an answer, Dana added, "One more thing, Sister." Dana decided now would be as good a time as any to insert one of her off-the-topic type questions. She found in her investigative work that when she changed the subject dramatically, taking the person off guard, more times than not she got truthful answers. "I was at your profession ceremony. Lovely indeed. Do you mind telling me, though, who the man was that tried to interrupt the service?"

The young nun's expression hardened, and Dana could see the woman's chest rise and fall as she inhaled and exhaled. "Name's Eddie Vineeti. I knew him from before I joined the order. He never wanted to give up the torch, I guess."

"Flattery to you for sure, but I hear he's married. Is that correct, Sister?"

"Is that so?" The nun's voice spoke of a bit of narcissism. "I wouldn't know." She turned her head aside. "I really must be going."

"Could we meet at another time to discuss things further?"

"I would be fine with that, Miss Greer. Oh, there is one thing I'd like to give you." She reached for one of the books in her stack and opened the cover. "Maybe, you'd like to have this."

Dana glanced at the card in her hand. "How did you know?"

"Know what?"

"I collect holy cards. Have ever since I was a child. Some people have photo albums of family and friends; guess for me, the saints have always been my heroes." Dana remembered the last one she had put in her album. It was the card distributed at her mother's funeral. The pastel painting of blue and pink showed Mary being assumed into heaven. On the reverse side was a black-and-white photograph of her mother with a prayer requesting eternal rest for her soul.

Sister smiled graciously. "If you collect holy cards, then you'll appreciate this one. It belonged to Bernadette. She got all *A's* on her last spelling test, and I told the children that those with a perfect score would receive a holy card. The children got to pick their favorites. Bernadette picked this, but before I had a chance to give it to her. . . ."

Dana could see tears fill the corners of the nun's eyes. She looked down at the card once again.

It was the scene of Abraham sacrificing his son Isaac on the altar. Seemed rather an odd choice of card for a young child. "Might you know why Bernadette chose this card?" Dana asked the nun.

"No, but maybe Doctor Thatcher might be able to help you. I've given her several of the child's drawings as well. The theme runs predominant in them."

"Which is?" Dana watched Sister's face; her mouth struggled to form words. She grabbed at the large button holding her cape closed and twisted it clockwise until it would no longer turn.

"Death," she said.

A shrill bell began ringing. Dana jumped when the door to the lounge opened. Two chattering nuns entered.

"Sister, when can we meet again?"

The woman bit down on her lower lip. "I must be leaving now," she said as she gathered her books.

Dana followed her into the hall filled with the noise of slamming lockers, students whispering among themselves, and classmates walking two-by-two along the tiled floor to their classes. It was obvious the students were well mannered and well disciplined. This was the way Dana remembered her own school days. There were hall monitors, hall passes. . .life then was structured, regimented, no one even considered stepping out of line.

Dana found the school office and asked the secretary where the auditorium was, as she planned to attend Doctor Thatcher's presentation on grief. The secretary had no sooner told her where the theater was than Dana turned to see Mrs. Artenelli, standing directly behind her. The woman wore a burgundy-colored coat with white rabbit fur trim and a hat to match. Her black spiked heels were shiny and the lines on her patterned hose straight.

"Mrs. Artenelli?"

The woman looked at Dana as if she were a town jester doing cartwheels.

"I'm Dana Greer, the detec—."

"I'm well aware."

"Pleased to meet you, too. In fact, I was hoping we might have a chance to get together for coffee. . . ."

The woman led Dana toward the wall, where a bulletin board was covered in fall leaves, and in an articulated and refined voice said, "I don't think your presence is welcome on the Cape."

Dana was about to tell her that she arrived on the Cape not in a voluntary capacity but as a hired private detective, when Mrs. Artenelli added, "What ferry do you intend to leave on?"

Dana stiffened, looked the woman straight on, and said, "I'll not be leaving until I find out who murdered Bernadette Godfrey. I'll be in touch to arrange an interview. We can conduct it at the station if you like." Then, she heard Opal's words, "They will not like what you have to say. . . . The hermit warns you once again: 'Be careful.'" Dana brushed past Mrs. Artenelli in silence and headed toward the auditorium. Little made Dana feel intimidated, but something about the woman's presence and the sound of her voice, made Dana feel as if she had no right to be there.

Chapter Eleven

The school bell rang, announcing the end of the morning class. Dana sat near the back of the auditorium on a gray velour seat. Like toy marching soldiers, the children began to file into the hall, two-by-two, the girls in the blue-and-green plaid jumpers, like the one found on Bernadette Godfrey's body, and the boys in navy blue trousers and pale green shirts. Each nun led seven or eight students. The enrollment of the private Catholic school numbered fewer than one hundred students, and those graduating eighth grade went on to high school on the mainland. The nuns ranged in age from the youngest such as Sister Mary Rose to the elderly, some of whom used ebony canes to guide them. Jay Harrison was the only layperson on the staff.

Dana could not but help but remember her childhood days at Assumption Grotto, at least six times the size of Holy Name Academy. Whenever a nun entered the classroom, all the students would rise and say, "Good day, Sister," and wait to be instructed before being seated. Whenever a sister would ask one of the girls what she wanted to be when she grew up, the child would proudly say, "I want to be a nun, Sister." Dana often wondered what life would have been like for her if she had chosen that route. She had pictured herself as a missionary, working on a far-away continent, using the money the school children had collected for the Pagan babies, as the unbaptized were called, to spread the word of God. Other times, she saw herself in the cloistered walls of a monastery, where she would pray for heartless souls. She reached into her bag and fingered the tiny tattered Bible.

When Dana looked up, she noted that all the students and teachers were seated. The principal, a stout woman with a cross-eyed face, walked down the aisle with a woman whom Dana assumed to be Doctor Polly Thatcher. She was dressed in a blue suit with shoes to match and carried a stuffed briefcase. The nun introduced her to the audience, and the doctor stood behind the podium. She began to speak in a clear but soft voice.

"Tears. We all shed them. There are tears of joy when you see grandma after a long time of being away. There are tears of fear when you're afraid what mother might say about the lamp you broke. And then, there are tears of sadness—those tears shed when we lose something or someone we know and care about."

Dana liked the woman's simple yet direct approach. She captivated her audience and continued to hold their attention during her fifteen minute presentation.

When she finished, everyone in the auditorium clapped and then began to file out. A tall nun reprimanded a few girls who whispered to each other. One of the boys following them stuck out his tongue and said, "Naughty! Naughty!"

After everyone left, Dana approached the principal and the doctor who were still on the stage, chatting with one another.

"Miss Greer has come to the Cape to solve the Bernadette Godfrey case," the principal said.

"Pleased to meet you, Doctor Thatcher. Could you spare a moment to speak with me?"

Before the counselor answered, the principal excused herself and left the room, and the two women sat down in the front row of the empty auditorium.

"I understand that you're from Boston?" Dana asked.

"Cape Cod to be more exact."

"Sister Mary Rose tells me that you had been counseling Bernadette Godfrey prior to her death."

"That's correct."

"Are you at liberty to tell me more about your visits with the child?"

"I can tell you this. Mr. and Mrs. Godfrey sought me out to work with their child to ease Bernadette's insecurities with the move. Anything more than that and you will have to speak with the Godfreys for yourself."

Doctor Thatcher was right. Dana needed to meet with the Godfreys in their home, not some coffee shop. And she needed to see the child's room. Often there were covert clues just waiting to be discovered in the homes of the homicide victims. Dana would call Mrs. Godfrey as soon as she left the school.

"Yes, of course. I'll arrange to speak with the Godfreys." Dana pulled the Abraham holy card from her purse. "Sister Mary Rose gave me this. She told me Bernadette had picked it out from several other holy cards."

"The familiar scene of total self-sacrifice," the therapist said, clasping and unclasping her hands.

"Or, as one might perceive it: murder," Dana said.

"You know Abraham didn't go through with sacrificing his son, don't you?"

"But to a child. . .a young child. How do you think it would be seen?"

"Do you really want to know?"

"Of course."

"A young child would question what the little boy had done that his father wanted to hurt him. You see, young children often blame themselves when a death or a tragedy occurs. . .whatever that might be."

"Really?" Dana paused for a moment studying the picture of Isaac with his father Abraham. "Sister Mary Rose told me that she had given you some drawings Bernadette made. May I see them?"

The woman thought for a moment and said, "Since the children's works were not part of her therapy session while she was alive, I see no harm in sharing the drawings with you. Why, of course."

The doctor opened her sleek, black briefcase. "Here are a few."

 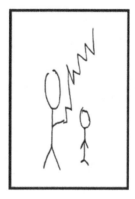 

Dana held the first drawing Bernadette had made. It was a black crayon sketching of a large headed person with big eyes and a large mouth. "What's this?" she asked, pointing to what looked to be a smaller stick figure near the character's mouth.

"Some might interpret this to mean that the smaller figure in the drawing is feeling overwhelmed by the larger image. . .well, almost to the point of being eaten up whole."

"And the second one?"

"Again this is done in only black crayon which we child therapists believe speaks to sadness or depression on the part of the artist."

"What's this?" Dana asked, pointing to a jagged line.

"This one is a bit more difficult to interpret. At first glance, the jagged line looks to be a lightning bolt, but when one studies the drawing more completely, the line radiates from the sky into the hand of the large stick figure while the small figure is left wondering what will happen to him or her."

"And the last one."

"A tall stick figure with very large hands symbolizing power of some sort. The fact that the little figure which appears to be a girl is near the large figure's foot, well, some might say that she feels belittled or small next to the all-powerful being."

"So, Doctor Thatcher if you were to give these drawings a theme or a universal motif, what would it be?"

"Getting back to the holy card you showed me, I would say that Bernadette is probably questioning what she has done to incur the larger stick figure's wrath. Taking it a step further, one might also wonder if the child feared for her life."

"Meaning death?"

"Yes. Some say that children are actually able to predict their own passing before it happens. Some believe it might be some innate sense that tragedy is about to befall them. Of course, these are only theories."

"Doctor, Sister Mary Rose told me the child got good grades, that she was a perfectionist, and always tried to do well. Would you say, though, that she was a happy child?"

The Doctor began to put the drawings back in her briefcase. "I'm not at liberty to go there, Miss Greer, but I will tell you one thing. All of these drawings show that the smaller figure saw herself to be in a dangerous place and without a doubt as a victim."

The Doctor stood, said it was good meeting Dana, and made her way up the tiled aisle of the auditorium, her high heels clicking like the keys of a typewriter.

Dana rubbed the back of her neck. She could feel her headache getting worse, yet instead of trying to get her mind off things even for only a moment, she mentally added up the pieces: Bernadette's poem, the holy card she had chosen, and her drawings; the sum could easily add up to a child who was introverted and shy for a reason. Fiona Wharton had a saying, "When you feel like you've fallen in a tar pit, you'll know what type of case you're working on." For sure, the Bernadette Godfrey case was going to be one of those.

Chapter Twelve

The early morning sun shone through the window of Logan's office. Smudges covered the glass, and tiny cobwebs lined the windowsill. The smell of fresh coffee lingered.

"But, Sergeant, the woman never even met me," Dana said. "To ask me what ferry I was returning on? Isn't that a bit boorish?" Dana threw the palms of her hands outward.

"You have to understand, Dana, the woman pretty much runs the Cape. Her philanthropy efforts have kept our medical center open, our library running, not to mention the generous donations she makes annually to Holy Name Academy. Gino Artenelli is an attorney with Bardley & Artenelli Brothers." Logan toyed with the badge on the breast pocket of his bluish-gray uniform. He sipped on the edge of a mug that bore the initials *CPPD* and the picture of a badge similar to the one on his shirt.

"Let me guess. The Artenellis live on the Pointe?"

"Correct. They used to have a home in Bay View, quite the mansion from what I'm told, but just recently purchased one on the Pointe to be closer to their daughter."

"Mrs. Artenelli's influence played heavily there, as well, right?"

Logan's eyebrows shot up. "What do you mean?"

"Angela joining the order. Wasn't Mrs. Artenelli influential in persuading Angela to join the convent?"

"If you care to believe everything you hear, I'd have to say that I, too, have heard the same."

Dana rubbed her index finger along her lower lip. "Whatever happened to Eddie Vineeti?"

"Wow! No segue there! Eddie went back to Waterville, where he's from. Better we get trash like him out of here as fast as we can." Logan stood up and jangled some lose change in his uniform pocket, then poured himself some more coffee. "Like a cup?"

"No, no thanks." Dana wondered if Logan was purposely trying to get off the subject of Eddie Vineeti.

"Why'd you ask about the scumbag?" Logan sat down.

"When I spoke with the guy, he blatantly made a threat against the woman—Mrs. Artenelli."

Logan's receptionist poked her head in the doorway. "Did I hear someone made a threat against Mrs. Artenelli?" Her voice rose like a squeaky violin when she said the word 'threat.'

"Don't think that's any of your business, is it, Janet?" Logan asked.

The young girl chomped non-stop on some gum. With an emery board, she filed the nails on her right hand. "Maybe yes, maybe no."

"Now what's that supposed to mean?" Logan asked, as he positioned a green pencil above his left ear.

Janet stopped filing her nails and pointed the overly used emery board at Logan. "I heard that kid mumbling to himself in his jail cell. He kept saying, 'I'm goin' get that woman if it's the last thing I do.'"

"He's all bark, ladies," Logan said. "I've seen his kind. A spoiled brat of a kid. If he can't get what he wants, he'll raise hell."

"I hope you're right, boss. He seemed pretty serious to me." Janet left the room as quickly as she had entered.

Dana could feel her nerves bristling. What right did this young secretary have to get involved in the middle of things, even if she was correct in her assessment?

Logan just nodded his head, obviously unaffected by Janet's rude intrusion. His tongue brushed across his upper teeth. "If I were a betting man, I wouldn't put money on it. The kid's probably as harmless as a flea."

Dana wished she could be as sure. From her experience in Bay View, she took all threats as serious unless proven otherwise.

"On another note, how have things been going with you? Everything okay down at the Harrisons'?"

"Been doing some background work on Loretta Harrison. Seems from what I've been able to gather, money talks." Dana tugged on one of her blond curls.

"You're referring to her rich daddy?"

Dana nodded.

"There's something about Loretta that strikes me as more than just odd. Like I told you before, it's one of the reasons I wanted you to board at the Harrisons; at least, that is until the Godfrey case gets solved."

"Are you saying that you think Loretta might have something to do with the case?" Dana edged closer.

"Not sure. All I know is that she and that pretty husband of hers sure gave the Godfrey girl a better than fair amount of attention and time."

"True, so I heard." Dana glanced at her wristwatch and stood. "Better get going, but there is one more question."

"Yes?" Logan asked.

"Do you have any idea how the Academy afforded that therapist to speak to the school children yesterday? I can't believe that she would have offered her services freely as I was told."

From his ear, Logan removed the pencil. He tapped it on his desk several times and then pointed it at her.

"Not Mrs. Artenelli?" Dana asked, as if she were reading Logan's mind.

He nodded, a huge smile covering his face, his gold incisor glowing in the light of the morning sun. Logan started to sort through some papers on his desk when Dana stopped him.

"Oh, one more thing, Logan." Dana bent down, bracing her hands on Logan's desk.

"That is?"

"Sister Mary Rose told me that Bernadette was being seen by Doctor Thatcher ever since her move over to the Cape. The Godfreys? Would you think they had that kind of money?"

"Hardly. Joe's got a miniscule job working the ferry line, and the missus works at an antique shop."

"So?"

"You're right on the money, honey, as they say."

"Mrs. Artenelli."

"Amen, Sister."

"But why?"

Logan threw his arms out and stood with his mouth open.

***

Almost three o'clock. Dana hoped to catch Sister Mary Rose before she left school for the day. If Dana was to do any questioning of Mrs. Artenelli, she could tell it would have to be through her daughter, and if that didn't work, she'd have no other choice than to involve Logan in the matter by bringing the woman down to the station for questioning. Dana liked to think she could do it on her own, however.

Dana found Sister in her classroom, erasing the chalkboard. She turned to the sound of Dana's tap on the classroom door.

"Sorry to disturb you, Sister."

"You're not, Miss Greer. Not at all." Again, the nun's voice sounded sing-song, almost, well, fake.

Dana looked around the room, decorated in gold and brown turkeys made from construction paper. The smell of fresh finger paints still lingered in the air. "Must be the work of your second graders?" she asked.

"They're quite the little artists. This one," she said, removing it from the bulletin board, "was the one Bernadette made. She called him Byron." The paper critter boasted real feathers of yellow and red, and his head was sloppily painted in a shiny green.

"That's an odd name for a turkey, isn't it?" Dana smiled.

The nun held her veil aside with one hand and said, "Byron is Father Sullivan's first name."

"Guess it makes sense then," Dana said, but she could not help but wonder why a child would choose to name her art project after the parish priest.

Sister eyed a desk in the front of the room. "I suppose I should box up Bernadette's things and return them to Mrs. Godfrey. Know she would like to have them."

"Have you spoken to Mrs. Godfrey since the funeral?" Dana shifted her weight from one foot to the other.

"No. They're private-type people. I wouldn't want to bother them. Not yet, anyway." Sister pinned the paper turkey back on the bulletin board and began to put some math problems on the clean chalkboard, ignoring Dana's presence.

"I agree with you that the Godfreys are private people," Dana said, convinced from her conversation with Mrs. Godfrey that she and her husband were closed people, not eager to entertain strangers into their home.

As an afterthought, the nun turned and asked, "Have *you* spoken to them?"

"Mrs. Godfrey, yes. She has no idea as to what motive anyone would have for wanting her child murdered."

"Is that so?" the nun asked. She tapped her chin with the piece of chalk as if trying to figure out what last equation she should put on the board. Then, she stopped and made eye contact with Dana. "It is strange, isn't it? Bernadette was such a beautiful child."

"And smart, from what you told me."

"Quite."

"From what the school psychologist told me. . . ."

"Doctor Thatcher. As I told you, a wonderful woman. Worked her darndest to get Bernadette to acclimate to the Cape."

"Do you think that was the only issue affecting the child?"

"Whatever do you mean?" The young nun's black eyes squinted.

"Just drawing at straws, I guess."

Sister picked up an English and a geography textbook from her desk and packed them in her black satchel. She began humming a hymn Dana couldn't recall the name of.

"Sister, was Bernadette a good writer?"

"Her poetry, you must mean? Ah, yes. See the drawing on the back wall? The children were to sketch a picture of the last poem they wrote."

Crayola pictures hung from a thin piece of twine like laundry on a sunny day. Dana walked to the back of the classroom and studied each one carefully. One child had drawn a picture of Santa Claus with colorful packages in his mittened hands. Another had drawn a man with gray hair and a matching beard. In broad-stroked red lettering, the student had written 'Grandpa.' "Any topic, in particular, they were to write on?" Dana asked. She ran her finger across the string holding the drawings.

"Someone who was important to them," the nun said.

"Bernadette's?"

"This is hers right here," the nun said, lifting it slightly.

"But, this looks like a place, not a person." Dana remembered the poem that Red Tanner had given her—the one that read:

I love the sea.

Its waves calm me.

I love the sea.

It's here he waits for me.

The nun bit down on her lower lip. "Oh, it's probably someone who takes her to the beach, don't you think?"

If Bernadette wrote about someone who waited for her at the sea, Dana hardly thought it was someone who took her to the beach.

A small point but important to make note of. Dana wondered why the nun didn't pick up on this minute detail.

Sister spun her gold band around her ring finger. "I must get going, Miss Greer. I'm in charge of the evening meal tonight." She wrapped her black cape around her shoulders and started to reach for the light switch.

Dana interrupted. "There is one thing, Sister, I'd like your help with."

Sister Mary Rose said nothing. She shut the lights off and looked at Dana with her dark, large eyes.

"I met your mother yesterday. Ran into her right here at the school."

"Mother likes to help out once in a while. Reads to the children. . .things like that."

"How kind of her. Do you think she'd like to meet me for coffee sometime?"

"Mother's a busy person."

"I can imagine, but I'd like to get to know her. You know, like you said, it's difficult for newcomers to feel welcome on the Cape."

"I'll ask, and get back with you."

Something about the nun's deliberate hesitation puzzled Dana. Like mother, like daughter. Mrs. Artenelli ran to the defense of her daughter when Eddie's behavior disrupted the chapel ceremony. Now the nun seemed to be so protective of her mother. But why?

Chapter Thirteen

To gain some insight into Bernadette's life, Dana considered speaking with some of the child's peers. What better opportunity than at the Parent-Teacher Open House. Dana busied herself walking through the halls of Holy Name Academy, fascinated with the projects the students had accomplished since the start of the semester. Masks made from brown paper bags, pipe cleaners, and buttons creatively became the faces of tigers and lions, Asian women and men, warriors and presidents. Another wall was covered in acrylic painted pictures of the various saints, each one attached to a lace paper doily. Dana was amazed at the vast assortment of the Church heroes whose lives the children must have studied from St. Rita and Luke to St. Andrew and Maria Goretti. There was a large rosary made with red construction paper beads. Someone had typed various personal intentions and affixed a prayer to each bead.

Between the multiple bulletin boards, glass display cases held trophies the students had earned over the years for drama and speech. Another contained the names of benefactors of the school, starting with those who had donated $20 or more. On a large gold medal at the very top of the pyramid arrangement was inscribed Carmelina and Gino Artenelli for their gift in the past year of $3,000. Logan was right. Mrs. Artenelli had a reason for her arrogance, especially when it came to wasting her time speaking with a humble private detective.

Near the rear double doors leading to the playground was the last of the glass display cases. Black cloth draped over the two shelves. In shiny silver cardboard letters the name Bernadette Godfrey enhanced the array of photos and belongings of the child. There was a picture of Bernadette with the principal and one with Sister Mary Rose.

Dana leaned closer to the window, trying to avoid the reflections that were being cast upon the glass when she saw a photo of Bernadette with a man. His black hair was slicked back with Brylcreem, revealing a wide forehead, and he sported a narrow, pristine moustache that appeared too long for the small mouth beneath. Her father. Dana remembered seeing him at the funeral. In the photo, Mr. Godfrey and Bernadette were standing on the shore, ocean waves engulfing their feet, the sun setting in the background.

I love the sea.

It's here

he waits for me.

Her father. Could Bernadette's poem be about her father? The only photo of Mrs. Godfrey in the collection was one with a nun, a Little Sister of the Poor. The nun stood next to Mrs. Godfrey with Bernadette in the middle. The Guardian Angel Orphanage, no doubt. On the bottom shelf, there was a small silver locket with the letter *B* engraved on the front. A charm bracelet lay next to it, trinkets of tiny silver animals hooked to the chain. A pearl-covered prayer book with gold edges and a rosary to match were propped up in a corner, probably Bernadette's First Communion gifts. Near the front of the case laid a stuffed black and gray kitten.

Looking at the child's personal belongings made the murder become too personal. Although Dana had never met Bernadette, after looking at her possessions, she felt an eerie closeness to her, a magnetism. The thought that someone, anyone, would take the child's life left Dana feeling intense anger. This wrath would lead her to finding the murderer; of that, she made up her mind.

She took a deep breath and walked back toward Sister Mary Rose's classroom and found parents and children wandering the room. Many of the lids to the desks were raised as children pointed out how organized their school supplies were. A boy with a blond head full of curls showed his father a math problem that he had done on the blackboard. Two giggling girls stood in the corner, practicing putting on a dunce cap. Dana stepped toward them and introduced herself as a friend of Bernadette's. The girls' bright eyes and faces full of mischief hinted that they might be willing to answer a few questions. Gregariousness radiated from them.

"I'm Karen, and this is Connie." The two girls looked at each other and started laughing all over again.

"Hello girls. How do you two like school?"

Karen was the first to answer. "We all love Sister Mary Rose. We think she is the prettiest sister at the Academy." Connie nodded.

"What is Sister Mary Rose teaching you?" Dana asked.

"My favorite subject is art," Karen said.

"Me too," Connie added. "Did you see the painting of St. Rita in the hall? I painted that one."

"She's the patron saint of anyone who gives up hope. Did you know that?" Karen asked.

"I must remember that," Dana said. "Saints are our friends in Heaven."

The two girls smiled widely, revealing almost the identical teeth missing from each of their mouths.

"Are you two friends?"

"Uh huh. So was Bernadette," Karen added, totally uninhibited. "She's our friend in Heaven now."

"What happened to her was sad," Dana said. She hoped to lead the girls into conversation about their former classmate.

Connie edged closer to Dana's side and tugged on her sleeve. In her ear, she whispered, "We know who hurt Bernadette."

"You do? Who?"

"Her daddy."

"Why do you say that?" Dana bent to be at eye-level with the girls, hoping they would feel comfortable enough to tell her more.

"Tell her, Karen. Tell her why we think Bernadette's daddy is a bad person."

Karen moistened her lips, scrunched her shoulders, and said, "He did bad things to her. Bernadette told us. She told us to keep it a secret."

Dana bent down on one knee. "Like what, honey?" She felt a harsh tap on her back, and turned to face a woman wearing a dark green sweater with a pin of holly branches on its collar.

"Why are you bothering Karen?"

Dana stood up and tried to introduce herself.

"I know who you are. Who doesn't by now?"

"I was only getting acquainted with the girls."

"They don't need to get dragged into this. Not after what happened to their classmate. They know better. Karen, come along with me."

The woman yanked on the girl's black watch plaid jacket.

"Mommy, don't."

"We're going, Karen. Now!"

By the time Dana turned around, she noticed Connie had slipped away and was standing with a man and woman who were speaking with Sister Mary Rose.

Sister eyed Dana's presence, nodded, and kept speaking to Connie's parents.

Dana decided to make her exit and to mingle in Jay Harrison's classroom directly across the hall.

"Dana, what are you doing here?" Jay asked. His voice spoke not so much of questioning as it did accusation.

Dana had a feeling the man was not about to forgive her for questioning him about his whereabouts the morning Bernadette disappeared.

"Did you get the message I left you?"

"Message?"

"I taped it to the door of your room. You must have left before I put it there."

"What message?"

"Sergeant Logan called. Said he wanted to speak with you as soon as possible. Gave me his home number in case you came in later."

Dana excused herself and began running back to the Harrisons'. She counted her steps as she ran. . .seventeen, eighteen, nineteen.

Without thinking, she stepped off the curb as a car whizzed past her at a high speed, honking its horn all the way down the block. She stepped back onto the sidewalk and took a deep breath. *That was close.* She reminded herself that she would have to be more careful. She had gotten used to there not being much traffic on the Cape.

When she finally got to the Harrison house, Loretta was reading in the parlor. She looked up. "Jay put a note on your door."

"Thanks," Dana said, and raced up the stairs two at a time.

Logan says there's been an important development in the case!

Call him at once. His home # is: 636-0044.

She took the number with her and dialed it from the kitchen. "Logan, it's Dana."

"We've got a real light bulb on the case. Tanner tells me that the body of Bernadette Godfrey showed signs of sexual abuse."

"What? Why. . . ."

"That's what I asked. Why did he wait until now to tell me?"

"His answer?"

"Tanner said Raymond McGregor paid him to keep his mouth shut. Didn't want the news hitting the paper. Said to let the kid rest in peace."

"But the motive?"

"Exactly, it sure would give someone grounds for murder. The last thing the perpetrator would want is for this news to be splashed all over the paper."

Dana could feel her adrenalin pumping and her heart rate accelerating. She paused to get her thoughts in order. "Wait one minute. Don't reporters go for the truth no matter how awful it may be to hear?"

"Unless it would pay for them to do otherwise."

"You don't think. . . ."

"I do. McGregor didn't do it for nothing. He stood to gain in the scheme just like Tanner. Only difference is Tanner came clean."

"Why do you think he did, Logan? Come clean, I mean?"

"The only thing that makes sense to me is that Tanner could have stood to lose his medical license."

"True, that makes sense. So, now the question is where did the blood money originate from? Either these two fess up, or we'll be forced to bring an indictment against them for interfering with the case," Dana said.

Chapter Fourteen

Here it was, November 5th—two weeks since Dana had arrived on the Cape. A freezing rain pelted her face like tiny needles. Intermittent fog and gray ominous clouds hung low in the sky. In many ways, her mind felt much the same: covered in a hazy mist. In terms of meeting people, she had met several. In terms of events, she had been to a few.

The only real clue she had as to the murder of Bernadette Godfrey had come from Bernadette's two school friends, Karen and Connie, who claimed that Mr. Godfrey had done bad things to his daughter. Added to that, McGregor and Tanner had accepted bribe money from someone who didn't want the sexual assault issue to hit the paper. That didn't necessarily mean that Mr. Godfrey had also murdered his daughter. Dana knew better than to jump to that conclusion.

She still pondered whether this would be yet one more case she'd walk away from with no closure, left wondering and transfixed endlessly. Memories floated back about the last days before the Myra Pembroke case went cold. That incompetent feeling submerged her like a wave washing her under and under until she gasped for air, doubting she'd ever come to the surface again. Coming to the Cape was to be her new beginning, her chance to resurrect herself, to prove to herself that she could successfully solve yet another murder case.

Dana pulled out her Bible and held it tightly between her hands as she stared out at the bay from the window of her room. Now would not be the time for self-doubt. She had the tendency to be much too hard on herself, to question her abilities, to second-guess her choices. The longer she held the tiny book between her clasped fingers, the more sustained she felt. As in the past, the small Bible brought her some assurance, a feeling like that of a mother kissing her child softly on the head, reminding her that everything would be okay. She allowed herself a few more moments to soak in the comforting feeling and set the book back in her handbag.

Investigative work can be so daunting that sometimes the most obvious clues become hidden in a dense forest. In the last twenty-four hours, the case had taken a new twist, one that shed light on a possible motive and maybe even a likely suspect. Dana took a sheet of paper from the roll-top desk and began to draw. Being a visual person, often if she saw some type of pattern, a connection, a relationship between people, it helped her to go the next step in discerning suspects with motives.

Certainly, the poem Bernadette wrote and the photo of her and her father at the beach might well fit together. Common that children write about their parents and their experiences with them, yet Dana recalled what Mrs. Godfrey had said about her husband; he had never considered himself a father to the child. An image of the young child with the Shirley Temple curls going down to the shore to meet with a man—her father—who waited in anticipation of what he could do to his own daughter sickened her. A boat house, a bathhouse, an abandoned cottage. . .who knew where he might have enticed the girl to meet. Scenes of Dana's uncle forcing her to get on her knees before him as he sat on the weathered Bayliner seat played before her like a repeat movie even after twenty-three years. The sea became rough and lightning streaks filled the dark skies. Dana had begged him to take her back to the cottage. The boat rocked with the white-capped sea. She panicked and stood up. That's when she fell overboard. Like a toy, she bobbed up and then went back down again. The final time her body rose, her uncle pulled her up by her hair. He said if she ever told anyone about that day he would drown her. Ever since then, water always spoke of death to Dana.

Then, she remembered Doctor Thatcher telling her that sometimes children can sense their imminent deaths. If Bernadette felt threatened by her father, it might make sense that she would have chosen the sacrificing of Isaac holy card from Sister Mary Rose. Perhaps, as Doctor Thatcher had said, Bernadette blamed herself for succumbing to her father's demands, and if he threatened her with death, the image on the holy card made even more sense.

As for the drawings the child had done, Doctor Thatcher had said that they revealed a sense of feeling overwhelmed, sad, depressed, even questioning as to what would happen next, and a possible fear for her life. If children can be trusted, Karen and Connie's comments about Mr. Godfrey being a bad person would make sense, too.

If Mr. Godfrey was abusing his daughter, he would, without a doubt, have a motive for murdering her. Open and closed case. But not that simple. Dana had no idea who would pay off Red Tanner and Raymond McGregor to keep their mouths shut. It didn't make sense that Mr. Godfrey would. That would be incriminating himself.

And even if it were proven that Mr. Godfrey had been abusing his daughter, the fact remained that it still did not necessarily mean that he murdered her.

The only person known to have plenty of money would be Mrs. Artenelli, but how would she know that Bernadette was more than the victim of a mere stabbing, and even if she did, why would she care to protect the integrity of Mr. Godfrey? As Fiona had said, "Eliminate the family first." Dana decided to make another call to Mrs. Godfrey; they needed to talk. As for Mrs. Artenelli, if Mrs. Godfrey refused to speak with her, she would get Logan involved.

As a child, Dana remembered going to a magic show by the great Houdini. She left the theater that night feeling irritated. While others commented on his ability to confuse and deceive his audience, she felt cheated, not understanding the rules behind his magic tricks. Solving a crime was not that much different for her.

If Tanner was willing to confess his sin to Logan, then he damn well should be willing to speak to her about it. If Dana was to get at the root of this case, it was time people realized that she had a right to not only question them but to expect answers as well.

She called Logan and told him of her intentions.

"Better you speak to McGregor. He's the one who took the money from the source and paid off Tanner. Like I said, the only difference is that Tanner confessed his guilt. Money must have burnt a hole in his soul."

"You mean McGregor still has his job after accepting bribe money?"

"Editor—guy by the name of James Worthington—runs the paper out of Portland. He ain't got no way of knowing the day-to-day bullshit that goes on, on the Cape. All he asks is that the paper get printed and sold."

***

After all, it was only $500 bucks between us," McGregor said, when Dana asked him why he resorted to a payoff.

"Why do it then?" she asked.

"What harm? The girl's dead. Who gives a damn how?"

"Who gives a damn why? Have you ever heard the word motive?"

"The fact that someone wants things kept under wraps about the child being abused doesn't automatically mean that it has anything to do with covering up the abuser." McGregor scowled at her, his face one of arrogance.

"Do you know that for a fact?" Dana asked.

"I do."

"Okay, let's forget, for a moment, the reason behind the blood money. What I want to know is where did the money come from?"

"Sure as hell in time, you'll figure that out, Miss Greer. You are the special investigator on the case, aren't you?"

Dana hated being taken for an idiot. "Let's get a few things straight, Mr. McGregor." She put her emphasis on *Mr.* "You really only have two choices here. You either tell me who paid you off or risk being arrested for interfering in a murder investigation. Last time I checked, that would be a felony."

"You're a pretty tough lady."

"You might say that. I call it doing my job."

McGregor looked like he had just swallowed a peach pit whole. He coughed several times into the palm of his hand and then cleared his throat.

"Well, the name," Dana inquired. Her patience waning.

"Mrs. Artenelli. . .but let me explain."

Although Mrs. Artenelli's name had crossed Dana's mind before because she would have the funds for a payoff, Dana couldn't quite figure out how a woman of her stature on the Cape would become involved in something so illegal.

As if reading her mind, McGregor said, "It's not what you think. Let me quote Mrs. Artenelli. She said, 'An innocent child should not be sent to her grave with the stigma of having been an abused victim. The public has no right to know this."

"How in heaven's name would Mrs. Artenelli even know that the child had been abused?"

"You got me there, Miss Greer," McGregor answered. "She is pretty connected on the Cape, so it didn't surprise me any."

Dana shifted her weight from one foot to the other. "It sounds as if you're telling me that Mrs. Artenelli cared about the image of the child, not out to protect the abuser's identity."

"Exactly. If you know Mrs. Artenelli, you'd know that she would not come close to being involved with anything that might speak of breaking the law."

Dana wasn't convinced of that. . .not yet anyway.

She thanked McGregor, and as she turned to leave, there were still two questions that perplexed her. Why did Mrs. Artenelli have such a concern for the murdered victim, and who told her about the evidence of abuse?

Chapter Fifteen

With a little persuasion, Dana was finally able to get Mrs. Godfrey to invite her to her home. Unfortunately, Mr. Godfrey was down at the ferry, just as Dana had expected, the day Dana arranged to meet with his wife. Dana would have to speak with him separately, more than likely at his work.

When Dana arrived at the Godfrey home, she found Mrs. Godfrey doing some needlework. She held a wooden embroidery hoop in one hand, and with her other, she meticulously pulled a needle with red thread through a white linen fabric.

"I make altar linens for Father Sullivan." She held up the fabric and showed Dana the three red crosses she had stitched next to a golden chalice. "Have you had a chance to meet Father yet? He's such a nice man."

"No, I've not introduced myself." Dana wondered if subconsciously she had had her reasons for staying clear of the pastor. Once he was to learn that she was a Catholic, she knew he would expect to see her at Mass. She'd rather not get into the fact that she had left the church years ago. It wasn't that she had a good reason for leaving, after all, she was raised in a strong, faith-filled home. Instead, she found it easier to put the blame on Nate and her failed marriage. Maybe, one day she would get over making excuses.

Dana watched Mrs. Godfrey's nimble fingers work the needle in and out of the altar cloth. Next to her on the floor was an open wicker basket filled with a rainbow assortment of threads. "Your needlework must bring you satisfaction."

"Keeps my mind busy. Don't have to think that way."

Dana appreciated Mrs. Godfrey giving her a segue into the case. There's nothing more difficult than speaking with someone who has recently lost a close family member to death. "I can understand why you wouldn't want to think about the loss of your daughter. Yet, if I can do something to relieve that pain, I want to help. Can you think of anyone who might have. . . ." Dana couldn't bring herself to complete the question. The Swiss grandfather clock in the small room chimed the hour, and a small, yellow chickadee flew out on his perch.

"Murdered my Bernadette?" Mrs. Godfrey looked away from her sewing. The tears in her brown eyes overflowed onto her cheeks like a small dam giving way. The woman continued to embroider.

"Yes, anyone you know? Statistics indicate that the perpetrator in most murder cases involving children is someone the child knew. You know. . .a teacher. . .a friend's parent. . . ."

Mrs. Godfrey looked up abruptly. "You're not thinking I murdered Bernadette, are you?" She stabbed her needle into the cloth on her lap and put it in the basket at her side.

"No. No, of course not. I was only hoping you might have some names. You know, acquaintances, anyone who played a part in Bernadette's life."

"We've not been on the Cape that long. . .only seven months."

"Anyone Bernadette played with, visited with?"

"Connie and Karen were Bernadette's two close friends, but Bernadette was a shy child, never went to their homes. Sister Mary Rose told me the girls played together during recess."

"Have you ever spoken to the girls or their parents?"

The woman shook her head, looked downward, and dabbed at the tears still flowing. "Oh, no. No, Joe wouldn't like that. My husband likes me to stay at home."

"I see. But I was told you work at an antique shop."

"That's strictly for money. We couldn't survive on Joe's paycheck alone."

Dana noticed the woman's hands shaking as she tried to hold them still in her lap. Dana decided to try another approach to her questioning. "Sister told me Bernadette was a wonderful student."

Mrs. Godfrey looked away. "She was. A perfectionist, always afraid she would make some kind of mistake." Mrs. Godfrey cleared her throat and stammered on her words, "Mr. Harrison helped her with homework. I don't get home from work until five, plus Joe and me don't have much schooling." She sniffled.

"What about your husband? What time does he get home from work?"

"Joe? He gets home at two-thirty, but he takes a nap."

"Hmm." Dana jotted quick notes:

Bernadette did not stay with Mr. Godfrey after school.

Was there another interest the Harrisons might have had in the child?

"I was grateful she had somewhere to go after school," Mrs. Godfrey said.

Why? Dana wondered. Was Mrs. Godfrey afraid of leaving Bernadette alone with her father? Then again, Dana knew that the

Harrisons had welcomed the child into their home on a consistent basis and wondered if that might have been a source of contention for the Godfreys. She continued her questioning. "Did that arrangement work, having Bernadette go to the Harrison home after school?"

"Oh, yes."

"What about Loretta? Did she enjoy Bernadette's visits?"

"Loretta can't have children. She loved. . . ." Mrs. Godfrey had trouble saying her child's name. "And Jay. . .he would have made a wonderful father. Not so sure about his wife, though."

"What do you mean?"

"She's lost somewhere in her past, I believe."

Dana's theory about Loretta surfaced once more. She wondered if Jay's display of affection onto a child who wasn't even his own might have caused some friction between him and Loretta. "The Harrisons treated Bernadette like their own, then?"

"Absolutely."

"Tell me more about Bernadette if you will." Dana noticed a painting of the child on a nearby wall. It was done in pastel oils and framed in white. The child resembled the angels on Dana's holy card collection; the child's face pale, her cheeks and lips a light pink, and her hair tightly woven curls of gold.

The thought of Bernadette coming late in Mrs. Godfrey's life and then taken in such a brutal way was intolerable.

Mrs. Godfrey eyed the photo of her daughter and threw her hands over her face.

Dana put her arm around the woman's shoulders. "I know this must be awfully difficult for you."

"My baby's in Jesus' arms now."

"I'm sure she is, Mrs. Godfrey." Like a typical mother recounting her past steps, asking how she could have done things differently, begging mercy for the mistakes that she made, Dana could see from Mrs. Godfrey's troubled face that she had been obsessing on these thoughts.

"Joe and me never should have adopted; none of this would have happened." Her chest rose and fell as she breathed heavily and sighed.

Dana sat down next to her. "It's not your fault. You did what you thought best."

Mrs. Godfrey's brown eyes were bloodshot and puffy. She looked at Dana and said, "My baby wasn't safe here."

"But isn't that the reason you moved from Bay View to the Cape. . .for Bernadette's safety?"

The woman looked at Dana. "That's not what I'm talking about."

Dana waited a moment, and then asked, "What do you mean?"

Mrs. Godfrey grasped at the fingers of her left hand so tightly that the tips turned a purplish-red.

Dana tried to comfort the woman. Mrs. Godfrey was second-guessing herself, making herself the brunt of guilt. "Try not to blame yourself."

The woman nodded as she ran her hand across her face, the nails on her chapped, reddened hands bitten low, her cuticles ragged, a narrow silver band on her left ring finger. "That's why Mrs. Artenelli suggested I get Bernadette help."

Dana attempted to follow Mrs. Godfrey's flow of ideas, which seemed to stray in many illogical directions. Mrs. Artenelli, the philanthropist, suggested the therapist, Doctor Polly Thatcher. What didn't Mrs. Artenelli pay for? For sure, Dana would find a way to speak with her.

Mrs. Godfrey continued. "Doctor Thatcher. She worked with Bernadette, got her to talk out her uneasiness. The doctor said Bernadette was coming out of her shell every day more and more."

"I met the doctor. Seems like such a kind woman."

Changing her thoughts yet again, Mrs. Godfrey said, "I owe so much to Mrs. Artenelli. Even the tuition at Holy Name. . .three hundred dollars a semester. There's no way Joe and I could have afforded to send Bernadette to Holy Name."

"Any idea as to why Mrs. Artenelli was so giving to your family?"

"Mrs. Artenelli is a faithful contributor to the Academy. She started a fund for families who want their children to have a good education yet don't have much money."

Mrs. Godfrey's voice became a mere echo in the background as Dana's mind flooded with ideas. The therapist, the school tuition, not to mention the institutions that were kept financially viable thanks to Mrs. Artenelli. She certainly would have the money to pay off McGregor, but the questions still remained. How did Mrs. Artenelli know that Bernadette had been the victim of sexual abuse, and why was she so concerned with wanting no one to know? It didn't make sense. "Mrs. Godfrey?" Dana looked at the frail woman before her. "I don't know how else to say this, but I learned from Sergeant Logan that your child had been sexually abused. Is that true?"

The woman quickly jumped up and clenched her fists, chewing on her thumb nail. "No! She died from stab wounds."

"I understand that that was the cause of death, according to Red Tanner's coroner's report, but it doesn't negate the fact that someone had sexually abused your child." Dana took a deep breath and waited. It was obvious such pointed remarks had to be painful to the mother of a murdered child, but Dana knew she had to ask the inevitable question. "You knew, didn't you, that someone had abused Bernadette?"

"Why, what difference does it make now? I mean, Bernadette is at peace with the Lord."

Dana smiled and gently tapped the woman's arm. "I'm sure she is, but whoever—."

Mrs. Godfrey pulled away and began to pace across the small room of the cottage-like home. The wooden floor beneath her feet squeaked. She chewed on her fingernails, first one finger, then another.

Dana watched the woman for a few moments before speaking again. "As I was saying, Bernadette is with the Lord, I am sure, but the abuser. . .do you have any idea who might have taken liberties with your child?"

The woman stopped her pacing and stood near the front window of the room. She pushed the heavy floral drapery aside and sobbed loudly, rubbing her hands up and down her face. Small dust particles filled the air.

Dana quickly got up and stood beside her. "Mrs. Godfrey, my heart goes out to you. You have had to carry a heavy cross, and I know this has to be difficult for you, but I'm sure you don't want the abuser, whoever he might be, to get away with the crime, do you?"

As the woman stared through the glass pane, she mumbled something under her breath, over and over.

"I'm sorry, but I can't understand you."

The woman let the drape fall slowly into place, turned, and looked at Dana. Like she appeared in the coffee shop, her shoulders bent forward. Her lips quivered. She tried to steady her hands. Even her neck was wet with her tears. "Don't you understand? He'll beat me; he'll beat me until he kills me."

It was then that Dana noticed the bruises on Mrs. Godfrey's neck, circular bluish-purple marks like those of fingerprints, fresh and newly formed. Next to them, the scratch marks of fingernails, left long red gashes in her flesh.

"Doctor Thatcher was the first to tell me. She mentioned that she saw symptoms that might speak of abuse."

"Such as?"

"Bernadette got her feelings hurt for no reason; she'd run off, cover her face, cry. Her shyness, her need for approval. . .her best was never good enough. That's when I confided in Mrs. Artenelli. I told her about my suspicions." Mrs. Godfrey reached for the arm of the Queen Anne chair to steady her shaking body.

"What did Mrs. Artenelli think?"

"She told me no child deserved to have her innocence taken from her, her purity robbed."

"Have you mentioned any of this to Father Sullivan?"

"In the confessional only. If Joe ever found out that I even hinted at him being involved with Bernadette, well, he'd. . . ."

"What did Father suggest?"

"He told me it is my duty to stay with my husband, to stand beside him, in good and in bad. It's what a loyal wife does."

"Let's get back to the abuse issue. Any idea where it might have occurred?"

"In a private place. . .a place where I'd never suspect. . .the bathhouses."

"You think your husband might have been abusing the child there?" The school drawing of the ocean, the poem about meeting someone at the beach. The pieces were fitting together nicely. "Mind if I take a look at your daughter's room?"

Dana followed the woman into the child's bedroom, which was wallpapered in pink sweetheart roses. A little girl's dream, she was sure. Baby dolls lined one wall; some were wrapped in flannel blankets while others sat in what looked like handmade doll clothes. A bassinet stood under the window, complete with tiny bars of soap and baby bottles of cream and shampoos. A wooden set of bunk beds stood near the closet door. Stuffed dogs, cats, and other animals graced another wall. Next to the child's bed, a huge corkboard hung, filled with Bernadette's artwork. Dana scanned the pictures from top to bottom, side-to-side. Not one depicted any person. All had a similar theme: water.

"Bernadette loved the beach," Mrs. Godfrey said, her voice nasal.

"She went there often, then?"

"Almost every weekend."

Dana stared at the drawings one more time. "Mrs. Godfrey, did Doctor Thatcher see these drawings of Bernadette's? Ever mention why the ocean was in all of the child's drawings?"

"Doctor Thatcher found it unusual, but only said it showed an obsession that Bernadette had with water. You know how some girls like horses?"

"A stage of development, you mean. Hmm. Or, a place to be alone, perhaps?"

Mrs. Godfrey's face turned a deep pink. Her lower lip trembled.

Dana had opened a door and needed to push ahead despite knowing it would be painful on the woman who had already bore so much despair. "Weren't you afraid to let Bernadette wander along the beach alone? Did she know how to swim?"

Like a river overflowing its banks, tears poured down the woman's cheeks and landed on the stiff, starched collar of her red and white checked housedress.

Dana waited for an answer for what seemed like several minutes.

"Bernadette wasn't alone. Joe was hired to do some repair work. He did it on the weekends when he wasn't working on the ferry."

"Repairing what?"

"The old bathhouses. Been down there on the beach for years. They're in need of new plumbing, some tile, roofing materials. You know, things like that."

"Your husband. . .he must be quite handy."

"And in need of money. The ferry job doesn't leave us with much. Joe likes to do odds and ends."

"I need to speak with your husband." Dana was not about to let him get away. Joe Godfrey was a person of interest, and she would meet with him wherever she had to, even if it meant she had to go to the beach alone. Avoidance wouldn't keep her from questioning him. Fiona's advice loud in her ears, "Eliminate family first." Mr. Godfrey had possible motive for wanting his daughter dead; that was for sure, and so far, he was her number one suspect.

Mrs. Godfrey blinked rapidly. "Joe works a lot."

The woman, as was common with abused wives, protected her husband, covered for him. To do otherwise might put her own life at stake.

"A good provider, I can see that." Dana smiled. Realizing that the weekend was upon them, before she left she asked Mrs. Godfrey, "Where might I find the bathhouses?"

The mere thought of going to the beach, the nearness of the water, the crashing waves coming to shore and pulling out to sea, made Dana's forehead perspire. Simple enough for anyone else to do, but not for her. She could hear the thudding of her heart loud in her ears. Tomorrow, Saturday, she would find Joe Godfrey. Tomorrow, she would confront him about his despicable deed.

Dana fidgeted with the fringe on her wool scarf. She thanked Mrs. Godfrey for her time, and as soon as she got out on the porch, she opened her bag and held her Bible tightly against her chest.

Chapter Sixteen

Dana arrived at the Station House first thing in the morning as she had done most mornings since coming to the Cape. It was her chance to update Logan on her findings and to let him brief her on any new happenings or changes. Officers Boyle and O'Neil stood at the door of the station, one eating a jelly donut, its peach marmalade dripping onto his fingers, and the other, smoking a cigarette, his pack of Lucky Strikes in his uniform pocket.

"Ah hah. Here she comes," Boyle said, "have gun will travel."

"Another busy day, boys?" Dana asked, and slipped past them.

Janet, the receptionist, sat at her desk curling her hair in small strips of rags.

"Looking to get some curls?" Dana asked, wondering how the woman could possibly feel comfortable sitting near the door, greeting those coming to the station, yet acting as if she were in her bedroom at home. Without waiting for an answer, Dana asked, "Logan in?"

Janet pointed with one finger toward his office while she busied herself wrapping another piece of gauze around her bangs.

Logan sat at his desk, a large black thermos sandwiched between his hands. He sipped from its lid. "How's my favorite investigator?" he asked. Dana told Logan about yesterday's visit with Mrs. Godfrey and that she planned to leave shortly to find Joe Godfrey at work on the bathhouses.

"Give me a minute, and I'll come along with you," Logan said. He put his drink down.

"No offense meant, Sergeant, but I'd rather tackle this one myself." Perhaps, that was a bit of a white lie. It wasn't Mr. Godfrey that she feared so much as it was the sea. Dana had battled this drama since she was seven-years-old, and the thought of going down to the shore filled her with apprehension. Her recollections still vivid of that stormy day when she had fallen overboard from her uncle's boat. While she glanced upward at the blurred bubbles rising to the surface, she had been convinced that there would be no escape from her sea sepulcher.

"So, you'd rather take on Joe Godfrey by yourself, would you?" Logan asked. Without waiting for Dana to answer, he said, "Okay, if you insist. The bathhouses are easy enough to find. Down the beach some near where the ferry comes into port; you're bound to see them. There's about six of them right near the shore, most dilapidated shacks. Or, better yet, walk to the end of Harrisons' street. There you'll find a set of stairs leading down to the beach. Sure you don't want my company?" he asked once more. "Or I'd be mighty happy to send one of my officers with you."

"Thanks but I'd rather do it alone."

"Okay but just keep your radio on if things get nasty."

"Will do." Dana liked Logan's willingness to protect, but if she were to make a name for herself in a predominantly all-male profession, she wanted to do it on her own, not have it said that it took a man to bail her out.

"There is one more thing I must tell you before I confront Mr. Godfrey."

"Yeah?"

"The mystery over who paid the blood money to McGregor has been solved."

"Good girl! Should I guess as to who it was?"

"I suspect you'd be a winner. Let me tell you anyway. It was Mrs. Artenelli."

"Why does that not surprise me?"

"That's how I felt. But the mystery doesn't end there. McGregor told me the woman was only trying to protect the girl's innocence; it had nothing to do with a cover. Wonder if that's the truth?"

Logan put his thumb and index finger at the corner of his mouth. "Now, now, that sure is a mystery. Why did Mrs. Artenelli give such a damn about that kid?"

"That's the next thing I plan to investigate, but first things, first. From everything Mrs. Godfrey told me yesterday, from the child's poem about the ocean that Tanner found in the girl's school bag, to some drawings Doctor Thatcher showed me, I feel I know the Bernadette Godfrey child quite well. Now, I need to get an idea as to what makes Joe Godfrey tick."

"Let's hope you do. That Joe Godfrey's a real Mickey Mouse. Odd ball, all right. Never could quite figure that guy out. Course that don't mean he murdered his own kid." Logan grabbed at a toothpick from a small container on his desk, and began to bite down on it.

"No, not every Mickey Mouse is a felon; I'll agree with you there. But Mrs. Godfrey pretty much put the cuffs on her own husband, admitting that he had been abusing their child." She told me that she thought the abuse was going on down at the bathhouses."

"She what?" The toothpick fell from Logan's lips.

"You heard me right. Not only that but Mrs. Godfrey said her husband would beat her if he knew she told me. I saw the bruises myself."

"Well, I'll be." Logan paused and said, "Makes me wonder if I shouldn't go with you to confront Godfrey."

"I'll be fine." Dana told Logan she'd be back in contact with him once she had a chance to speak with the man.

"You keep that radio on now, you hear me?"

***

Dana headed down the splintered stairs, covered in beach sand and seagull dung. To avoid slipping, or so she told herself, she grasped the railing tightly, feeling her fingers ache from the grip. The veins in her hands rose rigid and defined. She watched her feet moving slowly down the steps, like a child on an ice rink for the first time. The smell of saltwater came closer. A gust of wind, cutting like a blade, blew across her face. It stung at her ears and took her breath away. The splashing sound of the tide grew louder and louder.

She forced herself to look up, to look forward, to look out over the navy-blue waves. Pointed white caps like the teeth of a shark hurled to shore and then back out again. She stopped, telling herself that she could do this, she must. The tip of her shoe touched the gritty sand at the bottom of the stairs, and she knew she could not go back.

Off to her left were the bathhouses that Logan described. They stood in a row about ten feet from the edge of the water. Each was supported on four wooden stilts that looked like fine, thin legs of a flamingo. One of the stalls was painted a bright earthy green, but the others looked like forgotten orphans waiting their turn to be attended to. Over the sound of the crashing waves and the cawing of seagulls, Dana could hear the pounding of a hammer.

She glimpsed over her shoulder at the rolling breakers and felt her body sway with their rhythmic movement. She breathed deeply, tightened the wool scarf around her neck, and pushed herself against the direction of the wind as she tried to venture closer to the small sheds. *Quite a nasty day to be doing renovation work*, she thought.

A man wearing a brown plaid jacket climbed down from the roof of one of the huts on a ladder braced in front of the shack. Dana knew immediately it was Joe Godfrey from the photo she had seen of him. His face was weathered red, his slick black hair blowing wildly, his moustache glistened with ice crystals, and he held a hammer in his gloved hands.

"Mr. Godfrey," she called out.

He turned at the sound of her voice, opened the door of the building, and went inside.

She tapped on the door, shielded her face with the edges of her scarf, and screamed over the sounds of nature, "Mr. Godfrey."

The splintered door flung open. Mr. Godfrey's eyes widened to reveal the white of his corneas. He still held the hammer in his clutches.

"I'm Dana Greer, special investigator for Sergeant Logan. May I speak with you for a moment?"

"Ain't got no time. I'm busy." He swung the hammer from side to side, like a clock pendulum out of control.

"I can see that, but I only need a minute."

"What's this about?"

"I'm trying to find the person who hurt your little girl, Bernadette."

"Don't waste your time asking me nothin'. I ain't got no idea who murdered the kid."

The wind's force picked up. Sharp grains of sand slapped Dana's cheeks as she stepped inside the deteriorating shack. Immediately, the door slammed shut. There she stood staring into the whites of the man's eyes. His breath smelled of cheap vodka. Along his bottom lip, saliva oozed, and he used his thick tongue to sweep it away.

In the corner of the bathhouse, Dana saw three bottles of liquor, one of which was empty and next to it a copy of *Frolic*, the cover of which displayed a voluptuous blond woman wearing only purple pasties, a thin string bikini, and black fishnet stockings. Lying among a pile of tools, near a black metal lunch box, was an issue of *Gala*, depicting another scantily-clad woman. Dana knew she would have to choose her words carefully. She was used to this kind of man—the type you didn't cross for fear he'd become violent, the type who saw women as mere objects.

"Look, like I said, I've got work to do. Better ask your questions elsewhere." Mr. Godfrey began to pound a nail into the framework around the door.

"But you're her father. Might you know of anyone who—"

"Let's get this straight. The Mrs. and me adopted the kid; she never was mine. The wife can't have kids."

How brutal that he should talk that way. Dana felt her adrenalin begin to pump. "Mr. Godfrey, Bernadette was an innocent child whose life never should have come to this. Have you no compassion?"

"Let's not give me no sermon; I get enough of that from the Mrs. I ain't about to fall for any God lectures."

"This has to do with evil, Mr. Godfrey, not God. Whoever did this to *your* child had to be evil."

"Well, I don't got any idea who that might be, Miss Grange."

"Greer. Dana Greer." She edged closer to him and pointed her finger. "Then let me ask you this. Word has it that Bernadette had been sexually abused. Do you know anything about that?"

He dropped his hammer on the floor, his hands calloused, blistered, and chapped, the hands that would be capable of stabbing a small girl mercilessly until she gasped her last breath. The corner of his right eye began to twitch as he wiped his nose in the palm of his hand. "Don't believe that was in the paper."

"I didn't say where my *word* came from."

"Sure as hell hope you're not listening to that old card reader. She's bad news. Let me guess, she left a card in Bernadette's grave?"

The comment startled Dana, her shoulders stiffened. She couldn't tell if he knew more than he said, or if he was just being sarcastic. "It was not Opal who gave me the information."

"I'd sure as hell like to know who. I'd like to put my gritty mitts around his neck." The man's face reddened, his opened mouth revealing three decayed teeth, blackened and chipped.

"The source is not what is important. Only the facts are. Did you know Bernadette had been abused?" Dana emphasized the word 'abused.'

"Lies, cheap lies. That's all this is. You gotta be pretty goddamn dumb to fall for that shit." He bent down and picked up his hammer.

"Are you saying that you refuse to believe Red Tanner, the coroner's, report? It's all there, Mr. Godfrey. . .not speculation but fact."

The color slid from the man's face like cherry liquid being poured out of a pitcher until nothing's left but its transparency. "Did the exam reveal who could of done such a thing?"

"Afraid medical knowledge isn't that sophisticated. Why'd you ask?"

In a hushed voice, Mr. Godfrey said, "Just wonderin'. Sure'd be nice to point a finger at who would've done such a thing."

"What about the morning Bernadette went missing, Mr. Godfrey?"

"What about it?" He raised his upper lip, looking like a fighter going into the ring.

"Were you at home when she left? When was the last time you saw her alive?"

"I never cared for the kid, raising kids is women's work. I leave by 6:00 a.m. to head out to the ferry."

"So, you were gone when Bernadette left that day." Dana made the statement less like a question and more like a note for her to remember.

Mr. Godfrey ignored her point. "Now let me tell you something, lady. If you don't high tail your ass out of here, I could make it look like a drowning. Simple enough. Call it an accident.

Dana blinked hard, the sand crystals making her eyes water. The man with the thin moustache and weathered face blurred for a second. The face she stared into looked like that of her Uncle Lou. She heard his words, "Do it, you little piece of shit! Now!"

Dana closed her eyes, then opened them and saw Mr. Godfrey, his shoulders hunched low, his lips in a scowl. Dana's return to reality made her realize that she was not about to let Mr. Godfrey intimidate her. "In addition to being a suspect in the abuse of Bernadette Godfrey," she said, "and possibly in the murder of the child as well, should I add threat to an officer of the law? Do you think you can lay a finger on me and make it look like an accident? So happens the Sergeant is fully aware that I'm here. There's no way you can get around this one, Mr. Godfrey. I'll see you at the station first thing tomorrow morning, where I expect to get a formal statement from you."

Mr. Godfrey stepped back; his mouth opened as if he were about to say something, but decided against it. His tongue swept across his lips.

Dana opened the door to the bathhouse and made her way toward the beach stairs, hearing the tide moving in and out. Her chest tightened; she had trouble breathing. She gasped and stumbled. She brushed the sand out of her eyes and got up again. When she made it to the top of the steps, she found the nearest tree, braced her arms against it, and swallowed the bile that had risen in her throat.

Chapter Seventeen

Dana glanced out her bedroom window. Ice crystals covered the tree branches and the glazed walk looked like a mirror. A perfect day to stay inside. After the harrowing time she had had yesterday confronting Joe Godfrey and exposing herself to the perils of the sea, she needed a day to relax. She would call Logan later and tell him about her encounter with Mr. Godfrey. She hardly believed that Joe Godfrey would show up at the station as she had asked; she figured Logan could order the subpoena. She found a stack of albums on the shelf in her closet and put a Frank Sinatra record on the phonograph. Then, she slipped back under her covers and reached for the novel on her night table, *The Cardinal* by Henry Morton Robinson. Although removing herself from the Church by choice, she still maintained a respect for the ritual and hierarchy. *The Cardinal* provided her with a magical tour into what life must have been like for a person of this status.

Her plans were abruptly circumvented by a knock on her bedroom door. Jay greeted her with, "What the hell happened to you? You look like something the cat dragged in. Shouldn't you be off playing 'cops and robbers'?"

"Yesterday was exhausting. Thought I'd take it easy today." She questioned why she needed to explain herself to the man. "Is there something you wanted to tell me?"

"There's someone waiting to see you in the parlor, I'm afraid." Jay had a slight smirk on his face as if he found some small delight in interrupting Dana's plans. "Should I send her away? It's Mrs. Artenelli."

Dana looked incredulous as Jay said, "I know. Mrs. Artenelli would never consider gracing our presence—mine and Loretta's. Keep in mind that our humble abode isn't on the Pointe. Whatever she's here for, it has to be something important."

"I'll be right down," Dana said. She quickly changed into some casual clothes and headed for the parlor.

Dressed in an aqua suit with a pencil skirt and a cropped jacket that revealed the woman's hourglass figure, Mrs. Artenelli looked like a fashion model on the cover of *Vogue* magazine. A navy blue-and-white polka-dot blouse completed her ensemble. Her fur stole lay on the sofa cushion next to her; the beady eyes of the red fox stared in her direction.

"Miss Greer."

"Dana, please."

"Dana, ah yes. Please, call me Carmelina. I'm delighted that you've come to the Cape to investigate this horrible crime."

Quite a contradiction in personas from the woman who only days ago had asked her on which ferry she planned to leave. Dana was eager to learn why the change of heart.

"Any leads, dear?" Mrs. Artenelli pulled out a cigarette from her handbag, which was covered in pearls and faux diamonds. She put the cigarette in an eight-inch holder covered in gold rhinestones, lit the cigarette with a lighter engraved with a fancy letter *A*, and took a deep drag. "Would you like one?" she asked.

"I don't smoke, thanks. And, no. No concrete leads on the murderer."

The woman continued breathing in and out deeply, daintily removing a small piece of tobacco from her tongue. She began to toy with her fur coat, petting the piece of fox as if it were a pet. The sound of her voice changed from one of questioning to one of worry. "Dana, there's something that's happened. I'm not quite sure where to turn, who to turn to. Thought maybe you could help me." Her forehead bore deep creases.

"With what?"

Mrs. Artenelli opened her small clutch again. "It's this," she said, handing a piece of paper to Dana. "Read it, please."

Dana opened the folds of what appeared to be a piece of school loose leaf and read:

We all know you got money for this and money for that. It's come to my attention that I'm running short of cash. Was wondering if you could spare me a buck or two. Here's my address:

4787 3rd Street

Waterville 36, Maine

Eddie Vineeti

"Wait a minute. Eddie Vineeti is the man who interrupted your daughter's profession of vows."

"Yes. He's always been quite immature for his age."

Dana pretended to know little about the man, hoping to learn more. "Tell me, Carmelina, exactly who is this Eddie?"

"He used to date my daughter, Angela, long before she entered the convent." Mrs. Artenelli smoked feverishly on her cigarette, finally snuffing it out in a small amber dish on the coffee table. "You must understand, Dana, the man is and will always be beneath our social standing. I just don't know what Angela ever saw in him in the first place."

"The convent? Why did Angela decide to join, if I might ask?"

"Praise the Lord, Dana. Do you have any idea what an honor it is to have your child become a bride of Christ?"

Dana noted that Mrs. Artenelli had deliberately skirted the answer.

"We're a strong Catholic family. I head up the ladies' auxiliary, the altar society, and the rosary guild."

The woman reminded Dana of a modern-day Pharisee, so eager was she to brag about all that she did for the Church. The question remained. What part did Gino Artenelli play in Angela's decision to join the convent? Why, he never even attended his daughter's profession of final vows.

"But what about Angela? Why did she want to become a nun?"

"She always wanted to be a bride of Christ. Never dated much, other than that rascal Eddie." The woman adjusted a small diamond pin in the shape of a tiger on her lapel.

"Hmm. So, it was Angela's decision?"

"Oh absolutely. And, she does make a beautiful one, don't you agree?"

How strange. Eddie had told Dana a completely different story, one where Angela's mother had forced the young woman to join the convent as a means to escape his affections. "Has Eddie ever come to you before for money, Mrs. Artenel—"

"Carmelina. This is the first. But if you knew Eddie like I do, I know this won't be the last. He's a pushy type."

"In what way may I ask?"

"Why I must have asked that scoundrel at least a half dozen times to leave my daughter alone, and then I'd find out the two of them were dating again. He said that he wanted to go steady with Angela, but you very well must know. . .or do you. . .that allowing a teenager to go steady is a mortal sin!"

"Sounds as if he wouldn't take no for an answer."

"No."

"How did the two of them meet?"

"At a party one of Angela's friends from high school had. Eddie isn't even from Bay View, lives in the small town of Waterville. He probably lives in one of those month-to-month trailer parks. Eva, Angela's friend, had no right inviting such a loser to the party in the first place."

Whether what Mrs. Artenelli was saying was true or not, Dana could not believe this church-going woman could possibly be so judgmental. "So, you think you'll hear from Eddie again, asking for money."

"I do; that's what worries me, Dana. The man has a temper. I worry if I don't send him money that he might turn hostile."

"I see. Any idea why he's come to you for money? I mean besides the fact that he's angry you broke the two of them up."

The woman smiled and adjusted the large polka dot bow below her chin. "He knows I have it." The woman lifted her head and pointed her chin outward. She blinked rapidly.

"Of course, but I'm thinking of other reasons."

"Such as?"

"Maybe, he blames you that Angela entered the convent."

"Ridiculous!"

"Or, maybe he plans to blackmail you."

"How silly! Whatever for?"

Dana began to wonder why the woman had even brought this to her attention. If the note from Eddie was merely a plea for money, why did Carmelina need to bring her into this? Dana remembered the threat that Eddie made that day in the jail cell. He had said, "I ain't through with Mrs. Artenelli yet. That bitch owes me one." Dana knew then that Eddie's threats weren't to be taken lightly, unlike what Logan thought. No, this man planned to retaliate, and his notes for money were only the beginning. "I suggest you take these letters, all of them that you have, to Sergeant Logan. He's got a file open on the guy, and should these notes become any more demanding, Logan could bring extortion charges against the man."

"You're scaring me, Dana. Maybe, it would be easier to send him some cash now and again. I mean, it couldn't hurt. Like I said, the man has a temper."

"Wrong. The stakes will just go up. If it's a couple of bucks this time, it might be a couple hundred the next time, a few thousand after that. Plus, I believe Eddie wants more than money."

Mrs. Artenelli arose, tossed the fur stole around her neck, and pulled out an elbow-length pair of rabbit-hair gloves from her handbag. With her eyes squinted, she looked at Dana and said, "You're not trying to tell me the man would intentionally hurt me, are you?"

Dana purposely chose not to answer, but did say, "There is something that concerns me, Carmelina, and it has to do with the deceased child."

"Oh, come now. Eddie may have a temper, but you're not insinuating that he would have anything to do with the child's death, are you?"

Dana shook her head. "No, no. . .at least, I don't think so. I was thinking of something else entirely. Something I heard."

"From Opal? The woman's got a God-given gift. If I were you, I'd pay heed to what she has to say. She's been correct more times than not."

"No, from the Sergeant."

Mrs. Artenelli's face looked like a rose in full bloom, hot pink.

"He tells me that the child had been sexually abused."

"And, you. . .you believe *him*?"

"Why would I not?" Dana decided not to get into the threat she had to make about arresting Tanner before he confessed, nor would she say Mrs. Godfrey had openly admitted her husband's secret.

"Miss Greer, why don't we just say, 'Let the dead lie in peace.' Bernadette's in the arms of God. What good does it do to go public about the child's tainted image?"

Beneath Mrs. Artenelli's heavily mascaraed lashes, her eyes began to glisten with tears. There was something about the pretentious woman that suddenly made her human.

"There is something I don't quite understand, Carmelina."

Mrs. Artenelli dabbed at her eyes, her fingernails polished a glossy red.

"I admire your feelings for Bernadette and for not wanting her innocence scrutinized, but I wonder why the child meant so much to you."

Mrs. Artenelli pulled out another cigarette from her beaded bag and lit it. She puffed on it for several seconds as she watched the smoke rise. "I love children, Dana. And I always admired the Godfreys for reaching out to give the girl a home." She puffed some more on her cigarette.

Mrs. Artenelli's explanation sounded weak to Dana. There are lots of people who love children, and many who open their homes to adopt. There seemed to be a link missing here, and Dana wasn't quite sure what. "Knowing the Godfreys as well as you did, did you ever think to ask them who the birth parents were?"

"Never! That would have been plain rude. A lack of manners. Have you never read Emily Post?"

"In order for me to solve this case, it will become necessary for me to find out this information. I was just hoping you might have been able to help."

"Sorry," Mrs. Artenelli said, snuffing out her cigarette, "but I'm certainly not the one you should be asking."

***

Back in her room again, Dana sipped on some warm milk and pushed aside the plate with her half-eaten sandwich. Although she had hoped to clear her mind and get some rest, life wasn't about to let her have it that way. She opened her notebook and began to write: *November 8th Three Weeks Since Arriving on the Cape*

- *Discuss Eddie's extortion of Carmelina Artenelli with Sergeant Logan*

- *Get a confession from Joe Godfrey regarding the part he played in the abuse of Bernadette Godfrey*
- *Investigate possible suspects in the murder of Bernadette Godfrey*
- *Introduce myself to Father Byron Sullivan*
- *Pay a visit to the Guardian Angel Orphanage in Waterville, Maine*

Dana was about to shut off the light when she heard some loud voices coming from the spare bedroom down the hall.

"I know, Jay. You're involved with that woman. Don't deny it."

From her room, Dana could hear Loretta's sobbing, stuttering on her words.

"That's ridiculous!" Jay answered.

"But she's a nun, Jay, a woman of God!"

"I told you once, and I'll tell you again, I'm not seeing anyone."

"You're lying, Jay. You're lying."

"Loretta, please, lower your voice. Do you want Miss Greer to hear?"

Chapter Eighteen

The next day, as soon as Dana arose, she took out her notebook and added the following to her to-do list:

- *Look into possible sexual relationship between Jay Harrison and Sister Mary Rose*

The thing that puzzled Dana, though, was why would the nun have agreed to profess final vows only a couple of weeks ago if she was carrying on an affair behind Loretta's back? Why wouldn't she have either postponed the vows or have gone so far as to leave the convent entirely? Something about her behavior didn't add up. On the other hand, perhaps all of this was simply Loretta's jealous imagining.

The day Dana stopped by the school to meet with the nun in the faculty lounge, Jay did seem a bit amorous around her, and then, there *was* the photo of the two of them Dana had found in the cedar chest. If Loretta was questioning her husband's behavior, it might account for her emotional state as of late.

Dana got up and stood next to the window overlooking the bay. During the night, several inches of snow had fallen on top of the remains of an ice storm. The sun was just coming out; its glistening rays shone on the carpet of white, making the ground look like a blanket of crystals, not yet baptized by human foot traffic. Dana made her way down to the kitchen for a cup of coffee when the phone rang.

"Miss Greer."

"Yes, who is this?" Dana waited but only heard hysterical crying and the words, "No, no, no."

"Please. Tell me, who is this?"

"It's Mia Godfrey. Something's happened. It's Joe. Please come."

"I'll be right there," Dana said. Thoughts flowed through her mind like a waterfall cascading down from a rocky embankment. Had Joe done something to hurt his wife? Had he found out that Mia had told Dana about her speculations involving his abuse? Did he learn that Mrs. Artenelli also knew? As Dana dressed, she found herself praying for Mrs. Godfrey's safety. She left the Harrison home and as in a nightmare, the quicker the strides she made, the slower her progress seemed to be, her boots cracking through the crunchy snow. When she finally arrived, Mrs. Godfrey opened the door before Dana had a chance to ring the bell. In her hands she held a bloody towel.

"My God, what's happened, Mia?"

Mrs. Godfrey's eyes were swollen and bloodshot. Her body trembled like the last of fall leaves withering on a barren branch. "Out back," she said, "follow me."

She didn't bother to put on a coat or boots and hastily made her way out the back door toward a metal shed in the rear of the yard. "In there," she said. Between sobs, she continued, "He's in there. Joe. He's in there."

The door to the shed was partially opened and the latch was covered in fresh blood. Dana entered the small space that was filled with garden tools, everything from rakes and pots to a rusted lawn mower in the rear. On the floor slumped next to a small window laid

Joe; his face totally disfigured, resembling a piece of raw meat. "My God, in heaven's name!" Dana shouted. It was then that Dana saw a Sport King semi-automatic pistol next to the body.

"I found him this way. I tried to revive him and then realized it was too late, too late." Mrs. Godfrey fell to her knees as if in front of a shrine ready to pray. "My Joe." Her whole body shuddered; she lay prostrate in front of him.

"Any note? Did he leave one?"

"This," Mia Godfrey said, and handed Dana a blood splattered piece of paper.

I can no longer live with myself and the monster I have become.
I hate myself and what I did to Bernadette.

The card reading that Opal had done came to Dana's mind. Opal said the card spoke to someone who felt guilty. Could Opal's sixth sense and the package that arrived at the Bay View radio station point to Joe Godfrey as the monster? Could it be that his guilt became more than he could bear?

Dana pulled out her Motorola handheld receiver and radioed Logan. "On site of a suicide. Joe Godfrey. Dana Greer over and out."

"Stay put. On my way. Logan over and out."

Dana did her best to comfort the woman who by now was hyperventilating and hysterical. "Help is coming," she said, as she led the woman back to the house. "Would you like for me to call Father?"

"Please," Mia said.

Dana took the phone on the kitchen wall and dialed the Holy Name rectory.

"Father Sullivan speaking."

"Father, I'm afraid we have not formally met. The name's Dana Greer."

"Ah, yes. Heard about your arrival on the Cape. Saw you at the child's funeral. May God's blessings be with you. Go in safety, my child. For surely, this is a wicked world that we live in."

A perfect segue, Dana said, "Father, I am at the Godfrey home. Could you come at once? Joe Godfrey is dead." Dana decided not to mention it appeared to be a suicide. She knew the Church's stance on suicides as well as Christian burials.

"Jesus, Mary, Joseph. I'll leave immediately," he said.

Dana held Mrs. Godfrey in her arms, the woman sobbed uncontrollably. Her heart went out to the woman who had been abused by her husband and had lived under his menacing control. He even referred to himself as a monster. Dana could not comprehend what man would refuse to accept his adopted child as his own. It seemed strange to Dana that the woman would shed endless tears over her husband's death.

Under her breath, Mrs. Godfrey could be heard calling Joe's name repetitively.

Fortunately, within a short time, Logan arrived accompanied by Officers Boyle and O'Neil as well as Red Tanner, the coroner.

The four men greeted Mrs. Godfrey and offered their condolences, then went immediately to the shed out back. Dana excused herself and told Mrs. Godfrey that Father was on his way.

Dana watched the men gasp at the sight of Joe's body.

Tanner hunched his shoulders and bent his knees to be eye level with the corpse. "Jesus Christ," he said, "this asshole wasn't going to take any chances he might miss."

"What'd ya mean?" Logan asked.

"Why look here. The bastard must have pressed the muzzle right up against his face."

Logan, Boyle, O'Neil, and Dana gathered closer to the body, staring into what was left of the man's face.

Tanner continued, "Look closely."

Dana bit down on her lower lip in hopes she could keep herself from getting sick.

"See this star-shaped pattern? The muzzle had to have been pressed right up against the skull where the hot gases and particulate matter were driven directly into the skin. . .er what's left of it." He turned to face Dana. "What time did the Mrs. say she found the body?"

"She didn't," Dana said, "but I assumed it must have happened shortly before she called me. The blood's still fresh and dripping."

"That's what I thought," Tanner said. "Rigor mortis is just beginning in the muscles of his neck. See how stiff it is?"

Logan, McNeil, Reynolds, and Dana nodded in agreement.

"Did he leave a note?" Logan asked Dana.

"One admitting to the girl's sexual abuse, calling himself a monster."

"Think he was responsible for her murder?" O'Neil asked. He directed his question to Logan as if Dana were invisible.

"Hard to say, but it sure would give him one hell of a motive for a suicide," Logan said.

Tanner said that he would make arrangements with Mrs. Godfrey to have the body transported to the morgue.

"How about an autopsy?" Dana asked.

"As long as I've been a coroner on Cape Peril, I've done five or six autopsies. With the high concentration of Catholics on the island, most frown upon the procedure as desecrating the body after its death."

When Logan, Dana, and the two officers returned to the house, Father Sullivan had already arrived. Mrs. Godfrey had her head on Father's shoulder, crying so hard that her entire body trembled. The priest patted her on the back.

Dana wanted to inquire if Mrs. Godfrey heard the gun go off but decided now was not the time.

The woman cleared her throat and looked at the priest. "Father, you remember me confessing. I thought Joe might have. . . ." Her lips shivered and her teeth chattered.

"My child, I am unable to speak publicly about your confession. Let us pray that eternal rest is granted unto Joe. May his soul rest in peace, oh Lord."

Mrs. Godfrey and the priest completed the prayer in unison, "And let perpetual light shine upon him," while the others stood silent with bent heads.

"Officers, might I go out to the shed to see Mr. Godfrey before his body is removed? I'd like to administer the sacrament of Extreme Unction. I've brought my oils with me."

"It's a pretty grizzly sight, Father," Dana said.

"Jesus, Mary, Joseph, no." He made the sign of the cross over his chest. The priest looked at Dana as if he were about to say something but decided against it. He nodded his head and walked away.

Dana heard him mumble, "May God forgive him."

***

"Quite a day, huh?" Logan said. "At least we got Godfrey's written confession. Checked it out, and it's his handwriting all right." Almost in the same breath, he asked, "Can I pour you a cup of coffee?"

"Please." Dana sat down opposite Logan's desk and held the mug between her hands, enjoying the heat radiating from it. "My heart goes out to Mrs. Godfrey, first, losing her only child and now the suicide."

"True, true. She sure has been given a load of crosses as Father would probably say." He poked at his gold incisor with his index finger. "Where do you go from here, Dana, in your investigation?"

Just then, Janet, the receptionist, wearing a tightly fitted, fuzzy pink sweater and poodle skirt, poked her head in the doorway. "Mrs. Artenelli on line one; for you, Sergeant."

Logan picked up the phone, and Dana watched his eyebrows rise and fall. "I see. I see," was all he kept repeating. When he stopped talking, he looked over at Dana. "No, she hasn't. . .not yet anyway. Will do." He hung up the phone. "I understand Mrs. Artenelli is getting money requests, huh?"

"Yes, that was one of the things I had hoped to discuss with you this morning before all of the commotion over Joe Godfrey," Dana said. "Came by yesterday and showed me a note that she received from Vineeti. I told you that guy smelled of trouble. He's got some kind of vendetta with that woman."

"What do you suggest be done? Arrest him on a ten-dollar extortion charge?" Logan laughed.

"Guess here's where you and I split, Logan. You don't see Eddie Vineeti's demands as being anything more than that; I say, the guy's got something up his sleeve, and it's not very pretty. I intend to find out what it is."

Logan's mouth opened, but before he had a chance to say anything, Dana went on.

"I'm planning on making a trip to Waterville to the Guardian Angel Orphanage. I intend to take a little side trip to surprise Eddie."

"Hmm." Logan began to doodle on a yellow sheet of paper, his pencil forming small fish, each shape in one movement. "Anything else you got planned?"

"I want to speak with Father Sullivan. Mrs. Godfrey told me that it was Father who recommended that she and Joe try to adopt an older child from Guardian Angel."

"I'll mind the fort until you get back, but don't be gone too long. We need you here."

Dana smiled. After only three weeks, maybe Cape Peril was beginning to feel more like home than she realized.

Chapter Nineteen

Dana had scheduled an appointment to see Father Sullivan before she left for the mainland. She waited in the Holy Name rectory. A plump, short woman with wet, gray hair wrapped tightly around black bobby pins opened the door from Father's private office and told Dana that Father would see her. The woman wore a red-and-green organdy apron with an appliqued white cross on its pocket. Her black dress reached to the middle of her calves, and her oxfords squeaked.

Father rose as Dana entered and extended his hand, a firm, strong shake. "Nice to see you again, Miss Greer." He motioned for her to have a seat. A life-size statue of Saint Michael the Archangel stood in the corner of the room.

Dana found herself mouthing the prayer to the patron saint: *Defend us in battle.*

Be our protection against the wickedness and snares of the devil.

She knew that that was exactly what she was up against. Whoever could murder an innocent, seven-year-old child had to be nothing short of Satan himself.

Father noticed her eyeing the statue and said, "A going away gift from my parishioners of Saint Michael's parish in Bay View, where I used to be pastor before coming to Holy Name."

"Lovely," Dana said, "how thoughtful."

"What brings you by, Miss Greer? Certainly, you have seen enough evil since arriving on the Cape."

"Quite. It's the survivors that demand the most sympathy. My heart goes out to Mrs. Godfrey. Have any plans been made for her husband's burial?"

"There will be no funeral, no burial." Father's words were cold and indifferent. He did not flinch.

It did not surprise Dana though, as she knew the Church's teaching: suicide victims were considered condemned souls by the Church and were not given the blessings of a traditional Christian wake nor were they allowed to be buried in a Catholic cemetery.

"From what Red Tanner told me, the body will be shipped to a potter's field on the mainland."

"Speaking of the mainland, I'm planning on leaving for Waterville in the morning, a visit to the Guardian Angel Orphanage. Mrs. Godfrey told me that you had put her and her husband in contact with someone there when the Godfreys were looking to adopt."

Father looked down at his desk and handed Dana a small pewter frame.

Dana looked at the image, a round-faced woman with tiny twinkling eyes who looked to be in her mid-nineties. She wore a white habit.

"Oh, you mean my Aunt Helen." Father laughed. "Let me explain. My Aunt, Helen, belongs to the Little Sisters of the Poor order. She's got to be a hundred years old by now." He laughed again. "Seriously, though, she's a caretaker at the orphanage, has been for years."

"Was she able to arrange the adoption for the Godfreys?" Dana asked.

"No, no, no. She's only a cleaning person there, helps with some of the cooking, too; well, you know, basic operational kinds of things."

Dana waited for Father to tell her more, as she jotted in her notebook.

"The Godfreys were well into their forties when they decided to adopt and did not have any luck in finding an infant. I suggested they visit the orphanage, and I put them in contact with my Aunt Helen."

"I understand that Bernadette, the child the Godfreys finally adopted, was six-years-old at the time that they met her."

"True. Sister Thomasina, the Mother Superior, thought an older child would be better for the couple because of their age. Most of the children are adopted at birth, so it was fortunate for them that Bernadette was among the children waiting to be adopted."

Dana jotted quickly as Father spoke. "Any idea as to the background on the child, Father? I mean why she was put up for adoption, by whom?"

"All adoptions at Guardian Angel are considered closed. That's why the home has as many children as they do. All information about the adoptive child is kept private; it's the way the people want it when they put their child up for adoption."

"Understandable." But in her notebook, Dana wrote: *Question Father Sullivan's Aunt as to what she might know about the Godfrey child.*

"I hope I've been of some help to you, Dana."

"More than you know, Father."

Dana started to put her notebook in her bag but decided against it. She looked at Father, a handsome man with thick black hair, a five o'clock shadow, and a face that spoke of kindness. "How well did you know Bernadette Godfrey, Father?"

The priest clasped his hands in a prayer mode. "As pastor, I have the chance to know all of the students at the Academy. Why?"

Dana sensed some irritation in the priest's reply as he put his emphasis on the word *all*. "Oh, I'm sure you do, but is there anything about Bernadette that stands out?"

He pondered for a moment. He chuckled. "Oh, come on, Miss Greer, we all have our favorites now, don't we?"

"How so, Father?"

"Bernadette was a model child. She tried to do her best at whatever she did. Well, Sister Mary Rose can vouch for that." The priest turned around a framed picture on his desk. It was that of Sister Mary Rose as a novice.

"Sister was a student of mine while in the novitiate, a prized student, as well."

Dana thought it odd that Father should have a photo of the nun on his desk as he must have taught several other novices beside Sister Mary Rose. Then she remembered seeing Father in the vestibule of the church the day that the professed nuns had greeted their families and friends. Father stood in the corner, in the shadows, watching, his focus on Sister Mary Rose. "Also one of your favorites?" Dana asked.

"Indeed."

Fiona Wharton had taught Dana that it paid to be persistent no matter how uncomfortable the person being questioned might become. Dana picked up from where she left off. "So, Father, why would you say Bernadette was a model child?"

The priest moved from side-to-side in his leather chair and peered through the large window overlooking the rectory courtyard. Several small wooden bird houses stood on tall posts, one of them resembling a small church complete with stained glass windows, a steeple, and a cross.

Father turned his attention back to their conversation. "Let's put it this way, Miss Greer. There was something unsettling about the child. Perhaps, that's why I was drawn to her. Her sweet, angelic face reached out to me."

"How so, Father?"

He shook his head. "Can't say."

Dana opened her notebook again and jotted:

Why did Father find the child unsettling?

Mrs. Godfrey told Dana that she had confided in the priest about Mr. Godfrey abusing the girl, but Father guarded his words so as not to touch on the subject. "Might you know who wanted the child dead?"

He rubbed his fingers across the dark stubble on his cheeks. "Afraid not."

Dana watched as the man's face cringed; he pounded his fist into the palm of his hand and looked toward the courtyard again. A lone chickadee flew away.

"There is one more thing I'd like to ask."

The priest's dark eyes riveted in her direction.

"Did you happen to recall seeing Mrs. Artenelli at the eight a.m. Mass on the morning that Bernadette Godfrey went missing?" Dana had also learned that technique from Fiona Wharton: abruptly change the topic, ask a pointed question, and observe the reaction.

"That was how many days ago?" he looked at Dana quizzically. "I would suppose she was; she comes to Mass every morning with the school children."

Dana scanned the collection of photos father had on his wall, smiling youngsters in their blue-and-green plaid uniforms. Each frame was of a classroom with the teacher in the background. Then Dana's eyes caught the attention of one of the photos in the middle row. It was of Bernadette and Father standing next to the Seaside Ferry. Dana made no comment other than to say, "Thanks for your time, Father."

Chapter Twenty

Spending her entire life in Bay View, Dana had never been to Waterville, about fifty-five miles from the city and Northwest of the Cape, with a population of slightly over 7,000 people. She had departed from Cape Peril on the ten a.m. ferry and arranged for a cab to take her to the hotel once she got to Waterville. She arrived in the middle of a blizzard, a veil of stark white before her. It was as though she was in a dream, lost, in a thick cloud, unable to find blue sky or her way out of the mystical maze. She asked the cab driver to wait while she went into the hotel to register.

A frail man with wired spectacles and black leather suspenders greeted her with, "You sure picked a cold one to come to Waterville. What's brings you to these parts?"

Dana ignored the man's inquiry, smiled, and asked for the key to her room. "I've got a cab waiting; I'm afraid I'm in a hurry.

When she came out, the taxicab driver asked, "Where to?"

"Guardian Angel Orphanage."

The tires of the cab skidded from the curb; the driver spun the steering wheel first one way and then the other. Someone honked his horn.

"Slippery as hell," the taxi driver said. "Sure you want to be out on a day like this?"

"How far is the orphanage from here?" Dana asked.

"In this weather, it's hard to say. Plus, the place is in the middle of nowhere, I'm afraid. When people got secrets to keep, they sure as hell don't want anyone knowing them." The man's New England accent was thick and barely understandable.

Secrets, an interesting way of putting it. Obviously there were secrets behind Bernadette Godfrey's adoption. Hopefully, the orphanage would have the answers Dana sought.

Almost an hour later, the taxi pulled in front of a four-story red brick building, the wide circular drive and walkways shoveled bare. Two nuns, each bundled in long, black coats, walked the path in front of the orphanage, their breaths rising upward as they spoke to one another.

Dana asked the cab driver to wait and saw him turn off his meter.

As she entered the building, soft music hummed in the background, accompanied by voices singing Gregorian Chant. A large wooden banister wound its way up the floors, each step trimmed in a floral carpet. Large framed oil paintings filled the walls. One depicted a pregnant Mary with child, making her way with Joseph to Bethlehem. Another was of St. Anne standing beside Mary, who was a mere child. From a long, golden chain hung a painting of St. Rita as a mother with her two sons, juxtaposed with one of her as the nun she finally became after her husband had died and her children had passed away, victims of the Black Plague. Interesting, Dana mused, that all the paintings were of mothers and children.

The furniture in the room, mostly of an Italian Renaissance variety, was arranged in small conversational groupings. Large crystal chandeliers hung every few feet from the ceiling, which was shaped like an opened umbrella rising to at least sixty feet in height. A pair of stained-glass windows, made of thousands of blue, green, and yellow mosaics, showed Elizabeth, Mary's cousin, and the boy John the Baptist. One window stood on each side of double doors that were marked overhead with the word *Chapel*. The entrance floor was a highly polished pink marble that reflected all the surrounding colors. A statue of Christ welcoming several young children to his side stood across from the chapel. Small blue votive candles sparkled along another wall, a picture of angels as dancing babies above it. If Dana had to picture what heaven might be like, she had a strong speculation that it might be something like this.

She went up to the oak counter in the far corner of the room and told the receptionist that she had an appointment with Mother Superior. Before she had a chance to be seated, a middle-aged nun dressed in the completely white habit of the Little Sisters of the Poor greeted her with, "Miss Greer, please come into my office; I'm Sister Thomasina."

The office was small yet embellished with Catholic sacramentals: crucifixes; statues of saints; and an open, red-leather Bible, which sat on a pedestal in the corner. The nun offered Dana a cup of tea, and before she had a chance to accept, the Mother Superior poured some into a tiny china cup, small enough for a child.

"How might I assist you, Miss Greer?" The nun adjusted her long veil and black wooden rosary beads before sitting behind her desk.

Dana told her about her newly acquired assignment on Cape Peril and that she hoped to learn about the child the Godfreys had adopted.

"I remember the Godfreys well," the Mother Superior said.
"Mrs. Godfrey, middle-aged, barren, and too old to be seen as a
possible adoptive mother by most agencies."

Nothing new there to add to her notes, Dana thought.

"Mr. Godfrey, a quiet man, did not have much to say, but I
could tell he was only going through the motions of adopting to
please his wife." Sister Thomasina wrinkled her nose. "A difficult
man, to say the least. But, then again, aren't most men?"

Dana found the nun's comment amusing yet, at the same time,
personally revealing. She obviously didn't care for men.

"And the girl. . .she was six. Were the Godfreys encouraged to
adopt her because she was older than most?" Dana asked.

"The staff and I recommended that Mr. and Mrs. Godfrey
would be better off to adopt an older child. Interestingly, though, the
child had her own share of challenges."

"How so?" Dana asked, eager to begin her note taking process.

The nun toyed with the large crucifix around her neck. "Well,
there were a couple of issues actually. The child seemed emotionally
delayed. I'm not a psychologist, but I would say the girl had
abandonment issues. Why, let's face it; the girl hadn't bonded with a
loving, significant other."

"I see." What the Mother Superior said made sense to Dana.
Although she had been raised by the nuns in the orphanage for the
first years of her life, certainly, it could not come close to the normal
relationship a mother and child would have.

"The girl suffered from low self-esteem," Mother Superior went
on. "Bernadette was also unusually shy, didn't relate well to others,

but our adoption coordinator felt that she could work with the Godfreys to make sure the child got all of the help she needed."

That must have been when Doctor Polly Thatcher came into the story. So far, so good; this was making sense.

"Sister, about the child's shyness, do you have any idea why the child had these issues?"

"Certainly, I am no therapist, however, it's my belief that when a young woman strongly admits that she doesn't want the child in her womb, it is as though the infant subconsciously feels unwanted."

Dana nodded as she continued to jot snippets of the Mother Superior's conversation into her notebook.

"There was tension; the birth mother had her own demons to fight. I'm convinced that if it had been up to her, the young woman never would have come to our doorstep to deliver her child."

"Are you saying that she might have aborted her child?"

The nun looked away. "Jesus, Mary, Joseph. . .yes."

Dana could see pain in the woman's face as if she had cut her own flesh.

"So, Sister, was the decision made for her. . .to have the child, I mean?"

The nun ran her fingers across her heavily starched wimple, her pale face suddenly taking on a warm glow. "Not only was the decision forced upon the young girl, but it went even further."

"How's that?" Dana asked.

"The girl's mother forced her to sign a document, saying that once her baby was delivered, it would be up to the girl's mother to decide which home the infant would go to." The Mother Superior shook her head from side-to-side. "Highly unusual."

"Which might explain why the child was not adopted until the age of six," I said.

"Exactly. I'm convinced the birth mother's mother hovering over the child the way she did, didn't help matters."

Dana edged her chair closer to the nun's desk, her notebook swaying on her lap. "So the girls give birth here. . .at the orphanage?"

"We are a Catholic institution that not only provides children for adoption but also welcomes single girls to stay with us until their babies are born. Here the likelihood of moral disgrace is removed from the families. No one need even know that the girl was pregnant to begin with."

Harsh thoughts for sure, but the thinking of the church, unfortunately. It brought back memories of the days when Dana thought she had conceived Nate's child and rushed into marriage. She had felt like a moral degenerate, an outcast. By the time she realized that she was not pregnant, it was too late for her to consider anything other than making their marriage work. Her efforts had failed miserably and when news of Nate and Myra Pembroke's relationship became public knowledge, she felt as if her life had been torn into pieces like a jigsaw puzzle.

"Miss Greer?" the nun said, bringing Dana back to the present moment.

"Sorry, Sister, my mind began to wander about these unfortunate girls."

The Mother Superior smiled, looking like a cherub on one of the holy cards in Dana's collection. "Oh, but you're wrong, Miss Greer.

These girls are hardly unfortunate; they are, after all, sinners in the eyes of God."

"I see." Dana forced herself to keep her thoughts private. "And, the deliveries. . .how. . . ?"

"There are midwives on staff who deliver the infants. La Petit Maison de Maria. That's what the second floor of the orphanage is called."

"Beautiful name."

"And as I was saying, here things are kept quiet for the families, so no one bears the shame."

Dana must have had a strange look on her face as she somehow couldn't quite equate a pregnancy, any pregnancy, with shame.

Sister continued, "We must pay for our sins, however, and the girls that come to Guardian Angel do just that; afterwards, for the services we provide, the girls stay with us for three years."

"Oh, and their babies? I assume most are put up for adoption?"

"Eventually, they all are. We do our best to place the right child with the right Catholic family, no matter the age. Some stay with us longer than others."

Bernadette Godfrey, Dana thought.

"And what about the girls after they give birth?

"They live on the third floor of Guardian Angel. They work in the kitchen, help in the conservatory on the top floor, or make rosary beads and religious artifacts. The church benefits from the profits of their labor."

"So, I assume this was true of the woman who gave birth to the Godfrey child? She worked here for some time, as well?"

The nun nodded. "Yes, if I recall correctly, the girl helped in the laundry facility." No sooner had she said this than she began to tap her lips with the tip of her index finger.

Dana echoed her words—"The laundry facility?" Dana was just about to ask her next question when the Mother Superior placed her hands on the edge of her desk and stood.

"Certainly, there's nothing more I can say, Miss Greer. You understand that we value the privacy of our birth mothers here."

"There is one more thing, Sister."

"Yes?"

"How well do you know Father Byron Sullivan?"

"You mean Sister Cyril Marie's nephew?"

Dana didn't answer. She felt confused. Father had said his Aunt's name was Helen. That had to be her name before entering the order of the Little Sisters of the Poor.

"Sister's been with Guardian Angel for about as long as the institution. . .1874." The nun smiled, revealing a set of perfectly lined teeth.

"I'd love to meet her. Any chance?"

"If you told her that you were a friend of Bryon's, I'm sure she'd love to meet you."

"I have only today. . . ."

"Let me place a call, won't you?"

Within minutes, the Mother Superior put down the receiver of the phone, and said, "Sister is in the atrium, watering our plants. She is so agile, even at ninety-six."

Dana followed the head nun onto an elevator. They exited on the top floor. There a glass-domed conservatory greeted them, complete with flying birds and colorful butterflies. A frail looking woman, stooped over, about four-foot-ten, forced her head upward as the Mother Superior introduced Dana, telling the nun that she knew Father Sullivan.

"Why don't you two have a small chat, and I'll get back to my work."

The little nun, dressed in the white habit of the order, wore open-toed black sandals with black stockings, and supported her weight on an oak cane. "So, you like my nephew, huh?"

Dana smiled. "I do." She waited until the nun invited her to sit with her on a wooden bench. "Sister," Dana said, "one of the children who lived at this orphanage from birth until six-years of age and who was recently adopted was found murdered on Cape Peril. I'm the private investigator on the case and wondered if I might ask you a question or two."

In a scratchy voice, the nun said, "How dreadful. Satan and all of his evil works."

"Do you think you might be able to help me?"

"I can try," she said, sounding like a little girl who aimed to please.

"Sister, Mother Superior told me that the child I'm speaking about was adopted to a Mr. and Mrs. Godfrey who lived in Bay View at the time."

"Yes, yes, such lovely people."

"And the child they adopted?"

"So shy," the nun answered. Sister Cyril Marie's eyes narrowed, to the point of almost closing. "Yes, yes, I remember the girl, one of the oldest ones still at the orphanage. Should have left long ago, you know." The nun spoke nonchalantly as if this was common knowledge. "She needed to bond with an adoptive family long before she did." The elderly nun fingered her rosary beads, her lips moving as if in prayer. Her face reddened. "Blame it on the family. It was the mother who forced the girl to sign some type of paper. It was to be up to her to choose the adoptive family the infant would go to."

"Do you remember the young girl's name. . .her family's?" Dana asked, hoping her voice didn't sound too much like prying.

The nun ran her thin fingers up and down her cane while her other hand grasped it tightly. "I'm an old woman; my memory doesn't work as well as yours," she said.

Dana patted the nun's right hand, her gold wedding band embedded deeply into the folds of her aged skin.

"Now, what were you saying?" she asked.

Dana repeated. "Her name. . .the girl's name? The name of her family?"

The elderly nun, with shoulders bent low, twisted her neck to look up at Dana, her face lined with wrinkles and covered in brown liver spots. Like a record whose needle got stuck, Dana listened as the woman began to tell her story all over again from the beginning, totally unaware that she had lost the context of her conversation. "Never should have stayed here; never bonded."

"I see," was all Dana said, before she thanked the nun and headed toward the elevator.

It was obvious that the adoption coordinator had abided by the terms of the document.

Dana entered the elevator and before she pressed the button for the first floor, she decided to press the number three, the floor where the girls who had delivered their babies lived. When the doors opened, she saw what looked like a long hotel corridor with doors on both sides. The floor was carpeted down the center in the same floral-print carpeting that was on the stairs. The doors to the rooms were painted a pastel blue, and each had a number on it or the name of what lay behind the door, such as maintenance, storage, and laundry. Several young girls who looked to be mere teenagers were standing about mid-way down the hall, speaking to each other. Other than the uniforms the girls wore, black dresses and white aprons, Dana could have pegged them as any other adolescents chattering outside their high school lockers. Before she was within three feet of the girls, one of them said, "Excuse me; are you lost?"

When Dana didn't immediately answer, the same girl said, "Are you looking for anyone in particular?"

"Sort of," she said.

"Do you have a name badge?" another girl from the group asked.

"I'm afraid not."

"You're not supposed to be on this floor unless you first obtain a name badge from the desk on the first floor. Mother Superior is quite strict about these kinds of things."

The arrogance in the young girl's voice was reprimanding with a hint of disrespect. Dana wondered if many of these girls had problems with authority figures, especially, with women.

"I can understand, but I was just speaking with Sister Cyril Marie. She sent me down here." Dana was surprised that her voice didn't waffle.

"For what?" the third girl asked.

Dana explained that she was a private investigator, showed them her badge, told them that she was doing some interviewing. She went on to explain. "There was a recent adoption of a six-year-old child. Adopted by a couple named Godfrey."

The three girls shared eye glances as if they were giving each other a secret code.

"You must mean Mary-485665. We've only been here a few months but heard it was quite the story around here," one of the girls said.

"How so?" Dana asked.

"The girl's mother, from what we've heard, is quite the controlling type. She demanded the girl deliver her baby, rather than have an abortion."

"So the mother is Catholic."

"Quite. A religious nut might be more appropriate," the girl said. "Then she forced the girl to sign some paper, saying that the adoption would take place only with the mother's consent."

"Might you know why the mother approved of the Godfreys?"

"They all went to the same church in the same city; they knew each other."

That made sense, Dana guessed. Thank God. She was finally getting somewhere. "The adoption coordinator. . .what's her name?"

"Sharon Nelson. She works here only in the morning if you plan on speaking with her."

"Thank you. I might do just that."

The elevator doors opened, and as much as Dana feared turning to look who might have gotten off, she did. It was a nurse, carrying a tray filled with syringes. As quickly as she appeared, she disappeared into one of the rooms off the corridor.

"Lunch time," one of the three girls said, her voice filled with mockery.

How strange. Were the young girls being injected with something? Something that might have a control on their behavior? Dana brushed the thought aside, telling herself not to get too carried away with her imagination. She lightly touched the girl's arm. "Please could you answer at least a few more questions for me?"

Two of the girls rolled their eyes and left, headed toward the room the nurse had entered.

"Do you know the name of the birth mother?"

"No, like I said, I've been at the orphanage only a few months. The girl you're talking about left three years ago."

"How silly. I should have been able to do the math."

"I'm the same way. I have trouble with fractions, decimals, and all that stuff."

Dana smiled and thanked the girl.

She looked at Dana and said, "You're some good investigator."

"Thanks."

"Don't forget now. Talk to Sharon Nelson. She'll be in, in the morning."

Chapter Twenty-One

Although it stopped snowing, the temperature was five degrees below zero and a sharp, brittle wind cut across Dana's face.

"What was that address again?" the cab driver asked, over the roaring of the car's heater, which was turned to full blast.

Dana repeated Eddie Vineeti's address and gave the cab driver his name.

"That hub cap? Well, you know that guy just got out of prison. He's not well liked around here. Why, everybody's got his number."

In a town of 7,000, Dana wondered how the cab driver could possibly know Eddie that well.

"That bird brain gets his picture in the *Morning Sentinel* once too many times for me."

Dana glanced over at the cab driver. "Mind if I ask what Eddie Vineeti did to get his photo in the local paper?"

"What didn't he do? He stole some money from his relatives."

Sounded like Eddie Vineeti, Dana thought.

"Yeah, his aunt and uncle live here in Waterville. There ain't a damn thing they wouldn't do for the guy, but he treats them like dirt."

"What do you mean?"

"Besides taking money from the old folks, he even pulled a knife on them once."

Dana raised her eyebrows. She realized the cab driver might be exaggerating, so she asked, "Seriously?"

"Yeah, the story hit the papers; he got some jail time, and the relatives dropped charges. I mean, what kind of people would do that? They obviously love the guy for some reason."

Dana wondered the same thing: *what kind of people would drop charges after being assaulted by their own nephew?*

The roads still snow-covered and icy, she listened as the tires of the cab tried to hug the pavement, crunching the snowy street.

"You sure you want to go to this guy's house?" The man looked over at Dana with a questioning glance.

Dana had no idea that Eddie could be as dangerous as the cab driver said, but she realized that she had to go through with her visit. "Yes, I do," she said.

"At least, the guy's got himself a pretty woman," the driver continued. "That Rayna could of got any guy she wanted. Don't quite know how she ended up with Vineeti of all people."

The cab pulled up to a small house, isolated by several hundred yards off the main road. A 1938 lime green Buick, mostly covered in snow, stood parked out front. The driver's door was dented in and the running board was missing. The house, in need of paint, had a shutter missing from one of the windows. As Dana looked closer, she saw that one pane of the window was missing as well, and a piece of cardboard from a carton of Lucky Strikes had been used to block the space. Hardly a solution on a day like today with digits below zero.

"Should I wait here? See if every thing's okay before I leave?"

"Not a bad idea. Please."

Dana rang the bell, hoping someone would come to the door before she froze. The strong winds pushed her from side to side. She slipped the strap of her handbag over her shoulder and rang the bell again.

The door opened a crack, and Dana was pleasantly surprised, as the cab driver had said she would be. A young woman with red hair reaching beyond her shoulders opened the door. A small sprinkle of freckles crossed her nose. "Who are you?" she asked.

"Friend of Eddie's. Is he home?" Dana tried to peer around her.

The red-haired woman opened the door the remainder of the way and motioned for Dana to come in. Dana was hoping she wouldn't have to show the woman her badge.

"Eddie, you've got a friend to see you."

Eddie, still looking as though he could be anyone's favorite grandson, came from a back room, his shirt unbuttoned, his black jeans cuffed, his feet bare. He ran his hands over his eyes as if he had just awoken. "What in Christ's name are you doing here? Is this a nightmare or what?"

"Doesn't matter, does it?" Dana asked.

"Must have a reason," he said, grabbing for a cigarette from his top pocket. "Rayna, get me a light."

Rayna picked up a match from the cracked coffee table and lit Eddie's cigarette.

"I actually was paying a visit to the Guardian Angel Orphanage."

"The what?" he asked, as he blew smoke curls in the air.

"Ever heard of it?" The Guardian Angel Orphanage was the largest institution in the small city of Waterville, and for anyone to admit that they were not aware of its existence was preposterous.

"Rayna, you got any idea what the lady's talkin' about?"

Rayna glanced at Eddie and then at the floor. She shook her head.

Dana knew the two were lying. The question now was *why?*

"Is that it? You came all the way here to ask me that?"

"No, actually, I did have another reason. Mind if I sit down?"

Eddie didn't answer, so Dana sat on a gold upholstered chair, the edges of the fabric frayed and worn with braided tassels along the bottom. Dana found she couldn't help but smile at this man who truly did look as innocent as the pure, white snow despite what she, unfortunately, knew about him. Meanwhile, Rayna hovered behind Eddie like a scared child.

"Let me guess? Who murdered that kid. . .right?" Eddie asked.

Although Dana couldn't quite see herself suspecting Eddie at this time, she thought it wouldn't hurt to ask him some questions just the same. "Now, that you mention it, Eddie, where were you the morning Bernadette went missing?"

"Humph. Want me to get out my diary, lady?" He bobbed his shoulders up and down. "Where was I? Hell, I've got a hard enough time figuring out where I was yesterday. Probably, I was in the garage. I'm rebuilding a '30 Chevy out there."

"There is something else I'd like to know, Eddie," Dana said.

"What?" He put his hands on his hips.

"It's come to my attention that you've been asking for some cash."

"Oh, hell. That bitch opened her fuckin' mouth?"

"Who, Eddie?" Rayna asked, peering from his side.

"Listen, I ain't got nothin' to hide. I could use some bucks. Who couldn't?"

"Is that all this is about, Eddie?" Dana asked, standing and throwing her palms outward.

"What the hell is that supposed to mean?"

"The money. . . . Is that all you want?" Dana looked Eddie straight on.

He thought for a moment. "Unless I don't get it. . .the money, I mean." His voice trailed upward on the word *don't*.

"What will you do then?" Dana asked, feeling as if their conversation was firing like a Gatling gun.

He smiled, revealing his tobacco-stained teeth. "I've got my ideas."

"Eddie, did you realize that threatening another person for money or services is called extortion and is a crime punishable by jail sentence?" Dana's question caused Rayna to hide behind Eddie again like a young child being reprimanded by her parent.

"Wow! You're pretty impressive, miss detective. But, let's just say that's between me and that fuckin' bitch, Artenelli."

"It won't be between just the two of you for long; that is, if you decide to take this any further." Dana grabbed her handbag and threw it over her shoulder.

Eddie's face turned stern as if it were made of cold, hard cement. "I ain't planning on drawing blood or nothin'. At least, not now. All I want is for a fair hand of cards."

"Mind if I ask why you think you haven't been dealt one?"

"Me?" Eddie started to laugh. "You kiddin' me? I've been screwed since the day I was born."

"Sorry to hear that, Eddie, but just like anyone else, you're not above the law. What is it you're really after?" Dana emphasized the word *really*.

"Secrets, lady. Let's just leave it at that. Secrets," he said, puffing on his cigarette voraciously. Then, he snubbed out its butt in an ashtray filled with other remnants: a Tootsie Roll wrapper, a store receipt, and a lone brown button. Eddie slipped another cigarette from his pack, and asked Rayna, once again, to light it for him.

The girl was quick to respond, to do what Eddie asked.

Odd, Dana thought, how often the word *secrets* had come up since she had left the Cape. She waved the smoke out of her eyes as Eddie gradually neared. "What is it you're hiding, Eddie?"

"Me?" He laughed so loudly the sound rang in her ear. "Why don't you ask the Artenelli bitch?" Eddie walked over to the ice box in the small kitchen, only feet away from the living room and got himself a beer. He took one long slug on the bottle and said, "Now, mind doing *me* a favor? Why don't you get your ass out of my house?"

"Eddie!" Rayna yelled, "But, she's your friend."

"Friend? Hell no." He pushed Dana toward the door, opened it, and said, "Nice seein' ya again."

"This won't be the last, Eddie," Dana said. She was glad she had kept the cab waiting.

Chapter Twenty-Two

The sun awoke as it streamed through the lace curtains in Dana's room. Just as well that she got up earlier than expected. She couldn't wait to tell Logan about her visit to Waterville, but first, she decided to organize the notes that she had taken, convinced that there were probably more questions than there were answers. She began to scribble her list:

November 12, 1952

- *Whoever the birth mother was, why was she fighting her own demons? And what might those demons be?*
- *Why did the birth mother not want to put her child up for adoption? Why would she consider the possibility of an abortion? Why would she consent to signing a document that left her mother in charge of the adoption?*
- *Why did the birth mother's mother feel she had a right to decide the best adoptive home for the child?*
- *Who from St. Michael's Parish might have chosen the Godfreys as potential adoptive parents of Bernadette?*
- *What was the secret that Eddie knew that gave him the possibility to extort Mrs. Artenelli for money, if not her life?*

She read and reread the list before her, knowing it would be by exploring these issues that she would become closer to solving the Bernadette Godfrey case. Just as she had thought, much had been learned in Waterville, but there still remained many unanswered questions. She needed to call the adoption coordinator, Sharon

Nelson, to find a time when they could meet. Her last attempt at contacting the woman had been met with her secretary's standard line, "I'm sorry. She's with clients right now."

Dana walked into Logan's station and greeted the receptionist, who sat there reading a *Little Lulu* comic book. "Logan in?" she asked.

"Huh?" the receptionist asked. "That Tubby character is quite the kid. He's a scream."

Once again, Dana wondered where Logan had found such an incompetent receptionist. Either she came cheap, or Logan was desperate.

Logan must have heard Dana speaking with the girl, as his voice called from the inner office, "Come right in, Dana. Good to see you again. How was the trip? Can I get you a cup of coffee?"

Before she sat down, Dana looked back at the receptionist who was now scouring the pages of a *Casper the Ghost* comic book, her attention lost in its colorful print. Dana just shook her head.

"The trip went well, if well means coming up with more questions than there are answers."

"Let's hear 'em," he said, extending his arms as if welcoming in a crowd.

As Dana went through the list, Logan tossed his head back, bracing his arms behind it until his fingertips met. "You sure have been a busy bee. Let's take these one-by-one, speculating, of course. If Bernadette Godfrey's birth mother had demons, as the Mother Superior said, what might these have been? Guilt over having a child out of wedlock, maybe? Regret that she hadn't done away with the child, rather than having taken it to the orphanage? Remorse at not being able to keep and raise her own child, maybe?"

Dana began to jot down these new points. Logan was making a great sounding board.

"From what the Mother Superior told you, the birth mother's mother forced her to deliver her child at Guardian Angels despite the fact that the girl wanted to abort the fetus. Interesting dynamics between the girl and her mother, I'd say."

"You are most helpful, Logan," Dana said, looking up from her notebook.

"It's called brainstorming. Freud called it stream-of-consciousness. Maybe, when you go to reread your notes, none of this will make any sense to you, but let's go on. Now, what was the next question?" He hunched his shoulders forward.

"I still am in a quandary as to what kind of person would allow her mother to decide the fate of her child."

"Indeed, you do look puzzled," Logan said. "I'm no shrink, don't get me wrong, but it appears to me that this is one passive chick with one controlling mother. As I've said before, the girl seems to be one who was easily threatened and must not have felt that she had any voice. Might want to give. . .what was that woman's name. . .the therapist?"

"Polly Thatcher?"

"Yeah, you might want to give her a call. See what type of individual would allow themselves to be so manipulated."

Dana liked that idea and made a note to call the woman. "As for the Artenellis, I assume they belonged to St. Michael's parish in Bay View before coming to the Cape?"

"Yep," the Sergeant answered. "The Artenellis owned quite a showplace there from what I've been told."

Dana's earlier question rang through her mind like a bell clanging in a church tower:

Who from St. Michael's Parish might have chosen the Godfreys as potential adoptive parents of Bernadette?

"A penny for your thoughts," Logan said.

"I'm wondering if Mrs. Artenelli isn't the mother we're talking about. A. She was a parishioner of St. Michael's. B. The Godfreys were members there also. C. Father Sullivan, who was pastor of St. Michael's Parish at the time, recommended that the Godfreys speak to his Aunt, Sister Cyril Marie, at Guardian Angel Orphanage about possibly adopting. And D. probably the most important point of all, if rumor is true and Mrs. Artenelli forced her daughter to join the convent, could it be that she also forced her to give birth to her illegitimate baby?"

No sooner had Dana completed her fourth point, then Logan, with his hand in a loose fist, hit the side of his head and said, "Sure makes sense to me." He thought for a moment, then, spoke again. "But if this is true, that would mean Sister Mary Rose is actually the birth mother of Bernadette Godfrey! Could that be. . .the young nun having given birth?"

The energy in the office felt like a vacuum had subtly sucked away Dana and Logan's breath, choking their conversation. Minutes passed before they spoke. They sat there staring at one another. Dana broke the silence with, "That would explain why Mrs. Artenelli forced her daughter to have the child and not abort it. It would also help to explain why Mrs. Artenelli hovered over the child as she did, even to the point of not wanting any word of the child's abuse going public. And, no wonder, she wanted the Godfreys as adoptive parents as Mother Superior thought it best the couple adopt an older child."

"Precisely," Logan said, "and it would also explain Sister's demons: guilt, regret, remorse. The fact that she was forced to deliver the child, rather than to consider any other option had to play with her psyche."

Dana decided to skip her last note about the secret that Eddie claimed to be keeping. That would have to wait for another day.

"You don't think I'm being too quick to jump for my gun, do you Sergeant?"

"Why would you think that?" Logan asked.

"It's easy to go off on a whim in this business, to see things the way you want and not necessarily the way they are."

"I'd say you're heading for pay dirt. Keep digging!"

"Thanks," Dana said, and left.

Chapter Twenty-Three

Dana found herself repeating the line from Robert Frost's poem, "And miles to go before I sleep." On one hand, things were starting to make much better sense than they had; and on the other, she found herself not knowing what to grab next in order to solve the case. There were still two issues that she hadn't discussed with Logan when she met him the other day. One pertained to the argument that she overheard the other night between Jay and Loretta, and the second point pertained to Eddie's threats to go public with secrets involving Mrs. Artenelli.

Plus, Dana had hoped to speak with Doctor Polly Thatcher, not to mention making one more jaunt to Guardian Angel Orphanage.

She threw some of her things into an overnight bag. She would see Logan and then catch the six p.m. Seaside Ferry for the mainland. Before she did so, she dialed the number for Doctor Thatcher.

After making some small talk with the woman, Dana got right to her question. Without using specific names, she explained how Mrs. Artenelli had influenced her daughter to sign a document that basically manipulated her. "What type of personality must a person have to allow herself to be controlled like this?" With the phone's receiver held in place by her shoulder, she got ready to take notes.

"There are a number of answers to your question, but more than likely, this person has a dependent personality disorder. The person needs to be taken care of and is fearful of being alone."

Dana wasn't sure that this applied to Sister Mary Rose, so she asked for some more details.

"This type of individual has difficulty making decisions, needs advice, and reassurance from someone else, usually someone he or she is close to."

"Go on," Dana said. She quickly flipped the page in her notebook and continued to scribble Doctor Thatcher's comments.

"The person wants others to assume responsibility for his or her actions."

Bingo! Angela Artenelli had a child out of wedlock, but she looked to her mother to resolve her so-called mistake.

"This type of person is afraid to state his or her own demands for fear the other will not approve. Is this starting to make some sense?" the doctor asked.

"Yes, actually it is," Dana said.

As if reading from a textbook on the topic of dependent personality types, the doctor continued, "This person will go to whatever lengths necessary to seek nurturance."

The incident in the teacher's lounge, Dana remembered, where Jay Harrison and Sister Mary Rose were present, showed the young nun to be needy of someone else's approval. The Sister had seemed to rely on the support of Jay's comments until Dana had asked him to leave.

"Let me go on," Doctor Thatcher said. "What I'm about to say goes along with the point I just made."

"Please," Dana said.

"A person with dependent personality disorder will go to whatever lengths necessary to seek out another relationship, particularly if the relationship he or she had with the original person has ended."

Another reason, Dana felt, why Sister would have sought the support of Jay. She might very well have felt separated emotionally from her mother; after all, the Mother Superior had explained how these pregnant girls are made to feel less than honorable and in many cases, social outcasts from their families. Dana remembered how Mrs. Artenelli had hovered over her daughter, not only at the funeral of Bernadette Godfrey but also at the young nun's profession of vows ceremony. But, Dana also knew that dependency breeds contempt and wondered if that was the relationship the two had presently.

"You have been most helpful, Doctor," Dana said. She felt that the doctor painted a more than thorough picture of Sister Mary Rose.

"Does that explain why someone might sign a document against his or her better judgment?"

"It does now, Doctor. I think the person had no self-image and, therefore, believed she had to do as she was told. If all along her decisions were made for her, and she was given no choice in the matter, it makes sense that she would be more than vulnerable, especially, in the context of a domineering individual."

"Well put, Dana. I think, you've got a good grasp of the characteristics of this personality disorder. Oh, there is one more thing." The woman cleared her throat, "Often times, these types of persons are only children. They become smothered by a parental figure to the point where they struggle with their own identity."

"Fascinating," Dana said, believing that she just had a crash course in dependent personality disorder.

"It would only make sense then that as an adult, this type of individual would need the approval of another."

"Interesting, indeed. Let me ask you one more thing if I may, Doctor Thatcher. Might this type of person ever rebel, turn on the parent, for example, who controlled him or her?"

"Ah, yes. Quite typical, actually."

Dana thanked Doctor Thatcher for all of her help. She sat down at the kitchen table and reread her notes. She felt that she had a good personality profile of the young nun, but despite that, she still had no idea who would have murdered her child. She began to reflect on what she already knew about the young nun. More than likely, she felt guilt over becoming pregnant out of wedlock. Although she had probably wanted to rid herself of her mistake, she lacked the confidence needed to make such a drastic decision. She probably was coerced into delivering her child, rather than aborting it. Once she had the child, her mother forced her to turn over the control of the infant to her. As punishment for her daughter's sin, Mrs. Artenelli must have talked the young girl into joining the convent. From what the young girl at the orphanage had said, Mrs. Artenelli was a religious fanatic. Quite possibly, she told the girl that the only way she could seek reconciliation with God was to give her life back to him. Yet could it be that Angela felt enough was enough? Would she go so far as doing away with her own child for the sole purpose of making her mother pay?

Dana headed to the station eager to share what Doctor Thatcher had told her about dependent personality disorder.

Logan's secretary was not at her desk, so Dana knocked on his door.

"Come in, please," he said. "What brings you out so bright and early?" Without asking, he poured her a cup of coffee and set it on the edge of his desk.

"You might say I've many miles to go before I sleep, Sergeant."

"Where you headed this time, Miss Frost?" he asked, and chuckled softly.

Before Dana explained what she planned to do, she said, "The other night. . .before I left for Waterville. I heard Jay and Loretta arguing. Jay was yelling that he was not involved with Sister Mary Rose. Loretta told him that was a lie."

Logan arched his eyebrows and edged closer to his desk. He put his cup down.

Dana could tell that he needed to gather his thoughts, so she remained silent for a few moments.

"I asked you to move in with the Harrisons, wanting to rule out that Jay may have had something to do with the murder of the Godfrey child. I guess I never expected you'd come up with this shocker. What do you make of it, Dana?"

She explained briefly what Doctor Thatcher told her about dependent personality types. "The points Doctor Thatcher made sure fit Sister Mary Rose and her mother. When Sister was ostracized by her mother for having an illegitimate child, she sought out someone else for love and support."

Logan fiddled with a pencil, trying to balance it with another as if playing Pick-Up-Sticks, a game Dana hated as a child. After a few failed attempts, he said, "That sounds like something to research. It would certainly fit in with your theory as to why the woman sought out Jay Harrison."

"That will be plan B." Dana sipped on her coffee, pleased that it was still hot, just the way she liked it.

"What's plan A?" Logan asked. He picked up one of the pencils and pointed it at her.

"I'm off to see a Sharon Little, who is the adoption coordinator at Guardian Angel."

"And the purpose?"

"I hopefully can verify that Angela Artenelli gave birth six years ago."

"Quite a plan," he said.

"That's not all that plan A involves."

"Go on," he said. He pressed his back against his chair as if ready to listen to a long story.

"I ask to see the document that Angela Artenelli was forced to sign. If lucky, I'll find Mrs. Artenelli's name somewhere on the agreement."

"Sounds as if you're on the right track, Dana. I wish you luck." Logan started to get up from behind his desk.

"Oh, there is just one more thing."

Laughing, Logan sat back down.

"We still don't know what secrets Eddie Vineeti is keeping, do we?"

"Here you go again, Dana." Logan wagged his finger back-and-forth. "The kid's just got a loud bark; that's all. If he thinks the lady's got money, he'll pester her until she gives him some."

"That sounds too simplistic, Logan. The guy may have an innocent enough looking face, but I say you've got him pegged wrong. Something about him tells me that he's more aggressive than you might think."

"Remember when you asked me before if you were jumping the gun? Why read into things?"

"You just wait and see. I'll prove you wrong." Dana set her half-filled coffee cup down. "I'll see you when I get back from Waterville."

***

Dana ran up the front steps to Guardian Angel Orphanage, passing by three nuns who were on their way down. Dana nodded her head in reverence; at least, that's what she had been told to do as a student in her Catholic elementary school. The three nuns didn't seem to notice. Before opening the main doors to the lobby, Dana ran her finger across the glass that enclosed the names of the orphanage's staff and office numbers until she came to the name: Sharon Little, 110.

Dana stepped into the lobby and turned down a long hallway to the right. The floor was tiled in the same pink marble as the massive entry. The sixth door down was marked with the number 110 along with the woman's name and the words, *Adoption Coordinator.* Dana tapped lightly until she heard a woman's high-pitched voice say, "Come in." A woman with a messy, brunette ponytail and heavily applied makeup stood from behind her desk, with her hand extended.

She wore an Immaculate Heart of Mary blue cameo ring on her left pinkie finger. Dana remembered having one exactly like it as a child, but she couldn't recall whatever happened to it.

"Hello, the name's Dana Greer." She shook the woman's hand.

"Sharon Little. From the message you left with my assistant, I understand you are underway in solving a murder case on the Cape. . .that of a Bernadette Godfrey. Please, have a seat."

"A child who was adopted from this orphanage, yes."

"How may I help, Miss Greer?" The woman closed a manila file folder on her desk and clasped her hands together.

"At this point in the investigation, I am not about to rule anyone out as a possible suspect. That's why I was hoping I might get some information about the birth mother of this child."

"I'm sure you must know that all of our adoptions are sealed. Guardian Angel is a private institution governed by its own rules, passed down from the hierarchy of the Catholic Church." Her words were like staccato notes on a piano.

Dana hoped she wouldn't have to listen to a bunch of political-religious jargon as she wanted to get to the bottom of this mystery, but it appeared that Sharon Little was versed in the same rhetoric as the Mother Superior. Both spoke confidently, assured of their words.

"Miss Little, I understand that the mother of the then pregnant girl had her daughter sign some type of document, stating that it would be up to the girl's mother to decide who would be suitable as adoptive parents." Dana made up her mind that she would not let the woman intimidate her with her knowledge of rules and regulations.

"That much is true. I'd be happy to show you the arrangement that was made between the daughter and her mother." Miss Little spun around in her chair to the two-drawer file cabinet. She found a red file folder and slipped out a piece of paper. "Here, you can read for yourself":

On the 6th day of January 1946, I ▆▆▆▆▆▆▆▆ *give my mother* ▆▆▆▆▆▆▆▆ *full permission to act in the capacity of guardian of my daughter until which time she determines suitable adoptive parents for my child. At that time,* ▆▆▆▆▆▆▆▆ *will relinquish full custody and responsibility for said child to the assigned adoptive parents.*

"As you can see, Miss Greer, there is nothing illegal here in this document. The daughter willingly signed the agreement, and the mother fulfilled her part of the contract when six years later she agreed to have Mr. and Mrs. Godfrey adopt the child."

The wording sure sounded legal to Dana and considering that Gino Artenelli was an attorney, she could see him drafting such a statement. The adoption coordinator was not making this easy on her. Dana felt as if the woman were dangling a carrot in front of her nose but refusing to let her bite.

"Miss Little, is there anything you could tell me that might help solve this case?"

The woman twirled her ponytail with her fingertips and said, "Not really, other than to say many girls pass through our doors wanting to deliver their babies and to put them up for adoption. This birth mother struck me as quite different from the norm."

Dana kept her persistence. "Why do you say that?"

"The birth mother was sixteen-years-old as are many of our girls, but I found her to be almost like a child herself."

"Interesting," Dana said. "How so?"

"So many of the girls who come to us, come out of rebellion, out of a need to prove their adulthood. A large number of them have no regard for their parents, no respect. The girl of whom you speak was much different. She exhibited a strong desire to please and to accommodate to her mother's wishes."

"Might you say that she was dependent on her mother?" Dana asked, remembering what Doctor Thatcher had told her about the personality type.

"Without a doubt, Miss Greer. How otherwise would you explain her willingness to put her infant in her mother's complete care, not knowing when and, even if, her child would eventually be adopted?"

"Anything else that stood out to you about the birth mother besides her dependency?"

Sharon began to smile, the corners of her lips widening. "I can say that the girl looked like an angel in her incredible beauty, long black hair with bouncing curls, brown eyes. . .well she looked just like her mother." Sharon reached for the rubber band in her pony tail and tugged on it with both hands. Staring off into space, she said, "Without a doubt, that young woman could have graced the cover of any fashion magazine."

"Yet the child, Bernadette Godfrey, had the blond curls of a Shirley Temple doll," Dana said, hoping it might prompt the woman to tell her more.

"Well, well, I met the father, too, Miss Greer. Good looking young man with a blond brush cut. . .good looking that is except for his stained yellow teeth." She smiled. "You know he wanted the girl to keep the child; actually, he would have married her if it weren't for her mother. The girl's mother did not approve of his social status. I often wonder how things might have worked out if the mother hadn't gotten involved."

"Social status?"

"Seems the people who adopted him weren't the most respected of sorts." Sharon edged closer over her desk, and glanced around the room as if she expected someone else to overhear her. She whispered, "You know…alcohol, drugs."

Could this be Eddie Vineeti? If so, he had outright lied to Dana when he told her that he did not know about the Guardian Angel Orphanage. Just maybe, he was the one who tried to prevent Angela Artenelli from giving custody over to her mother. More questions surfaced. "Do you ever hear from the girls again? I mean, do they drop a note, make a call?"

"Usually not. Most want to forget their past and move on. In this case, though, I have a feeling the girl would do whatever the mother demanded, whether it was something she wanted to do or not."

As in entering the convent, Dana mused. No wonder the girl still pined for the single life; she had never wanted to join the convent in the first place. That good looking man with the blond, brush cut sure would fit the picture of Eddie. His attempt to prevent her from taking her final vows was likely an indication of a love—or perhaps a need to control—that hadn't died, even though he had gone on to marry Rayna. This might well explain the secrets Eddie spoke of if, indeed, he was the father of Angela's child. Finally, Dana felt as if she were getting somewhere. She might still be at a loss as to who the murderer was, but she was learning a lot about possible motives.

Chapter Twenty-Four

Dana sat at her desk and looked out over the bay. The sea was a deep emerald, and despite the beauty of the hue, there was something about its vibrant green color that made Dana associate it with jealousy. Loretta was jealous of Jay's attention toward Sister Mary Rose; she had every reason to be. Dana still wondered if Loretta wasn't also jealous of the child that Jay had brought into their home, if only under the guise of tutoring. Dana decided at that moment she would have to secretly follow Jay to find out for herself what, if anything, was going on between Jay and the nun. As for Loretta's jealousy of the deceased child, Dana would have to question those who knew the woman better than she. Would it mean a trip into Aberdeen before she could rule Loretta out as a possible suspect in the case? Although innocent appearing, Loretta's demeanor might just be a cover-up for a guilty conscience.

More immediately, though, Dana needed to do some spying on Jay.

As she entered Holy Name Academy, the chattering of children's voices was gone, and some of the classroom lights were already turned off for the weekend ahead. The scent of pencil erasers greeted her. Near the showcase in the hall, the one that had been dedicated to Bernadette Godfrey, was a man in blue denim overalls and a long-sleeved yellow shirt. He hummed a tune without melody until he noticed Dana's presence.

"Miss Greer? You're that pretty investigator lady." He removed his hand from the rim of a large green trashcan and shook hers. "The name's Buzz Meechum."

Dana could tell from peering into the trash can that Buzz had been busy disassembling the memories from within the glass-doored cabinet. On the top of the pile lay the picture of Bernadette with her father at the beach. Deep in thought, Buzz focused on the photo in the trash and shook his head. Then as if taking out his anger, he ripped and yanked at the black construction paper that lined the walls of what had been a shrine in honor of Bernadette Godfrey.

Dana said, "It's difficult for me, too, to believe anyone would go so far as to murder an innocent child."

"You see this," he said, changing topics. In his hand, he held the Mother-of-Pearl prayer book that was to be part of Bernadette's First Communion ceremony. He flipped through the golden-edged pages with his thumb. "In here, it says to trust the Lord with all your might, but how ya goin' have faith after something like this?"

Dana thought for a moment as she watched the janitor's trembling hands and his head, which bobbed involuntarily. "Maybe that's what faith is all about in the first place."

He glanced at her, his face questioning.

"It's holding on when it seems there's nothing left to hold onto." After Dana had said the words, she wondered where they came from. Somewhere in her Catholic past, she was sure.

"I hear you, lady." Buzz carefully removed the silver charm bracelet from the case and put it in the front pocket of his overalls. "A gift to the girl from Mrs. Artenelli."

"Seems Mrs. Artenelli took a real interest in the girl and her family," Dana said.

"She did, she did." Then, Buzz's eyes narrowed as he began to scratch at a small wart on his neck. "But like it or not, I say that woman's got her reasons."

Maybe for once someone was willing to share some secrets with Dana, rather than leaving her with one more question unanswered.

"Are you saying Mrs. Artenelli had a motive for being nice to the girl?" Dana found one of the most difficult tasks in being an investigator was to pretend to know less than she did.

"Mrs. Artenelli has a motive for everything she does. Right down to her daily church going and her rosary reciting in the convent garden." He looked at a small piece of skin that he'd rubbed off from his neck, rolling it in his fingertips.

Down the hall, classroom doors could be heard slamming shut, and the sound of a floor polisher revving up on the linoleum flooring.

"You're saying that the woman isn't who she appears to be?"

"She's got money, Miss Greer, and people who got money can be whoever they wanna be."

"Mind if I ask who *you* think she is?"

"She's a phony baloney, that one. Listen," he said, as he moved closer. "That woman don't do a thing if she don't think she's got somethin' to gain."

"Like?"

"She likes all the hoopla that goes with being rich and all the money she donates. She likes for people to see her in church." Buzz began to dance in small circles as he continued, "and prancin' around the Ladies Auxiliary meetings."

Dana thought she'd use this as an opportunity to expand on some things she had already learned. "By chance, do you know what her connection is with the Guardian Angel Orphanage?"

Buzz took a picture from the case of Mrs. Godfrey, Bernadette, and the Mother Superior at Guardian Angel and stared at it. "I ain't one for spreading gossip none, but from what I've heard over the years, Carmelina Artenelli gave up a baby herself once. Whether it was guilt or what I can't say, but I know she gives a lot of her money to the place now."

Dana felt skeptical. How could Buzz be privy to so much knowledge? "Are you implying the woman might have had a child out of wedlock?"

He nodded his head. "She sure is *one* to talk. I mean, she's always pointing her finger at this sinner or that one, always judging." He scratched at his head as small pieces of dandruff fell onto his shirt collar. Buzz looked up and down the hall. "Why don't we go in here?" he asked, pointing to the chapel behind them.

Dana followed Buzz. The chapel felt like a darkened cave, where the only hint of light came from the late afternoon sun reflecting through the narrow stained glass windows, casting shadows of red, green, and blue. They sat down in a pew near the rear. Attached to the back of the seats were wooden racks filled with various holy cards and a note that read:

Help yourself.

Dana chose one of Saint Alphonsus Liguori, who was known to give sermons to those who had lost their faith in an effort to bring them back to the Church. Somehow, Dana felt that she could relate to the man's mission. Maybe one day, he could help her find her way back. She tucked the card into her notebook, planning to add it to her collection. "So, you're telling me that Mrs. Artenelli gave up an illegitimate child?"

"Sure as shootin' she did."

"This is unbelievable! How do you know all this?" Dana's questioned how Buzz had more knowledge of Mrs. Artenelli than even Logan had.

"My mother, bless her soul, used to clean the Artenellis' home in Bay View and, later, once Gino opened practice, his law office, too."

Someone who had known the Artenellis for a long time might be just the route Dana needed to further her investigation, but Buzz had indicated that his mother was deceased. "I'm sorry to hear about your mother," she said.

"Why? What'd ya mean, sorry? She's ain't cleanin' for them no more. No, she's long retired."

Dana laughed. "Guess I assumed your mother had passed away. . . I mean, you said, 'bless her soul'."

"Heck no. My mother's strong as an ox."

"Might it be possible for me to speak with her, Buzz?"

"Sure as hell, you can. Mother always was one for gab. She'd love a visitor."

It had been some time since Dana felt what she was feeling now—that adrenaline moment, that heart racing minute, that mind bolting instant, when she realized that there might be light at the end of the tunnel after all.

Buzz grabbed a pencil from the pocket in his overalls and scribbled a name and number on the back of the photograph he was about ready to toss in the trash. "I'll tell mother to be expectin' a call from you."

Their conversation was interrupted when Jay Harrison poked his head in and said, "Oh, sorry. Didn't realize anyone was in here."

"Getting ready to lock up," Buzz said.

Jay waved goodbye and said, "Pile up some *Zs*, Buzz."

"I will, I will," Buzz responded, his head still moving up and down. Buzz waited until the back doors to the school slammed shut. "Nice enough guy, that Jay, but a player."

Dana chose to appear dumb. "Oh that can't be. Must be just a rumor. Jay Harrison is a married man."

Buzz motioned for Dana to get up. He led the way out, banging the large wooden doors of the chapel closed. He pulled a ring of keys from his rear pocket, then locked the place of worship.

"Now you're opening up a can of worms, aren't you?" He returned to the showcase, slipping a piece of black velvet that had lined the shelves from the case and letting his fingers slide over it as one does with the fur of a cat. "Don't say I told you none, but that pretty daughter of Carmelina's? She's cruising for a bruisin'. People say the only reason Angela joined the nunhood is because her mother forced her to; the Mrs. was afraid her daughter would get herself in a heck of a lot of trouble if left to her own choices. You know, one illegitimate is one too many."

So, even Buzz knew that Angela had a child.

"Besides, I've even heard that Carmelina threatened to take Angela out of her will if she didn't do as told."

"Really?"

"Nice woman, that Carmelina, eh?" He gently pulled Dana closer by the sleeve of her coat. "That hep teacher, Mr. Harrison? He's ape over the sister."

Just the confirmation Dana was looking for. "But Loretta. . . ."

"Everyone around here knows Loretta Harrison is a wet rag. Jay never should have married her in the first place, but here again, you get down to money."

"So I've heard."

As Buzz tossed the last of the disposable items from the showcase, Dana could tell he was finishing his work, so she said, "Let's just hope these stories are only rumors. I mean, the one about Jay and Sister Mary Rose."

"Wish I could, lady, but you see that room over there?" He pointed to a door that looked like an entrance to a broom closet.

"Uh huh."

"That's where the two of them make out when no one's around."

"Are you serious?"

"Refused to believe it myself until I found the raincoats in the trashcan."

"Raincoats?"

"Yeah, you know. . .the rubbers. I don't mean to offend you none, but you know the old saying, 'no glove, no love,' don't you?"

Dana could feel her lower jaw drop and a flush race up her neck and onto her face. The separate bedrooms at the Harrison home, Jay's flippant attitude toward Loretta, Loretta's persona of victim. . . . It made sense. Loretta's father might have paid off Jay to marry his daughter, but that was as far as the relationship went. It was strictly a marriage of convenience. Loretta got to leave Aberdeen and hide from her sin, and Jay got the money to allow her to do so. It didn't matter how Loretta felt about Jay. Jay had his sights set elsewhere.

"By the way, if you don't believe me, you might want to speak with Harold Baylor, the pharmacist at Rexall's."

"What do you mean?"

"He's my brother-in-law before the wife died. I got the word from the bird."

"Meaning?"

"He's keeping a running tab. Jay Harrison has gone through more boxes of rubbers than that greaser down at the Hubcap Auto Shop."

Dana stared at Buzz with a blank look.

"It's pretty common knowledge that a number of those rich ladies up on the Pointe not only get their cars serviced, but they also get a heck of a lot more from that mechanic. But Jay's even beat him."

Buzz sure seemed to have his connections. First, his mother used to clean for the Artenellis, and his brother-in-law was keeping Jay Harrison supplied with condoms.

Chapter Twenty-Five

Dana rounded the corner, finding herself directly across from the entry of the cemetery, where only months earlier Bernadette Godfrey had been laid to rest. In the midst of the heavily falling snow, Dana almost missed seeing the small white house with black shutters that already was decorated for the Christmas holidays: a holly wreath with bright, red berries on the front door and a string of unlit bulbs hung from the spindled porch.

Through her mittens, Dana felt the cover of her tiny Bible in the pocket of her coat. She took a deep breath and rang the bell to Mrs. Meechum's house. The wind whistled and whipped around her, so she couldn't hear whether the bell had rung or not. She pressed it again.

The door flung open, and a short woman dressed in fluffy blue slippers and a pink-and-blue checked robe grabbed her by the arm. "You come in here right now, you hear. Buzzy told me you were coming, Miss Greer. You must be freezing out on a day like today. Take your boots off; there's a hook for your coat."

Dana could smell fresh wood burning and the scents of barley and mushroom.

"Here you make yourself at home," Mrs. Meechum said, as she sat Dana on a dark green corduroy couch, in front of the crackling fireplace. A small Christmas tree stood in the corner decorated with what appeared to be homemade, crocheted ornaments. A rat terrier lay on a cushion beneath the branches. The woman left the room, her voice trailing, "Don't you mind Nelli none; she was born stone deaf and couldn't hurt a flea. Buzzy got her for me last Christmas; she's only a year old."

After living in the historical Victorian house of the Harrisons ever since coming to the Cape, Dana welcomed the cozy atmosphere of Mrs. Meechum's house. She immediately liked the woman, who had to be in her late eighties. Mrs. Meechum returned holding two bowls of steaming mushroom-and-barley soup and offered one to Dana and took one herself.

"Homemade soup. . .how nice," Dana said. "Thank you."

"Warms the body and the soul. Now, tell me. My Buzzy said you'd be coming by. How can I help?" She sipped on the tip of her bowl.

Dana set her soup on the coffee table in front of her, where several Catholic magazines lay. That's when Dana noticed a large crucifix on the wall opposite her and a statue of Mary in an alcove in the side wall. "I see you're Catholic?"

"Why, who isn't on the Cape?"

"Have you always lived here?" Dana asked, knowing full well that if she had cleaned early on for the Artenellis that she had to have lived in Bay View. The question should get the woman to speak of her past.

"Why, no. I'm from Bay View. Born and raised and taught by the good sisters of St. Michael's parish." She set her soup bowl down.

"Then, you must have known the Artenelli family."

The woman hung her head, and when she raised it, she had a big smile. "Who doesn't know the Artenellis? Well, did Buzzy tell you that I used to clean for them in that big, old house? Twelve bedrooms, six bathrooms, and even a heated summer porch. Why, it was quite the job, but they paid me well. I must say that."

"How long ago was that, Mrs. Meechum?"

The woman put her hand across her lips and thought for a moment. "That had to be almost twenty years ago. Time sure does fly."

"That must have been the time when Mr. Artenelli was still in law school, right?"

She nodded. "There was money in that family right from the start, I say. I often wondered how they afforded that magnificent home. They were only newlyweds back then."

Dana could tell the woman was getting off track from where she hoped to lead, so she steered the conversation along another direction. "Did Mrs. Artenelli have a child at that time?"

"Oh, my yes. Sweet little Angela, only a babe in arms." The woman stared in the distance as if picturing the child. Then, she added, "But you know it wasn't her first, don't you?"

Dana could feel her eyebrows rising.

"Before she and the Mr. married, only a year or so prior to Angela, the Mrs. had a son."

"How do you know this? You weren't working for the couple then."

"The arguments! Why after little Angela came along, the fights didn't stop there. No! Whenever something went wrong between the Mr. and Mrs., the Mr. would say, 'I should have known better than to marry such a cheap whore.' Oh, he could be mean, all right. He'd tell the Mrs. that one day her child would come back to haunt her, if not in this life, than in the next. I heard it all with my very own ears."

Dana could not believe what she was hearing. "Do you think Mr. Artenelli wanted his wife to keep the child?"

"Gracious no! Mr. Artenelli already had his connections, even back then. The Mrs. was sent off to Holy Angel Orphanage in Waterville when she was about eight months along, and as soon as the baby was born, she came back to Bay View, married Gino, and within only months got pregnant with Angela."

"The child. . .the boy. . .her son. . .was he Mr. Artenelli's child?"

"Oh my, yes. An accident you know. Young lovers. Well, you know how that can be. Mr. Artenelli forbade her from keeping the child. He didn't want any bad gossip surrounding his name. I felt sorry for her. Well, that's when she turned to the Church."

"The Church?" Dana took some of the hot soup.

"She began to devote her days and nights to St. Michael's. She joined the Women's Auxilliary, the Rosary Society. . .why she practically lived at the church. There are those who say she used the Church as a front. You know, to show how religious she was."

"I see."

"She even got the Mr. to join, and he could care less about God or the Church for that matter—one of those Catholics in name only." She put the palm of her hand on the side of her mouth and whispered, "He's a gangster, you know. Alcohol, drugs, and women. Always out with his *boys.*" Mrs. Meechum sipped on her soup, and then setting it down, went over to the Christmas tree. She picked up the small terrier and placed the dog in her lap, petting its ears. "But that isn't all. Near as I could tell, the Mr. got Mrs. Artenelli involved in his illegal business."

"How so?"

"Mrs. Artenelli used to come-and-go to the Holy Angel Orphanage even after Angela was born. Near as I could tell, she was some kind of go-between at the place."

"Like some sort of business?" Dana rustled in her chair.

"Mrs. Artenelli would chastise young unwed mothers, yet on the other hand, she would bring them to the orphanage. It was all a sham."

Dana could tell Mrs. Meechum, as an employee of the Artenellis, knew much more than she at first wanted to tell.

"Why do you say it was a sham?" Dana leaned in closer, sure to not miss a word of what Mrs. Meechum had to share.

"I don't know how much of this I should get into, Miss Greer. You know, the Artenellis would not hesitate to send one of the *boys* over here if they ever thought I said a word about this."

"I understand your fear, Mrs. Meechum. Know, though, that you can trust me."

Without any more coaxing, the woman went on. "The Mrs. and her husband made money off of the girls. For every girl Mrs. Artenelli brought through the orphanage doors, she got a certain percentage once the child was adopted."

Dana began to scratch the back of her neck.

"It gets worse. The Mrs. went about selling the babies to rich families, who would pay top dollar."

"But the orphanage. . .it's run by Catholic nuns."

"True but there were families who were desperate to have a child. It became a money-making proposition for the Artenellis as well as the nuns. The real parents got rid of their children, skipping the whole adoption step, and the orphanage and Mrs. Artenelli split the money that came from the sales. Why it's like these babies were nothing more than a piece of produce."

Dana rubbed her hands over her eyes. "How awful."

"I always knew when business was good because the Mrs. offered to give me a bonus. Why, I couldn't accept. How could I? I would be no better than the two of them." Mrs. Meechum kissed her terrier's head and continued petting her.

"Understandable. And the baby that Mrs. Artenelli had. Might you know about when he was born?"

"I sure enough do. It was the same date as my wedding anniversary: May 10." She toyed with her fingers as if trying to add a sum. "Let's see; that would have been 1928. Yes, May 10, 1928." She looked at Dana with a questioning look. "Why'd you ask?"

"Oh, you might say, I'm trying to put a puzzle together."

"From what I've heard, the whole ordeal was a puzzle."

"What do you mean?" Dana asked.

"If you're one to believe gossip, and there's plenty of it that goes 'round on the Cape, I've heard the baby that the Mrs. gave up for adoption still lives in the town of Waterville. It's a darn shame, but I heard the child was adopted by a none too good family. His mother's supposed to be into drugs, and as for his father. . .why not any better. It's a crying shame that the Artenellis hadn't kept the poor boy. At least he might have stood a chance to make something of himself."

Dana chewed on the tip of her thumb. "Do you think Mrs. Artenelli knows what's become of her son?"

"I doubt it; she's not one for listening to rumors. You know, gossip is a sin and all."

"True." That made sense to Dana. After all, if the woman was known to be such a religious fanatic, wouldn't it only go to prove that she wouldn't have the ear for idle talk?

"And maybe it's just as well. I hear the boy's been in more trouble with the law than one can shake a stick at. Can't imagine the Artenelli family would own up to someone like that being part of their family."

"That's too bad. . .I mean, it sounds, if one can believe rumors, that the young man didn't turn out very well. Any word on what kind of trouble he's been into?"

The woman shook her head. "All I can say is I wish you luck, dear. If I were you, I'd be careful. The Artenellis aren't a family to fool with." She edged closer. "Those two got a lot of money and power; they wouldn't hesitate to use either if they knew someone was foolin' around in their business."

Dana felt a sudden chill and reached for her soup. Mrs. Meechum got up and threw a log into the fire and then sat down. The two women finished their broth in silence, staring at the blue-and-orange crackling flames. In a town of 7,000 people, what would be the likelihood that a twenty-four year old man in Waterville who came from a troubled home life and, himself, got in trouble with the law, could possibly be Eddie Vineeti? Dana realized she might very well be jumping to conclusions; she couldn't say for sure, yet she knew what her next step would have to be.

Chapter Twenty-Six

Eddie chewed on a piece of tobacco and scratched his cheek with his thumb. He wished his curiosity hadn't gotten the better of him. Ever since Rayna told him that his mother had called while he was on the Cape, he debated whether he should return the call.

When his inquisitiveness would not leave him alone, he broke down.

"Yeah, Maw. Rayna tells me you called me. I was out."

"Eddie, so good to hear from you. How long has it been?"

"Maw, let's just get to the point. I'm busy and don't have much time to waste." He was glad that at least this time his mother sounded sober.

"I need to speak with you, Boy. It's something important."

"So. Go ahead!"

"Not on the phone, Eddie. I need to see you."

"Maw, quit making this some big deal. What is it you got to say to me?"

"Eddie, I'm telling you I need to see you."

Eddie went over the conversation in his mind. At first, he thought he'd just stand his mother up, leave her waiting for him. Did he really care what she had to say? He never had in the past. Yet this time, he called it a sixth sense. He told Rayna that he had decided to meet with his mother after all.

"Why can't she come here? We got a real nice place and all," Rayna said. She glanced around the small room filled with items from the local Goodwill: most of which were torn, scratched, broken, or worn.

"Because God damn it! I didn't invite her. Do you really want her here after the way she treated you last time? I ain't all that happy going out to meet her, but somethin' in her voice told me she might have somethin' to say this time. Hey, maybe she won some money or somethin' and wants to share it with us." Eddie's eyes got real big, and he put on that little boy charm that Rayna was so fond of.

"If that's the case, Baby, I say we sell this dump and move to that place on Cape Peril where all the rich people live."

"Let's not count our chickens until they hatch, Rayna," Eddie said. He put on his plaid hunter jacket and a knit cap and headed for his truck. He lit up a cigarette and turned up the radio. Bill Haley and the Comets were blasting "Rock the Joint," and he sang along bouncing in his seat as he made his way toward a small diner on Messalonskee Street along the Kennebec River. He swore he would have to get the crack in the passenger window fixed as cold air flowed in. He turned up the heater until the rickety noise overshadowed the Comets.

When he arrived at the diner and stepped out of his truck, the smell of greasy chicken hit him in the face. A jukebox was playing some unknown country song, which Eddie considered hillbilly junk. The cigarette smoke was so thick that even Eddie's eyes watered and blinded him for a second.

"Eddie, honey," his mother said as she came out of the crowd. She put her arms around him in an attempt to hug him.

"Aw, Maw, not here, not now," he said, shrugging her off.

She led him by the hand to a corner table where the lights were dim and the music not quite as loud. "What can I get you to eat, Son?"

"I ain't come here to eat. I only came because you insisted I do. What's the urgent message?"

The waitress, dressed in a skimpy red-and-white checkered skirt and a red halter top, rolled up to the table on white high-top skates. "Get cha anything, folks?"

"Bring us a couple of Cokes," Eddie's mother said.

"Don't tell me. You gave up the bottle, Maw."

Eddie's mother's face turned pink even in the dim light. "I'm tryin', Eddie. Really I am. I ain't had a drink in six months."

Eddie bit down on the gum of his lower lip and watched the cute waitress as she whizzed about the diner delivering orders.

"But, Eddie Boy, I do have somethin' really important to tell you, but I ain't sure how to go about it."

"How 'bout you tell me," Eddie said. Without having to make any effort, Eddie's sarcasm crawled into his speech like a dusty worm making its way through the grass.

"You remember Auntie Tillie and her husband Uncle Roy?"

Eddie nodded. He considered them to be two of the biggest hillbillies he ever met.

"I don't know how better to say this than to tell you that they ain't your real relatives."

"Well, I'll be. That's a pleasure to know."

"Eddie Vineeti!" his mother scolded, as if he were five years old.

The drinks came and Eddie blew a kiss to the skater who returned one and stuck it on her butt.

His mother sipped on her straw and said, "Eddie, you ain't my boy either." Her voice cracked and her eyes instantly filled with tears.

"What are you saying? You lying to me again?" Eddie's face got red and sweaty. His cheeks pulsated as if they had a heartbeat of their own.

"No, it's true. Me and Daddy. . . ."

"Let's not talk about that bum."

"Okay, well, I never was able to have a baby. That is until one of the ladies at the church told me about those girls up on the hill."

"Girls?" Eddie's face lit up.

"The pregnant ones. The ones who got banged up and ain't wantin' to keep their babies."

"Wait just one minute," Eddie said. He pushed his chair away from the table. "You tryin' to tell me I'm one of those bastard kids?"

"Eddie, please, keep your voice down. Do you want someone to hear you?"

"I don't give a shit who hears me!"

"Eddie, please." His mother reached across the table and tried to grab at his arm.

He pulled away.

"It's a nice place. . .Guardian Angel. The nuns takes good care of the girls, even have midwives who deliver the babies. You weren't cheap, Eddie. That's where Auntie Tillie and Uncle Roy come in."

"Don't tell me. Don't tell me. Do those two God damn hillbillies have something to do with you payin' for me?" He turned his head aside and scowled.

"Eddie, Aunt Tillie and Uncle Roy. . .they got big money. They live in a big trailer. Those Airstreams don't come cheap. They never even asked me to pay them back. They just gave me the cash."

"Great! So, now you're sayin' I was a real bargain. I knew I shouldn't have come. Every time I get within two feet of you, I can smell trouble."

"Don't say that, Son. I love you. I never would have taken the money if I didn't want a baby so bad."

Eddie pretended to think for a moment. He lit up a cigarette and blew the smoke on the floor, covered in peanut shells. "Let me guess. Do the good nuns do returns, too? Maybe you'd like to trade me in."

Eddie's mother began to cry. "Don't say such horrible things, Son. I love you."

He picked at his front tooth with the nail of his index finger. "If you loved me so much, then why did you wait until I was twenty-four years old to tell me?"

The woman pulled the small napkin from under her drink and wiped her nose. "I didn't know how to. . .didn't know how you'd take it. . .didn't know when the time would be right."

"My, my. You see how I'm takin' it, don't you? I ain't never thought too highly of myself to begin with, but knowing I'm a bastard child, well my, my." He didn't bother to complete his sentence. He stood up.

"Wait, Eddie. Don't leave. We can work this out. Give me time."

"I got news for you, lady. You betcha I'm leavin', and you'd better stay out of my life. You ain't nothin' to me. Do you hear me: nothin'." He got up and walked through the crowd of people lined up at the bar. In a loud voice, he screamed, "Hey, everybody. Look at me. I'm a son of a bitch." He laughed like a crazy man. People whispered to each other as they stared at Eddie.

His mother stayed at the table, her tears so heavy that they began to drip across its edge.

Chapter Twenty-Seven

S o were you able to prove that Sister Mary Rose is the mother of the Godfrey girl?" Logan asked, as he chewed on the pink eraser at the end of his pencil.

"Maybe a better way of saying this, is that I have strong speculation to believe just that. After I spoke with Doctor Thatcher, I understood much better why a girl would turn the control of her child over to her mother."

"Mind filling in the blanks for me?" Logan asked. "Last time we spoke, you mentioned a dependent personality type would look for love elsewhere if it no longer was provided by the original person."

Dana couldn't wait to tell Logan everything that Doctor Thatcher had told her. "There's more, lots more. The adoption coordinator, Sharon Little, confirmed just about everything I learned about dependent personality types from Doctor Thatcher."

Logan repositioned himself into his leather armchair as he folded his hands under his chin. "Shoot. I can't wait to hear what you found out."

"From what Little told me, the birth mother aimed to please her mother and to abide by her mother's wishes."

"Explaining why she'd go along with signing the document."

"That's right."

"What else did you learn?" Logan began to twirl his thumbs.

Dana opened her satchel and pulled out her notebook. "Listen to this," she said, "a personality type like this has difficulty making decisions, needs advice, and takes reassurance from someone else, usually a person he or she is close to." She glanced up at Logan.

"Fascinating. Go on."

"Point number two: This person actually likes others to assume responsibility for his or her actions."

"Ta-da!" Logan shouted. "You're onto something here, for sure." He brushed the palms of his hands along his hairline.

Dana continued to read from her list. "The last point: This person is afraid to state his or her own demands for fear of disapproval."

"Ah hem. That would explain why Angela Artenelli. . .I'd prefer to call her by her biological name rather than Sister Mary Rose. . .wouldn't even consider going the abortion route. With a controlling mother as she has, it would make sense why she would fear her mother's disapproval of that choice. What a moral insult, I'm sure, to a woman of Mrs. Artenelli's standing."

"Perhaps."

"What's that supposed to mean. . .perhaps?" Logan asked.

"Do you mind looking up something for me in your police log?"

"Sure. What is it?"

"Could you check the birthdate of Eddie Vineeti?" Dana asked.

"Oh, let's not get into this again, Dana. You know how I feel about that weasel."

"No, please. It's important. I need to know."

"If you say so," Logan said, breathing heavily, as he got up and called his secretary. "Janet, could you find the recent police report on Eddie Vineeti?"

"That guy?" Janet yelled back.

Logan waited while Janet rummaged through the file cabinet behind her, spilling a jar of hand cream on the floor.

"And clean up your mess," Logan ordered, a scowl on his face, as he almost slipped on the greasy spot on the floor.

"Sure thing, boss," Janet answered, handing him a manila folder.

Logan sat back down. "What'd ya need to know about this culprit, Dana, that I don't already know?"

"Just his birthdate, Logan. That's all."

"Ah, let's see here. He reported that he was born on May 10, 1928. Why?"

Dana gasped. She told Logan what Mrs. Meechum had told her about Mrs. Artenelli's illegitimate son, about his adoptive parents, his run-ins with the law. "It all fits. Mrs. Meechum was positive about the date. She said it was the day she married, May 10."

"C'mon, Dana. I mean *how many* people live in Waterville?"

"Around 7,000 but the real question is how many men born on that very date have had their names make the front page of the *Morning Sentinel* for an illegal act?"

Logan thought for a moment. "Hmm. Guess you got me there. So Carmelina Artenelli ain't no saint herself! Like mother, like daughter."

"Exactly," Dana said, "you've got it! But there's more." Dana told Logan what Sharon Little had told her about the birth father of Bernadette."

"Well, I'll be a monkey's uncle! Angela and that miserable freak Vineeti are blood relatives."

Dana nodded. "And, if my assumptions are correct, the biological parents of Bernadette Godfrey."

"I'll be damned. Do you think either of them know this?"

"That still needs to be determined, but if they did, it sure would give them a good motive for murder, wouldn't you say?"

"What can I say? You're a gem, Dana. A real gem." Logan rubbed his hands together.

"I wouldn't go that far. . .er, at least not until I solve the case."

"For some reason, I have the feeling there's even more to your story, Dana."

"There is. Listen to this."

Logan smiled and tapped his knuckle above his lip.

Dana explained the conversation that she had with Buzz Meechum's mother, and what she told her about the Artenellis being involved in some type of baby trafficking scheme.

Logan picked at his front teeth with the nail of his index finger. "A syndicate, the mob, gangsters. . .you bet! This sure isn't anything new, Dana. The Cape used to be an innocent, little haven, but that's history."

"When did it change? I thought Gino Artenelli only moved to the Cape since Sister Mary Rose came to the Academy?"

Logan picked up the pencil on his desk and used it as a pointer. "Let me put it this way. These kinds of guys can operate anywhere. Actually, the more out-of-the-way kinds of places the better. Who'd suspect?"

"Why not crack down on the guy? Sounds as if you've enough to get him on."

"For one thing, it's not as simple as you say; and for another, let's just say some things are worth looking the other way."

"I don't understand."

"Dana, our force here on the Cape consists of me and Officers O'Neil and Boyle. Small potatoes like us don't take on the Mob, nor are we interested in dragging in the FBI to do so."

Sounded like a weak excuse to Dana, but she had come to the Cape to investigate a murder, not to wrestle down the Mob alone. "Well, I don't know that I necessarily agree with you, Logan, but the syndicate is a bit out of my league."

Logan bit down on his lower lip and nodded. "Got anything else for me, Dana?"

There was more. There was the whole story Buzz had told her about Sister Mary Rose and Jay Harrison's presumed affair. But until she could prove it to herself, this would be one thing Dana would refrain from mentioning. "Nothing other than doing some math work on the case" she said, "the usual just trying to put two and two together."

"I sure wish you luck with your calculation."

Before Dana responded, Logan's secretary knocked on the door, and without waiting to be asked in, she said, "There's someone waiting to see you."

"I'm busy, little lady, but who's out there?"

"Guy by the name of Amhurst. . .a William Amhurst."

"Hmm. Don't recognize the name. Tell him to wait. I'm with someone."

The secretary, her hair in a poofed up bob, shook her hips and left the room.

"You were asking me where I go from here?" Dana asked.

"Right, where are you headed?" Logan spun the pencil around on his desk. "And where she stops no one knows." He smiled.

"To make sure I'm not running off on a whim, I need to do some investigating of my own. No sense listening to some idle gossip until I have the facts."

"Ah, yes. Sounds to me as if you've heard an earful. Good idea to weigh the truth from rumor. You know how quickly hearsay can spread on the Cape."

Dana didn't have a chance to comment before the secretary re-entered the room. "Sorry to interrupt," she said, chomping on a piece of pink bubble gum, "but this guy out here is demanding you see him now, Logan."

Logan looked at the secretary and then at Dana. "Do you mind?"

Dana shook her head.

"Okay. Send him in."

A man, who looked to be in his early fifties wearing a three-quarters length gold wool coat with oversized pockets and toggles for buttons, walked in and sat down next to Dana. "The name's William Amhurst."

Amhurst, Dana thought. The name was so familiar, but where had she heard it?

"I'm Loretta Harrison's father."

"Indeed," Logan said, "the mayor of Aberdeen, South Dakota."

Dana gulped. That was it. She remembered reading Loretta's maiden name on her marriage certificate to Jay. She had heard that

Loretta's father was a significant figure in Aberdeen. . .a mayor no less.

"What brings you to Cape Peril, Sir?" Logan asked.

The man tossed a glare in Dana's direction.

"Oh, forgive me, Mr. Amhurst. This is Dana Greer. She's a special investigator hired to solve a recent murder that took place on the Cape. Hope you won't mind if she sits in with us."

The man eyed Dana from head-to-foot and did not look pleased with Logan's suggestion.

"I suppose," was all he said, as he straightened his blue-and-red striped tie.

"What can I do for you?"

"It's not about me; it's about my daughter." The man pulled a cigar out of his pocket and proceeded to suck on it, paper and all.

"Would you like a light?" Logan asked and lit a match he found in his desk drawer.

"Certainly. Thank you," Mr. Amhurst said, as he lit the cigar and filled the room with the scent of sweet cherries.

"So, you've come to speak with me about Loretta?"

"More importantly, about Jay, her husband," the man said, sucking on the cigar.

Dana could feel the tension escalating and wanted to scream out what she had reason to suspect, but instead, waited patiently for the man to complete his thoughts.

Mr. Amhurst glanced over at Dana and positioned himself sideways in the chair. "Loretta has written me that she believes her husband is involved with another woman."

Although Logan's right eyebrow shot up, he said not a word. Neither did Dana.

"What you need to understand, Sergeant, is that no one hurts my daughter." He narrowed his eyes.

"Understood," Logan said. "But I don't understand what you want of me, Mr. Amhurst."

"You're a police sergeant, aren't you? You uphold the law, don't you?"

"Why, of course, I do. . .I mean, we do. But an extramarital affair? Well, can't say that's exactly in my line of work."

"Then, I suggest you make it." The man reached into one of his large pockets and pulled out his brown leather billfold. He put a one hundred dollar bill on the edge of Logan's desk.

Logan put up the palm of his hand. "Whoa! Wait a minute, Sir. Is this some kind of bribe?"

"Not at all. Let's just say it's for your services," the man said.

"Look, I've already told you that what your son-in-law does in his free time is not, in any way, considered to be breaking the law."

The man reached into his wallet again. He put another one hundred dollar bill on the desk. "Then, find me someone," he said, as he now glanced at Dana, "who would be willing to prove my daughter's assumption to be correct."

"You're looking for a private detective?" Dana inquired.

He smiled sweetly. "And, let me guess, there just happens to be one on this small island."

"Why no," Logan said.

"Then, I suggest you're hired," the man said to Dana, putting the two bills in her hand. "An investigator should be more than capable of doing a little detective work on the side."

"Exactly what do you want, Mr. Amhurst?" Dana asked.

"Follow Jay Harrison. See where he goes, what he does. If after a week, you find what Loretta tells me is true, I will personally pack up my daughter's belongings and escort her back to Aberdeen."

"What if I don't find any misgivings? Then, what?"

"The money is yours either way, and Loretta will be seen by a shrink. But I feel highly confident that what my daughter tells me is not a lie."

Dana stared at Logan and he at her.

"This is highly irregular you must understand, Sir, but the decision is up to my special investigator." Now, Logan and Mr. Amhurst were staring at Dana.

Since she had planned on doing just what the man was requesting anyway plus she had hoped to learn more about Loretta, Dana nodded and agreed to help him out. Why, she had heard of cops moonlighting as security guards. Why not an investigator as a private detective? "Before I get involved in any so-called private detective work, Mr. Amhurst, I'd like to sit down with you and learn a little bit more about your daughter."

"When do we meet?" he asked.

Chapter Twenty-Eight

As soon as Eddie left the Waterville Pub, he drove his truck down along the Kennebec River south toward the Mobile Trailer Park. He knew the place only too well. He had spent a lot of time as a kid with his so-called relatives who lived in a rusted Airstream that smelled like charred hotdogs and mustard inside. He never did know what the two did for a living, but rumor had it that the couple had inherited a large sum of money from Roy's side of the family. Eddie often wondered why the couple hadn't moved out of the trailer park. In his opinion, it was home to nothing more than a bunch of scumbags. He remembered once when he was only about six years of age, he and a friend of his had gotten locked into an empty icebox someone had set out next to the trailer. Fortunately, the police found them before they had suffocated in the thing. Eddie recalled how for the Christmas holidays, the trailer park owners would try to make money off their used stuff by offering it for sale as gifts. Cardboard signs in their yard would read:

Phonograph for Sale – Records Included

Aunt Jemima Cookie Jar – Original

Philco Radio

Even as a child, Eddie thought the ploy was tacky. Aunt Tillie and Uncle Roy always chose to put a faded Nativity set next to their trailer with red, green, and blue bulbs twisted around the figures. In the summertime, most of the kids ran naked through the sprinklers, chased by stray dogs.

As Eddie pulled into the park, he noted that nothing had changed over the years. Most of the trailers were the originals, the owners had their Christmas 'For Sale' signs already posted in their yard, and out front of Aunt Tillie's and Uncle Roy's place was the same faded Nativity set with its blaring red, green, and blue bulbs. He parked in a snow-covered, muddy rut and went to the door; a small wreath with holly berries and mistletoe hung from a nail.

The door opened a crack, and Aunt Tillie, a woman in her sixties with bleached blond hair, peered out. "Yes, what do you want?"

"Aunt Tillie, it's me, Eddie. Rosie's boy."

The woman opened the door wide, and put her plump arms around Eddie's neck, kissing him over-and-over again on the cheek. "How long has it been? How have you been?"

The woman reminded Eddie of Rayna with her nonstop questions, not stopping long enough for him to even answer one. Her boisterous voice brought Uncle Roy from the back room. "Well, holy shit, if it ain't Eddie."

"A little taller but not a day older with that baby face," Aunt Tillie said, squeezing his cheeks as if he were a five-year-old. "Come on in. Have a seat."

The place still reeked of hotdogs and mustard, and the cheap, brown upholstered furniture showed its wear.

"Can we get you a drink, boy?" Uncle Roy asked, as if he were speaking to an animal.

"No, no. I'm fine," Eddie said. "Don't intend to stay long or to take your time."

"Stay as long as you like; you know, we still got that cot in the back room."

Eddie could feel his face cringe. "This won't take long. It's about maw."

"Your maw? Is she alright? Is she sick? Is there a problem?"

"Nothing like that. I met with her the other night, and she told me the truth. No more secrets."

Uncle Roy patted his wife's knee while the three of them sat on the conch. "What'd ya mean, boy. . .secrets?"

"Just what I said. The woman ain't my maw any more than you two are my aunt and uncle."

"Whoa! Just a minute here," Uncle Roy said, abruptly standing up.

"Wait a minute, Roy, let the boy explain."

"I found out everything. That I was born up on the hill at that orphanage. . .Angel something."

"Guardian Angel, why of course, Eddie," Aunt Tillie said, running her hand back-and-forth over the upholstered arm.

Roy tried to quiet the woman by lifting up the palm of his hand.

"There's no sense keeping the truth from the boy, Roy, if Rosie has already told him."

"You're going to cause trouble, Tillie. I tell you to shut your mouth."

Tillie got up and motioned for Roy to back away. "We helped your maw, made it possible for her to have a boy."

"Yeah, yeah, I know all about your contribution to the cause. What I want to know is who in the hell is the bitch that gave me up in the first place?"

"Now, listen here, Eddie, there'll be no swearing in my house," Roy said.

Tillie chose to ignore Roy and continued. "It's a secret. The Good Sisters of the Poor keep it that way, so girls can feel free to deliver their babies with no disgrace."

"My, my, now. Isn't that the sweetest thing I ever heard," Eddie said. "The only reason I got out of the damn place to begin with is because you and Roy had the money to buy me."

"It wasn't like that at all," Roy said. "You got it all wrong. Rosie couldn't have no child."

"Well somebody did, and I want to know who. What is the name of the damn bitch that had me?"

"Like Tillie said, Eddie, it's kept secret."

"Is it or is there a price for knowing?" Eddie asked.

"You don't mean. . . ."

"Sure enough do, Aunt Tillie and you got plenty of dough to do just that."

"Are you asking me to bribe the good sisters?"

"That's putting it nicely. And I'm sure they'd appreciate your kind generosity," Eddie said.

"Don't put us in the middle of this, Eddie," Roy said.

"You were in the middle of this from day one.

"What if I refuse?" Aunt Tillie asked.

"That's not an option, is it?" Eddie widened his eyes and pulled a long-bladed switchblade from his rear pocket. "Now, what'd ya say ya take a drive to see the good sisters?"

"Wait a minute," Roy said. "We dropped charges on you once before for pulling a knife on my Tillie here."

"Shut up you shit hole, and do as I say. Tillie, you get in the cab of my truck; Roy in the back, but not before you fill your wallet, you bastard."

The two people began to stutter so badly that their words made no sense. Eddie followed Roy into the back room, where the old man opened the combination lock to his safe. Folded in neat, crisp piles were bills marked with one hundred on them. Eddie poised the blade of his knife over Roy's neck as he bent to grab some bills. As Roy was about to get up, Eddie pushed him back down. "Get another handful for safe measure."

***

Eddie was glad about one thing—that he had worn his blue serge suit. Hopefully he would be taken seriously by the Mother Superior of Holy Angel Orphanage, and not as some young shit head who came to stir trouble. . .not as some criminal who had come to bribe the holy woman of God.

"Sir, you must understand that sometimes it is in the best interests of a child that he or she be taken from his or her birth mother shortly after delivery. You see, we want the child to bond with his or her adoptive parents."

Oh, she had the words all right. . .the words that made her sound all legitimate, not to mention kind and giving.

Eddie tried to guard himself from using his usual swear words...the ones he used when angry.

"That's exactly what we tried to tell Eddie, Sister," Aunt Tillie said.

Eddie bit down hard on his lower lip until he drew blood. "How do you explain this bein' in my best interest, Sister?"

"Your adoptive mother was unable to have children, Sir. Can't you see how the orphanage provided her with a blessed service?"

Eddie's patience was being tried to the limit. He decided not to get into the payoff by Aunt Tillie and Uncle Roy that made it possible for him to be adopted in the first place. No matter which way he looked at it, money was the common denominator in all of the transactions. People paid money to buy a kid, and the real mother paid money to forget her kid. Somehow in the midst of it all, Eddie felt that he had gotten lost in the shuffle.

"Let's get back to the woman I was given to."

"You mean your adoptive mother, Eddie? Rosie Vineeti?" the nun asked.

"Yeah. You tellin' me that she was a good choice? Let me tell you a few secrets, Sister. Not only did Rosie Vineeti lie to me all these years, but she was a far cry from being a good mother to me."

"Eddie, please," Aunt Tillie shouted.

"No, let me talk. Let me tell the way it really was. I was nothin' more than a burden to her. When she wasn't cleanin' someone's house, she was livin' off the streets, using whatever money she made to pay for her habit."

"Eddie, I'll hear nothing of this," Uncle Roy said. "Your mother loved you."

"Don't give me that shit! Let's put it this way, Uncle Roy. You sure wasted your money buying a kid for her. She didn't know the first thing about bein' a mother, let alone love."

Uncle Roy at that point tried to quiet things down by telling the Mother Superior that he and Tillie had come to donate a gift to the orphanage for all the good that the sisters had done over the years.

Eddie shook his head. Bullshit! Why in the hell doesn't Roy come right out and tell the nun that he's paying her off for some information?

The Mother Superior's jaw dropped when she saw the roll of bills that Roy took out of his wallet.

"God will bless you royally," she said.

Aunt Tillie cleared her throat. "My nephew here. . .well, Sister, he's come to learn the identity of his birth mother."

The Mother Superior's pleasant expression of gratitude quickly turned to one of irritated understanding. "You see, Mr. Vineeti, your birth mother was young and unmarried. Why, she was confused and didn't know quite what to do."

"I see," Eddie said. "Is that really the truth, or is the truth that she didn't want her good name smeared. I mean having a kid illegitimately. . . ."

"No, you don't understand," Mother Superior said. "Your birth mother actually married the man she had fallen in love with. Only they got married a few years later when she was older and knew that he was the man she would vow to love in good times and in bad times." The nun looked down. "I must tell you all that this is highly unlikely that we reveal the identity of a birth mother. Guardian

Angels Orphanage prides itself on the bond of secrecy that it keeps with each and every adoption."

Uncle Roy started to slip the roll of bills back in his wallet.

"Then, again, there are always exceptions, aren't there?" the Mother Superior asked, her chin lifted, and her eyes on Uncle Roy's wallet. The nun spun around in her chair and opened the file cabinet behind her. Once having retrieved the file she was looking for, she handed it to Eddie. "Your birth mother, Mr. Vineeti, is a well-known woman on the island of Cape Peril. She has donated much to Holy Angels both in time and financially. Why, her own daughter chose to enter the convent."

"Her name?" Uncle Roy, interrupted, making a gesture toward his pant pocket.

"Why, of course. Carmelina Artenelli." The Mother Superior's lips trembled when she said the name.

It was clear to Eddie that the nun had known the truth for the past twenty-four years. Eddie wondered how a religious woman could have lived with herself, knowing that it was merely a bribe that that made her finally willing to tell him the truth. For a moment Eddie couldn't speak. His birth mother married his birth father a few years after he was born? Wait a minute, he thought. There was one small detail that wasn't being spoken of: His birth mother went on to have another child shortly after she married. Same mother, same man, brother and sister. His chest tightened. He felt a pain run down his left arm, a sharp pain. He breathed in and out rapidly. Then, he said, "How then do you plan to explain this. . .that you told me the truth?" Eddie asked.

"Quite simply, I won't. I will write a letter to the Diocese of Bay View and inform the bishop that there had been a break-in. That someone had found a way to get into the files. It will be simpler that way."

"A lie on top of a lie," Eddie said, and smirked. "Unholy secrets to hide the truth."

Mother Superior looked up at him. Her steel blue eyes appeared cold like pieces of ice, frosted and sharp at the edges. Her face hardened like stone. "Trust me. It is better this way."

When Eddie left the orphanage, he drove Tillie and Roy back to the trailer park in silence. Before they stepped out of Eddie's truck, Tillie tried to hug him. Uncle Roy said, "As sad a day as this is, I hope it won't mean we'll never see you again, boy."

Eddie looked into their faces and laughed. "Let's put it this way. Maybe we got more in common now than we ever did, but money can't buy love. Now, get the hell out of my truck before I shove ya out." He watched as Roy put his arm around Tillie's shoulders. The woman cried and scurried to her trailer door.

Chapter Twenty-Nine

The windows of the Sip 'n Stay were covered in moisture, and someone had drawn some silly faces on the glass. Dana stepped inside, stomped the freshly fallen snow off her boots, and waved to the waitress, who was busy running between the kitchen and the customers. Dana spied Amhurst, sitting in one of the booths close to the restrooms. He stood as he saw her coming.

"Good to see you, Miss Greer. May I order something for you?" Amhurst had already ordered—a cinnamon roll and a cup of tea.

"Just a coffee. . .black, please."

He flagged down the waitress and placed Dana's order.

While they waited, he wasted no time in getting to the point of their meeting. "After you left the station yesterday, the Sergeant explained to me that you are staying at Loretta's place."

"Correct." Interesting that he put it, "Loretta's place."

"Then, you've probably had the chance to get to know my daughter quite well by now."

Dana nodded, but her inner voice told her quite the contrary. Loretta was no more open today than she had been when Dana had first arrived on the Cape. Her secrets were well kept, or at least, she thought so.

"I hope you understand, Miss Greer, that I only want what's best for Loretta."

"Certainly."

"She has written me that she believes Jay is involved with another woman." His voice raised as if asking a question, rather than making a declarative statement.

"When did Loretta first write you about her suspicions?" Dana asked, as she took the cup of coffee from the waitress and pressed it against her lips.

"Only recently but she made it clear that she felt convinced."

Dana planned to play devil's advocate for a while. "Why's that?" she asked.

"He's not been honest with her, leaves at odd times of the night, doesn't return for long periods of time, tells her not to wait up."

"Hmm. Seems those all point to a legitimate suspicion."

"Loretta has not told me who the other woman might be, but I assume she knows and has purposely chosen not to tell me. What I'm asking from you, Miss Greer, is that you tail this guy's ass, find out if Loretta is correct in her assumptions. . ."

The waitress returned before Mr. Amhurst completed his thought. The woman stared at Dana. It was obvious from the waitress's expression that she had hoped to eavesdrop on the conversation. When Amhurst thanked her, she mumbled something under her breath, and walked away.

Dana continued where Amhurst had left off. "And what happens if your daughter is correct, and Jay is involved with another woman?"

"For starters, Loretta takes the train with me back to Aberdeen." He pushed his roll aside as if he suddenly lost his appetite.

"I see. Loretta did tell me that she missed South Dakota."

"She's always loved Aberdeen."

"Then, why did Jay and Loretta decide to come to Cape Peril in the first place?" Dana hoped that she might get Amhurst off guard and, by so doing, he might offer the truth.

"Well, you see," the man said, humming and obviously choosing his words with the utmost care. "Loretta is a quiet girl, always has been, never had very many friends back in Aberdeen. I suggested a new place, a new start, might change all of that." Amhurst sat rigidly against the vinyl booth. Then, he pulled a cigar from the pocket of his coat. "Got a light?"

"No. I don't smoke."

He motioned for the waitress, and she returned with a book of matches marked:

Sip 'n Stay

Where Coffee and Chatting Go Hand-in-Hand

He lit the cigar; a musky, earthy smell filled the booth. He continued. "Loretta, you see, is a perfectionist. That's why she'd make a wonderful homemaker for any man."

Dana nodded. She hoped to give Amhurst enough time to tell the real story behind his daughter, who obviously carried a dark history.

"She fell in love with a local boy who she trusted and admired. He got her pregnant; she lost the child." He raced his statements together like a White sewing machine at full speed, probably hoping that Dana wouldn't interrupt to ask anything specific.

"Sorry to hear that." Dana thought it a perfect time to interject some of her questions about Loretta and Bernadette Godfrey's relationship. Perhaps, Amhurst's answer might help to explain whether Loretta saw the Godfrey child as a replacement for her own or whether she saw the child as an interference in her relationship with Jay. "Mr. Amhurst, did Loretta write you very frequently?"

"Probably a letter a week, I'd say. Why?"

"Did she ever mention anything to you about Bernadette Godfrey, the little girl whose body was recently found on the Cape?" Dana held her pen tightly ready to jot down Amhurst's reply.

"Loretta had written me about how she and Jay had helped a shy child, much like herself, adjust to the Cape and to the Academy."

"Anything in particular you remember her saying about the child?" Dana tapped her index and middle finger on her chin.

"Loretta was never happier than when the child visited their home. My daughter often told me she felt like a mother to the girl. She said the child reminded her of herself."

Interesting. This sounded more as if Loretta bonded with Bernadette, rather than having felt any animosity about having the girl in her home.

"So, she never felt imposed upon?"

Amhurst stiffened in his chair. "Absolutely not." His words staccato-like and sharp, he said, "She loved that little girl as if she were her own."

"Loretta say anything about how she felt when the child was killed?"

Amhurst's face saddened. He held his hand above his lip. His eyes began to glisten, his voice lowered. "She was devastated. She told me she had no reason to live. She wanted to come back to Aberdeen. . .even more so."

Unlike Amhurst's cover-up about Loretta's self-inflicted abortion, Dana believed that he was being truthful to her now, that he told her exactly the way his daughter had felt about Bernadette. Loretta was basically a shy woman, depressed over her own past actions at aborting her child, and welcomed Bernadette into her life as a substitute for the child she would never have. It made sense.

"Loretta lost Bernadette, and now she fears she is losing her husband as well. Is that what you're telling me?"

Amhurst nodded. "You stole the words from me, Miss Greer."

For the time being, Dana ruled out the need to travel to Aberdeen. On the other hand, she was not about to rule anyone out as a possible suspect, not even Loretta.

"Let's get back to Jay. How did Loretta meet her husband?"

"I met Jay through a friend who's a college professor at Northern, where Jay was a student. The professor and I are good friends. Why, he knows enough about Jay to write a book. He told me that he was a fine, young fellow, a bit older than Loretta by ten years. I introduced them, and the rest is history."

"Any chance you could get me some information on Jay?"

"What'd you have in mind?"

"Oh typical things. . .what'd his high school yearbook had to say about him, ever make the news for anything, ever involved with the law, things like that."

"My pleasure, Miss Greer. If I can smear this ass's face in mud, nothing would give me greater pleasure."

"So, do you blame yourself for what happened. . .introducing Jay to Loretta?"

Amhurst thought for a moment. "To a certain extent, I do. Let's just say, I was misguided by my choice."

"Are you saying that Jay was your choice but not Loretta's?"

The man sighed and took a deep breath. "Loretta knew all along that the only way she could get a fresh start would be by leaving the area. I only facilitated that move for her."

Sounded like a strange comment. The way he put it, Loretta didn't have much to say about whether she wanted to marry Jay or not. Her father had decided that for her once he thought he found a good match. Surprised that Amhurst had told her as much as he did, Dana decided to move forward, both hands hugging her coffee cup. "If Loretta leaves to go back to Aberdeen, what will she say to Jay?"

The man arched his back like a cat approaching his prey. "Why, of course, she owes the man no explanation. No, I'll take care of that."

"Meaning?"

"There's an old saying, Miss Greer. Perhaps, you're too young to have heard it. It goes something like, 'No man can ever walk from his foul deeds.'"

Dana didn't like the look in the man's face. His eyebrows suddenly appeared bushier than she had at first noticed; his upper lip raised at the corner, his right eye began to twitch.

"I'm afraid I don't understand. Are you saying you'll take the house away from Jay?"

"For starters, absolutely. Consider it sold."

"Anything else?"

"Well, now. The Cape certainly doesn't need a man of Jay Harrison's caliber."

"What does that mean?" Dana finished the last of her coffee and set the cup down.

"I plan to speak to the pastor. . .Father Sullivan. See to it the man no longer teaches at the Academy. For that matter, that he no longer teaches anywhere. The Sixth Commandment, Miss Greer, 'Thou shalt not commit adultery.'"

There was something about the man's tone of voice, the expression on his face, the way he pointed his cigar at Dana, that made her believe every word he said.

Chapter Thirty

Dana had dinner with the Harrisons, something she hadn't been doing too much of lately, especially, since the tension between Jay and Loretta had seemed to escalate. She usually just made herself a sandwich or a bowl of soup and took it to her room. A restless, uneasy feeling permeated the home, and she chose to remove herself from it as gracefully as she could, whenever she could.

When Loretta, Jay, and Dana had finished the meal of pork roast and red potatoes, the young woman cut a piece of chocolate cake with white sprinkles on it for Dana.

"No, thanks, Loretta. I'm plenty full. Think I'll go to my room and do some reading." A bit of a white lie, Dana knew, but in the end, she hoped it would benefit Loretta.

Loretta stood with the plate in her hands, watching while Jay fumbled around, opening and closing the kitchen drawers. He banged them so hard that the dishes in the cabinet above clanked. Dana had a feeling that Loretta knew what Jay was looking for in the drawers.

"Where you going, Jay?"

"As if it's any of your damn business," Jay responded, a small key in his hand. He reached for his coat, hanging on a wooden hook next to the kitchen door. "Don't wait up." The door slammed, the small panes of glass rattled.

"Loretta," Dana said, "May I. . . ."

Loretta brushed past her, the dish of desert falling onto the floor. The china plate shattered. Loretta never looked back but hurried up the stairs.

Dana suddenly felt torn. She wanted to comfort Loretta, yet she realized that this might be as good a time as any to tail Jay to see if the accusations against him held any truth; furthermore, the woman was in no state of mind for Dana to speak with her. Dana got her coat from the front closet and stepped outside. A foggy night, she could hear the horns blowing in the distance. . .an eerie, lonesome noise, the way Dana assumed Loretta must be feeling. She only wished someone could have told the woman early on that she was making a big mistake to marry Jay, a man who valued money more than relationship. Better still, Dana felt perplexed as to why Loretta's father, a man who supposedly loved his daughter, would succumb to such a scheme to marry her off.

The Cape, where everything was conveniently located, meant it only took ten minutes for Dana to arrive at Holy Name Academy. She hid close to the building in the dark shadows. After a few minutes when Jay hadn't arrived, Dana scurried to the front of the school. She could see a light on in the entrance. She scrunched down close to the ground and peered into the corner of the window. She could see Jay about halfway down the hall, opening the door opposite the chapel. . .the door that Buzz Meechum had pointed out to her. She waited until Jay entered the room. She took a deep breath, opened the front door to the school, and stepped onto the thick black mat with the words:

Welcome to Holy Name Academy

Where God is with Us

Afraid her boots might make too much noise on the tiled floor, she slipped them off and began walking on stocking feet. Although she had spent many years involved in crime scenes, being a private detective was a first for her. Snooping struck her as inappropriate; as if in some way, she was no better than the one being spied on, yet the investigator in her told her she had no choice. It was the only way to prove whether Sister Mary Rose and Jay were indeed having an affair. Only weeks prior the woman had professed her final vows, doing so because of her mother's pressure.

Only inches outside of the closed room, Dana pressed her ear against the door. The sound of cardboard boxes being shuffled around was all she heard at first. Buzz Meechum had told her that it was a storage closet of some kind. Dana pictured a floor polisher, some brooms, a ladder, possibly some cleaning supplies. Certainly, an out-of-the-way place, where one could enter and leave without arousing much suspicion.

Dana listened more intently.

"She knows, Angela. Loretta suspects. . .she's onto us."

"How much longer, Jay?" It was the soft-spoken nun's voice.

"Not yet; now's not the time. It would make things appear too suspicious. Do you want them to think you had something to do with the murder? I mean, think, Angela. If you and I suddenly disappear, what's one to think? For sure, it will put the suspicion of guilt on one of us if not both."

"No, Jay! No! Of course, I don't want that."

"We'll find a time. I promise you but just not yet."

"It's hard, Jay. I feel like I have two faces. I don't like having to be so secretive, so clandestine."

Just then, something fell to the floor, a loud clamor. . .a container of some sort. There was the moving of furniture, scraping noises. Dana could hear rustling; the small noise of static electricity, the sound cloth makes when it is tossed into a pile, the kisses of feverish lust, the whispering of passionate voices, the utterances meant only for lover's ears; then, the rumpus of bodies moving, slipping, sliding against the door.

The accusations, the suspicions confirmed. Dana now had the truth she had come looking for. Surely, Amhurst would take his daughter back to Aberdeen. But what consequences would Jay face, if any? And, equally significant, what would the future hold for Sister Mary Rose?

Chapter Thirty-One

Logan offered Dana a glazed donut from an open box that sat on his desk. She was surprised to find Amhurst seated across from him.

Dana eyed the container from the bakery and chose, instead, a maple-frosted Long John. "Is there any cause for celebration?" she asked, as Logan poured her a cup of coffee and motioned for her to have a seat next to Amhurst.

Logan's cheek was stuffed like a chipmunk's. He pointed toward Amhurst.

"We're anxious to hear your news, Miss Greer. The Sergeant, here, says you usually stop by the station to give him an update." The man's bushy eyebrows shot up like two ragged arches. "So, what did you find out about that scoundrel, Jay?" He tore his sugar donut in half and took a hefty bite.

"I'm afraid I'd have to agree with Loretta. Jay Harrison is involved with another woman."

Amhurst dropped the other part of his donut. He grabbed at the knuckles of his left hand, snapping each and then repeating the ritual several more times. He bit down on his inner lip. "I knew it; I just knew it. I should have known better all along." He pounded his sugary fist into his hand and scowled. "For Christ's sake, who's the woman?"

Logan coughed into his hand.

"I'm not sure that knowing the woman's identity would do you any good, Mr. Amhurst."

The man's face turned a deep red. He sucked his breath in, pursed his lips until the corners of his mouth tightened into a straight slit, and exhaled. "It would if I could break her legs in two, not to mention what I'd like to do to Jay."

"Believe me, I can certainly understand why you're upset, rightfully so, but I ask that you try to be civil about this. Seeking revenge won't be the answer." Dana sipped on her coffee and took a small bite of her donut. She tried to give him the impression that she was composed. If Amhurst knew that Sister Mary Rose was Jay's lover, she knew the man would probably be at the convent's door.

"Why. . . ." Amhurst began to stutter on his words. "I helped that squirrel get established here, helped him find a job. I bought a home overlooking the bay for them. I only wanted Loretta to be happy. That's it! Loretta takes the train with me back to Aberdeen."

Logan spoke up, "Whoa, just wait a minute. I hardly think that's the answer. At least, not now while we're in the middle of a murder investigation."

Amhurst's shot a look at Logan like an arrow headed for a bullseye. "Whatever are you talking about? You don't think Loretta has anything to do with this case do you?"

"I didn't say that, Mr. Amhurst. But what I am saying is that until Miss Greer, here, has a better idea of who the suspects in the case will be, there's no sense anyone leaving, including Loretta, until the investigation is complete. Wouldn't you agree, Dana?"

"Absolutely. It isn't that I'm pointing a finger at anyone but only gathering information. You never know who might know something, no matter how little, that could help crack the case."

The man scowled. "Well, I'll tell you one thing. That house goes on the market, and that two-time gets his ass out of there!" Amhurst got up and headed for the door. He looked back. "Thanks for the roll."

Logan paused and then said, "At least he sees the reasoning behind leaving Loretta on the Cape." He took a gulp of his coffee. "So, Dana, who is the *other* woman?"

Dana got up and shut the door to Logan's office.

Logan edged closer, folding his hands into a steeple.

"Just what Buzz Meechum said. The woman Jay is seeing is Sister Mary Rose."

Logan swallowed, his Adam's apple bulging. He stood up. "My God, no. Not a nun! Whatever is he thinking?" Then, he added, "But I could have guessed."

"What's that supposed to mean?" Dana asked.

"That woman is gorgeous. The thought that she would be locked behind some convent door is almost ludicrous."

"If I hadn't tailed Jay myself, I would have questioned Buzz's lead. But, it's true."

Logan put his hands in the pockets of his uniform and swayed back and forth, biting on his lower lip. "So, the morning the girl went missing. . .where exactly were the two of them?"

"Jay's alibi is that he had forgotten a book and returned home to get it, but no one was around to confirm it."

"Hmm. Another reason why it won't hurt to keep Loretta right here on the island."

"Agreed," Dana said. "I'd have to say that I doubt she is a suspect, but at a bare minimum, there's still the possibility that she might know more than she's saying."

"Think there's a chance the nun and Jay were together on that morning?"

"An interesting thought. As for now, the nun has her own alibi as to where she was the morning Bernadette went missing. She claims she was ill that day and never reported to school."

"Oh, the webs we weave," Logan said, twirling his index finger, making larger and larger circles in the air. Logan rattled on. "No matter what, Amhurst sure isn't going to lose any time in making Jay pay for his adulterous behavior." He grabbed for a second donut.

"And it should prove interesting to see how Father Sullivan deals with the news."

"Help yourself to another," Logan said, glancing at the last three donuts in the box.

"No thanks," Dana said. "I've got a full day ahead of me."

"Where you headed next?"

"Off to see Mrs. Godfrey."

"Thinking she may have a motive, too?" He laughed.

"No just hoping to learn some more as to why Mrs. Artenelli chose the Godfreys as the parents of her grandchild."

"Good girl! Don't leave a rock unturned."

***

It was a mild day on the Cape for mid-November, so Dana decided to take a walk through the park on her way to Mrs. Godfrey's. Bundled toddlers shrieked joyfully as they slid down the slides and flew high into the air as their mothers pushed them on the swings. Two boys wrestled each other on the monkey bars as each tried to make his way to the top. A black Cocker Spaniel puppy, tied to a metal bench, barked at the antics of the children. Such an idyllic setting, so simple, unlike the complicated situation Dana found herself enmeshed in.

Dana found Mrs. Godfrey in the middle of decorating her home for Thanksgiving when the woman welcomed her in. Dana noted the paper turkey, named Byron, the one that Bernadette had made, sitting in a centerpiece the woman had on her dining room table. Sister Mary Rose must have returned the child's artwork to Mrs. Godfrey.

"Please have a seat," Mrs. Godfrey said, pulling out a Queen Anne chair from under a heavily polished table.

They sat across from each other.

As Mrs. Godfrey fingered the red feather on the paper turkey, she asked, "Any closer in solving the case, Miss Greer?" Mrs. Godfrey's face looked drawn and the wrinkles aside her eyes were etched deeply. Long lines outlined the corners of her mouth.

"I can say that I'm not at a loss for suspects these days, but then again, it's not until one is proven to be the murderer of Bernadette that we can all breathe more easily."

"Praise the Lord Jesus."

"I do have a few questions regarding your daughter, Mrs. Godfrey."

"Such as?" The woman continued to run her index finger across the red feather. She hummed the tune "Jesus Loves Me" to herself.

"From what you told me before, Father Sullivan put you in touch with Guardian Angel Orphanage." Dana could see the woman had mentally removed herself from Dana's presence. "Is that true?"

Mrs. Godfrey smiled. "Bernadette is finally at peace, you know."

"I'm sure she is, but could you please just answer my question. Did Father Sullivan give you a contact at Guardian Angels Orphanage?"

"You know, it was all a mistake. I never should have listened to Father. Joe never wanted me to go to the orphanage, but I told him it would be a sin not to obey Father."

"Go on," Dana said, hoping the woman would be more willing to share what she knew.

"Mother Superior, Sister Thomasina, encouraged Joe and me to adopt an older child, rather than a newborn. Joe didn't have any patience, you know. His nerves never would have tolerated a crying baby."

"Makes sense. How did you decide upon which child to adopt?"

"A woman. . .Sharon Little, the adoption coordinator, worked with us. When she learned that we were from St. Michael's Parish in Bay View, the woman said she had a perfect contact for us. Sharon's the one who introduced Joe and me to Mrs. Artenelli. She used to belong to St. Michael's, too."

"I'm afraid you've lost me, Mrs. Godfrey." Dana hated lying; it wasn't her style.

"Sharon put Joe and me in contact with Mrs. Artenelli. We had seen her, of course, at church. She sang in the choir, was a member of the ladies' auxiliary, and occasionally sewed altar cloths, but Joe and I had no idea of her tie-in with the orphanage."

"Tie-in?"

"She's like one of God's angels." Mrs. Godfrey smiled. "She does so many wonderful things. She helps support the orphanage, too. When Sharon told her we were from St. Michael's parish and wanted to adopt an older child, Mrs. Artenelli said she knew the perfect child. . .and perfect she was, my sweet baby; that is until. . . ." The woman began to weep, chewing on her thumb, her lips trembling.

Dana got up and put her arms around her. "I know this must be terribly difficult to talk about, Mrs. Godfrey. There really is only one other question I have for you."

In between sniffling and dabbing at her nose, Mrs. Godfrey looked at Dana, her eyes brimming with more tears.

"How did Mrs. Artenelli happen to know the child that you adopted? I mean, she didn't work at the orphanage, did she?"

"No. . .why. . .I guess, I never thought of that."

***

When Dana arrived back at the Harrison home, a middle-aged woman with her hair in a French Twist, who was carrying a tattered briefcase, was just on her way out the door. They nodded to each other.

Loretta was sitting at the kitchen table, a pile of printed documents in front of her. At her side sat Amhurst.

"Ah, we meet again, Miss Greer. Did you happen to see the realtor on your way in?"

"Oh, I wondered who the woman was."

"I'm helping Loretta fill out these forms. The house goes on the market first thing tomorrow," he said, a large grin on his face.

Dana was amazed that Amhurst had worked that quickly to not only find a realtor but to also list the house for sale. Dana wondered what Jay's fate would be with the quick decision making. "What about Mr. Harrison? Will he stay until the house is sold?"

"For God's sake no! He stopped at the house this morning, packed, and got the last of his things. Once Father Sullivan learns of this scandal, he'll have to find a substitute to take Jay's place. In the meantime, he'll be living at the Sea Cliff Motel near the entrance to the ferry."

Just as Dana thought. Amhurst was a man of his word. She excused herself and went upstairs.

In only days, Jay Harrison was found to be conducting an illicit affair with Sister Mary Rose and, as a result, lost his wife and home. And, in only days, Dana learned that Mrs. Artenelli was directly involved in the adoption proceedings of Sister Mary Rose's child. Dana had to admit that she felt more reassured than ever that Mrs. Artenelli not only had complete custody of Sister Mary Rose's child, but that she had deliberately chosen the Godfreys as the adoptive family. It made sense that Mrs. Artenelli would want to be close to the child both in proximity and as the grandmother that she was. Not only had she assisted with the Holy Name Academy tuition, but she also found Doctor Polly Thatcher to work with the child in helping her adapt to her new surroundings on the Cape. It also explained why she had chosen to pay off Tanner and McGregor, so as to keep the news of the child's sexual abuse out of the paper. But there was one thing Dana wasn't that sure about. She wondered just how well Mrs. Artenelli and Mrs. Godfrey knew each other. Could it be that they were more than past parishioners of the same parish? There was something about the way Mrs. Godfrey spoke about Mrs. Artenelli. . .almost too admiringly that made Dana feel uneasy.

Chapter Thirty-Two

Dana Greer, please," the caller said, a sound of urgency in his voice.

"This is she," Dana said.

"This is Gino Artenelli, Carmelina's husband. I'm sorry to bother you, but my wife. . .well, she's locked herself in her room. She keeps screaming, 'He's going to kill me!' Do you have any idea what this might be about? She has some kind of letter in her hands."

Dana quickly began to put two-and-two together and wondered whether the woman might have heard from Eddie Vineeti yet again, but this time, it sounded as if his threats might have gone too far. "Mr. Artenelli, is it possible that I can speak with your wife?"

"She won't speak to anyone, not even our maid."

"I'd like to try. I have a feeling I may know what this is about," Dana said. "Might I stop over to see her?"

"Please, please do. We live on the Pointe, two-fifty Overlook Drive."

Dana hung up and called a cab. If all of her speculations about Angela Artenelli and Eddie Vineeti being blood relatives and possibly conceiving a child together were correct, Dana could only surmise what the letter Mrs. Artenelli had received must have said.

***

The Cape was shaped like a child's drawing of a boot. The Pointe was located at the northern-most tip of the island, about two miles from the Harrisons'.

A long, black asphalt drive round its way like a thick snake up to the front door of the Artenellis' home, a white brick mansion with Doric columns and forest-green shutters.

"Mr. Artenelli's been expectin' you," the maid said, greeting Dana at the door. She led her toward the rear of the home, where floor-to-ceiling windows showcased the ocean, which in the early morning autumn sun looked like shining crystals rolling in and out. The gold-painted walls were covered on all sides by several heads of wild game. An RCA Victrola played soft classical music in the background.

Gino Artenelli jumped when Dana and the maid entered. He rose from a zebra-striped sofa, a cocktail in his hand. "Miss Greer, pleased that you have come so quickly." He motioned toward the maid. "Can Lydel get you anything to drink?"

"No, thank you."

The maid curtsied and left the room.

Gino set his drink on a glass coffee table, its legs that of a taxidermied chimpanzee lying on its back with its appendages supporting the weight of the table.

Dana glanced around the room. Elephants, rhinos, and leopards stared back at her.

"My wild game collection," he said, "I shoot in India and Africa." In the same breath, he said, "My wife. . .I've never seen her this upset. Like I said, all she keeps repeating is something about a letter and someone trying to kill her." Under his breath, he muttered, "Let me get my hands on this jerk."

Dana assumed Carmelina must not have told her husband about the prior letter that she had received from Eddie, asking for money. "Where is your wife, Mr. Artenelli?"

"She's locked herself in the master bedroom. Here, follow me."

Gino led Dana down a side, inconspicuous hall, where the two of them got into an elevator.

"She's in here. She's got the door locked. Carmelina, you have a visitor. Please, open the door."

"Go away! Please, just go away!"

"Carmelina, Miss Greer is here with me. She says she may be able to help. She may know what this is all about."

Seconds later, the two of them heard a light click as the door opened a crack.

"You, you go speak to her. See what you can find out," Gino said.

Dana gently pushed her way inside. She could hear noises coming from the adjoining bath. When she knocked and received no answer, she opened the door to find Carmelina, her head hung low over the toilet, retching. Her face pale, sweaty, and her normally long, black hair pulled into a tight bun on the top of her head. She was still in her nightgown and next to her on the black, marble floor lay an open vial of pills and a razor.

"My God in heaven. It can't be," Carmelina cried out. "He'll kill me!"

Dana helped the woman's unsteady body over to the chair next to her bed.

"Carmelina, have you taken any of these pills?"

The woman continued to shake her head.

"Are you sure?"

"No."

Dana carefully looked at the woman's white wrists, which revealed no evidence that she had tried to use the razor's blade on them.

"I wanted to. . .I wanted to end this nightmare, but God would condemn me to Hell." Carmelina looked upward at the twenty-foot ceiling as if expecting the plaster to break open and a voice to declare that she was still His beloved.

"Carmelina, your husband told me that you are upset over a letter you received. Might I see it?"

"It's over there, on the dresser, under the mirror."

A mother-of-pearl brush, a handheld mirror inlaid with ivory and ebony chips, and three atomizers of perfume lay on the lace-covered bureau. Next to the items lay an envelope addressed to Carmelina. Dana took the letter out and read:

I don't know how to say this. Where do I begin? I ain't much for writin'. I know you never cared for me and hated me for gettin' Angela pregnant and all. We were in love. I still love Angela with all my heart. I understand why you never wanted me to have nothin' to do with Angela right from the start. I don't come from much, never was lucky enough to have a life like Angela. My father was nothin' but a drunk, and my mother a run-around who did drugs. But, hell, they tried to give me a home, took me in as one of their own. After that detective lady came snoopin' around here askin' me questions and tellin' me she was involved with some damn orphanage in Waterville, I did some investigatin' of my own. I needed to know where I came from. My mother finally broke down and told me everything. I don't know how better to say this, Mrs. Artenelli, but you're one frickin' liar and hypocrite! You forced Angela to the nunnery, wouldn't let us marry, took control of our kid, when all along you were no better than the rest of us. May 10, 1928. . .does that day mean anything to you? How about December 3, 1932. . .does that day mean anything to you? A son, a daughter. . .who fell in love never knowin' that my roots came from the same tree.

Your son,

Eddie

Inside the envelope, Dana found an official copy of Eddie Vineeti's birth certificate, dated May 10, 1928, and naming Carmelina Artenelli and Gino Artenelli as the parents. Just as Dana had suspected, Eddie was the son Carmelina had out of wedlock. Once she had delivered the child at the Holy Angel Orphanage, she thought her secret was behind her. Little did she know that it would surface years later.

"I can understand why you're shocked by this news, Carmelina. Who wouldn't be? Someone from your past suddenly reappears, and. . . ."

Carmelina inhaled, her face stiffened. "What are you talking about?"

"Eddie, your son."

"Don't tell me you're foolish enough to fall for these accusations. Are you telling me that you believe what this scoundrel has manufactured?"

Dana swallowed hard and moistened her lips. "You're saying Eddie made this all up, that these are all lies?" Dana could not believe what she was hearing.

Carmelina's dark brows hovered over her eyes. "What kind of person do you think I am, Dana? Some kind of slut?" She paused for a moment and an icy stare covered her face. "Don't you see, Dana, this monster will go as far as he needs to, to extort me, and if I don't give him what he wants. . .well, he'll kill me." Carmelina burst into tears.

Dana quickly reread Eddie's letter. "But there is no mention about money or even a threat in this letter."

"It'll only be a matter of time before he spreads this nonsense around the Cape, trying to ruin the Artenelli name. Don't you see? He's out to destroy our family, and he'll do whatever it takes." Carmelina looked down and thought for a moment. "Even if it means murder."

Dana was at a loss for words. She could not believe the woman would outright lie to her when based upon all that she had learned both from Buzz Meechum and his mother, the facts stacked up that Eddie Vineeti, born on May 10, 1928, was the son that Carmelina had delivered at the Holy Angel Orphanage, only to be put up for adoption. Even Eddie had the exact date in his letter.

In between her sobs, Carmelina kept repeating, "He'll kill me."

Dana bent down and put her arm around the woman. "Carmelina, have you ever considered speaking to Eddie yourself?"

Carmelina stiffened and sat upright in her chair. Through her tears and the black strands of hair that had fallen across her cheeks, she looked at Dana and said, "Never!"

Dana needed to get a reaction from the woman. "What I mean is, if you think this man has made a mistake and claims to be your son. . . ."

"There's one thing that is certain. The man is insane, crazy, and who knows what he is capable of?" She wiped the last of her tears off her face and stared long and hard at Dana. "There's only one solution to this problem. My husband will know what to do."

Dana realized there was no more that she could say. It was clear the woman was in a state of denial, and once she had been able to clear her mind of emotions, she resorted to her husband for putting an end to what she referred to as Eddie's lies. Dana placed the letter in her coat pocket and left. She couldn't wait to show Logan the proof that Eddie Vineeti was the son that Carmelina had put up for adoption over twenty years ago.

***

Logan's secretary, Janet, was flipping through the pages of an August issue of *Photoplay*. Esther Williams graced the cover in a vibrant purple dress with fresh lilacs gracing her neckline. The office clerk peered up from the edges of the magazine and with a yawn said, "He's with someone."

"Oh, do you know how long he'll be?" Dana asked.

"Would you like a magazine?" the girl said, as she pointed to a stack of outdated *Photoplays* on the corner of her desk.

Dana grabbed a July issue, one with Betty Grable on the cover, sat down on the bench outside of Logan's office, and began to read 'Betty Hutton's Wonderful Love Story.' After about ten minutes, Logan's door opened, and Amhurst stepped out. The man's face reddened, his lips in a scowl, it was evident that he was more than irritated.

"I was just telling Logan that I stopped in the rectory to see the Father Sullivan."

Dana motioned for the man to step outside. The receptionist pursed her lips and continued to flip through the pages of the magazines on her desk, pretending to be occupied. Amhurst understood and opened the door to the station. The two huddled close to the building to avoid the blustery winds.

"He accused me of being too quick to judge Jay. Why, he quoted something from the Bible," Amhurst said.

"Let us not judge, lest we be judged," Dana said.

"Yeah, yeah, something like that. Sullivan told me that he'd known Jay for five years, ever since he arrived on the Cape, and was not about to let some gossip soil his reputation."

"But it's not gossip," Dana said.

"I told the man I had proof."

"And?"

"He said he'd have no part in this blasphemy. He began to ramble on about Jay being an outstanding teacher and a man of high morals. Why, he even hinted that Loretta might be delusional! Can you believe this?"

Dana didn't comment. Loretta was hardly delusional. Nervous, depressed, yes, but not delusional.

"I said, 'Father, are you telling me that you have no intention of even investigating the matter?'"

"What was his answer?"

"He just said that my request was foolhardy and that he'd do nothing of the kind." In an exasperated voice, Amhurst said, "The priest's a fool. I don't care whether he is a man of the cloth or not."

"What do you plan to do, Mr. Amhurst?"

"We need more definite proof. Something less circumstantial and more concrete."

"What are you suggesting?" Dana asked.

"A tape recording, photographs, some evidence. . .for starters."

Trying to solve a murder case, going over motives and means, not to mention potential suspects seemed to fill Dana's cup to overflowing. "Any chance you might be willing to help. . . with the evidence, that is?" Dana asked Mr. Amhurst..

"I'm staying at the Cape Peril Inn. Why don't we meet at the 'Second Mate' right across the street from the hotel. Let's say, at one o'clock?"

"Looks as if Father Sullivan isn't going to budge that easily."

"We'll make a believer out of him yet."

Dana was afraid that she didn't feel as optimistic as Amhurst.

She stepped back inside the station and found Janet busy typing. She paused and looked up at Dana. "I'm writing a letter to Tab Hunter. Isn't he just the coolest cat you've ever seen?"

Dana didn't bother to answer but, instead, knocked on Logan's door.

"C'mon in," he said. Before Dana had a chance to sit down, Logan filled her in on his visit with Amhurst. "Seems the guy's pretty damn hot under the collar. He's bound and determined to prove Jay's involved with another woman."

"So he says. Not sure what it will take for Father Sullivan to finally believe, and wait until he learns that one of his own, Sister Mary Rose, is the other side of the denominator."

Logan nodded.

"And speaking of not wanting to believe, I just came from Mrs. Artenelli's place. Gino called me, saying his wife was hysterical, claiming someone wanted to kill her."

"What? What's this all about?"

Dana showed Logan the letter from Eddie.

"Ah hah! So, Buzz and his dear ol' mom were right on about Carmelina's unwanted pregnancy."

"It gets worse, though. Carmelina is in a state of denial. She's calling Eddie Vineeti a liar and threatening to get Gino's boys involved."

Logan scratched the hairs on the top of his head. "Doesn't surprise me in the least. The Artenellis will go to whatever measure they need to in order to keep their name from being tarnished."

Chapter Thirty-Three

During the night, mother nature had covered everything in sight with a white blanket at least a foot deep, so what better day Dana decided, to stay inside. And, furthermore, she needed some time to sort through all that had been happening since her arrival on the Cape. She opened her desk drawer and found the photographs she had taken of Bernadette Godfrey and the burial site. One by one, she loosely taped them to the lid of the roll-top as she focused on each. She pulled out a piece of yellow lined paper and began to write down what she remembered about the crime scene.

The grave site had been meticulously dug, almost as if a tape measure had been used to gauge just the right size for a small body, yet whoever had prepared the shallow grave obviously had not tried to hide the body. No, someone was hoping the girl's corpse would be found and, quite possibly, before it had a chance to decompose or be eaten by wildlife. Whoever had prepared the site used precise care to dig away any weeds, long grasses, or pine branches that were part of the natural landscape. Then the body was covered, not with a soiled piece of burlap or a blue tarp, but with a clean white cloth.

Dana went down to the kitchen and found a piece of cheddar cheese in the ice box. While nibbling on it, she thought about what Logan had said earlier about Tanner's handling of the sheet. The sergeant questioned whether or not Tanner had gotten rid of the cloth that had covered Bernadette's lifeless body. Now Dana asked herself the same question: *Had he?* Dana had seen firsthand Tanner's casual attitude toward evidence in the way he had destroyed the Tarot card that had been found with Bernadette's body, saying it was just mumbo-jumbo. If lucky, Tanner might have stored the cloth somewhere. She decided to give him a call.

"Tanner speaking here."

"Red, it's Dana."

Before she said anymore, he said, "Let me guess. You've figured out who the murderer is."

"Wish that were the case but actually, I'm still working on it, which brings me to the reason for my call. By chance, did you happen to keep the cloth that was covering the body of Bernadette Godfrey?" She expected the man to hem and haw and then to say, "No."

"Actually, I do think I've got it around here somewhere. Hold on one second."

Dana heard the man whistling a jingle from the hair tonic Brylcreem, then bursting into song, something about a little dab'll do ya. She heard doors opening and slamming shut.

"The thing was so soaked with blood that I let it dry out in an upper cabinet. Yeah, got it right here. . .nice and stiff."

Dana tried to remain calm in the midst of the man's ignorance, telling herself he was a coroner, not an investigator, but even then, she was dumbfounded that the man could have been so careless with a key piece of evidence. "Red, can you tell if the cloth is a bed sheet, a tablecloth?"

"Let me check." When he came back on the phone, he said, "Yeah, it's a sheet alright. Not too big. . .looks like it would have fit a twin bed."

"Any labels on it, brand names?' Dana waited, trying not to reveal her lack of patience.

"Nope, doesn't appear to be any that I can see," Tanner said.

A dead end, Dana thought. She thanked Tanner and hung up the phone. She focused on the photographs once again. The girl looked to be no more than forty-five pounds, slightly smaller than average for her age Dana guessed. The child had been stabbed in the chest, not once but multiple times in what looked to be a frenzy, out-of-control act, an overkill. The girl's blouse was intact with only one button missing at the neck. Still wearing the blue-and-green plaid uniform of Holy Name Academy, the child looked tidy, aside from the gruesome dried blood stains and one missing white anklet and a saddle shoe. By her side lay her navy-blue school bag buckled shut. Dana recalled Bernadette's missing shoe had remnants of wet grass and broken pine needles on it. She believed the girl must have willingly walked to her own grave. Whoever anonymously wrapped and sent the saddle oxford to the station had to have known that one of the child's shoes was missing as none of this information was published in the local paper. Dana wondered whether the murderer might either have been feeling guilty for the deed or had hopes of being caught. She jotted down some additional questions:

- *How long would it have taken to prepare the grave? Was this a premeditated murder, preparing the site in advance of the kill?*
- *Who might be tidy and a perfectionist, wanting everything just so, complete to readying the grave?*

- *Why would someone cover the child in a clean cloth? Was it a last act of kindness on the part of the murderer?*

Dana made herself a note to call Red Tanner in the next day or two. Knowing Tanner the way she did, she wondered if he might have overlooked a small tag.

- *Might the child have known who her killer was? Might it have been someone the child trusted and went with willingly?*
- *Did whoever sent the shoe want to feel in some sick way that the body was now intact, that the child could go on to the next world in her complete uniform? If not, why wouldn't the person have just destroyed the shoe?*

Dana reminded herself that she must also pay a visit to Opal. There was still something unsettling about the High Priestess Tarot card, the one Tanner had found with the body and had destroyed. Dana studied the photos some more and then carefully pulled them off the desk and placed them back in the drawer. She'd see if she could bounce her questions off Logan but not until she took a cat nap. She could feel one of her migraines coming on, and she had found over the years that the best way of warding them off was to get some sleep before the pain had a chance to escalate. She fell into a light sleep and saw herself crossing and re-crossing things off a list that had been carved into a stone tablet; then she'd start the ritual all over again. Unexpectedly, the rock on which she had been writing fell to the floor with a loud bang; she woke up startled only to realize that someone was banging on the front door. Dana hurried down the stairs, but when she opened the door and looked out, all she could see were deeply formed holes in the snow in front of the house.

Across the street a black Oldsmobile was parked, but she couldn't make out if anyone was behind the wheel, nor could she see the license plate number. At her feet, on the concrete stoop, a package lay wrapped in brown butcher paper and tied with a piece of twine. It was addressed to Dana, but it had no return information on it.

She brought the box into the kitchen and carefully cut it open with a pair of scissors. Several photographs fell onto the table, scattered like cards in a deck. She held up one of the black-and-white pictures. Bernadette Godfrey and Father Sullivan were in a field, where the priest held a small daisy beneath the girl's nose. Her chin was propped in the priest's cupped hand. The second photograph showed the two of them outside a church, which Dana assumed might be St. Michael's in Bay View, where he had been pastor. The third showed them at a table, eating a meal together, Father putting a small morsel of food into the girl's mouth. The fourth photo displayed Bernadette in her school uniform, standing with Father in front of Holy Name Academy, his arm around her shoulders. When Dana picked up the last of the photos, her jaw dropped as she gazed at Father Sullivan in swim trunks and a striped T-shirt and Bernadette in a polka-dot swimsuit, tossing a red and blue beach ball, by the shore. The last photo, also at the water's edge, showed Father and Bernadette building a sand castle.

The poem, the one Bernadette had written and that had been found with her body, resounded in Dana's mind:

I love the sea.
Its waves calm me.
I love the sea.
It's here

he waits for me.

Could it be that she had been writing about Father Sullivan? Dana sat motionless, an utter shock immobilizing her. Then, she began to fumble through the box. She had hoped to find a letter, a note, an explanation as to who sent the photographs, but there was nothing. Joe Godfrey confessed to abusing his adoptive daughter, but might he not have been the only one to abuse the child?

Recalling an earlier conversation Dana had with Father when she had asked him how well he knew Bernadette, he had responded with, 'Oh, come on, Miss Greer, we all have our favorites now, don't we?' But how much of a favorite was she? From the photographs on the table, it was quite obvious that Father had felt closer to the Godfrey child than most other children at the Academy.

But, then again, Dana recalled how Father Sullivan had stood in the shadows in the vestibule of Holy Name Church that day the young brides of Christ had exited the ceremony. He never approached Sister Mary Rose to congratulate her, yet he looked infatuated with her, eying her from the distance. Dana still thought it odd that Father had a photograph of the nun on his desk. Days ago when she spoke with him, he had said, 'Sister was a student of mine while in the novitiate, a prized student, as well.'

The more Dana thought about it, she wondered if someone was trying to set the priest up for murder. She took a deep breath and put a pot of coffee on the stove, as she nursed a dull ache, lingering from her migraine. She ran her fingers under the faucet and let the cold water drip over the back of her neck. Her thoughts ran wild like a locomotive out of control. She poured the steaming coffee into a china cup and sat at the table. Snowflakes fell from a steel-colored sky, and the howling of winds shook the bare tree branches. She shivered at the view, gripping her hands around the hot cup. She cleared her throat and placed her hand on her chest. She could feel her heart pounding.

Dana glanced at the photos in the box one more time. Even if someone was trying to set the priest up for murder, Dana had to admit that Bernadette and Father Sullivan did appear very comfortable with each other, considering the child had been described by the Mother Superior at Holy Angel Orphanage as being quite shy.

Dana returned the pictures to their box and remembered that as much as she wanted to stay inside that she had agreed to meet Amhurst at the Second Mate at one o'clock.

***

The smell of malt vinegar permeated the air along with the scent of salty fries. At lunch time, the Second Mate always had a full house. Dana squinted as she quickly scanned the restaurant for Amhurst; she was five minutes late. As she came through the crowds of people standing around the bar, Amhurst appeared, dressed casually in a pair of wide-whaled corduroys, a brown sweater vest, and yellow broadcloth shirt, and motioned her to his table.

"What will you have, Dana? It's my treat."

She quickly looked over the one page menu that was covered in spots of grease. "I'll have the salmon sandwich, please, with a cup of coffee."

"That it will be," he said, as he motioned for a waiter to take their order. "Got some great news for you, Dana."

"I could sure use some of that."

"I've found a way to outsmart Father Sullivan. I've found a camera. . .one with a timer. . .that will take photographs along with a tape recorder that'll do the same. You just tell me where the scoundrel sets up his shop, and we'll catch him in the act."

"There's nothing like proof to get a nonbeliever to see the light."

"Agreed. If this priest can't believe what he sees with his own eyes, nothing will convince him."

Dana did have one worry, though, that she could not broach with Amhurst. Once his photographs were developed, he would find out that Sister Mary Rose was Jay's lover. She couldn't allow herself to think what that might mean.

The waiter came to the table with their orders, and for a few moments, they enjoyed their sandwiches and drinks without conversation. The timing could not have been better as Dana hoped Amhurst wouldn't confront her as to who Jay's secret lover was.

"I do have some more news for you. Remember, my professor friend. . .the one who introduced me to Jay Harrison?"

"Yes, of course."

"Sounds as if Jay is not new to this lowlife existence."

"Oh?"

"He's been a lady's man ever since his college days. From what my friend tells me, Jay can't keep his hands off the ladies."

A handsome man. . .Jay. It didn't surprise Dana that he would be the type to have women around him.

"There's more. Jay was president of his fraternity—Phi Sigma Nu—and was arrested for some immoral act that he and a number of his fraternity brothers were involved in. Had something to do with pledges."

"Any more details on that?"

"Best I could find out, it caused Jay to be thrown on his ass by the fraternity and to be put on suspension from school for a semester." Amhurst's eyes narrowed, and he scratched at the side of his nose. "I should have guessed the guy was bad news when he accepted. . . ."

Amhurst chose not to complete his thought, but it was easy enough for Dana to fill in his missing words: 'I should have guessed the guy was bad news when he accepted a bribe from me to marry my daughter.'

"Sure sounds like Jay has a trail of bad deeds," Dana said.

"And I'm just about to hang his skinny neck out to dry. When I go public, which is what I intend to do, Jay Harrison will be history."

As before, there was something about the intensity of Amhurst's voice that almost frightened Dana.

He motioned the waiter for the bill, and said, "Now, when can we plan to set up my equipment?"

Chapter Thirty-Four

According to the weather forecaster at WXYZ, the radio station in Bay View, a major winter storm was headed toward Cape Peril due to hit by noon. By the look of the black clouds overhead, Dana wondered if the snow might not arrive earlier than anticipated. She braced the box of photos under her crossed arms and hurried toward the station. The wind whistled like a lone train in the distance, and the overheard bare tree branches swayed wildly as if ready to snap.

As usual, Dana was greeted by Janet who actually seemed to be busy this morning with more than her outlandish antics. She looked up from her typewriter. "Got a gift for Logan?"

"Not exactly," Dana said.

"Have a seat. He's got Mrs. Artenelli in with him. Man alive, she looked like she just saw a ghost. You know, the woman is usually such a fashion plate. Why, I've never seen her look so bad." Janet edged over her typewriter. The top of her red brassier inched out of her black blouse. "Might you know what's going on with the woman, Dana?"

"I assume that must be between the Sergeant and her."

Janet went back to her typing, cussing over a typo she had made.

After about ten minutes, Logan's door opened, and Mrs. Artenelli stepped out. Her face looked flushed and her eye makeup smeared.

"Carmelina," Dana said, "is everything okay?"

Janet quit typing and glanced upward at the woman, her jaw dropped.

Carmelina motioned for Dana to come closer and in a whispered voice said, "No, dear, it isn't. It's Eddie." Her voice rose and fell like the octaves on a sheet of music. "I've gotten another letter. . . ..more threatening."

"I was afraid of that," Dana said.

"He's asking for more money, thousands."

"You don't intend to pay him, do you?"

"Not a cent, dear, but now he claims that if he doesn't receive the money delivered by tomorrow, that he will. . . ." The woman grabbed a lace handkerchief from the pocket of her leopard coat.

"What did Sergeant Logan suggest you do, Carmelina?"

"He says that this is the last straw. He's threatening my life if I don't comply. The Sergeant says it is enough ground to arrest the man."

Dana noted that the woman still refused to refer to Eddie as her son. "I'm so glad the Sergeant plans to take action. Eddie Vineeti runs on a loose fuse, that's for sure."

Mrs. Artenelli attempted a smile, left the station, and got into a waiting black Oldsmobile.

Dana tapped on Logan's door, and before she had a chance to even sit down, Logan said, "I know. I know. You told me so. I should have listened."

Dana only nodded.

"I've got Officer Boyle issuing a warrant for Eddie Vineeti's arrest as we speak."

"Wonderful," was all Dana said.

"Let's get on to more important things," Logan said, a slight chuckling sound under his breath.

Dana opened the box with the photographs of Father Sullivan and set them on Logan's desk. "What are your thoughts about *these*? They came in the mail with no return address." She watched Logan pick up each picture and eye it for a few seconds.

"Holy God! I mean, Father Sullivan at the beach with the young girl? How out of character for a priest." Logan put both hands on his face and spread his fingers widely. He shook his head.

"These things do happen, Logan, as much as we'd like to think otherwise. But as you've told me before, we shouldn't jump the gun. There could be an explanation for these, and it could be all innocent."

As Logan scanned the remainder of the photos once again, he asked, "Where was Father the morning the Godfrey girl went missing?" he asked.

"Saying the eight a.m. Mass for the school children."

"Hmm."

"But I'm beginning to think the time frame I've been going with.
. .the time that Bernadette left for school that morning and the time she never showed up at school, approximately fifteen minutes, may not be the one I should be working from."

Logan twirled his index finger in his left ear.

"If the child went with someone she knew and went willingly, it doesn't naturally have to follow that the girl was murdered during that time, does it?"

"I hear you."

"Going on the premise that the girl was captured, she may or may not have been kept against her will."

"I get the drift, though, speak to the ears of the deaf monkey if you will."

"What if Bernadette was preoccupied doing something for her murderer during this time. . .something that would have kept her from attending morning Mass?"

"Now, here's an interesting theory. Go on," Logan said, rubbing the edge of his nose.

"It could be anything, Logan. Maybe she was asked to help with some task. I don't know."

"And Tanner. What does he say about the time of death?"

"According to temperatures drawn on the environment, where the body was found, and Bernadette's temperature, Tanner feels convinced that the body was probably in its grave for only several hours, at most."

"That would account for approximately the time McGregor found the body while he was out hunting, right?"

"Precisely."

Dana could hear Logan's shoe tapping under his desk. "I remember you commenting earlier on the condition of the grave."

Dana pulled the notes she had made only days ago out of her satchel. "That's exactly where I was headed."

"The perfect grave site," Logan said.

"Exactly." Dana glanced at the questions she had formulated and read from the list. "How long would it have taken to prepare the grave? Was this a premeditated murder, preparing the site in advance of the kill?"

"Impressive, Dana. You're shooting for a strike. Who might have had the time to arrange the burial site? From what I recall, the grave was shallow yet tidy."

These were the times in Dana's job when she felt most excited. It usually happened this way. . .slowly to begin with, but after reassessing the facts, new insights surfaced like digging shells out of the sand.

"That leads to my second point. Whoever planned the murder and took great pains to cultivate the grave in such a meticulous fashion had to be someone who was a perfectionist, complete to covering the body with a clean, white cloth."

"That is odd about the covering over the body. Oftentimes, a murderer will do this so as to symbolically hide his guilt. But a white cloth? It doesn't make sense."

"I spoke with Tanner. Seems he kept the cloth but was unable to find any labels on it—only said it was a sheet, probably a twin size."

"If you can find out where it was manufactured, you could be onto something." Logan pulled at his lower lip with his thumb and index finger. "I've going to meet Officer O'Neil for lunch. Feel free to stay and use my phone if you'd like."

The thought of not having to call from a phone booth on a blustery, cold day nor having to return to the Harrisons' home appealed to her. "Think I'll do just that. Thanks. I'll keep you posted if I find out anything."

Logan stood up and tapped her on the arm, mumbling to himself, "Grave is prepared ahead of time; child is kidnapped and preoccupied until time of murder." His voice ended on a high note as if he were struggling to complete his sentence.

Dana continued Logan's chain of thought. "The wounds left in the child's chest, multiple stab wounds. . .whoever murdered the child, frantically and continually stabbed at her. Was the murderer in a mad frenzy, out-of-control, maybe even facing temporary insanity? Who from the list of possible suspects was known to be fond of the child? Dana jotted the names into her notebook yet one more time:

Jay Harrison
Carmelina Artenelli
Father Sullivan
Sister Mary Rose

The thoughts pelted through her mind like hail on a thunderous day.

Jay Harrison would certainly fall under the category of an organized man, being a teacher. But was he a perfectionist? Carmelina Artenelli certainly was a fashion statement who took great care and emphasis with her appearance and could easily be seen as a woman who paid attention to the finer details in life. As for Father Sullivan, Dana really didn't feel she knew the man well enough to determine just how much a perfectionist he was. Sister Mary Rose, a teacher like Jay, would also be organized. Could any of these suspects have entertained the child before murdering her? All of the names on Dana's list would be people Bernadette knew well, and she would have gone with any of them willingly. This would go along with the fact that all of these individuals had an alibi as to where they were at the time the girl went missing. She scribbled into her notebook:

Jay claimed to have returned to his home to look for a forgotten book.

But with no witnesses, who was to say where Jay had gone the morning that Bernadette disappeared on her way to school?

Carmelina Artenelli claimed to have been at eight a.m. Mass.

Dana had already asked Father Sullivan to verify this fact. He claimed that the woman came to morning Mass daily and that he supposed she was there the morning the Godfrey child had disappeared.

Father Sullivan was celebrating the eight a.m. Mass.

Certainly that would be a given as the children of Holy Name Academy attended Mass each morning before school.

Sister Mary Rose claimed to have been ill that day and had a substitute teacher filling in for her.

Dana wrote herself a note to find out from the principal who the substitute was that filled-in for Sister that morning. If the nun was not in school that day, the other sisters at the convent should have been able to substantiate Sister Mary Rose's presence.

Dana looked at Jay's name again. It struck her as odd that Father Sullivan was so careful to protect the man's image. What was it about Jay that made Father Sullivan so unwilling to accept the accusation of Jay's affair? Could it be that he couldn't get himself to believe something so inconceivable, or was it more than that? Dana thought about the mysterious photographs she had seen of Father. Could it be that each of the men was covering for the other. . .a scheme to conceal the sins of the other? And as for Sister Mary Rose, a nun who had only recently professed her final vows, might she have hoped to hide the fact from Jay that she had borne a child out of wedlock? Then, too, would Mrs. Artenelli have tried to cover her own daughter's mistake by murdering the child? There were still missing links. It wasn't time for Dana to count her chickens just yet.

Dana picked up the phone on Logan's desk and dialed Tanner. The phone only rang once before he picked it up. "Red Tanner, coroner," he said.

"Tanner, it's Greer."

"Your ears must have been burning. I was just going to give you a call."

"Oh?"

"Looked over that sheet one more time. Found a tag on it."

"Just give me the name, please."

"Made in the U.S.A. by Ladybug."

"That's what I need," Dana said, and hung up the phone. Now she'd have to figure out a way to inquire about each of the suspect's taste in linens. But first things first, she needed to see Father Sullivan's reaction to the box of mysterious photographs.

***

It was one thing to confess one's sins to a priest but quite another to ask a priest to confess his. Dana sat in the waiting room of the rectory, feeling much the same way she did while waiting for a dentist appointment, restless and anxious.

The elderly caretaker asked if she could get her something to drink, but Dana refused. Instead, she toyed with her black leather gloves, wrapping them in-and-out of her fingers as though weaving a pot holder. In her lap lay the large package containing the photos that had been anonymously placed on the front door stoop. Dana had no idea how she would broach the subject with Father Sullivan. She kept reminding herself that to question the priest was in no way any different than to question anyone else about the case, yet she knew that this would be probably be one of the most difficult challenges she had to face. She needed to be non-accusatory, non-threatening. The photographs were nothing more than pictures of the priest with Bernadette Godfrey. They could be purely innocent, after all.

"Father will see you now," the caretaker said, while she rearranged her gray hairnet.

The priest stood, shook Dana's hand, and asked her to be seated.

Dana could tell he was in the process of putting the weekly church bulletin together as small pictures of chalices, crosses, and circular hosts lay next to a bottle of glue as well as a sheet of advertisers who supported the newsletter.

"Just about ready to send this off to the printer. Most pastors have a committee to do this sort of work, but I rather enjoy doing it myself."

Dana smiled.

"But this can wait. Your time is valuable, too, I'm sure," he said, as he pushed his work to the side of his desk.

Dana continued to smile and as her mother used to often accuse her, she felt like the cat had her tongue.

The priest lifted his chin and brought it down with a nod. "Now, is there something I can help you with, Miss Greer?"

Dana's hands moist and clammy, not to mention trembling slightly, she handed the package wrapped in twine to the priest. "It's this," she said.

"Why, let's have a look, why don't we," he said, in a pleasant, uplifting voice. In only minutes, his expression of surprise turned instantly to one of grave concern. He bit down on his lower lip as he flipped through the photos several times. Through his prickly black facial hairs, Dana could see blotches of red. His large, dark eyes looked piercingly at her. "Where in heaven's name did you get these, Miss Greer?"

"Someone dropped them off on the front porch of the Harrison home."

"Did you see anyone?" He ran his index and middle fingers over his lower lip.

"Only fresh footprints in the snow."

"Any note in the box?"

"Nothing, only the photos."

"I see. I see."

"I'm not accusing you of anything, Father. It's just that. . . ."

"What is there to accuse?" he asked, his voice gravelly.

Dana immediately regretted what she had said. It was just what she didn't want to do. . .to act, as though, she were accusing the priest.

"This is most difficult for me, Father. I hope you can understand that. I only wanted to ask if you recall these times spent with Bernadette Godfrey?"

"Of course, I do. I told you before that I took a special interest in the child. She was new to the Cape, new to the Academy, not to mention being utterly shy. I tried to befriend her, nothing more than that. I wasn't alone in trying to help the child adjust."

"I know that, Father."

The priest threw his arms outward. "And do you know, Miss Greer, that I'm not a child molester if that is where you're going with this!"

Now, Dana could feel her face heat up until it felt moist to the touch. She ran her hand over her forehead and upper lip. "I'm not suggesting that, Father, really, I'm not. I'm more concerned with who sent the photos and why."

"I have no idea who would drop these off on your porch, but I have an idea as to why. It's quite obvious someone is trying to set me up, to make this look like much more than it is. There are sickly souls out there; I see them every day."

"But do you have any idea who might want to do this? Why you, I wonder?"

"Just a scapegoat. There are those who enjoy smearing another's reputation, especially, when it comes to someone who is known in the community, respected."

Dana shook her head.

"If it's any comfort to you, you can take the pictures to Mrs. Godfrey. I'm sure she'll tell you that she recalls each of these photos being taken. After all, it was she who took them, Miss Greer."

Dana's left eye began to twitch, and she felt a stream of sweat rolling down her cheek. She had an idea how it must feel to be on the other side of the desk, the one being interrogated, especially, when one was innocent. Suddenly, Dana felt incredibly absurd for thinking the priest might just be a child molester. She felt like such a fool. "I don't know what to say, Father."

"You needn't. I understand that you're doing your job. I watch 'Dragnet' on Friday nights, you know." His attempt at a lighthearted joke seemed to cut the tension in the room. He slipped the photos back into the package and handed it to Dana. "Take these to Mrs. Godfrey. Do yourself a favor. Trust me. You'll feel much better. I guarantee."

Dana tried to smile. Her eyes refused to make contact with the priest. "Thank you," she said. Then, she remembered one thing. The day the photos came, she recalled seeing a black car across the street; no one was in it as far as she could see, and she was unable to see the license plate number. "Father," she said, "might you know anyone who drives a new black Oldsmobile?"

He laughed. "On the Cape? You've got to be kidding me? How many cars would you say there are, total, not counting the two police cruisers? Probably fifty at most. A black Oldsmobile, you say? New? Anyone who drives a car around here is more-than-likely wealthy and lives up on the Pointe."

Dana about to leave spun around on her heel. "Father, I did think of one more question."

Father smiled. "You are an investigator, aren't you?"

Dana returned Father's smile. "You're sure you recall having seen Mrs. Artenelli at the eight a.m. Mass the morning Bernadette Godfrey disappeared. . .October 25?"

"No doubt about it. The woman always sits in the center, front pew. Yes, she was there as she is every day."

Chapter Thirty-Five

The yellow cab, the only one on Cape Peril, waited out front of the Harrison home as Dana ran out to greet it. "Two-fifty Overlook Drive," she said to the driver, who was a different man than the previous one who had taken her to the Artenelli home.

The driver turned and fixed his gaze on her. "The Artenelli place?"

"Why, yes. How'd you know?"

"Simple. The houses up there are all numbered in ten-digit figures. You know, two-ten, two-twenty, and so on."

"Interesting."

"There are those who joke that the addresses match the millions the folks own."

Dana glanced at her watch: eight-thirty-nine. She hoped to catch Gino Artenelli off guard with a surprise visit.

The driver was still mumbling about something.

"What was that you said?" Dana asked.

"Do you know how many people live on that street?"

"I have no idea," Dana said, staring out the side window.

"Three, Ma'am. Exactly three. The Rivosellis, the Gavonis, and the Artenellis."

"Please, could you just drive me to Two-fifty Overlook."

"You're sure now? You're really sure?"

Dana was getting tired of the driver's jibber-jabber. "Why wouldn't I be?" she asked, hearing the sting of sarcasm in her voice.

"Not too many people go up there, is all I'm saying."

"Okay, you win. Why don't too many people go up there?" Dana felt as though she were playing some riddle game with a six-year-old.

"They're the boys. That's what they're called anyway."

"You mean the Mob?"

"You got it, lady. Those damn shysters are the only ones rich enough to afford that kind of property. There ain't a room in their houses that doesn't have a view of the sea. Mind if I ask why a nice lady like you would want to go up there?" he asked, as he made a sharp left turn.

"I just want to speak with Mr. Artenelli if he happens to be in," Dana said.

"Hell, yeah, he'll be in. The boys do most of their work after hours when the rest of us are sound asleep."

Dana watched out the window as the driver made his way up the circling road. Large brick homes, unlike the typical clapboard ones on the Cape, sat along the hillside, looking as if someone had just perched them there for appearance's sake. Long black asphalt drives wound their way to the front doors of the homes. With each tight turn the driver made, the homes seemed to increase in size until they almost looked like overnight inns.

"You can see why these are the only folks who need cars around here. Can you imagine trying to get down these hills by foot? Cadillacs, Lincolns, and Oldsmobiles, they all got 'em."

"What do you mean?"

"You won't see much else up here. Only the biggest and the finest the auto industry makes. Most of the folks up here run businesses on the mainland, and these here are their summer resorts. Unless, of course, you're talking about the doctors who work on the Cape. A few of them got houses up here, too." The driver swung another tight curve, sending Dana to the other side of the back seat. "Two-fifty Overlook Drive, Ma'am," he said.

The last time Dana had been to the Pointe, when Gino Artenelli had placed the urgent call about his wife, Dana hadn't even noticed the other homes wrapped around the edge of the Cape, like pearls on a chain, all with double doors and shutters.

"Here you go, Ma'am. The middle one, that white-brick one with the columns, is the Artenellis'. Looks like the White House, eh?"

Parked in the circular drive out front sat a black Cadillac. Out front of the red-brick house was a black Lincoln, and out front of the gray-brick house sat a shiny, black Oldsmobile. Dana could see what the driver meant. The boys. . .the Mob. . .who had everything that money could buy. "Who did you say lives in this house?" Dana asked the taxi driver, as she pointed to the house on the right of the Artenellis'.

"The Gavonis. . .like I told you, all part of the Syndicate. It ain't bad enough they all make their money by illegal means, but they even gotta live next door to each other like bees in a hive."

Dana began to wonder if that black Oldsmobile was the same one that had been parked out front of the Harrison house the day the secret package arrived. If so, the Gavonis might have had something to do with the delivery. One of the boys. . .Gino could very well have given the task to one of them to conceal who actually was behind the drop off. If her presumptions were anywhere near correct, the Artenellis were setting up Father Sullivan. What kind of people would do such a thing? Overtly, Gino's wife was the pious and active churchgoer; however, covertly her husband would sell the priest's soul for thirty pieces of silver if it meant they were to be seen as innocent. Traitors all in the name of power and money.

"Need me to drive up to the door, lady?" the driver asked.

"Please do."

Dana asked him to wait as she stepped out of the cab. Two brass fox heads graced the large wooden doors. She tugged on the door knockers several times until a woman dressed in a black uniform, a white lace apron, and a small lace doily on her head came to the door. Dana remembered the woman from the last time she had called upon the Artenellis.

"Welcome to the Artenellis'," she said. "May I help you?"

"Yes, the name is Dana Greer. . .private investigator Greer." Dana showed the woman her badge. "I'm here to see Gino Artenelli."

"Is he expectin' you?" she asked, her voice sounding shaky and uncertain.

"He is now," Dana said. "Please, is he in? It's important."

"Come in," the maid said. "I 'member you from da last time." She left Dana standing in the vestibule, which immediately spoke of wealth. An enormous crystal chandelier hung above her head with matching sconces on each side of the wall. Mahogany crown moldings lined the ceiling and the baseboards. The walls, painted a light yellow, were covered with framed mirrors, and beneath Dana's feet, the wooden floor was covered with a wool Oriental rug in shades of green.

She could hear heavy footsteps coming down the hall.

"What in the hell does that woman want?" Not expecting Dana to be waiting in the foyer, Gino Artenelli's voice suddenly changed as he tightened a maroon belt around his bathrobe. "Miss Greer, what a pleasure. Come in. Come in."

He led Dana down the long hall and stopped outside his room of wild game. "I like to hunt in my spare time. These folks," he said, pointing to the various heads, "are from my last excursion to India. But, then again, I believe, I told you that on your last visit, didn't I?"

Dana wondered how many times the man bragged about his room to others as well.

He offered Dana a drink from his bar, and when she refused, he poured himself a Vodka Tonic. After a few gulps, he said, "By the way, that culprit who sent my wife that incriminating letter, is up to no good again."

"So I've heard," Dana said.

"Here, have a seat, won't you?"

Dana sat down on a zebra-striped sofa with red and orange toss pillows. It was quite apparent that the home had no particular decorating scheme as the wild game room seemed totally out of place with the formal entrance.

"What brings you by today?" he asked, nonchalantly. "Any leads on your investigation?"

"Oh lots of leads. In fact, it's one of the reasons for my visit."

Gino's eyebrows shot up. He removed a cigarette from a silver engraved box and lit it with a matching lighter that sat on a table made from a Cobra's coiled body. As an afterthought, he said, "Do you smoke?"

Dana shook her head. "Mr. Artenelli, I just came from the Holy Name rectory. Seems an anonymous visitor dropped these off on my doorstep." She handed him the package containing the photographs of Bernadette and Father Sullivan. "Might you be familiar with these?"

Gino took out a few pictures and placed them on the table. Then, he puffed on his cigarette, raising his head as he blew small smoke rings toward the ceiling. Clearing his throat, he said, "Sure, Miss Greer. Thought they just might help in your investigation. You know, sort of a community thing. One hand helping another. Do you have a problem with that?"

"No, I don't have a problem with someone trying to help, but these photos seem to me to have another purpose."

He laughed, removing a bit of tobacco from the tip of his tongue. "What in heaven's name do you mean?"

"I'm talking about a set-up, Mr. Artenelli. Why else would you think someone would drop these off where I'm staying?"

He stood up and walked over to the ceiling-to-floor window that overlooked the ocean. The waves matched the overhead clouds, grey and ominous, with white-caps. He continued to puff on his cigarette. When he turned to face Dana, he said, "If I were you, Miss Greer, I'd be grateful for any serious leads you can get." He emphasized the word *serious*.

"What makes you think Father Sullivan might be a lead in the murder of Bernadette Godfrey?" Dana asked.

"Let the photographs speak for themselves. Aren't pictures worth a thousand words, Miss Greer?" He sneered. Then, he called out, "Ladel!" He shook a small bell that matched the silver of his cigarette case.

The maid entered the room.

"Ladel, Miss Greer was just leaving. Will you show her out, please?" He turned to face the sea once again, snuffed out his cigarette, and crossed his arms against his chest.

"But when were these. . . ?"

"I believe Mr. Artenelli's askin' me to show you to da door, Miss Greer," Ladel said.

Dana thanked the maid and left.

When she got back into the taxi, the driver asked, "Well? What do you think?"

Dana deliberately ignored his question and sidestepped it with, "Actually, I've seen quite enough," she said. "The Pointe. . .lovely, quite lovely, indeed. Now, would you drop me off at Mia Godfrey's house?"

***

Mrs. Godfrey welcomed Dana into her home, so different from the days when Joe was still alive and didn't like visitors in his house. Scents of pumpkin and cinnamon wafted from her kitchen—the familiar smells of Thanksgiving in the air, only two days away. Hopefully, Dana's visit with Mrs. Godfrey would confirm whether or not Father Sullivan had been telling her the truth about the photographs. For his sake, Dana hoped he was. The thought of Gino Artenelli having one of his 'boys' anonymously deliver the pictures in order to implicate the man on murder charges, or at the least abuse charges sickened her.

"Please, let me have your coat; make yourself at home," Mrs. Godfrey said. As she went to hang Dana's coat in the hall closet, she looked back at her and said, "Oh, what a lovely skirt." She cupped her cheeks. "You always look so stylish."

"Thank you. You're very kind," Dana said. Personally, Dana found the stiff crinoline petticoats that helped flare her skirts to be quite uncomfortable.

Dana started to make small talk about pumpkin pie when Mrs. Godfrey stopped her and said, "My, my, what have we here?" eyeing the package that Dana had in her lap.

"Oh, this. Last week, someone dropped this package off on the Harrisons' porch, addressed to me, with no return address. I found these pictures inside." Dana decided to stop there. Mrs. Godfrey didn't need to know who the anonymous party was.

"May I look at them?" she asked, wiping her hands in a yellow canvas apron that she had tied loosely around her neck.

Dana handed the package to her. She needed to see Mrs. Godfrey's immediate reaction. It would tell her more than words, she was sure.

The woman slipped the photographs onto the coffee table in front of them and spread the pictures out like cards in a deck. Dana watched as she ran her hand above the array from left to right. Her first thought was that the pictures saddened the woman, to see her deceased daughter who looked happy and full of life on the photographs. Dana observed the woman more closely. Her expression went from forlorn to a hint of a smile.

"Yes, yes, I remember these," she said.

"Remember what, Mrs. Godfrey?"

"These photos. The visit down to the shore. The picnic. . .why such fond memories."

"Bernadette, then, spent time with Father Sullivan?"

Like one of those rubber-faced rings children found in a box of Kellogg's cereal, the Snap, Crackle, and Pop ones, the kind whose expressions could be manipulated in seconds by the touch of small fingers, Dana noticed Mrs. Godfrey's appearance change once again. Her jaw tensed, and she clenched her teeth.

"Could you tell me what you remember?"

In a voice, cold and indifferent, she said, "It's Joe's fault." Mrs. Godfrey stared past Dana as if she were alone in the room. "If Joe hadn't been gone so much. . .why he hardly spent time with her. . .never wanted her to begin with. . .never bonded with her. . .never saw her as his child." She paused.

It was clear that Mrs. Godfrey had kept her emotions bottled for too long, probably too fearful to express them to her husband for what he had done to her in the past.

"I see. That's why Bernadette began a friendship with Father Sullivan," Dana said, moving the conversation back to the photographs.

Mrs. Godfrey refocused her attention on Dana and said, "He was one of the few, real friends Bernadette had. The man took time from his busy schedule to spend time with her, with us."

"So, Father Sullivan was your friend, too?" Dana asked, wondering if she would admit to having taken the photos.

The woman's brown eyes blurred, filled with tears that stubbornly refused to fall. "Yes, I. . .I love that man."

"I see. You saw Father Sullivan as the father Bernadette never had. Is that what you mean?"

Mrs. Godfrey covered her face with her hands and nodded her head.

Dana waited a minute to let the woman regain her composure. "Then was it *you*, Mrs. Godfrey, who was on the other side of the camera, taking these photos of your daughter and Father?"

Without removing her hands from her face, the woman continued to nod, mumbling something about, "I bet you think I'm some kind of fool. . .spending time with a priest."

"No, not at all. It makes sense to me why you turned to someone whom you could trust. After all, life with Joe was far from satisfying." Dana could see why the woman might have transferred her need for love and acceptance onto the only man in her life who provided it. . .Father Sullivan.

"By chance, did Father Sullivan ever spend time with Bernadette alone?"

"Oh no! Of course not. I hope you're not thinking. . .I mean, Father Sullivan is a man of God. He wouldn't. . .no. His intentions were only to make Bernadette and me happy."

A sad story but one that confirmed what Dana had hoped. Father Sullivan was every bit the man that he said he was, but Gino

Artenelli was set on proving him otherwise. The question left to answer was why.

Dana tried to comfort Mrs. Godfrey as best she could but realized that the woman needed someone who was trained in the skill of therapy. Dana could only hope Mrs. Godfrey would seek out the help of someone like Doctor Thatcher. Meanwhile, the smell of burning dough filled the air. Mrs. Godfrey appeared totally oblivious of the charred scent. Dana quickly went to the kitchen to find small curls of grey smoke rising from the oven door. She grabbed a pair of hot pads, shut off the oven, and pulled out what was left of two licorice-colored pumpkin pies.

Chapter Thirty-Six

Dana still had questions as to what part Jay Harrison played, if any, in the death of Bernadette Godfrey. Dana recalled him telling her that he was late to class the day the girl disappeared, as he went home to get a forgotten book. But with Loretta already at the antique shop, he had no witness. Dana remembered Sister saying that she was ill that day and had a substitute teacher take her place. Dana needed to meet with the principal of Holy Name Academy to find out who the substitute was. If lucky, this person might be able to provide her with details concerning the morning the child went missing.

Dana headed for the school office. The principal, a chubby nun with a bad case of crossed eyes, was seated behind her desk, file folders piled before her and what looked to be contracts. If these were teacher contracts, there might be two second-grade openings coming up sooner than the principal knew. Dana excused herself for interrupting her, and the elderly nun asked her to be seated. Dana told her she was interested in learning more about the substitute that was hired to replace Sister Mary Rose on the day that Bernadette Godfrey went missing.

"Excuse me," the nun said, and whirled her chair around to face the gray file cabinet behind her. "Hmm, let's see. Letter *S*. Ah, yes. *Substitutes*." She turned and placed the file folder on her desk, licked her thumb, and began paging through the thick stack of papers within. "October 25, correct?"

"The day that Bernadette didn't arrive for classes," Dana said.

"Hmm, looks like we hired Martha Engel that day. She's a fine, older woman, works well with the children."

"Any chance I could have her number?" Dana asked.

"Any chance I might ask why?" the principal asked, giving Dana a big frown, her crossed-eyes unblinking.

"I'd like to know some general things. You know, such as the time Martha Engel arrived at the Academy, if she took the children to morning Mass."

"Humph. Sound innocuous enough." The nun scribbled a number down on a small piece of note paper. "Hope you're not going to cause any trouble for Sister Mary Rose. You know, she called in ill that day. The sweet thing never cancels class. She had to be truly sick to do so."

"I understand," Dana said. "Thank you for your help."

Immediately upon returning to the Harrison home, Dana called Martha Engel, explained who she was, and the purpose of her call.

"The principal called me that morning and told me Sister Mary Rose had called in ill and wondered if I would be available immediately. I'm an early riser, so I had no problem with dashing over to the school," the woman said.

"I'm sure the principal appreciated that. What time was it when you arrived?"

"Weekday Mass is at eight a.m., so I'd say I got to the school at about five till. Getting all of those little bodies hustled over the church was no easy task."

"I can imagine," Dana said. "By chance, did you happen to see the other second grade teacher. . .at school. . .at Mass?"

"Oh that handsome Mr. Harrison? As a matter-of-fact, he was late getting to school that day, so I took his little sweethearts with mine to Mass."

"I see, so did he eventually show up?"

"Ran into the church, out of breath, just when Father Sullivan was about to begin his sermon."

So, Dana thought, Father Sullivan's alibi was confirmed. At the time Bernadette Godfrey went missing, Father was, indeed, celebrating the eight a.m. Mass. "What time might that have been when Mr. Harrison arrived?"

"I'd say about 8:15. Father likes to say the Mass quickly on weekdays. You know, the little ones just don't have much of an attention span."

"Understandable," Dana said. If Jay's alibi about going home to get a book was the truth, that would mean he had made the trip from school to his home and back to the church in about fifteen minutes. That would not have given him time for much else. "Miss Engel. . . ."

"Mrs. . . George is my husband."

"Mrs. Engel did you by chance happen to hear what kept Sister Mary Rose at the convent that day?"

"Why no, nor did I feel it was my place to ask." She paused briefly and then added, "But Sister wasn't at the convent when she got sick. . .er at least that's what the principal told me."

"Oh?"

"No, Sister had spent the night with her parents. You know, they live in one of those big mansions on the Pointe. . .the ones overlooking the ocean."

"So, I know. Wonder why she was there. . . ." Dana let her voice trail off, hoping Mrs. Engel could fill in the blanks.

"From what I've heard, and you know how gossip is on the Cape, the Artenellis purchased a home on the Pointe so that they could be closer to their daughter. Such a close, loving family, you know."

Without a doubt, Mrs. Engel was more into the happenings on the island than she had first admitted.

"Yes, that was it. The Sister got sick. You might like to call the Artenellis. I'm sure they'd be happy to give you whatever details you need."

Dana thanked the woman and hung up. She should have known. If Gino Artenelli tried to indict Father Sullivan with the murder of Bernadette Godfrey by sending the photographs of the priest and the girl, it would be quite believable that the family would also cover for the nun's whereabouts on the day the girl went missing.

Dana felt like she was finally getting somewhere, but there was one more thing she needed to do before she would head over to the station to speak with Logan, and that was doing some research on the manufacturer of the Ladybug sheets, the type used to cover the body of the Godfrey child. She searched for the phone book and looked up the number for Sears Roebuck on Stillwater Drive in Bay View.

"Sears Roebuck. Which department would you like?"

"Linens, please," she said.

A woman with a scratchy voice answered, "Bedding, towels, rugs, curtains. . . ."

"I'm interested in bedding, Ma'am," Dana said. "I'm going to a bridal shower and would like to purchase a particular brand of sheet. Do you happen to carry Ladybug?"

"No, Ma'am, we don't."

Dana was just about to hang up when the sales clerk continued.

"Ladybug is a commercial brand, not sold to retailers."

"Might you know. . . ."

"Those sheets are sold in bulk. You sure won't find them in any store."

"Who might purchase them, then?" Dana asked.

"Hospitals, nursing homes, boarding schools. . . ."

Not another litany. Dana thanked the woman and hung up the phone. As far as Dana knew, the possible murder suspects of Bernadette Godfrey had nothing to do with a hospital, a nursing home, nor a boarding school. But the suspect might very well be connected to the Guardian Angel Orphanage. Sister Thomasina had told her that Angela Artenelli had served her three mandatory years after the birth of her child at the orphanage. The Mother Superior said that Angela had worked in the laundry room of the institution. Dana placed a call to the orphanage and asked for the laundry. She waited a couple of moments while the girl who answered went to get her supervisor. Dana could hear the grinding of several washing machine wringers, the running of tap water, and the banging of metal pails. The sound of clothes whirling around in dryers completed the picture of the busy laundry room that cared for the entire orphanage.

"Sister Monica," an out-of-breath nun's voice answered.

Dana introduced herself to the nun and explained what she was after.

"A Ladybug sheet?" the nun asked, her voice confused. "Are you telling me that you think one of our girls confiscated a sheet from Guardian Angel?"

The question, as Sister Monica put it, sounded ridiculous, but that was exactly what Dana was asking.

"I'm afraid the brand Bedtrex is the only one I'm aware of."

"Might the orphanage have changed brands more recently?"

"I've been here twenty-five years, Miss Greer, and the only sheets I've seen come in and go out of our laundry are Bedtrex."

A dead end until Sister Monica offered a possible solution. "I can give you the manufacturer's number, Bedtrex that is, and maybe they can tell where the sheets you're looking for are made."

"Thank you. That's a wonderful idea," Dana said, as she jotted down the phone number. She dialed the number, a number out of Salem, Massachusetts, and the operator connected her to a Mr. Oliver, the sales representative for Bedtrex.

"Industrial bedding, Oliver speaking."

"Sir, I am desperately trying to find a phone number for the manufacturer of Ladybug sheets. Might you be able to help me?"

"First, let me tell you that if you're looking for the best quality made industrial strength linen for your institution, you're not going to find better than Bedtrex."

"I'm sure that's the case, but. . . ."

"Fifteen-hundred thread count. . .you can't find much better. They wear, wash, and dry like no other."

"I'm sure they do, but I need the manufacturer of Ladybug linens."

"Just a moment, then," he said.

Dana could hear his frustrated breathing on the other side of the receiver. He obviously was a good salesman and couldn't see her bothering with his competitor. He came back on the phone and gave her a number.

"Company's based out of White Plains, New York."

Dana had to admit that as an investigator she had tracked down many things over the years, but this was a first.

"Ladybug industrial linens, Wayne Brill, speaking."

Once again Dana explained her dilemma, asking if this particular brand of sheet was purchased by any institution in or near Bay View, Maine.

He excused himself, saying that he needed to consult his inventory book. When he returned to the phone, he said, "Ah yes, we supply sheets all over the East Coast, but it looks as if the nearest place to Bay View that we service is a small, out-of-the-way place called Cape Peril."

Dana sighed deeply, feeling her heart flutter like a butterfly fresh out of its cocoon. "Yes, yes, where on Cape Peril?" she asked.

"You familiar with the Holy Name Convent, Ma'am? Our company's been providing sheets to the good nuns. . .why it looks as though it's been ever since the order started," he said, laughing at his own attempt at humor.

"Holy Name Convent, why yes, I'm very familiar with the place."

"Do tell the good sisters that Wayne Brill gives his best regards."

"I'll do that," Dana said, and hung up the phone.

It was time she paid Sister Mary Rose a visit.

***

Classes had dismissed for the afternoon, and the lights were out in Sister Mary Rose's classroom. Running the floor polisher was Buzz Meechum. He waved from down the hall and shut off the overpowering motor of the machine. His forearms continued to vibrate even after the polisher was shut off.

"Miss Greer, you looking for the pretty nun?" he yelled, his voice trailing like an echo down a long tunnel.

Dana waited until he got closer.

"Saw her walking toward the convent with one of the other sisters," Buzz said, his head involuntarily nodding. "Don't want to wish nobody no ill will, but Carmelina Artenelli sure has it comin' to her. Keeping secrets all these years like she did. I bet mother gave you an earful!" He waited for Dana to comment and when she didn't, he continued as if speaking to himself. "Angela, excuse me, Sister Mary Rose ain't much better, sneaking around with the Harrison man. Did cha ever prove me right by that one?" he asked.

"I did as you said, yes."

"Inside the storage closet, right? Just like I said."

"Just like you said."

"Well, it ain't any of my business, but I think it's time someone better blow their cover. Like I said, that whole family's nothin' but a bunch of sinners."

Not wanting to waste any more time, Dana said, "I'd better get over to the convent before the dinner hour."

"Don't expect the sister to tell you a word. Like I said, that whole family's got secrets that could fill an old trunk."

"Maybe not but it's worth a few questions," Dana said, and turned to exit through the main doors.

"Listen." The doors opened behind her.

Dana turned.

"If you need any help from me, just let me know." He pulled out a slip of paper and a broken pencil from his bib overalls and began to scribble with the short nib. "Here's my telephone number. Like I said, give me a call if I can help you out. Don't get me wrong. I'm no snitch, but it's about time the truth be told."

Dana thought of Amhurst and his plans to spy on Jay and Sister Mary Rose. "I may just do that," she said, and hurried out the building toward the convent.

The narrow path leading from Holy Name Academy to the convent looked like something found in a painting. The walkway was shoveled clean. Several bushes outlined the walk, and a few bristly branches poked their heads through the snow. Intermittent trees formed arches overhead with their bare leafless branches. Four more long months until spring, Dana thought.

She rang the bell on the front door and a nun wearing a white apron carrying a wooden spoon greeted her.

"Miss Greer, how nice. Please come in," she said. A faint smell of stew filled the entryway.

The nun stood several inches shorter than Dana, who had to crook her neck to be at eye level with the woman.

"I'm Sister Thomas. You know the doubting one."

Of course, Dana knew. Something about those Catholic roots never died. She could still recite the names of all twelve apostles and list the various events in the Bible.

"How can I help, Miss Greer?"

"Sister, I hope I'm not disturbing your dinner time."

"We eat promptly at five forty-five," the nun said, her voice sounding as authoritative as a ringing dinner bell.

"I was wondering if I might see Sister Mary Rose."

"Certainly. . .that is unless she's in the chapel. We sisters each take turns at Adoration. Round-the-clock, you know. Father Sullivan was good enough to arrange that for us with the bishop. Such a good man, that Father Sullivan," she said. "Please, have a seat." She left Dana in the parlor of the convent, where a roaring fire warmed the room. Above the mantle was a framed picture of the sisters who occupied the Holy Name Convent, about thirty-four sisters in all. Some were dressed in the solid white habit of the novice, and the others were in the black veils and dark blue habits of the professed. Their faces stared straight ahead as if they had been told to look right into the camera. In the third row, the fifth from the left, stood Sister Mary Rose in her professed habit, the picture having been taken quite recently. The young woman had her mother's outstanding features, and as Logan had said at the nun's profession of vows, it did seem a pity that someone as beautiful as she would resign herself to a life of poverty, obedience, and chastity. Sister Mary Rose must have thought the same and found it easier to give way to temptation.

Dana turned when she heard the rustle of a habit and the clinking of wooden rosary beads. "Sister Mary Rose, how good to see you again," she said.

"Likewise. Sister Thomas tells me that you need to speak with me." Her voice rose as if asking a question.

"As a matter-of-fact, Sister, I would. Might we sit down?"

They sat on the oversized gold-and-green striped Victorian sofa that stood in front of the fire, each of them at one of the ends. The reflection of the orange flames danced in Sister's dark irises. The young nun rested her hands in her lap, folded, angelic.

Dana wished that she had prepared better for this conversation, maybe even have gone so far as to have prepared an outline to organize the thoughts that rambled through her mind. Where to begin? Was one place better than another?

"Is there something in particular that you wanted to speak to me about?" the nun asked, her gaze on the dancing fire as it crackled and snapped, logs repositioning themselves as they fell onto each other.

Again, where to begin. . .from the particular to the general maybe?

"Sister, as you know, I have been working on resolving the murder of Bernadette Godfrey, trying to find motives, analyze alibis, and narrow the field of suspects."

"Are there many. . .suspects, I mean?" The young nun unclasped her hands, digging her nails into her soft flesh.

She asked the question so innocently that Dana felt as if she were speaking to a law enforcement officer, not a beautiful nun who might very well have a motive for murder.

"There are some," Dana said, "but more importantly, it's the loose ends that I wrestle with. You know, the things that don't come together as easily as I would like."

"Hmm," the nun said. She stood up to stoke the fire, arranged her habit so as not to crease it, and sat back down. "I see," she said, shaking her head from side-to-side.

Dana sat for a moment analyzing the young woman's composure. The nun chose not to make eye contact; that was obvious. And, her words did not fit with her gestures. *Lying, by chance,* Dana wondered.

"The day I went to the gravesite, Sister, I took photographs, spoke with the coroner, and later revisited the site in my mind."

"Do you not just love fires? They're so mesmerizing; do you agree?" The nun continued to stare at the flames, her eyes fixed as if in a trance.

Sister's diverted attention was beginning to bother Dana. She repeated her last statement about the gravesite and Red Tanner.

"Raymond McGregor. Was it not he who found the body?" Sister asked. She looked down at her lap.

"It's the burial site that has me even more concerned," Dana said.

Sister Mary Rose turned toward Dana and folded her arms into the habit's loose sleeves, a practice Dana had seen many nuns do. The nun's pupils contracted, her face one of concentration. "Why so, Miss Greer?"

"The grave was shallow but perfect, not a stray weed or broken branch anywhere."

"Interesting. Your work, I mean."

"The girl was stabbed multiple times as if the person who murdered her had lost control and repetitively thrust the knife into the child's body."

The nun began to hum the lyrics to "Amazing Grace," her head nodding, while her focus, once again, became that of the blue-and-orange flames.

Years ago, when Fiona Wharton had begun to teach Dana what she thought every good investigator needed to know, she had gone through a list of characteristics of a liar: the lack of eye contact, words not befitting the gestures given, the ability to change the subject radically and indifferently, and even the avoidance of contractions. Dana remembered the list as if it was a litany to one of her favorite saints, and now she found herself mentally checking off the same traits that Sister Mary Rose exhibited.

"Sister, you probably read that the girl's body was covered in a white cloth." This would be Dana's perfect ploy to see if, indeed, Sister was lying to her. The newspaper account never mentioned the fact that the body was concealed by a sheet.

"Yes, I had."

Dana worked at maintaining her composure, though she felt that the nun was slowly incriminating herself. "I did some checking with Red Tanner, the coroner. He was able to give me the name of the manufacturer of the sheet that covered the girl's body."

At the sound of the word sheet, Sister spun the gold band on her right ring finger, the one that represented her marriage to the church and to God.

"I was able to track down the manufacturer as well as source of the order."

Dana watched the nun cover her lips with her fingertips. Another subconscious movement to counteract the obvious anxiousness and uncomfortable way that she had to be feeling at the moment.

Speaking through her hands, the Sister asked, "And what did you find out?"

"The Holy Name Convent buys these, Sister. They're the only institution near Bay View that deals with this supplier."

The nun squinted her eyes like a cat surveying its prey, continued to stare at the fire, and in a rapid rate of speech blurted out, "Are you saying someone used one of the convent sheets to cover the body? But who? Why?"

To make the question less accusatory, Dana said, "Not necessarily the murderer, but someone who had access to the convent."

The young woman looked toward Dana for the first time and said, "I can think of no one here who would have done such a despicable thing, Miss Greer! We are, after all, servants of God, called to lives of virtue. How dare you think one of my fellow sisters could do such a thing. I suggest you take your questioning elsewhere. You will not find the answers you are looking for here, I am afraid."

Just then, Sister Thomas walked by and hearing the heated exchange, entered the parlor. "Is everything okay?" She eyed Dana from head-to-foot, obviously protecting her own.

"Everything is fine, Sister," the young nun answered. "Miss Greer was just leaving."

"Would you like for me to show her to the door?" Sister Thomas asked.

Without answering the nun, Sister Mary Rose held the edge of her veil back and grasped tightly the crucifix that lay on her chest. She stood.

Not only had Sister Mary Rose's behavior added up to a woman who was hiding what she knew, but the more Dana thought about it, the more convinced she became that with a domineering mother as she had, lying must have been a part of her life. Rather than deal with the wrath of her mother, it had to have been much easier to deny any wrong doing.

With the thought of lies in her mind, Dana said, "Oh, Sister, before I go. The Guardian Angel Orphanage must use a lot of sheets." The sing-song sound of Dana's voice made her comment appear innocuous.

Sister Mary Rose looked at Dana over her shoulder. "I have no idea."

"But, Sister, didn't you work in the laundry at one time?"

Sister Thomas crinkled up her nose, her body stiffened. She threw her hand across her chest.

"That had to be someone else you are thinking of, Miss Greer. I have never been to any orphanage."

Like Eddie, Sister Mary Rose was denying knowledge of the orphanage, yet it was there that Angela Artenelli had given birth and where Eddie Vineeti had tried to convince her to keep the baby. In some strange way, it was the nun's lies that told Dana the truth. She was, however, not quite ready to charge the beautiful nun with the death of Bernadette Godfrey.

Chapter Thirty-Seven

Thanksgiving with Loretta and Amhurst passed by uneventful other than a rather dried out bird, which Loretta had overcooked, and yams with too much sugar. Her father apologized for her, saying that Loretta's mother had never taught the young woman to cook as they had always had culinary help in their home. Dana was glad that she had purchased a pumpkin pie from the local bakery; at least the completion of the meal was tasty.

On Friday morning, with much to inform Logan about, she hurried over to the station.

"I can't believe Gino Artenelli would actually admit to sending me the anonymous box of photographs. He actually was bold enough to tell me that he thought they might help me in my investigation. He called it a community thing. . .one hand helping another."

"Doesn't surprise me in the least. Cover-ups are all part of a day's work for the Mob, Dana," Logan said.

"Gino acted as if he were doing me a service, and as he called it, offering me a serious lead on the case."

"Serious meaning?"

"As in implicating that Father Sullivan was involved in the murder of Bernadette Godfrey." Dana swallowed hard.

"Maybe more like having his boys cover up for Carmelina or Sister Mary Rose," Logan said. He scratched his head. "I'm not about to cast a vote yet, but I've got a feeling you might just have the horse by the tail."

"That's what I'm thinking, but there's more," Dana said.

Logan raised his eyebrows. "Really?"

"I stopped by Mrs. Godfrey's place to show her the photographs."

"And, what was her reaction?"

"At first, the woman looked about to burst into tears and then she smiled. She admitted to taking the pictures of Father Sullivan with her daughter."

"What!" Logan jarred his neck upward.

"That's what I thought until she went on to explain just how much a part of the family Father played. Sounds from what Mrs. Godfrey told me that Father almost became a surrogate for the real father Bernadette never had."

"Rather sad, I'd say."

"So true." Then, Dana went on to inform Logan that she had confirmed the whereabouts of both Father Sullivan and Jay Harrison the morning Bernadette Godfrey went missing. "So, that leaves me back at square one: Sister Mary Rose and Carmelina Artenelli."

"Splendid," Logan said.

"I can go on." Dana told him about what she had learned from the manufacturer of the Ladybug sheets. "According to the factory representative, Cape Peril's Holy Name Convent is the only recipient of the sheets in the Bay View area."

"Sounds to me Sister Mary Rose is going to have one hell of a time denying her involvement in the murder of Bernadette Godfrey." He stared out the window looking at the storm clouds which promised another winter blizzard by nightfall. Then he spun his chair around, faced Dana, and said, "About those sheets. . . .speaking about cover-ups, no pun intended, what would prevent someone from trying to make it look as if the nun were guilty? On second thought, it does seem inconceivable to think that a nun would commit murder and of her own child."

"There is one small detail that leads me to believe Sister knew more than one might think," Dana said.

Logan peered at Dana, his eyebrows hovering over his eyes, studying Dana's face.

"The *Peril Post* never made mention of the sheet when it ran the story about finding Bernadette Godfrey's body. No one would have known that small bit of minutiae except for McGregor, who found the body, and Tanner, the coroner. Yet when I asked Sister if she had read about the newspaper account of the body being covered in a white sheet, the nun replied that she had."

"Good strategizing, Dana—twisting the truth and letting the nun admit to the lie. What can I say? You're one doggone investigator. I'll get ahold of Officer Boyle. Think it's time we do an undercover surveillance on the good ol' Sister Mary Rose. We sure don't want her getting out of our sight."

"Agreed." Dana was about to get up when the receptionist poked her head in the door. "Officer Boyle is on the line, Sergeant. Says it's an emergency."

Logan picked up the receiver. His face grew grave. "Good God," he said. "Where? I'll be right there." Logan slammed the phone down. "There's been a hit and run on the corner of Port and Reef Streets, right near the Ferry."

"Oh my God!" Dana said.

***

Logan pulled his police cruiser out of the garage beneath the station, and as the siren wailed and the blue overhead light flashed, he and Dana skidded through three intersections and around two corners. At the scene of the accident, an ambulance from Cape Peril Memorial had already arrived, its horn screeching and its red lights blaring. Two men in white lifted a gurney, but Dana could not make out who was on it. Shards of broken glass, pieces of lime-green metal, and a rusted hubcap lay on the pavement. Officer Boyle had a tape measure and was measuring the black rubber marks left on the road.

Logan stepped up to the man and asked, "What the hell happened?"

"A hit 'n run. From the looks of these streaks on the pavement, someone was in a hurry to get away but not before gunning down a pedestrian. That's the problem around here. . .most residents are just that—pedestrians—and the few that are drivers must have gotten their licenses in a Cracker Jack box."

"The ambulance," Logan said. "Who?"

"For God's sake, Logan," Officer Boyle said in a nasal voice, looking up with tears in his eyes, "it's Carmelina Artenelli. A witness heading for the ferry said he saw Arenelli's chauffeur drop her off as she crossed the street. The next thing he knew, he heard a thud and saw her on the asphalt."

Logan shook his head. "Jesus Christ, no. How bad?"

"She's in pretty ugly shape from what I could see, and all she was trying to do," Boyle pointed, "is cross this here street."

Dana stared at the accident scene. . .a leftover piece of metal, which appeared to be part of a running board, lay near the curb. Lime-green. Eddie Vineeti drove a 1938 Chevy of that same color. Dana began to speculate. May be Vineeti had asked Carmelina to meet him at the pier in Bay View. He must have known approximately the time that Carmelina would have been crossing the corner of Port and Reef Streets on her way to the Seaside Ferry and had watched in wait for her there, ready to run her down

***

At around nine p.m., in the dilapidated shed out back of his house, Eddie wiped the front fender of his 1938 Chevy with an oil-soaked rag in order to get a better view of the damage. He was just beginning to clean the underside of its grit, tar, and dirt particles when Rayna opened the door to the shed. She wore a plaid coat, a hat with a pom-pom on top, and mittens.

"What 'cha doin', Eddie? It's ten degrees outside." She wrapped her arms around herself.

Eddie kept working deliberately, avoiding the intrusion of his wife who seemed to have a knack for finding him whenever he wanted to be hidden from sight.

She came closer to him and tried to put her arms around his shoulders.

"Back off, broad! Can't you see I'm busy?"

Rayna did as she was told and distanced herself by a few feet. Her curiosity, though, still lingered. "What's wrong with your Chevy?"

"Just fixin' some paint that got chipped off the front fender. Now, leave me alone." He hoped she'd do as she was told. He had work to do. He grabbed the dolly block off the shelf behind him, ready to smooth out the jam in the fender, when Rayna spoke again.

"I've been meanin' to tell you, Eddie. Remember that rich woman who you said owes you some. . .the one you wrote the letter to?"

Eddie quickly turned and stared at Rayna. "Yeah? What about her?"

"She's in the hospital. Was crossin' a street on the Cape when some jerk took too quick of a turn and hit her."

"Hell no," Eddie said.

"But that ain't all, Eddie. The person who hit her never even stopped to see if she was all right."

Eddie could feel his face burning like hot acid and his knees felt like trembling twigs. "What else do you know?"

"I just heard all about it on the radio."

"Humph."

"It said that a lime-green car hit her. Eddie?"

"Yeah, so?"

"How many lime-green cars do you suppose there are?"

As if a wild storm overtook him, he scowled and gritted his teeth while grabbing Rayna by the sleeves of her coat. He began to shake her.

Rayna cried out, "Eddie! Stop! Stop!"

He watched as tears streamed down the woman's face, which had gone white, but found he couldn't stop himself. Finally, she fell onto the dirt floor of the garage at the same time that a loud bang could be heard at the side door of the building.

"Open up! It's the police!"

Rayna looked up at Eddie but didn't move or say a word.

Eddie opened the squeaky door but only a crack.

"Open up or I'll break the door down," the officer's voice said. Eddie did as he was told.

Office Boyle said, "You're under arrest for the hit 'n run of Carmelina Artenelli," while Officer O'Neil slapped handcuffs on him.

"Wait a minute. What in the hell is this all about?" Eddie asked, shaking his shoulders and twisting his back as if in some attempt to escape.

"You oughta know, buddy," Boyle said. "Extortion was bad enough but murder will put you in the clink for a long time to come."

Eddie tried to spit on the officer but missed.

Rayna had braced herself up against Eddie's Chevy. "Eddie, it was you, ain't it? God, no, Eddie. How could you?"

O'Neil shoved Eddie out the door. He looked back over his shoulder and yelled out, "Shut your mouth, you little bitch!"

Chapter Thirty-Eight

It had been almost forty-eight hours since the hit 'n run had occurred. Now, at ten a.m. Sunday morning, Dana sat next to the bed of Carmelina Artenelli at Cape Peril Memorial. On the night table next to her sat a vase with murky water and a wilted bouquet of pink roses. The note read:

All my love, Mia Godfrey

On another table near the window sat a tall vase filled with a mixed bouquet of red and pink roses, purple and yellow daisies, and sprigs of baby breath. The card read:

From your loving husband, Gino

Both of Mrs. Artenelli's legs were suspended in milk-white casts that ran from her hip to her ankle. Her head was bandaged, hiding her entire face from her forehead to her chin and concealing her hair. Dana picked up a copy of the *Cape Peril Post* and there on the front page, making headlines, it read:

Hit 'N Run Driver Strikes Down Cape's Philanthropist

Dana began to read:

Friday morning at eleven thirty-four a.m., Mrs. Carmelina Artenelli, well-respected and loved philanthropist on the Cape, was struck down by a hit and run driver on the corners of Port and Reef Streets. Police records indicate that Mrs. Artenelli was attempting to cross the Southeast corner of the street on her way to the Seaside Ferry when a lime-green car sped around the corner at a high rate of speed, knocking Mrs. Artenelli to the payment. The woman is recovering at Cape Peril Memorial Hospital, suffering from a broken pelvis and thirty-six stitches to her face. Doctor Beret, Mrs. Artenelli's attending physician, said, "With serious complications such as those of Mrs. Artenelli, I would anticipate a minimum of twelve weeks' hospital stay." Officer Boyle, the police officer at the scene of the crime, studied the evidence left from the accident and with the help of private investigator Dana Greer, was able to make an arrest late Friday night. A man, age twenty-four, from Waterville, named Eddie Vineeti was arrested and brought into custody at the Cape Peril Station. No further information is available as to the motive for the accident.

Beneath the headline, a photograph of Carmelina Artenelli showed her bandaged face.

Dana held the woman's frail hand in hers and listened as she tried to mumble something from beneath the multiple strips of gauze.

"It's him," she muttered. She nodded her head ever so slightly and groaned as if the mere movement caused her grave pain. She mumbled something that Dana couldn't discern.

"What? What did you say?" Dana asked, moving closer to the bedside of Mrs. Artenelli.

"Don't let them hurt him." With each word, Dana could feel the anguish in the woman's voice. "He's my son, my boy."

Dana stood motionless, speechless. The woman finally admitted the truth and hoped to protect her son as any loving mother would. Dana's convictions were verified. Eddie Vineeti was indeed the son of Carmelina and the father of Bernadette Godfrey. Even with all of Mrs. Artenelli's funds, she could not buy herself out of this tragedy, Dana thought. Eddie Vineeti would be charged not only with extortion with evidence of threat, but with attempted murder as well.

The handsome young man who physically radiated an innocent, boy next door kind of image could hardly support that stance now, proving that appearances can be deceiving. He would soon, by legal terms, be charged with an attempted murder. Ironically, as for the secrets Mrs. Artenelli kept, they were far from confidential. With the help Dana had gotten from Buzz Meechum and Guardian Angel Orphanage, she felt she had learned much about Mrs. Artenelli. There couldn't be too many more skeletons in her closet.

Dana was about to leave when a candy-striper entered the room, pushing a cart with yet more floral bouquets. The young girl looked pleased with her delivery. "Mrs. Artenelli, let's see what we have here. Is it possible to put any more arrangements in your room?" With her brightly painted pink fingernails, the girl began to lift each of the note cards, one at a time. "This assortment is from the staff and children at Holy Name Academy. This one's from the ladies' auxiliary. Let's see. This is from the parishioners of St. Michael's Parish in Bay View. Now, where should we put all of these? Oh, I missed one. This one's from the sisters of Guardian Angel Orphanage."

Mrs. Artenelli's torso seemed to stiffen slightly at the girl's last announcement. Other than being a faithful monetary contributor to the orphanage, it was evident that Mrs. Artenelli would understandably prefer not to be associated with the place.

"Why don't you let me help you?" Dana said to the candy striper. Within minutes, the hospital room looked more like the front window of a floral shop and smelled like a collection of fine perfumes. Dana stooped over Mrs. Artenelli to whisper that she'd better be on her way just when Gino Artenelli entered the room, wearing a three-piece, gray pin-striped suit with a bright red silk handkerchief in his breast pocket marked with a *G*. Like his wife, he too was a fashion statement, to say the least. Up close, the man's bulbous nose covered in broken blood vessels spoke of his long addiction to alcohol. He glanced at Dana as if he had never seen her before, and as Dana sat back down, she watched the overweight man struggle to plant kisses on his wife's bandaged face. "We'll get to the bottom of this, Carmelina. That son-of-a-bitch won't have to worry about a trial, I'll see to that." Then the man quickly glanced at Dana and said something to Carmelina under his breath. Dana could have sworn she heard him say something about *his boys*. As quickly as he had arrived, he left, saying, "Good day, Miss. . . ."

"Greer," Dana said.

Mrs. Artenelli's eyes fluttered slowly, a lone tear ran down her bandaged cheek. The trauma of the accident added to the pain medications she was on caused her to doze off. From Gino Artenelli's threat, it was apparent that he had no idea that Eddie was his own flesh and blood. Dana left the room, walked down the long corridor which smelled of rubbing alcohol and mercurochrome, and made her way down the steps of Cape Peril Memorial, located less than a half mile from the Pointe. She squinted as she started walking home, the sun bright like a summer's noon. The snow crunched beneath her boots and looked like tiny chips of diamonds. November 28[h]. . .Dana could not believe all that had happened in the four weeks since she arrived on the island. Truly, it could make a book. She pulled up the hood of her red coat and shielded her face from the badgering northern winds as she hailed a cab back to the Harrison home.

***

After all that happened with the unexpected accident, Dana's nerves felt frazzled, yet she remembered that she still had to call Amhurst; it was time that he learn who Jay's lover was and that Buzz Meechum would be just the person to help set up Amhurst's camera and tape recorder to prove it. Buzz had, after all, offered to help in any way that he could.

Amhurst answered on the first ring and was eager to meet Dana immediately at the Second Mate restaurant.

Dana sat at a round table with high-backed seats that looked like something out of a Medieval Castle. Running about ten minutes late, Amhurst entered, wearing a tailored blue suit with a pink oxford cloth shirt, his wool overcoat draped over his arm. He came toward Dana.

"Sorry I'm late." His salt-and-pepper hair was parted neatly on the side, and as before, his persona spoke of confidence and professionalism.

The waitress, dressed in a blue-and-white striped nautical looking uniform complete to the white Sailor hat, came to take their drink order. Dana ordered a glass of Sherry and Amhurst a glass of white wine. Before the woman walked away, she eyed Dana from head to toe and then did the same to Amhurst. Dana wondered if she wasn't one of those gossipy types who liked to spread rumors on the Cape. By now, most people recognized Dana as the private investigator who had come to the island to solve the murder case of Bernadette Godfrey.

"So, you said you had something to tell me about a Buzz. . .Buzz. . .what's his name?" Amhurst tossed his open hand into the air.

"Buzz Meechum. He's Holy Name Academy's janitor."

"Okay. Might I ask what in the hell he has to do with all of this?" Amhurst spoke his mind; that was for sure.

"Buzz told me about Jay's affair," Dana said, deliberately going slowly with her explanation in hopes of keeping Amhurst's blood pressure from rising. By the look of his red face, she could tell he was quickly growing impatient.

"How would a janitor know anything about Jay's behavior other than what he does when he's at school, possibly?" Amhurst narrowed his eyes and, for a moment, resembled the face on the painting of a pirate behind him, his words sharp like the swash buckler's sword.

Dana moistened her lips, guarding each word before she spoke. "It's at school that the affair takes place, Mr. Amhurst."

Amhurst edged closer and shielded his mouth. "Jesus, Mary, with a teacher? Is Jay involved with another teacher? Is that what you're telling me?"

Dana pressed her index finger to her lips, feeling like an elementary school teacher in the library with a class of students.

Amhurst's face turned a bright scarlet, and he rubbed the palms of his hands together. "So, continue."

"In answer to your question, yes, Jay is carrying on an affair with a teacher. According to the janitor, they meet regularly in the storage closet of the school."

A couple sitting across from Dana and Amhurst glanced over at them.

"Have they nothing better to do than to join in our conversation?" Amhurst asked.

"I doubt they've heard a word we've said," Dana answered. "Looks as if they are waiting for their bill." Dana assumed Amhurst's paranoia stemmed from him not wanting a word of this to leak. No, he wanted to spring the news on Jay Harrison when the time would be right.

"Well, this news is absurd! Ridiculous! Preposterous! I'd think the man would be smarter than that!" Amhurst said.

The waitress arrived, bringing Dana and Amhurst their drinks and asked if they'd like to order.

"No! Not now!" Amhurst said, causing the woman to crinkle up her nose and walk away. "So, who is this woman? I thought the staff at the Academy was predominantly nuns."

Dana cupped her hand around her lips and bent across the table. "Correct again."

"Jesus Christ, no. Are you telling me Jay is involved with a nun?" He threw his upper body back, rocking his chair as he did so. "When I'm done proving this tale to be fact, everyone will be reading it in the *Peril Post,* I guarantee you."

Just as Dana had surmised.

"Are any of the other sisters aware of this?" he asked.

"Not that I know of."

"But why? Why in the hell would Jay get himself involved with a religious of all people, for God's sake?" He pounded his fist on the table, spilling some of his wine onto his white linen napkin.

Dana lowered her voice to just above a whisper. "I wish I had an answer to that question. I suggest we meet with Buzz Meechum in order to discuss a strategy for setting up a secret camera and tape recorder in the Academy's storage closet. Once we have visual and auditory proof that Jay and the nun are involved in an illicit affair, those concerned will be hard pressed to deny it."

"I suggest we call the man immediately," Amhurst said, standing up and tossing a few bills onto the table. "We need to talk at once."

The waitress noticed that the two of them were leaving and said, "Was there something wrong with the service? Your drinks?" she asked, as she adjusted the Sailor cap on her head.

"No, nothing. Thank you," Dana said. "Just in a hurry."

Across the street from the restaurant was a phone booth. Amhurst slipped on his overcoat and said, "Do you have the man's number?"

Dana nodded and fumbled in her handbag for the slip of paper that Buzz had given her.

"Let's call him from there," Amhurst said, his head nodding in the direction of the phone booth.

Dana dialed the number as Amhurst stood, bracing the glass door open with his brown wing-tipped shoe.

"Buzz, it's Dana Greer. I'm with Mr. Amhurst. Is there a chance we could meet with you at once?"

Buzz invited them to his home, a block from the Second Mate. "Fourteen Rudder Street," he said.

"We'll be there in a minute," Dana answered.

Amhurst raised his shoulders stiffly, his posture rigid and erect and began walking next to Dana. She turned to look back at the restaurant; the waitress was standing by the door shaking her head.

Buzz's home looked like a cottage from a fairy tale with its low lying, red-shingled roof and matching red brick, a typical Snow White kind of place.

"Come in," he said. Without waiting for introductions, he introduced himself to Amhurst and shook his hand.

Amhurst eyed the small living room as Buzz told them to take a seat. A small gray-striped cat leapt off the cushion just as Amhurst was about to sit down. He dusted the fabric off, and small strands of fur rose in the air.

In his usual style, Amhurst wasted no time in getting right to the point. "What is this? Miss Greer tells me that my son-in-law is involved with a nun."

Buzz glanced over at Dana.

She nodded to give him approval to speak.

"That's true. Sister Mary Rose. "

"How in heaven's name would a woman of God who took the vow of chastity lower herself to becoming sexually involved with a married man?" Amhurst asked. He balled his hands into tight fists.

"I only know what I seen," Buzz said. "Every Tuesday night, the two of them. . .why, Mr. Harrison comes first, unlocks the storage closet, then the Sister arrives."

"Sounds pretty suspicious to me, but how are you certain?"

"The raincoats, Mr. Amhurst. Week-after-week, when I empty the trash can in the storage room, I find them. Why, the man ain't going to take no chances gettin' a nun pregnant."

"Pure disgust! What more can I say?" Amhurst said.

Dana wondered what Amhurst would say if he had known the nun had already gotten pregnant long before she gave her life to God.

"And my dear Loretta. She trusted Jay; she loved him. How could he do this to her?" Amhurst pounded one of his fists into the palm of his other hand. He ground his teeth together until his lips parted and saliva oozed from the corner of his lip.

"Buzz here has a plan. Why don't you tell Mr. Amhurst, Buzz?"

"What have you got in mind?" Amhurst asked, his voice one of arrogance and annoyance.

Dana was getting more and more upset with Amhurst's behavior. He might be mayor of Abilene, but he had to realize that Buzz and she were only looking out for his best interests.

"It's easy. We set up a camera, setting a timer to it, so that it snaps a picture, catching the two rascals right in the act. I'll have a tape recorder rolling, so their conversation will be easily understood. Other than that, it's up to them to provide the rest," Buzz said.

Amhurst sucked in his lower lip, his face one of disdain. "I have no more time to waste on this nonsense. It's time we hang up Jay's ass on a clothesline for all to see. The man is a disgrace to marriage, to religion, and to his profession."

Despite his haughty behavior, there was something to be admired about Amhurst, Dana thought, something about him that she actually liked. He was stern, yet level-headed, and definitely committed to his cause.

"When's the night all of this occurs?" he asked, in his state of anxiety forgetting that Buzz had already told him this.

"Tell him Buzz," Dana said.

"Near as I can tell, the two of them meet in the early evenings, usually on Tuesday nights. Don't ask me why that is. Maybe it's 'cause the school don't schedule no events on that night. Like I was saying, Mr. Harrison's got the key to the closet; he always arrives first, unlocks the door, and Sister follows shortly after." Buzz looked up at Amhurst. "Why don't you drop off your camera and recorder here on Monday, and I'll do the rest."

Dana looked from Buzz to Amhurst. The two men nodded and shook hands.

As Amhurst and Dana left Buzz's and were about to go their separate ways, Amhurst snickered and said, "I can't wait to see Father Sullivan's face when he finally has the proof."

Chapter Thirty-Nine

Dana, Amhurst, and Buzz gathered around the red oilcloth that covered his kitchen table. In the middle sat the tape recorder.

Amhurst fidgeted with his fingers, rubbing his thumb with his index finger, and moistened his lips with the tip of his tongue. "Before we begin, did everything go as planned last night?" he asked.

"Indeed, just as I said. Other than for the photo, which a friend of mine is developing in the dark room of his home, everything went fine."

"A friend? Who is this person? I don't want this becoming a public spectacle!" Amhurst shouted.

Buzz said his friend was one who could be trusted to keep his mouth shut and that he should have the picture by tomorrow. "Otherwise, things went exactly as planned. Jay arrived, looking over his shoulders as usual, unlocked the door to the storage closet, and waited for Sister. A few minutes later, Sister arrived. She seemed more anxious than I'd seen her before, hurried, restless," Buzz said, his head nodding more than usual, some type of neurological disorder Dana was convinced.

"Do you think she sensed something wasn't quite the same?" Dana asked. "Perhaps, a sixth sense kind of thing?"

"The equipment, the camera and recorder, were hidden on a high shelf. No, there was no way either one of them were aware of what was up," Buzz chirped in.

Buzz plugged in the tape recorder, and each of them crunched their shoulders as they lowered their bodies nearer to the table. The tape began with some scratching sounds and what sounded to be the moving of items and furniture. Then, the voices.

"Angela, I'm afraid we're going to have to stop meeting like this." Clearly, it was the voice of Jay Harrison.

"I don't care if she knows, Jay. I love you too much to lose you now."

"That bitch," Amhurst yelled out. "She's talking about my Loretta."

Dana tapped her hand on his raised knuckles in an effort to calm him.

The voice of Sister Mary Rose continued. "Why can't we just leave, Jay? Start anew somewhere else? Somewhere, where no one knows us."

A loud sigh came from Jay. "I told you, Angela, if we leave now, it will make things look too suspicious. Not until that Greer broad solves the case will it be safe for us to leave. You know I want nothing more, don't you, baby?"

"Baby? For Christ's sake, she's an adulteress, not a child," Amhurst said.

Buzz raised his index finger, covered in the blisters of a day laborer, and said, "Shh."

"What's solving the case got to do with us, Jay? We're not suspects," Sister said.

Dana wondered if this wasn't yet another of Sister's lies. She had to have known that she was definitely a likely suspect or, at least, a possible accomplice.

"Don't you get it, Angela? If we run now, everyone will think we have something to hide."

"But it's Byron, Jay, you know that, don't you?"

"I know. You've told me that a million times. Father Sullivan was behind the crime. But it doesn't matter." Jay's voice started to escalate. "He is, after all, a priest. What if no one believes us? Do you really think people will think he was capable of murder?"

"That's hogwash!" Amhurst yelled. "Now, the two plan to put the blame on the priest?"

"Shh," Buzz reiterated.

"So, you're saying the public will believe *I* did it. . .a bride of Christ, for God's sake? Is that what you're telling me?" The rage in the nun's voice was sharp and accusatory.

A moment went by with no rhetoric, only the scraping sounds like a table sliding across the floor. Dana's imagination pictured Jay shoving the nun against the wall, more-than-likely, smothering her face in kisses—all in an attempt to calm his lover.

"Of course, I'm not saying that, baby. You're the most innocent person I've ever met. You're like. . .why an angel, Angela."

She began to laugh loudly. "With all of the virtues but purity," she mocked.

"That's what I love the most about you, baby. Underneath those blue woolen robes of yours, you're the most seductive, sensual woman I've ever known."

"Jesus Christ. God have mercy on me!" Amhurst shouted. "This is pure disgust." He threw his fists into the air.

Sounds of the two of them kissing, storage items falling onto the floor, and a light thud could be heard.

"For God's sake, what's he done, pushed her onto a table?" Amhurst asked incongruously.

Buzz nodded. "Probably," was all he said, in a matter-of-fact tone.

"I've heard enough!" Amhurst said, and started to stand.

"Wait," Dana said. "There could be more."

Ruffled sounds came. Clothing being haphazardly torn off, the noise of keys falling onto the solid floor, the jingle of Sister's large crucifix and heavy rosary beads sacrilegiously hitting the vinyl tiles.

"Angela, you're all I want. When this is all behind us, I'll get the divorce I promised you. It'll be just you and me."

"And. . .what about Mother?" her voice filled with sarcasm.

"Just as far away from her as we can get," Jay said.

The two of them laughed. The tape elicited more sounds of their obvious lovemaking, and Dana realized the developed film would only serve as further proof of what was already known. To Dana, it was clear that Sister Mary Rose was going along with her father, setting up and blaming Father Sullivan for the death of Bernadette. To the nun, Jay might only be a tool to what Sister Mary Rose hoped would be her ticket as far away from Cape Peril as she could get.

"He's nothing more than a fool if he thinks he can get away with this," Amhurst said.

Amhurst was correct in his assessment. Jay was nothing more than a fool getting involved with the nun. But if Dana's suspicions were correct, she predicted his role as fool would go much further than just his lovemaking.

Chapter Forty

It was almost ten a.m. when the phone rang. "Dana Greer, speaking."

"Dana, it's Buzz. Can you meet me at the school? I've got the photo."

Last night's blizzard had dumped a good two feet of snow, and most homes and businesses hadn't gotten around to shoveling the mess. Beautiful, pure, and untouched, but near impossible to tread through. Dana felt as if her legs were trudging through canisters of molasses as she trucked toward the Academy. She remembered dreams like this, where she had tried to hurry along, always running late, and yet unable to move her feet any faster.

When she finally arrived, she found Buzz washing the interior glass of the front doors to the school.

"These lousy kids, always putting their mitts on the glass. It's a vicious circle trying to keep these doors clean," he said. He set his rag down on the edge of a large metal pail and hushed Dana into the empty chapel. The scent of roses filled the small space, and Dana's attention was drawn toward the pew in which they sat. Holy cards picturing Saint Rita lay on the bench, the patroness of hopeless cases. She slipped one into her coat pocket.

"I've got it," he said, the excitement in his voice causing his head to nod more rapidly than usual. "The photo my friend developed. If Amhurst is looking for more proof, he'll have it now," Buzz said, as he pulled the picture from the top pocket of his bib overalls. "Take a look at this."

Dana studied the black-and-white picture, looking first at the floor in the photo. In a crumpled heap were the nun's white coif and wimple along with her black veil. In another pile lay Jay's clothing, and on top of them, Sister's holy blue serge habit. In the background were her sacramentals: the large crucifix and her wooden rosary beads next to a ring of keys. As Dana's eyes scanned upward, just as Amhurst had said, a wooden table stood in the middle of the storage closet, surrounded by shelves and shelves of various cleaning supplies. Propped in a corner were a broom, dust pan, and mop. Off to the side was a large metal pail and a matching trash can. Dana glanced again at the table, after being sidetracked by the arrangement of the storage closet or maybe just too afraid to eventually see for herself what she believed to be true. There lay Sister Mary Rose and Jay. There was no doubt that the two of them were adulterous lovers.

Buzz looked at Dana assuredly. "Well, what'd ya think?"

"I think, you did great work, Buzz. This is exactly what Amhurst will need to prove his point."

"You go ahead and see to it the man gets it," Buzz said.

In the back of Dana's mind, she wondered again as to what this would all mean for Sister Mary Rose. Amhurst had said that Father Sullivan refused to believe Jay could be involved in an affair. The priest had said that he had known Jay for five years and wasn't about to let some gossip soil the man's reputation. Father Sullivan had told Amhurst that Jay was a man of high morals, but Dana pondered what Father Sullivan would think of Harrison now when not only was there an explicit photo of him and Sister together, but there was also a tape of their heated conversation. Dana had no idea how the priest would react when he realized that Jay's lover was Sister Mary Rose. Dana knew the priest had been infatuated with the nun ever since she was a student in his class. In Father's eyes, the woman was a model of perfection. Surely, he would be shocked to see the woman who he had put on such a pedestal not only fall from grace but who also was attempting to implicate him in the murder of Bernadette Godfrey. Cape Peril was to hear one of its biggest scandals, of that Dana was sure.

She thanked Buzz for his work.

On Dana's way out of the chapel, Sister Mary Rose passed by her. The nun was leading a group of children out to the playground behind the school. She pretended not to see Dana.

"Come along, children," the Sister said, and motioned for the class, walking in single file, to follow her. In the nun's wake, all Dana heard was the rippling sound of Sister's long habit against the tiled floor and the hushed whispering of the children, anxious to play in the snow.

The minute Dana got back to the Harrison home, she called Amhurst and told him that he would have all the proof he needed to convict Jay of the sin of adultery.

"That's great news, Miss Greer, but I'm afraid when it comes to Jay, the news might be a bit too late."

"What do you mean?"

"He's gone, nowhere to be found."

"But that can't be. What about his class?"

"I pretended I was a concerned anonymous parent and called the school's principal. The nun told me that Mr. Harrison had not showed up for classes this morning and that she had a difficult time finding a substitute at such a late notice. She said it was out-of-character for Mr. Harrison to miss class." Amhurst went quiet for a while. "Now, I'm concerned about that little tramp. The two of them had talked about leaving the area together."

"I just saw Sister Mary Rose at school, so we know she hasn't left with him." Dana hesitated to tell Amhurst that Logan had the nun under surveillance. As far as Amhurst knew, Sister Mary Rose was an adulteress, not a possible suspect in the murder of Bernadette Godfrey. "Let me call Logan and tells him Harrison's on the lose," Dana said.

"What the hell?" Logan said, shocked by Dana's news. "Harrison's taken off? For where? Let me call Ed Laboure, the ticket master at the ferry, and see what he can tell me."

Logan dialed the ferry and Ed Laboure answered. Logan quickly filled him in on the disappearance of Jay.

"Saw the man on the ten a.m. ferry," Laboure told Logan. "Told me he had a plane to catch. The guy seemed angry that the ferry was being delayed. We had an unusual amount of cars riding over this morning."

Logan thanked Laboure and dialed the airport in Bay View. He spoke with the ticket supervisor. "We've got a guy on the loose from the Cape, a Jay Harrison, wanted as a person of interest in the Bernadette Godfrey case. He may very well be at the airport, purchasing a ticket."

"Got any idea what airline?" the supervisor asked.

"Unfortunately, not."

"I'll notify all of our ticket agents at once, Sergeant Logan."

Logan hung up and gave the same message to Sergeant Middleton of the Bay View State Police Department. Middleton offered to send some of his officers to the airport.

When Logan called Dana to update her on the news, she said, "Sounds like we've got a Bonny and Clyde on our hands."

"And I'm not sure how far Clyde will go to protect Bonny." Logan added.

"Especially if Bonnie's convinced Clyde that she's innocent." Dana had no sooner put the receiver down about to brew a pot of coffee, when Amhurst called.

"Any news on the scoundrel?"

"Jay Harrison might very well be on his way to purchasing a plane ticket out of the country."

"What! Probably two tickets, I'm sure."

"Don't worry. Logan and I have things under control. I'm confident we'll have Harrison back on the Cape in no time."

"I like your attitude, Miss Greer. Once the authorities nail the bastard, I say you and me head over to Father Sullivan's. There shouldn't be any doubt in the padre's mind this time that Jay Harrison is nothing more than a dirt bag, and wait until Father finds out who Harrison's girlfriend is. That ought to shake up his confidence in the goodness of humanity."

Dana reserved her comments. It was not as if Amhurst didn't have his own issues, paying off Jay to marry his daughter Loretta and even going so far as to buy them a house and to give Jay a monthly stipend to stay with Loretta. Now that deal, too, would backfire. Dana no sooner poured herself a cup of coffee with thoughts about paying Mrs. Artenelli another visit at Peril Memorial, when the phone rang yet again.

"Dana, Logan here. Carmelina Artenelli called from the hospital. She said she needs to see you at once."

"That's interesting. I was just about to pay her another visit."

"Hope I wasn't too presumptuous, but I took it upon myself to call a taxi for you. Plus, the call sounded urgent."

Dana set her cup on the edge of the sink. She could not even see the trees in the backyard, a blizzard of white. In only minutes, the doorbell rang, and Dana opened the door to a man covered in snow from head-to-foot. "You ordered a cab?"

"Why, yes. I'll be right out," she said, as she hurried to put on her coat and scarf and struggled to zip her fur-cuffed rubber boots. The cab's engine was running, and the heater blowing full blast when Dana entered. "Peril Community Hospital, please, hurry." She had no idea what all of this could be about, but she knew Logan would never send her out on a day like this unless it was important. The cab skidded away from the curb.

Dana opened her bag and ran her fingers across the cover of her miniature Bible. These were the times in any private investigator's life that one waited for. Questions finally with answers, suspects with authentic motives, arrests on suspicion of possible murder, yet she found herself feeling anxious as if an unknown boulder was ready to fall in her path but she had no idea when and from what direction.

"Got a sick one at the hospital?" the driver asked, his neck crooked in her direction.

"I do," Dana said, wishing that were the case. Mrs. Artenelli wasn't calling upon her as a visitor; that much was for sure.

The cab driver pulled up in front of the red-brick building, Dana paid him his fee, and hurried up to the third floor of the hospital.

The door to Mrs. Artenelli's room was slightly ajar. Dana knocked, and Mrs. Artenelli said, "Dana, please. . .come in."

Both of Mrs. Artenelli's casted legs were still hoisted in the air. Most of the bandages had been removed from her face, and what flesh was exposed was bruised and swollen.

"I'm so glad you came," she said, her voice cracking. The radio on her bed stand played Johnnie Ray's hit, "Cry." He pelted out the words as if singing to an audience of one.

Dana pulled the chair in the corner closer to Carmelina's bedside.

Mrs. Artenelli rubbed the tears from her puffy purple-ringed eyes. "My Angela. . .such a sweet girl but so naive. I told her to watch herself with the boys. You know, Angela is a beautiful young woman."

"She is," Dana said.

"She never should have gone to that party that night. . .I told her. . .I warned her. That's when she met Eddie." Carmelina struggled with her words. "The two started going steady right away. Well, you know, it's a mortal sin; the Church forbids such activity and for good reason."

"Yes, I know."

"The inevitable happened. My Angela got pregnant. Eddie wanted Angela to keep the baby. I absolutely refused! Why Angela was only sixteen-years-old. What could she possibly know about motherhood?"

Dana continued to respond with short interjections. "True."

Carmelina's eyes filled with tears, her chest rose and fell. "Angela would have done away with the child if it hadn't been for me."

Dana reached for a tissue and handed it to the woman.

"That's when I stepped in and took charge of the future of the baby, waiting until I felt I had found a perfect, Catholic home for the child." Quickly, Carmelina jumped to the present. "When I learned that the Godfreys were moving to the Cape, I felt that I was obligated to tell Angela that Bernadette was the child she had given up for adoption, her child."

Dana let the woman catch her breath between her tears.

Carmelina continued. "At first, Angela wanted to do away with her own life, but I convinced her otherwise. I told her that I, too, had been in her situation when I was a young woman. . .Eddie, you know." The woman shook her head from side-to-side as if she herself couldn't believe that history had repeated itself.

Dana nodded and suddenly felt a deep pang of sympathy for the woman before her who chose to bare her soul, sins and all. "Then, Angela learned that Eddie was actually her brother?"

"Of course, I had kept telling myself that it wasn't true, that Eddie couldn't be my son. I denied it to the last minute until I couldn't face myself in the mirror any longer. Then Eddie contacted me and said he wanted to talk to me in person and asked if I'd meet him at the pier in Bay View. My husband. . .well. . .Gino. . .once he found out that Eddie was after me for money, he had his boys threaten Eddie."

Just as I thought, Dana mused.

"Eddie watched for me, planned to run me down." In a hushed voice, she said, "My own son wanted his mother dead." The woman sobbed uncontrollably. "My Eddie, my boy."

"I know this must be hard for you, Carmelina. Take your time. Breathe deeply."

Carmelina asked Dana for another tissue, and in a soft voice as if speaking to herself said, "Bernadette, the poor child. May her soul rest in peace."

"You did what you thought best at the time," Dana said.

Carmelina swallowed her tears. "When Angela found out Bernadette was her child, she went to Mia Godfrey, told her the whole story."

Dana tapped her fist against her lips. It was all making sense now.

"At first, Mia wouldn't believe Angela. She called me, asked me if what Angela had told her was the truth. I had no choice; I had to tell her; I said, 'Yes.'"

"Did Mrs. Godfrey tell you exactly what Angela had told her?"

"She did. Angela told Mia the child was born of the devil, that she was a grave mistake, marked by God as a child of Satan! Angela said that the child should have been disposed of before even being born. Don't you see, Dana? My daughter is blaming me for all of this."

"That's dreadful. What did Mrs. Godfrey say to all of this?"

"That was when she told Angela the God-awful things Joe had done to the girl. Mia said the child's soul had been tarnished. Mia said that it got to the point where she couldn't even look at Bernadette any longer." Carmelina choked on her own tears, coughing into her tissue. "My Angela convinced Mia that child needed to be destroyed."

Dana shook her head and wiped a bead of sweat from the woman's brow.

"That was in the middle of September. On October 25, Bernadette's body was found." Carmelina burst in to tears again, the veins in her neck protruding and blue, hyperventilating, unable to catch her breath, gasping.

Dana put her hand on the woman's shoulder. "Try to breathe through your mouth, slowly, very slowly." Dana could hear her own heart pounding in her ears, the spoken words so unbelievable. She waited until the woman's breathing became more regular before she went on. "Are you saying that Mia Godfrey is the one responsible for Bernadette's death?" Dana could not believe her own question.

Carmelina nodded. "I'm positive. Angela came and stayed with Gino and me, the night before the girl went missing; that morning, Angela awoke late. I had come home from morning Mass just as she was getting up. Oh, my God, my holy God!" Carmelina cried.

Dana placed her hand on Carmelina's cheek.

"Angela told me that morning. Mia had taken Bernadette to the grave site that only days earlier Angela had prepared, and it was my Angela who told Mia that she was like Abraham, offering her only child as a sacrifice to God."

"This is unbelievable. . .Mrs. Godfrey doing away with her own child. I don't know what to say." Dana gripped at the corners of her mouth. She sat dazed for a moment, a feeling of light-headedness coming over her.

"The two made a pact," Carmelina continued. "Angela prepared the child's grave, and Mia sacrificed her only child."

The image of Abraham and Isaac on the holy card that Angela had given Dana came back. Dana remembered God's words from the Bible. "Abraham, I want you to take your only son Isaac—the one you love so dearly—up to the mountains, and there offer him to me." The story went on to say that Abraham was sad, that he had waited so long for a son, that he didn't want to give him away, but that he obeyed. The words of Doctor Thatcher also came to Dana's mind, "Sometimes, children can sense their own deaths." If that were the case, it might explain why Bernadette had chosen the holy card from Sister Mary Rose, the one with Abraham offering Isaac on an altar to God.

Carmelina held her hand against her chest. In between her sobbing, she said, "Angela told me before Mia stabbed the child, Bernadette cried out, "Mommy, what's the hole for?"

Dana could hear the words that Isaac had asked his father, "But where is the lamb for our offering?" Dana now knew the answer that she had come looking for. Dana could not wait to get back to the station to inform Logan of what she had just learned from Mrs. Artenelli. Without a doubt, there were two accomplices to the murder of Bernadette Godfrey: Mrs. Artenelli for keeping such unholy secrets to herself and her daughter, Sister Mary Rose. Somewhere in the pit of Dana's stomach she had a feeling what it must be like to be a priest, hearing another's confession. The only difference was that Dana was free to tell what she had just heard.

***

By the time Dana returned to the station, Logan told her he had gotten a call from the Bay View Police. Jay Harrison was found at the TWA counter buying two tourist tickets. He was handcuffed and arrested and was due back on the five o'clock ferry.

"Did they say where he was headed?" Dana asked.

"Somewhere in Hawaii."

"Interesting, so off to the South Pacific and with two tickets."

"More-than-likely out of Gino Artenelli's wallet," Logan said.

"Makes sense."

"Speaking of the Artenellis, what'd Carmelina want?"

Dana explained that the woman had given her a full confession. The sheet taken from the convent, the meticulous grave preparation—all the work of Sister Mary Rose, Dana told Logan. When Dana proceeded to inform him that the nun had been an accomplice, but that Mia Godfrey was the one who actually stabbed her child to death in order to rid herself of a child of Satan, Logan bolted up from his chair. "God in heaven, no! An innocent child taken by the hand of her own mother? Not Mia Godfrey. I never. . .well, I," he shook his head several times, "certainly didn't see that one coming."

"I have to admit. I didn't either. It's evident Sister Mary Rose is nothing short of a monster."

Logan sat back down. He brushed the palm of his hand over his face several times. Minutes passed as Dana and he sat in silence, in disbelief. . .a case solved, a murderer identified but hardly one would ever suspect. . .Mia Godfrey, a mother, a murderer.

When the startling news finally settled, Logan looked at his watch and said, "Nearly three-thirty. I suggest we meet Boyle who's over at the Academy shadowing the nun. It's time we bring her down to the station, where we'll need to get her confession, so she can be charged as an accomplice in the murder of her daughter. I'll have Frank O'Neil arrest Mrs. Godfrey and charge her with the murder."

***

Dana rode along with Logan as he sped toward Holy Name Academy, turning on the patrol car's screeching siren along with the whirling blue light atop the roof of the vehicle.

"Do you think that's necessary?" Dana asked.

"Around here we don't see that much action. Trust me. The locals will get a kick out of it," Logan said, sounding like a high school student out on the night in his zooped-up car.

Logan parked his police cruiser in front of the school. Boyle was parked in a side lot, bopping his head to some music station unaware of Dana and Logan's arrival.

Logan and Dana made their way to Sister Mary Rose's classroom, where they found her humming a Christmas carol and erasing the blackboard. All of the children were gone for the day. The nun seemed startled when Dana and Logan entered, totally unprepared for their visit. Logan took out a pair of handcuffs as Dana said, "Sister, you are under arrest as an accomplice in the murder of Bernadette Godfrey."

"What are you talking about? Bernadette was my student, my favorite student." Trying to hide her alarm, Sister Mary Rose continued to erase the board, making large up-and-down movements with her arm.

"I'm afraid she was more than just your student, Sister," Dana said.

The nun spun around. Her black eyes glared like those of a panther. She blew off the chalk crumbs from the eraser and banged it down on the tray. "I suggest you let me speak with my father before you dare touch me. Daddy won't want you laying a hand on me."

"Right now, you will have to come with us to the station, Sister," Dana said, as she watched Logan twist the nun's white wrists behind her back as he snapped the cuffs.

"There's some obvious mistake here. I'm not the person you want." She wiggled about as if she thought she could break free of the handcuffs.

Logan and Dana looked at each other and then at the nun.

"I suggest you'd better find Jay Harrison; he's the man you'll want for the murder of Bernadette Godfrey." The words clipped off her tongue sharply as if they could slice.

Lies and more lies. Like her parents, Sister Mary Rose would do whatever it took to hide any guilt she might have, even if it meant turning in her own lover. She had, indeed, played Jay Harrison for a fool.

"No worry," Logan said, "the Bay View Police are bringing him back to the Cape on the next ferry."

"Bringing him back?" the nun asked, her voice surprised.

"From the airport," Dana said.

"What in heaven's name would he being doing there?"

"I believe you know the answer to that one," Dana said to the nun. Logan and Dana escorted the nun out of the school, Logan behind her and Dana beside her. She bowed her head, forcing her black veil to shield her face.

The principal came running out of her office. "What's going on here? What's happened?" she asked. "Sister, are you okay?"

"Read all about it in tomorrow's paper," Logan said. The three stepped out of the building. Boyle exited his cruiser, a look of surprise covering his face. The low lying gray clouds overhead, a background for despair.

Cameras from the *Peril Post* snapped photo after photo of the young woman who only months ago had professed her final vows as a bride of Christ.

By this time, a group of people had gathered around the sidewalk in front of the school. Others mingled near the police cruiser whose blinking blue light continued to spin. Mixed in the crowd of bystanders was Father Sullivan. "Sister," he called out. "I'll meet you at Logan's."

On the trip to the station, Sister Mary Rose repeated some Bible verses over and over as if she were in some sort of trance. Logan parked the cruiser and escorted the nun from the back seat. "It's a good thing we've got four cells here," he said over his shoulder to Dana. "Looks like we'll soon have a full house."

Janet, the receptionist, put down the lid to her compact and under her breath said, "Holy cow! A nun in handcuffs!"

The clanking of iron bars from the first cell could be heard. The nun turned her head in the direction of the noise.

"Well, well, what do you say, Sis? Looks like we're a twosome after all," Eddie said, running the wedding band on his finger across the door to his cell as if playing a banjo. "How's mom doing? Heard she's going be laid up for a while."

In the background, a radio announcer already privy to the arrests announced the news to the public.

The nun scowled at Eddie while Logan shoved her into her cell and slammed the door. Dana and Logan made their way down the narrow corridor of the station that housed the cells. Logan locked the outer, concrete door as he and Dana walked toward his office.

"Logan," Janet said, "you've got a visitor. He wouldn't wait; he's in your office."

Rubbing his hands together and blowing his breath into his palms sat Father Sullivan. He got up as Dana and Logan entered. "Sorry to intrude like this, but what's going here? First, I see Sister Mary Rose being led out of the Academy, her hands behind her back, a police cruiser taking her away." He sat back down.

"You've got it, Father," Logan said, positioning himself behind his desk. "By now, the news has probably traveled around the Cape."

"So I've heard. . .Sister is being charged as an accomplice to murder? Nonsense! This just can't be."

"I'm afraid it is true, Father," Dana said, placing her hand on his arm as she sat next to him.

"May I see her? Can I talk to her?" His shiny black shoe tapped involuntarily on the floor, his leg shaking.

Logan went to tell the nun that she had her first visitor while at the same time leading Father down the dark corridor toward her cell.

"Father, I'm so glad you've come. There's been a mistake," the nun said, in a childlike voice.

Father Sullivan sat down on the metal bench next to the nun. He held her hands in his. "Tell me all about it, my child."

"It was Jay, Father." She began to cry. "He's trying to put the blame on me. I was home that morning. . .the morning Bernadette never showed up for school. I was with Mother; you can even ask her yourself."

"But why would Jay want to harm the child, Sister? He tutored her, invited her into his home."

"Don't you see? It was only a sham. He was upset that Loretta and he could never have a child of their own."

"Cause enough for murder? This doesn't make much sense, Sister, I'm afraid." He ran his hand along the folds of her black veil.

She looked up at the priest, a picture of innocence. "He just couldn't take it any longer, Father. Don't you see? It does make sense." Sister's eyes squinted.

"I suppose, but murder? I mean, it seems like a long shot."

Sister pulled aside from the priest. "Are you saying that I'm lying, that you don't believe me?" She grabbed at the rosary beads hanging from her side.

"Why, it's just that. . . ."

"You're no different than the others, are you? How dare you, a priest, be so quick to judge. Sergeant, Sergeant, take this hypocrite away from me."

Logan opened the cell and led Father away. He looked back at the nun peering through the bars of her cell. A tear fell down Father's cheek. "How wrong I've been."

Chapter Forty-One

Dana had had a restless sleep. She found herself at the grave site of Bernadette Godfrey, the little's girl's face staring up at her, her wee voice squealing, "Mommy, Mommy." The girl's arms reached upward toward Dana, longing to be lifted from the grave. Dana awoke to the screaming of the telephone. She ran down the stairs into the kitchen and picked up the receiver.

"Dana, it's Amhurst. I say we take the proof over to the priest. Now that he sees his holier than though nun locked away, it's about time that he learn what other sins she's committed."

Dana agreed and an hour later the two of them found themselves seated in the rectory across from Father Sullivan. The normally handsome man looked haggard, the corner of his eyes sagging and the color of his complexion white as the wall behind him. Amhurst played the tape that Buzz had recorded.

"Angela, I'm afraid we're going to have to stop meeting like this."

"I don't care if she knows, Jay. I love you too much to lose you now."

Pure hypocrisy, using Jay as a foil, Dana thought.

The priest clasped his hands to his face, his fingers pointed upward in a prayerful mode. "Good, God, no."

The tape moved ahead.

"Don't you get it, Angela? If we run now, everyone will think we have something to hide."

The nun's voice answered, "But it's Byron, Jay, you know that, don't you?"

The priest lowered his hands cracking his knuckles. "Mary, Mother of God, no!"

"You've told me that a million times; Father Sullivan was behind the crime. But it doesn't matter. He is, after all, a priest. What if no one believes he was capable of murder?"

"Please, please, I've heard enough," Father said.

"There's more, Father," Amhurst said, placing the photograph of the two lovers in front of the priest.

Father lifted the picture and stared at it. His eyes glossed over as he blinked hard. "Surely, the last twenty-four hours have been a source of disillusionment for me."

Amhurst was about to speak, but Dana motioned his silence.

The priest went on. "I taught Angela Artenelli as a novice before her profession of final vows. There were so many times that I questioned her vocation, wondered if she were truly being called."

"Guess you have your answer," Amhurst said.

"You must understand, Mr. Amhurst, that any woman as beautiful as Sister would be tempted by her vows." Father looked over at the photograph of the nun on his desk. By his expression, he might well have been speaking of his own temptation by the young nun's charm. When he spoke of her, a morose look came over his face. He seemed to be more troubled about the nun's adulterous love affair than he was about the accusation the nun had made against him.

"With the proof before you, Father, what will be your plan of action?" Amhurst asked.

His abruptness bothered Dana, but she remained quiet, letting Father speak.

"It's obvious that the law will now take care of Sister. The incident will surely bring shame upon the good sisters and the Church, but we must remember the captain of the ship is divine. It is the crew who are human. None of us is perfect, Mr. Amhurst. In God's eyes, we are all sinners."

Amhurst brushed a piece of lint off his coat sleeve. "I suppose. I suppose," he said. He looked downward and continued to rub the wool of his sleeve.

"From the latest news report, Jay Harrison was brought back to the Cape, questioned, and is soon to be released, Father," Dana said.

"So I've heard. I will pay him a visit immediately. Let him know that no matter how serious his offense, merciful God is always willing to forgive."

***

As Dana neared the station, she could hear the loud shouting of men's voices. It was Gino Artenelli. Several Cape Peril residents hovered on the sidewalk, gaping at the activity. Ray McGregor snapped his camera several times.

In the doorway to the station stood Gino, wagging his index finger at Logan, as he stepped inside. "What are you trying to tell me. . .my daughter murdered that school child?"

"Your wife confessed to everything, Mr. Artenelli," Dana said, as she entered the building.

"Oh, it's *you* again. What confession? What are you talking about?"

"She asked me to see her at the hospital. She told me everything," Dana said.

"The woman's suffered a head injury. Are you about to believe her?"

"Early this morning, Mr. Artenelli, your wife told us everything she knew. It was Mia Godfrey who murdered her child." Logan said. "It was your daughter who prepared the grave of the child."

"What in the hell are you saying? My daughter? A nun, for God's sake, preparing a grave? I've never heard of anything so outlandish? The child was her student."

"The child was more than just her student, Mr. Artenelli. I suggest you speak with your wife," Dana said. It was evident that Carmelina was accomplished at keeping secrets. Not only had she not told Gino that Eddie Vineeti was the son they gave away years earlier, but she also never told Gino that Bernadette Godfrey was Angela's child.

"What are you saying? I intend to get to the bottom of this, and when I do, you'll all have a lawsuit on your hands. Slander! That's what this is. How dare you try to take the Artenelli name down! I won't hear of it." The man stormed out of the station.

Logan looked at Dana. "Better get to the hospital at once. Gino Artenelli is about to confront his wife. I don't trust the man."

***

"What are you doing here?" Carmelina asked, yawning and with an expression of surprise as she stared at Dana.

"It's your husband. . .he's on his way over. He wants to know the truth about Bernadette Godfrey. He's refusing to believe that your daughter was an accomplice in her murder."

The door to the hospital room banged open. Gino's face red, the veins in his forehead pulsating, he grabbed his wife by the arm.

Dana shot up. "Let's keep your hands off of her." Dana pressed the nurse button next to Carmelina's bed.

"She's my wife, you little piece of shit!" With his fists clenched, he asked, "What right do you have being here?"

"Logan sent me. I'm here to protect your wife."

Gino glared at Dana. He stepped closer to Carmelina's bedside. "Carmelina, what's this about?"

Just then a nurse burst into the room. "Is there something wrong?"

"Please send for security," Dana said.

"Why don't you leave, Miss Greer. This matter is between my wife and me!"

The nurse took one look at the sweating man and ran out of the room.

"Gino, I can explain. I can explain everything," Carmelina said, her voice wavering.

"Maybe you had better!"

Carmelina began at the beginning. "The baby I gave up for adoption?"

"Yeah, yeah."

"His name is Eddie Vineeti."

"That monster who put you in this hospital bed? How can that be?"

"Trust me, Gino. He is our son."

Gino raced to the window and peered out. He wiped his forehead with the palm of his hand. He paced across the width of the small room. "You're sure?"

"Positive. I saw the birth certificate. But that's not all, Gino. The child. . .Bernadette. . . ."

"Wait a minute!" He threw his hand against the side of his head. In a loud, doubting voice, he asked, "Are you going to tell me that she is the child Angela gave away?"

"Yes. Yes. Bernadette was Angela's child. She was also Vineeti's child."

Gino instantly fell to his knees at the bedside of his wife. "Did she know? Did Angela know?"

"No, not until recently. . .the whole truth came out."

Gino clutched at the hospital sheet, his fingernails turning red. "The Artenelli name. What will come of the Artenelli name? It's been destroyed. Don't you understand, Carmelina? It's been destroyed." The man began to weep.

At that moment a hospital security guard entered the room, took one look at the man on his knees, helped him up, and led Gino out of the room and down the corridor toward the elevators.

***

On her way to Mia Godfrey's cell, Dana ran into Jay Harrison on his way out of the station. The man appeared flushed, his eyes bloodshot.

"Jay," Dana called. She wasn't quite sure what to say to the man.

He looked sideways at her, his face blushed, a small twitch in his cheek. "Someone once said, 'No one ever found wisdom without also being a fool. Guess that pretty much sums up my time on the Cape.'"

Dana assumed she knew exactly what the man was referring to.

"Logan told me. To clear her own name, Angela tried to put the blame on me."

"Try not to be too hard on yourself, Jay. Hopefully, we all stand to learn from our mistakes."

"It sure took a real lesson to teach me." He looked up, but his eyes focused away. "I mean, I've lost my wife, the woman who I thought loved me, and even my job."

Not knowing quite what to say to the man, Dana patted his sleeve and only said, "I wish you the best from here."

He sniffled and walked down the block headed toward the ferry.

Dana knew there really was no reason to feel sorry for the man as he had brought his own sorrows upon himself, yet for some reason, she felt empathy for him.

She walked into the station, where the receptionist was brushing her hair at her desk. "Quite the stories around here, eh? Too bad you're an investigator and not a writer."

Dana smiled.

"That Harrison guy is quite the hunk, wouldn't you say?"

"I think that might be part of his problem," Dana said. "Now, I'd like to visit with Mia Godfrey."

"Logan's gone for the afternoon, but he left me the keys to the cells in case you stopped by." Janet handed the key marked *Cell #3* to Dana.

When Dana entered Mia Godfrey's cell, she found the woman flattening her hair with her hand and pushing the gray strands behind her ears. "I'm so sorry. I should have told you. I've wasted your time." The woman huddled against the concrete wall, her frail, shaking body blending in with the mortar.

Similar to Father being more concerned over Sister's secretive affair with Jay Harrison more so than her erroneous accusation against him, so, too, Mia Godfrey exhibited more guilt for having deceived Dana than the woman felt sorrow for murdering her own child.

Dana did not respond, only stared at the woman as she continued.

Like an RCA record that spun on its turntable round-and-round, Mia's words flowed. "Once Sister told me. . .said Bernadette was conceived in haste, marked by the devil as one of his own, I couldn't bear to look at the child any more. Sister hated her, as well. She blamed her mother. Sister had only wished that she had done away with the baby from the beginning." The woman toyed with a loose thread on her orange prison garb. "Don't you see? Sister and I had no choice. The child was soiled from the beginning. It explains why Joe. . . ."

Dana found herself growing angry at Mrs. Godfrey's deplorable explanation, her words too difficult to listen to. For a mother to take the life of her innocent child was beyond belief.

"Sister was the one to find the spot, a beautiful place in the bog lands. The marshy ground was easy for her to dig."

Dana pressed her fingernails into her upper lip, her eyes squinting in disbelief as the woman continued to confess her horrendous deed.

"I felt like Abraham, offering his only son. You know, he only did what God asked of him, don't you?" A peculiar smile crossed the woman's lips. "I laid Bernadette in the grave. I only meant to stab her once, but Bernadette wouldn't lay still. She tried to break free from my grip." The woman cast her eyes to the floor, and in a quiet voice said, "I stabbed her again, and again!" The woman glanced at Dana, a simple child-like expression crossed her face.

Dana studied the woman's posture. Her body folded in half, her shoulders shivering. Dana had the confession she had come to the Cape for, yet she wondered if Mia Godfrey would be mentally stable enough to stand trial.

As Dana was about to leave the station, she bumped into Father Sullivan.

"Praise, God, Miss Greer, for the work you do. Your reward will be great."

Dana smiled. The look on Father's face told her that he was carrying a heavy cross. "And yours, Father. The weight of sinners can't be an easy load."

"It never is. . .it never is," he said.

***

The following morning, Dana went down to the pier to buy a copy of the *Cape Peril*. She had just put the folded paper into her bag when she saw Amhurst and his daughter, Loretta, walking toward her.

"We're pulling out on the ten a.m. ferry, Dana," Amhurst said. Loretta stood by her father's side. She stared into the distance. They each had a brown piece of luggage.

"That quickly?" Dana asked. "I had no idea. Headed back to South Dakota, are you?"

"After all that's happened, Loretta and I couldn't get out of here fast enough. Let's just say the Cape has left us with some bad memories. But, listen. The house, as you know, is on the market, but with the understanding that you stay in the home until the trial."

"How kind of you," Dana said.

The ferry's horn honked.

"We'd better be going," Amhurst said. He took his daughter by the hand. Loretta smiled.

Dana looked back at the two of them. Perhaps, this was the best decision. Amhurst would be able to continue protecting and watching over his daughter, and as for Loretta, she would be happier in her father's care than she had ever been while married to Jay. Dana went back to the empty house and felt that if walls could speak, these might very well be saying, "Amen." She put on a pot of coffee and pulled the newspaper from her bag as she sat down and read:

Mother Murders Daughter, Nun Assists

Mia Godfrey was arrested yesterday after confessing to the death of her seven-year-old daughter, Bernadette Godfrey. The child went missing on the morning of October 25 as she left her home for the Holy Name Academy.

According to Ray Tanner, coroner, the cause of death was multiple stab wounds to the child's chest.

Sister Mary Rose, the former Angela Artenelli, was also arrested as an accomplice in the case.

Dana scanned over the article and noticed that there was no mention as to Sister Mary Rose being the mother of the deceased child, probably some kind of payoff by her father to keep that part of the news out of the paper. Dana continued reading.

It was announced yesterday that Holy Name Academy will be immediately interviewing candidates for two second-grade classrooms at the school. Mr. Jay Harrison, former second-grade teacher, left the Cape unexpectedly, reportedly for somewhere in the South Pacific. He was released from jail and is not believed to have been a suspect in the case.

Dana noted that no word was made of the relationship he had had with the nun.

Mrs. Artenelli, mother of Sister Mary Rose and a recent victim of a hit and run accident, only said that she was shocked to hear the news. When asked if she would comment further, Mrs. Artenell asked to be left alone, so she could pray for the two women's souls. At this time, no charges are pending against Mrs. Artenelli for her prior knowledge in the case.

Sergeant Logan offered his congratulations to Dana Greer, Private Investigator, for her work in solving the case.

No date has been set as of yet for the trial of Sister Mary Rose and Mia Godfrey.

Eddie Vineeti, the man responsible for Mrs. Artinelli's hit and run, has been sent to Bay View, where he awaits trial for extortion and attempted murder.

Epilogue

Three Months Later – March 2

Ray McGregor snapped photos of Dana and Logan, who stood shaking hands in front of the Cape Peril Police Station. Several people from the Cape gathered around them on the sidewalk.

"What a bittersweet moment this is," Logan said, his breath forming white clouds in the single-digit temperatures. McGregor jotted down his words. "Our gratitude goes to Dana Greer who brings closure to the Bernadette Godfrey case. Yet, on the other hand, I speak for myself as well as the residents of the Cape, that Miss Greer will be sorely missed."

The crowd applauded.

Logan put his arm around Dana's shoulders and pulled her closer. "On an island such as Cape Peril, where crime is essentially non-existent, an investigator must devote herself to an intense scrutiny of possible suspects, including its residents, yet at the same time being willing to live among and bond with its people. Dana Greer has accomplished both. It is my honor, however, to announce that Miss Greer will be leaving immediately for Punkerton, Texas, where Archbishop Floyd J. Boretti of Dallas has asked for her assistance in solving the murder of a ten-year-old boy, a resident of the Saint Aloysius Gonzaga Home for Troubled Youth."

One of the bystanders said, "How tragic. . .a ten-year-old boy. Whatever has come of this world?"

Someone else added, "Let's just be glad Miss Greer will be on the case."

Then the applause continued.

***

Days later as Dana caught the Seaside Ferry to the mainland, the same boy who had greeted her when first she arrived, dressed in his knickers, muffler, and stocking hat, called out, "Read all about it. Read all about it. Convictions in the Bernadette Godfrey Case."

Dana paid the lad twenty-five cents and boarded the ferry. Distracting herself from the ferry's rocking movements while it waited to leave the dock, she sat down at one of the inner benches on the second deck of the boat and opened the paper to the front page. The headline read:

Justice Served – Peace Restored to Cape

Yesterday the jury in the Bernadette Godfrey murder trial reached a verdict after three months of testimony. Mia Godfrey, mother of the child, was deemed unfit to stand trial and has been committed to the St. Dymphna Home for the Criminally Insane in Portland, Maine. Sister Mary Rose, the former Angela Artenelli, was sentenced to ten to twenty years in the Portland Women's Prison for her part as accomplice. She admitted to not only preparing the grave site of the child but also to being involved in the murder plot. The Immaculate Heart of Mary Order, of which Sister Mary Rose is a member, refused to comment on what the status of the nun will be after serving her prison term. Mrs. Carmelina Artenelli, mother of the nun, who is recuperating at home after being the victim of a hit and run accident in November, was tried as an accomplice and acquitted. Jay Harrison, former second-grade teacher at Holy Name Academy, was arrested and shortly afterwards released due to his non-involvement in the case.

Dana looked out the smeared window of the ferry, reminiscing over the past several months. Finally, she felt that she had been validated. She had come to the Cape from Bay View, where the memories of the cold Myra Pembroke case involving her unfaithful husband always haunted her and made her question her own competence. Now, she knew she could move onward; that there were those who believed in her abilities as an investigator; and, better still, she believed in herself once again.

Enjoyed reading *Unholy Secrets*?
Here's a preview of what's to come in
Delphine Boswell's second novel in the Dana
Greer Mystery Series

Silent Betrayal....

When a ten-year old boy, convicted of bludgeoning his parents to death, is found murdered in his cell at the St. Aloysius Gonzaga Home for Trouble Youth, Dana Greer, P.I. is called onto the case by the Archbishop of Dallas. Her efforts to solve the young boy's murder are thwarted at every turn by the corruption, intolerance, and narrow-mindedness of the town of Punkerton, Texas. *Silent Betrayal* takes you behind the damp, dark walls of boy's prison run by an order of Catholic monks, where no one is quite who they appear to be. *Silent Betrayal* is guaranteed to prove that deceit is something easily hidden...hidden until it's too late

Prologue

March 19, 1952

"I heard a high-pitched screech. The MG's tires smelled like burning rubber. The next thing, I see the car crash through the metal barrier and roll down the embankment. Dried weeds, dirt, and metal car parts flying in the air. Hell, the thing burst into a ball of flames!" the man in the Fedora hat and tweed sportscoat told the police officer.

The story made front page news the next day once identifications had been made.

Movie Star's Sports Car a Flaming Inferno

The article describing the event followed.

Movie star Chantel DeBour, one of the biggest box office attractions on the silver screen, and her chauffeur, Hamilton Jackson, were involved in a fatal automobile accident yesterday, at 3:10 p.m., on Route 1. The sports car Mr. Jackson was driving careened off the road, through a road barrier, and plunged 600 feet into an embankment, exploding upon impact. Cause of the crash is under investigation. According to an eye witness, the brakes on the vehicle appeared to have malfunctioned, and speed may also have been a factor.

Funeral services for Miss DeBour will be announced shortly. The handling of her multi-million dollar estate will be by her executor, Theodore Prussia, Esq.

***

He rattled the newspaper and threw it onto the floor. "The damn broad sure got what she deserved. The plan was foolproof, appearing like an ordinary car malfunction, thanks to Max Freda. But, now, the payoff is all mine!" He danced the chicken around the small room, swinging an imaginary partner in his arms, and sang the lyrics to "Happy Payday" by Little Willie Littlefield and the Jivin' Jewels. He bent down and picked up the paper, hoping to find an address for the attorney handling the estate. There in small print at the bottom of the article was the key to his fortune:

Theodore Prussia, Esq.

One Liberty Street

Utica, New York

Suddenly, his rock 'n roll moves stopped. His inner voice screamed, "Get a grip, you stupid idiot. Chantel might have been a bit ditzy, but do you think she'd be that dumb? I mean leaving her estate to you?"

Chapter One

February 28, 1953

Timothy Laughton, the first to notice, let out a blood curdling scream. Behind the rusted bars on the cold concrete floor, lay the bloodied body of ten-year-old Douglas Clifford, visible only by the light of a full moon; its rays peeking through the narrow, overhead window.

Brother Calvin, the Head Warden on Wing G, Level 1, where the most incorrigible of the troubled youth were housed, heard Laughton's call for help and came running down the long corridor. Here the boys who bore the sin of murder on their souls were locked away from the outside world. Here is where they...mere children yet with the intellect of the most hardened of criminals...spend their days and their nights.

"Step aside!" The brother unlocked the cell and rushed inside, his rubber-soled shoes skidding in the pool of blood on the floor. He braced his fall by reaching for the wall. "Go! Get help!"

Laughton, his wrists shackled together, hurried toward the infirmary trusting he'd find Doctor Hansen. But it was too late for the young victim. On February twenty-eighth, at approximately ten p.m., the small boy's body was placed upon a gurney and wheeled out of sight by two monks in brown habits. In the dark corner lay the boy's tattered rabbit, the only personal item that the boy possessed.

Brother Calvin provided the Laughton boy with a pail, a mop, and a bottle of Spic and Span. "What are you standing there for, gawking like a vulture? Get to work!"

The Laughton boy scrubbed the floor and the walls on his hands and knees, all in hopes of washing away the memory of that night.

Made in the USA
Coppell, TX
17 January 2020

CPSIA information can be obtained
at www.ICGtesting.com
Printed in the USA
BVHW08s2000131018
530050BV00001B/1/P